Well, there you go!

by

Hugh Chare

Publication data
Well, there you go! © Hugh B. Chare 2020

Book and Cover design by Hugh B. Chare.
ISBN: 978-1-940012-02-5
 Kilihune Books

The James Martin series
African Encounter
Across the Zambezi
Just off the Great North Road
Well, there you go!
Back to Africa
We don't make glass
The Sagitta Mishap
Carbon Copy
Flight 5 to Johannesburg

Marieke Englebrecht mysteries
Death in the Mopane
Revenge after twenty years
Death in a Bush Camp

Other books
The journal of Jan Englebrecht
British Spy in the Bushveld
Federica
First to the Cape

Preface

This is a work of fiction. Names, characters, businesses and incidents are fictional except for obvious references to historical figures, companies or events. Any resemblance in the featured characters to actual persons, living or dead, is purely coincidental.

The company James & Brown, which is featured in this work, is wholly fictional. It has no relationship with the automobile maker James and Browne, who produced cars in England in the early 1900s. There is no relationship between the fictional character, James Martin, who appears in this book and in four earlier novels, and James Martin of Martin Consultants, author of *Surface Mining Equipment*.

Contents

Chicago - February 1975

"Well, folks, we're on our final approach into Chicago's O'Hare airport. If you look out of the left side of the plane, you'll have a great view of the Loop," suggested the pilot of the TWA flight that James and Katrina Martin had taken from London. James had been looking out of the window as they descended into Chicago, but, as they were seated on the right-hand side of the plane, was unable to see the famed Chicago Loop. What he could see was the coastline of Lake Michigan, stretching off to the north towards Wisconsin, their ultimate destination. The ground was partially covered in snow, and where it was not white, it was brown, light brown for fields and open spaces and dark brown where there were trees. He could see houses arranged in neat rows, with occasional larger buildings that he surmised could be shops, offices or factories. There were also many motorways, or expressways, as he would later learn they were called in Chicago. The lake was bluish-grey with no evidence of ice, but perhaps because it was the end of February, the end of winter was in sight, and the ice was melting. The sky was similarly grey, and it was hard to distinguish where the lake ended and the sky began. James was amazed at the sheer size of the lake; it was almost like an inland sea. It did look cold, but he had no way to gauge just how cold.

On the ground, they discovered just how cold it was. The plane taxied into the Chicago International Terminal and had to be towed in the last few feet to avoid destroying with the blast from the jet engines the small business and private planes parked near the terminal. The ground crew pushed stairs up against the plane and opened the doors, allowing in a blast of frigid air. The pilot had cheerfully announced that the temperature was 25 degrees Fahrenheit, but that the wind chill was much lower, in the teens. All this really meant little to James and Katrina. Having recently come from Zambia, in Central Africa, they had little comprehension of what was in store for them. Even their brief stay in England had not really prepared them for Chicago

1

winters. The walk across the tarmac into the arrivals building was thankfully short, saving them from too much exposure to the bitter cold wind, but they did get a small taste of why Chicago was named 'The Windy City.'

Customs and immigration procedures were relatively straightforward, unlike Zambia, where one never knew what might happen. James and Katrina were welcomed to the United States and told to 'Have a nice day!' Because their final destination was Milwaukee, they had to check luggage back in with the next airline, North Central, a smaller local airline that ran the Chicago to Milwaukee route. As it transpired, it would have been quicker to drive up to Milwaukee. The two-hour wait for the plane and then the quick thirty-minute hop into Milwaukee far exceeded the time it would have taken to drive, but they did not learn that until later. When they did fly to Milwaukee, it was on a twin-engine turboprop plane, a Convair 580, so much smaller than the Boeing 747 they had taken on the flight from London. James was convinced that the Convair had to be thirty years old if it was a day. The plane was not in fact that old. It had been put into service in 1960 as a Convair 340/440 and then re-engined in 1967 and put back into service as a Convair 580, so was really only fifteen years old. Apart from a few bumps because they were flying so low and the noise of the propellers and engines, the ride was comfortable enough and allowed them to see the ground below very clearly, which was possible as they were seated in row three just forward of the wing. James studied the ground below and was surprised to see how much open space there was and how much farmland. He had expected everything to be really built up. As they flew north from Chicago to Milwaukee, they essentially followed the expressway which ran between the two cities. Just before landing, the plane made a couple of turns that took them back out over Lake Michigan, and they landed towards the west.

At the Milwaukee terminal, James spotted a young man with a sign that read 'Martin, James & Brown.' He and Katrina introduced themselves as the Martins and learned that their contact was Tony Wildelski.

"Welcome to Milwaukee," said Tony. "We'll get your bags and then I'll run you downtown to the Pfister."

"Thanks," said James. "What's the Pfister?"

"Oh, sorry, it's one of the better hotels in Milwaukee," Tony explained. "We've put you there while you are here. David Brooks and Tony Whitaker will be joining you for dinner at about seven."

"Have you seen our bags yet?" Katrina asked James. "I've been watching bags come out, and I haven't seen ours yet."

"No, maybe they didn't make the flight," suggested James. "So now what?"

"No problem," Tony promised. "We'll talk to the North Central baggage people and get them to deliver them to the hotel when they arrive. Just give me your bag tags and I'll talk to the baggage people."

That done, Tony took them out into the car park, or parking lot as he called it, and led them to the car.

"Man, look at the size of this thing," said Katrina. "How many people will it take?"

"Six comfortably," replied Tony. "In a pinch, seven."

Tony drove them out of the airport and north up Howell Avenue before turning west onto Layton Avenue, then joining the expressway. Almost immediately, they came to an expressway intersection of the I-94 and I-894 highways.

"What's the significance of the numbers?" James asked.

"Well, the I-94 runs east/west from Michigan to Montana, even if here it seems to be going north. Here in the US, even-numbered Interstate highways go east/west and odd-numbered highways go north/south. The I-894 is a route that runs around the city of Milwaukee and joins the I-94 again on the west side," explained Tony.

"That's a lot simpler than trying to work out the motorway numbers in England," commented Katrina, who had been confused with the M1, M6, M4 and M40 and had never really worked out how they had been

3

numbered. Soon enough, they were at another intersection, and Tony forestalled the obvious question with a quick answer.

"The I-794 is a route associated with the I-94, but it runs into the city centre rather than around the city. The system of numbers is essentially the same everywhere, even-numbered prefixes mean routes around a city, odd-numbered prefixes mean routes into the city centre, so if you see a highway number you can work out where it goes."

"I hope you're taking note of this, James," commented Katrina. "If we have to find our own way around, you'll need to remember where to get on and where to get off these motorways."

"Tony, we saw a lot of snow on the ground between here and Chicago. Do you get much snow here?" James asked.

"We get plenty," Tony laughed. "A lot of what we get is what we call lake effect snow. The lake's big enough that it affects the weather, and the moisture is picked up off the lake and dumped on us, so ten to twelve inch storms are not unusual."

"So, who clears all the roads?" Katrina asked.

"The expressways are done by the state, and in the city, the city people take care of those roads," Tony explained. "They do a pretty good job, but sometimes it's coming down so heavily that they can hardly keep up."

"Are there many accidents?" Katrina asked.

"Usually right at the beginning of winter, when everyone has forgotten how to drive in the snow and ice, and then we get a bunch of fender benders," Tony explained. "Okay, we're here."

The Pfister Hotel was an imposing edifice on the corner of Wisconsin Avenue and Jefferson Street. The lobby was very ornate and hot. That had been a shock, walking in from the cold air in the street. They stopped at the front desk to register and were told that they were expected and that all charges would be taken care of by the company. James told the desk clerk that their luggage had been delayed and should be delivered later. Tony said his farewells and reminded them that they had a dinner engagement at seven that night. Their room was spacious with a view across part of the city to the lake, but it was hot.

James tried to open a window without any success. He then went looking for a thermostat and reset it to a much lower temperature. Katrina told him to come to the window and look at something outside, but when he reached for her hand, he got an electric shock.

"What was that?" Katrina exclaimed in surprise.

"Static electricity," James explained. "It must be so dry in here that any movement across the carpets builds up static electricity, and I discharged through you."

"Well, next time, discharge somewhere else first!" she commented. "Will it always be like this?"

"If it's dry like this, yes," thought James. "If it were more humid, we wouldn't have the problem."

"I need a bath," Katrina announced. "Do you think they'll deliver our bags soon?"

"I've no idea," he replied. "It's possible. There were enough flights from Chicago on the departure board at O'Hare."

"Well, I'm going for a soak, and if the bags arrive, I'll change; if not, I'll have to put the same clothes back on," she said.

Katrina had not been soaking for long when the hotel porter knocked at the door and delivered the bags. James surmised that they must have arrived on the very next flight. With the potential distraction of bag delivery out of the way, James set the room alarm clock for six forty-five and then joined Katrina in the bath. It was a bit of a squash as the bath was not very big.

"This bath is only small," commented Katrina.

"I think Americans must go in more for showers than baths," James thought. "I wonder if anywhere has decent-sized baths big enough for two?"

"Well, we're not going to get very far here," said Katrina. "There's no room to move, we'll just have to try the bed."

"What do you have in mind, *Suikerbossie*?" James asked.

"I need to check that you haven't forgotten how!" she replied. "After all, it's been a couple of days since we last got together."

"Well, why don't you go and pull off the blankets and such while I quickly wash?" he suggested.

When James went back into the main room, the curtains had been closed and the covers on the bed had been pulled back. Katrina was lying on the bed waiting for him. She held her arms out to him, and they made love.

"So, *ou man*, did you ever think we would go to the US?" she asked.

"No, never in my wildest dreams. It always seemed a faraway place that I would never go to," he replied.

"Well, even if it doesn't work, we've been and we will have done it in one of the better hotels in Milwaukee," she added, laughing. Then she rolled them over and climbed on top of him. "I like it on top," she said. Things progressed to their natural conclusion, and afterwards, they lay spent but happy.

The alarm going off brought them back to the present. "We've got fifteen minutes to get ready," James reminded Katrina. "We don't want to be late for the first interview!"

"I'll be ready in ten minutes," she boasted. "I need a quick shower, then I'll get dressed. What should I wear?"

"I don't know. What do you have? Probably should be something fairly conservative. We don't know these people yet." James thought.

"Okay, what about this?" she asked, holding up a black top and trousers.

"Looks great to me," James replied. "Do you want to shower first, or shall I?"

"You go first and get ready, and I'll be out just now," she said. When she came out of the bathroom, James was dressed in his best suit, well, his only suit.

"Is my tie straight?" he asked.

"You're fine. Who are the *ouks* we are meeting?" she asked, while she dressed.

"David Brooks is the vice president of sales, and Tony Whitaker is the application manager," he replied. "I was referred to them by George

Murphy, you remember George, he's the regional sales manager for Africa for James & Brown, we met in Mkushi a couple of times."

"Well, are we ready?" she asked, quickly brushing her hair into some sort of order. "Do we look as if we've been having it away?"

"No, you look great. Let's go *ou frou*," he said, laughing.

"Less of the *ou frou*," she said, prodding him in the ribs. "Or, I'll tell these people what you've been up to for the last hour or so!"

In the hotel lobby, James looked around and saw two men looking towards the lifts. One of them waved, came over and said.

"You've got to be James and Katrina Martin! Is it James or Jim? I'm David Brooks, meet Tony Whitaker."

"I've always gone by James," replied James.

After handshakes all around, David suggested that they get a drink in the bar before dinner.

"Good trip over?" he asked.

"Fine, thanks," James replied. "Our luggage took a later flight from Chicago, but it arrived soon enough."

"Ah, you must have come up on the Blue Goose," commented Tony, referring to the common joke name for North Central. James had noticed that the company logo on the tail was a blue duck or goose, so he understood the reference. "What do you think of Milwaukee so far?" Tony continued.

"It's cold," said James, laughing. "It's bigger than I thought it would be, particularly as it's so close to Chicago."

"What about you, Mrs Martin, or is it okay to call you Katrina?" David asked.

"Katrina's fine," she replied. "I actually never thought I'd come to the US, let alone Milwaukee."

"So what's your poison?" Tony asked.

"I'll just have a beer if I may?" said Katrina.

"The same for me," added James.

"So what'll it be, Schlitz, Pabst, Miller or Budweiser?" Tony asked.

"I've no idea," said Katrina. "What do you suggest?"

"Well, Bud is not made here, so I'd pick one of the others, try Schlitz, we should support the local brewers," suggested David.

When the drinks arrived, the conversation changed from the general chit chat to more directed questions.

"So, James, tell us about yourself?" suggested David. "George speaks highly of you, by the way."

James then launched into a very summarised version of his career to date, starting with his most recent experience.

"I was working at an open-pit copper mine in Zambia until recently," he started.

"What happened there?" asked Tony.

"They closed the mine," James explained. "The economists forecasted a dramatic drop in copper prices, which would make the operation non-economic. So they anticipated the market and shut down early. There were also problems with Zimbabwe freedom fighter chaps in the area."

"That's what we heard from George," confirmed David. "My guess is that they made a smart move."

"Why didn't the mine give you another job?" asked Tony.

"They made me an offer of working underground again, at a lower grade or taking a buyout of my contract. I didn't really see eye to eye with the bloke I'd be working for, so I took the buyout," James explained.

"David, don't you just love the Brit words?" Tony said. "Blokes and chaps!"

"What was wrong with the guy you'd be working for?" David asked.

"I knew him from some years ago, and his style was very autocratic and he was not very open to suggestions or ideas not his own," James elaborated.

"Well, here we expect you to have ideas and to think," commented David.

"If your mine closed, do you expect that other open pits will cut back this year or next?" Tony asked.

"Probably," James thought. "My guess is that Nchanga will be fine for a while, as will probably be Chambishi, but some of the smaller operations, like Kalengwa and Mkushi, will also have to shut down."

"We'd better make some plans with George for a smaller-scale operation," commented David. "Ah, well, coal is going gangbusters in South Africa, so it'll take up any slack!"

"Do you know what we're looking for?" asked Tony.

"George said something about application engineering," replied James.

"That's right," Tony confirmed. "I've found that I really need someone to work with me in application engineering, working with the field sales guys to figure out what equipment is needed for what job."

"Of course, calculating things to match the sizes of equipment we make," added David, laughing.

"So, we've started an application engineering group, small at first, that will provide us with the expertise to compete with the guys at Bucyrus, Marion, Page and Harnischfeger," Tony explained.

"Right now we're looking for a guy to help with that function," added David. "Think you could handle that?"

"I should think so," James assured them.

"What about you, Katrina?" Tony asked. "What do you do?"

"I used to work in a family transportation business," she explained. "And then after it was sold and James and I were married, I worked for a small industrial minerals operation selling their products."

"What did you transport?" David asked.

"We had a heavy machinery transportation business," she elaborated. "We moved things like D-9s, mining trucks, crushers and other heavy equipment."

"You said industrial minerals, what did you sell?" Tony asked.

"China clay, glass sand, mica fillers and feldspars," Katrina listed.

"What do you think about a move to the States?" David asked.

"I think it would be fun," she replied. "As I said earlier, I've never been before, but I think I prefer it to England."

"That makes sense," commented Tony. "The Brits are so stuffy, no offence, James, but sometimes they can drive you up the wall."

"Well, what do you say we go to dinner?" suggested David. "Maybe you should get some coats, James. We'll be going out from here."

"I'll be down immediately," James promised.

"We've only got a block to go," said David when James rejoined them with coats in hand. "We thought we'd go to Karl Ratzch's, it's a famous restaurant here in Milwaukee."

"It sounds rather German, is it?" Katrina asked.

"Many of the restaurants here are either German or Polish. They reflect the immigrant communities that came here over the past years," explained Tony. "You'll get used to ski names. It seems almost every other engineer we have is a something ski."

"Does that also account for all the breweries?" James asked.

"Sure, those and the heavy metal working that goes on around here, they seem to go hand in hand," commented David.

Outside, it was cold, and there were snowflurries in the air. They walked up Jefferson Street and then turned onto Mason Street and found the restaurant.

Over dinner, the conversation and questions continued. "Say, James, what do you know about James & Brown?" asked Tony.

"I know you never made cars, unlike your namesake in England, who once did. This company was founded in the latter half of the nineteenth century by Albert James and Theodore Brown and builds electric mining shovels, walking draglines and blast hole drills, large cranes for railways and some other heavy machinery and has a line of construction equipment," he replied.

"Right, we're in there in the thick of it right now with the aftermath of the Arab oil embargo, coal mining is in, and you can't find mining engineers for love nor money," Tony added.

"I saw from your résumé that you have a mining engineering degree, right?" asked David.

"Yes, that's correct. After I graduated, I went out to Zambia to work," James explained.

"Ever seen a walking dragline?" asked Tony.

"Yes, there's one in Zambia, a Bucyrus-Erie 1260-W at Maamba Collieries," replied James. "I also spent a summer before I went to college working at an iron ore mine near Corby that had a Ransomes and Rapier W1400 machine."

"What about shovels and drills?" Tony continued.

"Well, the iron ore mine had shovels, and there is any number of shovels and drills in Zambia, most of them, I'm sorry to say, are Bucyrus-Erie or P&H, very few James & Brown. It seems to me that the application is essentially a function of bucket size, truck capacity and how well rock is blasted," thought James.

"True enough," commented David. "What we have set up for you this week is a series of interviews with our sales, engineering and personnel people, all from the mining machinery division. Then why don't we meet on Friday to see how things have gone?"

"Say, Katrina, I've got my wife, Margaret, set to pick you up tomorrow and show you some of the neighbourhoods," said Tony. "She'll be by around ten."

The waitress who had been hovering around them finally interrupted and asked for dinner orders. After each had indicated their preference, she started into the options. Options for salad dressings, Thousand Island, Blue Cheese, Italian, Ranch or plain oil and vinegar and then options for those having baked potatoes, did they want them with butter, sour cream, chives or all of the above. James looked at Katrina, and she shrugged; neither of them knew what Thousand Island was or Ranch, and they had never eaten baked potatoes with anything but butter. Then the waitress started to list bread options: rye, whole wheat, sourdough or pumpernickel. It was all rather overwhelming. There were just too many options. James felt that he was ordering at random at times, just to forestall the list of options that would otherwise come. Conversation continued over dinner and covered world affairs, mining, the history of the company, the current backlog of orders, the state of the roads, the amount of snow that had fallen so far in the season and how much more might come. In all, a wide-ranging and all-encompassing conversation.

Later, when James and Katrina had returned to the hotel, they talked about the evening and the two people they had met.

"These people seem nice enough, James," Katrina thought. "It's almost as if they are trying to sell you on the job."

"You're right," he agreed. "I wonder who I'll see tomorrow and where you'll go?"

"What do you think?" she asked.

"About the job?" he asked in return.

"Yes, that and moving here?" she continued.

"Unless there's something that I haven't thought of, or the salary is too low, I think it would be a great opportunity," James replied. "What about you?"

"Well, you're the one who's going to make the most money, but if it were up to me, I'd rather live here than in England," Katrina said, then she continued. "It's a big change from actually working in mines. Are you sure you want to make that change?"

"I think so," he replied. "I know it's a change from the normal career path in mining. I could always find another job at a mine, or I could go back to college like a lot of blokes and do a master's and then look for another job. I'm not sure. This is one of those chances that comes along, and maybe we just have to take the chance and see what comes of it."

"Well, whatever you decide, you know I'll be here with you," she promised. "I'd like a shower before bed. What about you?"

"Good idea," he agreed. He followed her into the bathroom and watched as she showered, wishing that it was big enough for two, but having to live with the reality that it just was not, and becoming aroused all the same. When she was done, he showered quickly while she dried herself, then when he was dry, they went back to the bed and he sat on it and she sat in his lap. They made love that way, then again later, lazily both lying on their sides, with her legs wrapped around him. It was a wonderful way to get introduced to a new country.

The next morning was bright and sunny with a dusting of fresh snow. Tony Widelski was in the lobby of the Pfister waiting for James, who had had just enough time to get breakfast with Katrina before Tony arrived. To get to the factory, Tony took regular streets that ran closer to the lakefront. James presumed that some of the names, at least, must have come from Indian tribes. He could not imagine that Kinnickinnic was either Germanic or Polish in origin. On the way to James & Brown, they passed the factory of Bucyrus-Erie, a machinery company that had been around for almost one hundred years and was a name very familiar to James from Zambia. When they reached the James & Brown factory, it was in Oak Creek, just on the border with South Milwaukee, somewhat south of the Bucyrus-Erie plant and headquarters. Tony delivered James to the office of Ray Pierce, the vice president of human resources. Ray asked James to take a seat and then went through a more formal review of his curriculum vitae, or résumé as the Americans preferred to call it. Ray then also went through a description of the organisation structure and who was in which position. He had a timetable laid out for the next couple of days, finishing up with a lunch with David Brooks and Tony Whitaker on Friday.

After his session with Ray, James was successively delivered to sales managers, product managers, accountants, engineers and contracts people, with a short break for lunch with Tony Whitaker and Richard West, the international sales manager. Richard was aware of his background, as it had been through him that George Murphy had passed on his recommendation. Richard was actually from Australia and had been assigned to Europe and Brazil before coming to the US. By five in the afternoon, James was tired and was ready for a break. It was only to be a short break because he and Katrina were to be taken out to dinner by Richard West, his wife, and Renato Castello, the current manager of the Brazilian company. Tony Widelski dropped James back at the Pfister and reminded him that he would be collected at seven by Richard. James had plenty to discuss with Katrina, and he was equally certain that she had lots to tell.

"So how was the day?" he asked her when he was back in their room.
"Busy!" she replied. "I was picked up at ten by Margaret Whitaker, or Maggie as she prefers, and we went for a tour of the suburbs."
"Which way out of the city?" James asked.
"I think mostly south and west," she replied. "We went through the cities of Hales Corners, New Berlin, and Franklin, then came back up through Oak Creek and South Milwaukee, where you were, along the lakefront."
"Did you get lunch?" he asked.
"Oh yes, we went to some restaurant, I don't remember the name, and met a gaggle of aunties, all with husbands that work for James & Brown," she replied. "How about you? How was your day?"
"Also busy," he started. "I must have repeated my life story ten times to different people."
"Did they feed you?" she asked.
"Yes, we had lunch at the company cafeteria in a small room that seemed to be used for visitors, customers and the like," he explained. "What else did you see on your drive around?"
"Oh, a major shopping centre, some of the aunties' houses, I wonder why it is that they all want to show you around their houses?" Katrina pondered.
"I've no idea," James admitted. "We have an engagement tonight at seven, so we need to be ready for that. Are you tired, or can you manage another night out?"
"I'm fine, I just need a quick bath and I'll be ready," Katrina promised.

Dinner with Richard, his wife Dorothy and Renato was in some ways relaxed, and it was at the Pfister, which meant that James and Katrina did not have to get out coats, gloves and hats. Richard and Renato had both been to Zambia, and had both lived in other countries, so understood what James and Katrina would be faced with, moving to a different country, a different culture and all the little things that would crop up. Neither James nor Katrina had been to Australia or Brazil, so they were the ones asking the questions. Richard and Dorothy came from Perth, and Renato came from a small town about a four-hours drive from São Paulo. Renato told them that the main mining industry in Brazil was for iron ore, but that there were other smaller operations going after different minerals and coal. James knew that Australia was coal, iron ore, gold, lead and zinc and copper. All three complained about the weather and how cold it was, and how hard it was to get used to the idea of having to dress up just to walk to the end of a driveway. Dorothy commented that it was almost as though she needed two complete wardrobes, a summer one and a winter one. James and Katrina understood that they had seen the need for better winter clothes than they had. Dinner ended quite late, and James and Katrina were ready for bed, so they showered quickly, then made love sitting on one of the chairs that was in the room, before repairing the bed and repeating the performance.

Thursday started out looking to be a repeat of Wednesday until James was delivered to the factory. Then he was whisked off to an office in Milwaukee to meet with the psychologist. The human resources people explained that this was standard procedure when hiring someone into the management of the company. James spent the next three hours doing word tests and interviews. He probably invalidated the tests by asking the test giver what different words meant. They dealt with occupations that he would rather have, comptroller versus controller and similar differences. James was unfamiliar with the term comptroller and had to interrupt the test to ask for a definition. The psychologist then asked him a series of questions about his life and experiences to date. He also asked him what was the best piece of advice that his father had given him. James's response was that he had been told how not to break his thumbs when using a starting handle on his Land Rover. That then led to a quick exchange of definitions, starting handle equalled hand crank! The psychologist seemed to think that was odd advice, but for James, it had had very practical application and no broken thumbs. James judged from the follow-up questions that the psychologist simply had no comprehension of Africa or his occupation to date, in the same way that James had no real understanding of American culture and values. They were two people

15

from very different worlds trying to be polite and understand each other.

Following that experience, it was refreshing to be delivered back to the factory into the hands of a young welding engineer who took him to lunch, then gave him a factory tour. James was fascinated by the size of the machinery that they had and the fact that most of the large machines were never actually fully assembled in the factory, but put together in the field. The factory floor was noisy, and there were lingering smells of weld rod and cutting oil in the air. In places, the floor was littered with huge chips of metal that were being turned off large pieces of steel, and some poor soul had the full-time occupation of shovelling them into a large bin for disposal. He also learned from the young engineer that the factory in Oak Creek made only the large mining machines; the smaller cranes, backhoes, shovels and other equipment were built at the company's factory in Pittsburgh.

That evening at the hotel, James and Katrina again swapped stories about their days. Katrina had spent the day in Milwaukee and had taken a brewery tour, visited the museum and walked through a few shops. She had had Dorothy as her guide, or rather companion, because Dorothy had not been on a brewery tour before, nor had she been to the museum. Dorothy had also told of some of her own experiences in moving to the US. They would be a little different for James and Katrina because Dorothy and Richard had been transferred by the company on a senior executive package and could afford to buy a house, cars and all the trappings of suburban living. Whereas James and Katrina would be coming into a new position, lower in the hierarchy, and therefore not receive quite the same treatment. Katrina had another day scheduled with Dorothy for Friday, and they would be visiting the James & Brown factory for a plant tour, something that Dorothy had not done before and was particularly keen to do. For all the years that Richard had worked for the company, she had never seen inside the factory, so when Katrina asked if it would be possible to take a tour, she had called Richard and he had arranged it.

Dinner that night was to be with George Murphy, who had arrived that day for scheduled meetings and a customer visit. At least with George, they did not have to explain where Zambia was, why Katrina was so light and that they did not generally speak Swahili in Zambia, all issues that had come up over the past two days. Dinner with George was a more relaxed affair than the previous two nights had been. He took them to a small family-run Mexican restaurant somewhere between Cudahy and St. Francis. Cudahy was a name that James was bewildered by; it was almost like going back to 1969 and the first time he saw a sign to Oudtshoorn. How to pronounce either name had not been obvious to him, and he needed help.

"So James, how's it going?" George asked.
"Fine, I think," James replied. "I hope I'm not going to be asked to list all the people I've met over the past two days."
"No, that's just standard procedure. We have as many people look at you as we can, I guess they figure that you can't keep up an act for that long and the real you will show," George continued. "What did you think of the shrink?"
"Oh, the psychologist," James replied. "Well, I don't think he had a clue about what I was talking about."
"Doesn't surprise me," commented George. "He struggles with all the foreigners. Where did you guys eat already?"
"Tuesday night, when we arrived, it was Karl Ratzch's, then last night another German-style place, I forget the name," James replied.
"All the guys in Kitwe say hi," George announced. "They all miss you and most are envious because the rumour mill is now going full blast with cutbacks and people reductions."
"What do you think, George, should we take a job if it's offered?" James asked.

"Absolutely! Once you have your foot in the door, what you do is up to you."

"Do you think I'll be offered a job?" James asked again.

"Sure, we wouldn't have flown you over here if we weren't going to do that!" George announced. "My bet is that they'll offer you the job with a starting salary of about $1,300 a month, plus you'll be part of the sales bonus scheme."

"What about work permits, visas or whatever?" James asked.

"Oh, don't worry, the company will fix that, probably get you a Green Card as soon as possible, so there'll be no problems for you and Katrina staying here," promised George. "So what do you fancy to eat, tacos, enchiladas, burritos or what?"

"I've no idea," admitted James. "What are all those things, and what do you suggest?"

"Well, they're all different Mexican dishes, why don't you try chicken burritos with refried beans and rice?" suggested George.

Over dinner, George continued the conversation by asking James and Katrina what they had been doing since they left Zambia.

"Well, we took a quick trip to South Africa to see Katrina's folks," James explained.

"And we spent Christmas in Italy with James's sister and her husband," added Katrina.

"Really?" George asked. "Where in Italy?"

"A really small town called Mommio Castello, it's near Viareggio, which is west of Florence and north of Pisa," Katrina explained.

"So, in Tuscany," George added. "Did you get to eat and drink much?"

"An amazing amount," James laughed.

"How did you get there?" George asked.

"We borrowed my mom's car, took the Hovercraft to Boulogne, then drove through France and Switzerland to Italy, then south to Viareggio," James explained.

"How long did that take?" George asked.

"We took a break at a place called Bourg in France before tackling the Alps and the snow," replied James.

"I'll bet that was fun!" George commented.

"Well, I'm glad the oil crisis that started in 1973 was resolved," said James. "Or, we might never have been able to go."

"I meant the snow in the Alps," said George.

"That actually wasn't so bad," James thought. "It's a little like driving on a really muddy road, but a lot colder and with the added risk of ice under the snow."

"Rather you than me!" George laughed. "So was it cold in Italy?"

"Not as cold as here!" laughed Katrina. "I suppose it was in the forties, dropping a little overnight with some frosts."

"You'll get used to the weather here," George promised. "Or at least so they tell me. I try to stay the hell away from here in the winter. Give me Jo'burg in December any day!"

After dinner, George dropped them back at the hotel, and they talked about what George had told them about the rumour mill and the likely job offer.

"It sounds pretty good, don't you think?" she said of the job.

"It does, doesn't it," he agreed. "We'll have to see what tomorrow brings and if they actually offer me the job."

"They will," she predicted. "I would."

"Yes, but you're biased," he said.

"I am," she agreed. "I think you're really smart, I think you could do whatever job they gave you, and on top of that, I really love the way we make love."

"I'm glad you think so," he laughed.

"Well, if nothing else comes of this trip, we can tell our grandchildren that we had it away in a fancy hotel in America," she said.

"Speaking of which," he said, reaching for her and pulling her close. That night, they only made love once before succumbing to sleep.

Friday morning was somewhat of the same until 11:30 when Tony Whitaker came to find James. He explained to the engineers that James was with, that he had an interview to go to. They left the factory and went to a small restaurant in Cudahy, where they met up with David Brooks and Ray Pierce. James had a hard time reading the menu he was given because it was so dark, atmosphere, David explained. The restaurant felt that the low-light projected atmosphere, but the real advantage of the place was that it was quiet.

"Well, James, whaddya think?" asked Ray. Or at least that is what it sounded like to James.
"It has been an interesting week," started James. "It's different to running a mine, but with some of the same issues."
"We've gotten good reports from the guys you talked to," Ray continued.
"We need people like you, James," added David. "We're prepared to offer you the job; that is, if you want to come?"
"Thanks, I would love to come," replied James. "I do have a few questions."
"Fire away," said Ray.
"Obviously, how much will Katrina be able to work, where could we live, when do you want me to start and probably a few more that I can't think of right at this minute?" James enumerated.
"Well, to the first, $1,300 a month plus the usual benefits, we'll get you a work permit right away, then we'll help you both get Green Cards, then Katrina may work. We want you to start right away, and we'll put you in touch with someone who'll help you find a place to live," replied Ray.
"What are the usual benefits?" James asked.
"Oh, participation in the bonus scheme, pension, social security payments, health and life insurances, expense accounts, all that kind of stuff," started Ray. "But, we can go over all that back at the office later."
"When can you start?" asked Tony.
"As soon as I have the appropriate documents," James promised.
"Why don't we send him back to the UK, sign him on with the Brits, then bring him back as a company employee?" suggested David.

"Great idea," agreed Ray. "James, why don't you go on back to Merry Olde? We'll get you signed up with the Brit sub, then come back here next week and start work."

"Is that legal?" asked James.

"No problem," thought Ray. "We have employees from foreign subs here from time to time, and we may put them to work while they're here. They'll have to create the job, and they'll bitch about that, but they'll back-charge us for the expense. Then we'll get right on the Green Card business."

"Can you tell me exactly what it is you want me to do?" James asked.

"We need a guy to help me with the field reps and the customers to size and type machines that we think the customers should buy," Tony explained.

"And this is for all types of machines?" James continued.

"No, just the mining machines, draglines, shovels and blast hole drills," David added. "The construction machinery line is sold through distributors, and they usually have their own guys to liaise with the customers. You'll have to tell us if we need more application engineers and how we're going to pay for them."

"Are we talking just the US?" James asked.

"No, we'll cover the world, James," Tony promised. "We have a lot of activity right now in Brazil, Australia and South Africa, but of course, I get to pick who goes where!"

"That means he goes to Florida in January and you go to Hibbing," laughed David.

"Do the other companies have similar people?" James asked, not really getting the joke at all, as he had only a vague idea where Hibbing was.

"Sure," Tony commented. "The Breaking and Entering guys have one, so does Marion and I'm sure the Poor and Helpless guys will soon do as well."

"I'm sorry," James interrupted. "Breaking and who?"

"Oh, just our pet names for Bucyrus-Erie and P&H, we don't really have a name for Marion, unless of course we call them the Maids," Tony explained. "So, if we're all done, why don't we make like trees and leave!"

21

Katrina wanted all the details when James arrived back at the Pfister. He explained everything, and then they talked about the next steps. First, they would fly back to the UK and on Monday sign up with the local company. There was a subsidiary operation in Didcot, not particularly far from where James's parents lived. They had been briefed and would be expecting him at ten. James had been warned that they would sign him up on a UK salary, which would be less than the offer he had been made, but that they would work to get him converted over to the US base as soon as possible. Meanwhile, his living expenses would be chargeable to an expense account, which should help to balance the difference in salaries.

For his part, James wanted to hear about her plant tour and what she thought of the place. She, like him, had been impressed by the sheer size of everything. She kept imagining what it would take to transport some of the parts of the machines and thought that her father would have been fascinated by it all. He would have been calculating loads and possible revenue that could have been made by transporting just one of the large machines in all its pieces and sub-assemblies. She told him that she had surprised the tour guide engineer by very closely guessing how many train trucks it would take to transport all the pieces of one machine they were looking at, to the mine site.

That evening, they were treated to a Friday night fish fry. Two of the sales trainees who were at a loose end had been co-opted to act as hosts, and they thought that a Milwaukee tradition might be a nice idea. James and Katrina were collected from the Pfister at seven by Dean Mason and Tim Bergstrom. It was not quite the fish and chips that James had grown up with, but was acceptable all the same. The sales trainees knew why James and Katrina were there and wanted to know if he would be back and what he thought of the job. James assured them that he would be back as soon as the appropriate paperwork was sorted out and that he would start immediately after that. James asked where they were from and learned that Dean was from a really small town in Wyoming called Bill, or rather, he was from a ranch that was close to Bill, and Tim was from Denver. They were both doing stints in Oak Creek before being sent off to their assignments, which for Dean would be Beirut and for Tim would be Singapore.

After dinner, James and Katrina sat in the bar of the Pfister and had a nightcap.

"So, what do you think?" he asked her.

"I think it's great," she said. "I like the idea of living here. We'd have to get used to the cold, but I'm sure we can get clothes, boots, all that stuff to make life easier. What do you think?"

"It'll be interesting," he said. "It'll be interesting to see where they send me and what kinds of places I see, but what will you do?"

"I'll find something," she said. "Maybe I'll even write a novel, I'll probably have time on my hands."

"That's an idea," he said.

"So, Mr Application Engineer, are you going to sit there all night and sip that drink, and are we going to go upstairs and celebrate properly?" she asked.

"Celebrate how?" he asked. She leaned over and whispered in his ear, and whatever she said, it caused James to look around to make sure that no one else could hear, and it was also enough that he paid for their drinks, but left them to hurry back upstairs to their room.

Flying back to London seemed almost pointless, as they would be turning around and flying back to Chicago soon enough. But rules are rules, and the US immigration authorities had to be satisfied. It was a question of getting the appropriate visa or authorisation to work in the US. Under other circumstances, they need not have gone back at all, because they had little in the UK to take care of, and such belongings as they had moved from Africa could be forwarded at any time. The flight back to London was an overnight flight, so they whiled away the morning making love and checked out of the hotel as late as they could and then took the flight down to Chicago to await the TWA plane. James was sure that the world would know what they had been doing all morning; he was sure that the satisfaction showed in his face, but Katrina assured him that he was giving nothing away.

James's father, William, was at Heathrow to meet them when they landed early Sunday morning. He was eager to know what had transpired during the trip and was interested to learn of the job offer. With James and Katrina moving to Milwaukee, the family was being further scattered. James's brother, William, and his wife, Bridget, were still in Johannesburg, and his sister, Alex, was living in Tuscany with her husband, Vincenzo. The drive back to Cores End, where James's parents lived, was punctuated by questions and answers about what they had seen in Wisconsin. Neither of James's parents had ever been to the US, and James was sure that he would have to repeat his stories as soon as they arrived at his parents' house to satisfy the curiosity of his mother.

"What was Milwaukee like?" was the first question that James's mother, Elizabeth, asked them when they arrived.

"Cold!" Katrina replied. "The wind cut right through you. There was snow on the ground when we got there, and some more came down while we were there."

"What about the town?" William wanted to know.

"I suppose I'd call it an industrial town," James thought. "There seemed to be factories everywhere and lots of breweries."

"Is it a nice place?" Elizabeth asked.

"I think so," Katrina replied. "The people were friendly enough. But it was all a little overwhelming. There's just so much of everything in the shops, the restaurants, even the houses."

"What about the job?" William asked, bringing everyone back to the reason that James and Katrina had gone to Milwaukee in the first place.

"I took the job," James explained. "I need to go to Didcot tomorrow and sign on, then they'll transfer us to the US."

"When?" Elizabeth wanted to know.

"They said as soon as possible," James commented. "I imagine it'll be sometime this week."

"So, you've really only just come back to England from Africa and now you're leaving again?" Elizabeth asked.

"I go where the jobs are," he replied. "If I got another job in the mines, it would probably be South Africa or Australia; either way, it would mean leaving. There are probably some jobs with the National Coal Board, but I don't fancy working for them. The iron mines around Corby are small, so the number of jobs will be limited and the tin mines in Cornwall are also small, so a limited number, there's just more opportunity elsewhere."

"I suppose so," Elizabeth agreed.

"When they go, then we can visit the States," William added. "I've always wanted to go. I should look up Wisconsin and see where it is and what's there."

Didcot

On Monday morning, James took the Land Rover they had brought back from Zambia and drove to Didcot in the drizzle. He had no problem finding the James & Brown yard and offices. Their forest of crane booms rather gave them away. There was a factory, and he could see partially completed machines sitting in the yard awaiting finishing. There were also track links, crane boom sections, buckets, steel wheels of various types and sizes and sundry other bits stacked up at one end of the yard. The offices were in a three-storey building that looked about fifty years old and had that feel about it inside as well. He introduced himself to the receptionist and was asked to take a seat. James took off his raincoat and sat down, and looked around. and there were pictures on the walls of machines, obviously fresh from the factory. There was a set of wide stairs that led up to the next floor. On the ground floor, there were corridors left and right, but as far as he could see, little obvious activity. While he waited, James flipped through some of the literature that was neatly placed on a table and wondered what the program for the day would be.

"James Martin?" a young lady asked him. She had come down the stairs while he was engrossed in one of the articles.
"Yes," he replied.
"Please come with me, John Williams is expecting you," she said. She led the way up the stairs to an office that overlooked the car park. "Please have a seat," she offered. "John will be with you shortly. Let me hang your coat for you." James took the offered seat and looked around. There was a large desk at one end of the office, stacked with papers, a table with four chairs at the other and a couple of easy chairs, somewhat in the middle. On the wall were maps of Africa, Europe, the Americas, Asia and Australia. On a low table in front of the easy chairs was a globe and some catalogues of the company's products.
"Hi, James," a middle-aged man said as he came into the office. "Sorry to keep you, these guys love meetings!"

"Mr Williams?" James asked.

"In the flesh," he replied. "Call me John. May we get you some coffee or tea?"

"Coffee would be great, thanks," James replied.

"Patty, can you get us some coffee?" John called out to the secretary in the outer office.

"Real coffee or American coffee?" she asked.

"Real coffee!" John ordered. "How about you, James?"

"That would be fine with me," James agreed, not really sure what he was agreeing to.

"In the States, we tend to make coffee rather on the watery side," John commented. "I like an espresso once in a while just to remind myself what coffee is supposed to taste like. So James, tell me a little about yourself; you really blew away the guys in Oak Creek."

James went through his life story to date in an abbreviated form. A few times, John interrupted him with questions that James hoped he answered intelligently.

"Ah, coffee's here," John announced. "You fancy biscotti with yours? Thanks, Patty."

"Thank you," James. "If you don't mind me asking, have you been in Didcot long?"

"About three years now, it seems much longer than that, but it's been fun!" John commented.

"How long have you been with the company?" James asked.

"Let's see, must be twenty years now," John thought. "I'll tell you, James, there are days that it seems like only yesterday when I started in Oak Creek as a sales correspondent, and then there are days when that seems so far in the past that it's hard to remember what it was like."

"Will you move back to the States?" James asked.

"Yes, we've got a plan that has me moving back in six months to take over from David Brooks when he retires; we just need to work out who's coming here," said John. "But what about you? Are you ready to move to Oak Creek?"

"Yes," James assured him. "I understand that I need a visa to work there."

"Right, and here's what we're going to do," John began. "Our personnel guy here, Howard Pitts, already has your information from Oak Creek, and we've given you the job title of sales technical engineer, and he'll go with you tomorrow to our embassy in London and get you a visa."

"Will I meet him in London or here?" James asked.

"I think London, but work it out with Howard," John suggested. "Why don't we go and get Howard and take a look around the factory?"

"Do I need my coat?" James asked.

"No need," John said. "We've only got a short walk to the factory, and it's under a portico, so we won't get wet. I've wondered since I've been here whether it does anything but rain, drizzle and rain some more."

"I was happy in Zambia that we had months with no rain at all," James commented.

"We could do with some sunshine here, Patty, we're going to get Howard and go walkabout," John said. With that, he led the way down the corridor to another office.

"Say, Howard, this is James," he said, introducing the two of them. "You ready for a walkabout?"

"Fine, yes, of course," was Howard's response. "I'm pleased to meet you, James," he added, offering his hand. James shook the proffered hand, and they quickly left the office, trailing after John, who was off down the corridor. He led them down some stairs, across an open space and into a hallway that led to the factory. Here he paused to pick up hard hats and safety glasses, then was off again onto the factory floor. As James had toured the factory in Oak Creek, he had some idea of what to expect, but this factory was a little different. The machines being built were smaller, and it was more of an assembly facility than a machine shop. There were cranes, shovels and backhoes lined up, all in various stages of construction. James noted that they all had notes on them that obviously denoted for whom they were being built.

"Are all the machines here sold?" he asked.

"Nearly all," John commented. "We have a few that we are building for stock and a couple for consignment to one of our major distributors in the Middle East, but otherwise we don't build it unless it's sold."

"How long does it take to get a machine if you were to order one today?" James asked.

"If it's a fairly standard machine with no peculiar options, we can usually crank it out in four to six weeks," John thought. "We do carry basic parts that are common to lines of machines, sometimes too much, but we're working on that."

"I noticed quite a few machines sitting in the yard when I drove in," James commented. "Are they waiting shipping or are they unsold?"

"There's a mix there," said John. "Some are stock, and some were built for an order that went south and left us with a bunch of inventory."

"What happened?" James asked the obvious question.

"Letter of credit issues, the customer had bank problems, and their letter of credit was rescinded, so no machines. No tickie, no laundry!" John elaborated.

"What will happen to the machines now?" James continued.

"We'll sell them, ex-stock," John explained. "It may take a little while, but we'll unload them, probably in the next three months."

"I suppose that the factory in Pittsburgh would look more like this one than the one in Oak Creek?" James asked.

"Right," John agreed. "Our Pittsburgh factory does all the smaller stuff, which is mostly sold through the dealer network. It's pretty close to an old locomotive works that was in Pittsburgh, where they used to build steam locos there. We should arrange for you to see that factory when you're in the States."

During their trip to the factory, James got the impression that Howard was along because John had told him to come, and it was not his habit to tour the factory floor. Although he obviously knew most of the employees, he was not comfortable in that environment and looked as if he would have preferred to stay in his office. John, on the other hand, was quite comfortable and seemed to know everyone and their families; he often asked a question that showed he had talked before to the employees and knew something of their lives. Howard was in his late fifties, or so James guessed, and rather reminded James of Alec Guinness, he had a sort of gnome-like demeanour about him, whereas John was more like Burt Reynolds and was expansive and given to large gestures and in some ways James could see him as a politician, not that that was necessarily a good thing.

Their trip finished at a loading dock where they saw a large crawler-mounted crane being manoeuvred onto a low loader. The boom and counterweight had been loaded separately onto another low loader, and they watched the final part of the operation as the machine was chained down to the trailer. John explained that the machine was on its way to Nigeria to an oil company and that he hoped it would arrive in one piece with all the parts intact. Apparently, it was not unheard of for parts to go astray; even parts affixed to the machine had been known to be removed between the docks and the customer site.

Back in the office, John ordered up more coffee, American this time. James arranged to meet Howard at the American Embassy at ten the following morning and then went with him to sign on as an employee and provide details of both his and Katrina's passports. By lunchtime, all the paperwork was complete, and James had an employee badge and number and was even shown somewhere to sit. It was suggested that he report to the office in Didcot until he went to the US and take the opportunity to start learning something about the company's products. They loaded him up with brochures and pamphlets and also found copies of back issues of the company magazine that featured products in use around the world. John suggested that they have lunch together and then proceeded to tell James what he was looking for in an application manager. His idea was for someone who would go out to the customer, learn about their project and then devise a mining solution that, of course, included the company's products. From John's point of view, also understanding how much and what kind of support the customer would need after the sale was important as well. Should the company place stocks of parts on consignment with the customer, or should they build a local parts facility that could serve several customers? Should they have service technicians in the field, or should they operate from a central location?

All those were things that James had encountered in one form or another in Zambia, and for him, there was no one ideal solution. He and John discussed the various companies that James had dealt with in Zambia, and which provided the better service and support, and did that make a difference when it came to buying decisions?

By the time James made it back to Cores End, it was six in the evening, and the family was beginning to wonder what had happened to him. He went through the events of the day and told them that he needed to catch the train to London the next morning to go to the American Embassy. Katrina needed to go with him to the Embassy as she also needed a visa for entry. They looked at train times and arranged to be dropped at the Bourne End station in time to catch a train that connected in Maidenhead for Paddington, from where they could take the tube to either Marble Arch or Bond Street. From either of those Tube stations, it was a quick walk to the embassy.

"So, now you're actually employed," Katrina said when they were in bed later that night.

"Better than being unemployed," he laughed.

"Much better," she agreed, nestling up to him. The nestling led to kissing, which led to other things, and they made love, not once but twice.

"That was wonderful," he said, as they lay looking at the ceiling.

"It was rather," she said. "I hope we don't get tired of each other and start to take one another for granted."

"I don't think we will," he said. "And for you, I'd do anything."

The next day, after an early breakfast, James's mother dropped them at the station and they caught the local train to Maidenhead. The weather had cleared up a lot, and although it was chilly, there was actually sunshine, making it a much nicer day for an outing to London. James and Katrina met Howard on the train from Maidenhead to Paddington. He had caught a train in Didcot earlier, changed at Reading and landed up on the same train that James and Katrina caught. Together they took the Tube to Marble Arch, via Notting Hill Gate, and walked the short distance to the embassy. There was a Marine guard at the door, but they were admitted and directed to the appropriate section. From there, it was straightforward. Howard had the paperwork already done and the money in hand for the fees. James and Katrina were issued the appropriate visa that would give them the right to work in the United States. Howard explained after they left that the US parent company would take care of converting their visas to permanent resident status, the so-called Green Card status. Getting the work visas had entailed submitting evidence that similarly qualified people were not available in the United States, and as Howard pointed out, finding graduate mining engineers was almost impossible, as they were snatched up by the mining companies as soon as they graduated. It was all fairly efficient, the only thing of note being the lines on the floor that designated where to stand and the instructions to stay behind the yellow line until called.

Howard then treated them both to lunch at a small but very elegant restaurant just off Regents Street. It was not the kind of restaurant that either James or Katrina had ever been in, far more elegant! Howard, however, was well known, and he informed them that when he came to London, it was his favourite haunt. James noticed that the menus had no prices on them, or at least the menus that he and Katrina had. He suspected that their host, Howard, had a different menu with pricing information. It seemed highly improbable that anyone would eat there without some knowledge of the potential damage. Several courses later, over cheese and biscuits, Howard passed the port around and asked James what he thought about going to the United States.

"I think it will be a great opportunity," James replied.

"You'll find the Yanks a bit different," commented Howard. "They're very much more open than people here typically are. But, I've found them, generally, woefully ignorant about the rest of the world."

"We did get asked a couple of questions last week that seemed odd at the time," James admitted.

"I'm not surprised," Howard commented. "They probably had no idea where Zambia was, did they?"

"Some did," James said, defending them. "Some had actually been to Zambia, to Chingola, to visit Nchanga."

"We're all a little concerned to see who they send when John leaves us to go back to Oak Creek," Howard said. "We're all a little afraid they'll send us an accountant instead of a marketing man."

"What's he been like to work with?" James asked.

"Has a wonderful memory," Howard began. "Remembers everyone's name, keeps little index cards on customers with names of wives and children and what kind of things they like to eat and drink."

"But what about as a person to work for?" James pressed.

"Not bad actually," admitted Howard. "He tells you what he expects and then helps you do it. I wish some of our British managers could be as helpful."

"Now that we have our visas, when do we leave for the US?" James asked.

"We've booked you on a flight on Friday on TWA," Howard replied. "That way, you'll have the whole weekend to recover before starting on Monday morning. We've also booked a room for you at a Ramada Inn in South Milwaukee. It's close to the factory and not as expensive as the Pfister."

"What about transportation?" Katrina asked.

"We've booked a hire car for James in Chicago, but I suppose you could use it while he's at the office," Howard thought. "So, when you hire the car, make sure that you're put on the paper as an extra driver."

"What about our household goods?" Katrina asked.

"How much do you have?" Howard asked her.

"Not too much actually," she admitted. "Only a couple of pieces of furniture and some boxes of things."

"We could box it up for you and ship it," Howard offered. "Can you bring it to the Didcot office?"

"I could manage that," thought James. "It'll fit in the Land Rover, it did when we left Zambia and drove to the Cape."

"Take as much as you can on the plane with you," Howard suggested. "Because, I think it'll be about a month before the rest of your things arrive."

"We'll do that," Katrina said. "Is there anything else we should know?"

"It'll be colder than here," Howard said."But you'll know that already. In the summer, it will be much hotter than here, so be ready for really sweltering heat and high humidity."

"Well, thank you for lunch," James said. "I suppose we should be starting back to Cores End. I'll see you in Didcot tomorrow."

"Right, we'll see you at eight tomorrow then," Howard agreed. "Have a good trip home."

After they left the restaurant, James asked Katrina if there was anything she wanted to do before they caught the train back to Bourne End. She thought that a winter coat might not be a bad idea. She had borrowed a coat from James's mother the week before, but could hardly spirit it off to America permanently. They walked up Regent Street and on to Oxford Street, looking at shops and coats. Katrina had to admit that most were priced beyond what she had imagined as reasonable, but they finally found one that was acceptable to her. She then decided that some boots would also be a good idea, and they spent the next two hours looking at boots until she found a pair to her liking. Before they bought anything else, James convinced her that they should start their journey back to Corse End, so steered her to the Tube station and thence to Paddington Station. Unfortunately, they had hit the beginning of the rush hour, and the train was quite full, but they were able to find seats. At Maidenhead, lots of people got off the train, and although quite a few left the station, there were still a large number waiting for the Bourne End train. James found a telephone box in working order and called his mother with their arrival time in Bourne End and asked for a lift from the station.

On the train ride between Maidenhead and Bourne End, James told Katrina stories of going to school when the trains had been pulled by steam locomotives. Obviously, to someone who had taken a steam train to school for two days and a night, the short ride between Bourne End and Marlow did not sound like such an adventure, but it was different. Katrina's trips had been on a school train that started in the Zambian Copperbelt and had finished in Bulawayo in Rhodesia. Whereas James's train had followed the Thames, her train had crossed the Kafue just south of Lusaka and the Zambezi at Victoria Falls with the spectacular view of the falls from the railway bridge. James's trips had taken less than thirty minutes, whereas Katrina's trips had taken two days. There had been times, though, when the line that James travelled on was flooded as the River Thames crested well above the level of the banks. James recalled twice when it had been high enough that the train did not actually run, but generally, with just a few inches of water over the tracks, the train just ploughed through, sending up sprays of water on either side.

James's mother met them at the station and drove home, all the while peppering them with questions about London, the American Embassy and what was in the parcels that Katrina had. James explained that they had flights booked for Friday and that Katrina had bought a coat and boots. Once back at the house, James set about organising their few belongings to take to the factory on the morrow. He explained first to his mother, then again to his father, that the company was going to crate it up for them and arrange shipping. While dinner was being prepared, James loaded their boxes and pieces of furniture into their Land Rover. It seemed to be very little to show for his time in Zambia and for Katrina's whole life, but they had brought with them only that that would fit in the Land Rover. Also, as they had lived in mine houses, they actually had very little furniture that was truly theirs, and for the rest, sheets, towels, china and crockery are easy to replace. One thing Katrina needed to do was visit a Family Planning Clinic and get birth control pills. She thought that a six-month supply would be enough until she could get signed on with a doctor in America.

"Howard's a funny little man," Katrina said to James when they were alone after dinner.

"Why?" he asked.

"He's my idea of Solomon Grundy," she said. "He obviously likes the good life, but he's not flashy about it."

"I was surprised at the restaurant we went to today," James said. "I shudder to think what the prices were."

"I wonder if he's married," she said.

"Probably," James laughed. "He's got that downtrodden look of a married man about him."

"What would you know about being downtrodden?" she asked.

"I'm your slave, subject to your every whim," he said.

"You are, are you?" she asked.

"I am," he confirmed.

"Well, Mr Downtrodden," she said. "Here's what you have to do to redeem yourself." She then whispered in his ear what she expected from him.

"I'll do the best I can," he promised.

"God, that was lovely," she said. "I'll never get tired of that."

"I have to say, I rather like this Katrina," he said. "What's changed?"

"I decided that life was too short not to enjoy every minute of it," she said. "What do you think it will be like living in America?"

"I really don't know," he admitted. "It'll be different, I'm sure, but we may not see all the differences immediately; we may come across things we don't understand, we may find words that are different. I remember in South Africa the first time I heard the word robot used for traffic lights, which threw me a little."

"They have large houses," she thought.

"I'm sure some do," he agreed. "But, I'm sure that many don't, we saw houses of people in the professional class, so I'm sure the house of a welder in the factory won't be as large."

"You're probably right," she agreed. "I'm still having a difficult time with all the choices, you go to a restaurant, and it's salad dressing choices, you get a baked potato and then it's all the choices of what you want on it, you ask for a bread roll and then get asked what type, that's hard to get used to."

"It is a little," he agreed. "I wonder what I'll see tomorrow at Didcot, who I'll meet?"

"Well, you can tell me all about it when you come home," she said.

The thirty-mile drive to Didcot took James a little longer than it had on Monday. He kept getting mixed up with rush hour traffic in the towns and villages that he passed through. First, it was Marlow, then Henley, then Wallingford, before he made the final leg to Didcot. Having driven it twice now, James was relieved to be going to the US. Making that trip every day was not something he would look forward to. His other option would have been the train, but that would have entailed a change in Maidenhead, thence to Reading and finally Didcot, a trip of probably an hour and a half, if the connections worked. At least the weather was still cooperating, and he had sunshine for the drive and no rain and no muddy spray put up by cars in front of him, but the forecast was for that to change and for less clement weather to move in quickly from the east and the North Sea.

At the office, James found his way to the desk that he had been assigned for that week. He had barely sat down when Howard appeared at the door.

"Good morning, James, how are we today?" he asked.

"Fine, thanks, Howard," James assured him.

"Do you have your belongings here?" Howard continued.

"Yes, in my Land Rover in the car park," James replied.

"I'll show you where to drop them off," Howard offered. He then went with James to the car park and then directed him to the loading bays where a couple of shipping agents were waiting. They emptied the Land Rover and assured James that it would be packed properly into a wooden crate and shipped to the US later that week. They told him to expect delivery in about a month. Because James had no home address yet in Oak Creek, they planned to ship his crate to the offices, and the US office could help him from there. That done, Howard then suggested coffee and a walk around the offices to meet people that James would probably be in communication with over the next year. Howard was a great believer in matching faces with names and told James that it made for better communications if you actually had met the person you were talking to. As much of James's communications with Didcot over the coming months was likely to be by telephone, he felt that it was wise to meet as many people as possible.

By lunch time, James's head was spinning. He tried to count up all the people he had been introduced to, and after thirty, stopped counting. He decided that he was likely to have some kind of communication with about eight people, and the rest were possible but not probable. Howard took him to lunch at the company cafeteria, where they joined John Williams and another American, Richard Zachowski. John introduced Richard as the chief engineer for the Didcot factory and explained to Richard who James was and what he would be doing in Oak Creek. Richard wanted to know where James had worked and with what equipment, then he wanted details on equipment performance, breakdowns and parts usage. James was able to answer in general terms, but told Richard that for more details, he would have to consult notes that he had kept. He would find a way to get some of that information to Richard in the coming weeks.

John told James that they needed to discuss things before he left for Oak Creek, so James followed him back to his office.
"James, here are your tickets for your trip on Friday," John started.
"We've put you up in the front of the bus now that you're with us."
"Thank you," James said, unsure if he had heard correctly that they would be travelling first class to Chicago.
"So, excited to be going?" John asked.

"Yes, but also a little apprehensive," James admitted. "I just hope I meet everyone's expectations."

"I wouldn't worry about that," John assured him. "Just do what seems right. I presume that has worked in the past?"

"Yes, I believe it has," James agreed.

"Well, there you go!" John told him. "Just do what comes naturally!"

"Do you have any advice?" James asked.

"Try to sort out what your priorities at work really need to be," John commented. "You'll be asked by everyone to go to their favourite customers and spend time. Many times, that will be a waste of your time. You'll have to learn how to read each salesman and gauge just how serious their prospective customers really are."

"So, rank each prospect as it comes in and assign a probability to each?" asked James.

"There you go," John agreed. "Tomorrow I've arranged for you to spend the day with our sales correspondents so that you can see what enquiries typically look like and how we weigh them and respond."

"Thanks," said James.

"You're welcome," John replied. "By the way, I'll probably see you later next week. I'll be coming to Oak Creek with some Brits to talk about some shovels and whether or not we can build them here."

"Is there anything else?" James asked him.

"No, James, not right now," he replied. "Do you have any questions?"

"What's Wisconsin like?" James asked.

"Typical Midwestern state," John replied. "Cold in the winter, hot and humid in the summer, moderated a little for those living along the shores of Lake Michigan. Lots of heavy industry, also lots of dairy farming, in the northern forests, not very diverse when it comes to races, so you won't see many black folks in South Milwaukee and Oak Creek; this isn't Zambia. Ethnic origins, Polish and German, probably make up the most."

"We flew into Chicago. I presume that any overseas flights would have to do the same?" James asked.

"They would," John confirmed. "It's too close to Chicago to make it another international point of entry. But, as you found out, there's plenty of flights from Milwaukee to Chicago, or to Minneapolis."

"What about wildlife?" James asked.

"Deer by the thousands," John said. "They have problems with too many, so there is a hunting season, but that's scary, a million guys out there with guns, half of them boozed up with brandy, so if you ever go, wear the brightest orange vest you can find and keep your eyes open, or you'll be taken for a deer."

"I'll remember that," James laughed. "Thank you, I shouldn't take up any more of your time."

"Be sure to stop in and see me tomorrow afternoon before you leave for Chicago," John said as James left his office.

James went back to the desk he was using and made a list of things he needed to do before leaving for America. Thankfully, it was a short list; they had no house to sell or rent out, they had no flat to terminate the lease on, their possessions were already taken care of, the Land Rover he already had a buyer for, one of the people at Didcot. Their bank account, they had decided to empty and close and take whatever cash they had in traveller's checks. He also sorted through all the documents and brochures he had been given and pared them down to a few that would give him the best overall view of the product line of the company. He could always pick up more when he was in America. Howard stopped by to see him with the shipping documents, the waybill that told him that their possessions were now in the hands of the shipper and also to complain that the sunshine had gone to be replaced by clouds and drizzle.

Later that evening, after dinner, James related his experiences of the day to Katrina and asked her what she had done.

"I got your mother to take me to Windsor Castle," she replied. "It was nice, but man, it was only cold standing on the battlements in the drizzle!"

"What did you do for lunch?" he asked.

"We went to Marlow and ate at this little place close to the bridge and the church," she said. "I think it is more of a tea shop than a restaurant, but it was fine. I think your mom is trying hard to accept me after our difficult start."

"Well, when we go to Chicago on Friday, we'll be going in style," he announced. "Look at these tickets, first class!"

"No man, really?" she queried.

"As you once said to me, *kyk* man," he said, waving them under her nose.

"That's only *lekker* man," she commented.

"I have to go to Didcot tomorrow," he said. "What are you going to do?"

"I'm going to the Family Planning Clinic to pick up pills, and I think I'll pack what we have left to take," she thought. "I'll leave out some clothes for you to wear on Friday. How many suitcases can we take?"

"I think all we have," he said. "We had no problem when we flew from South Africa a couple of years ago on our long leave, and that wasn't First Class. I would imagine that First Class passengers on TWA get a bigger luggage allowance, like they do on BA."

"I'm sure they do," she agreed. "I wonder if the TWA first is better than the BA first. Remember when we got to fly back to Zambia in first?"

"That was fun," he agreed.

"You know what's more fun?" she said, grinning at him.

"I can guess," he said. "What would you like to do?"

"Let's see if we can match the lions," she said. "I'm not going to hold you to every thirty minutes, but let's see what we can do."

James drove to Didcot the next day and would take the train home as he was handing over the Land Rover to its new owner. His day was spent looking at letters of enquiry and responses. He was fascinated by the pricing structure that they used. To the factory cost, they added something for administrative costs, shipping costs, profit margins and, depending on the destination, various fees and dealer add-ons. It was explained to him that, of course, they would never be party to bribery and corruption, but certain dealers in certain countries operated with different margin structures. That explained the extra five and ten per

41

cents added to the overall price for equipment destined for certain countries. He had lunch with the sales correspondents, and they told him stories about salesmen who sent in leads that were so far removed from reality as to be laughable and also some that seemed improbable but that led to ultimate sales. After lunch, James stopped to see John Williams. They agreed on how to send back expense reports, and John suggested that James take an advance of £300 against his expense account and take it along in the form of traveller's checks. That way, he would not be in contravention of the 1966 regulations on exchange control facilities regarding monies exported outside the United Kingdom. He would take along his allotted £25 in cash, as would Katrina. But all in all, traveller's checks were more convenient and more negotiable. His ride home on the train took a lot longer than the drive to Didcot. There were changes of trains involved and everything took time, so it was almost six-thirty by the time he reached the Bourne End station, but he did come home some £800 richer.

That evening, James called both his sister, Alex, in Italy and his brother, Will, in Johannesburg to tell them that he and Katrina were moving to the States. He had threats of visits from both of them, but promised that the visits would not be imminent. He told them to at least wait until the winter was well and truly over unless they fancied freezing to death! Katrina called her parents in South Africa and gave them the news. All her mother wanted to know was how cold it was going to be where they would be going and how far it was to California. Her father, now that he was a grape grower, rather fancied the idea of a trip to California to visit vineyards and winemakers. He knew that his Hannepoort grapes were nothing like those grown in California, but he was curious to see how vineyards were managed there. Both parents wanted to know if Katrina would be working there, and Katrina was able to tell them that when immigration formalities were settled, then she indeed could work if she chose to do so. She thought it likely; otherwise, she would get bored with not much to do all day, particularly as children were not something that they planned on.

"So, we're ready for tomorrow?" Katrin asked James that night.

"As ready as I'll ever be," he replied. "Are you excited?"

"I am," she said. "It'll be new, different, and I'm looking forward to seeing more of the States when you get some time off, you do get holidays?"

"Two weeks a year to start with," he said. "That plus public holidays."

"How many of them?" she asked.

"No idea," he admitted. "But, I would think American Independence Day, Christmas, New Year and maybe some others."

"I wonder where we'll find a place to live?" she said.

"I'm sure there's places we could rent," he said. "Then we'll have to buy a car as well. I didn't see too many buses out where the James & Brown factory is."

"I'd like to find a job as soon as I can," she said.

"I'm sure that as they sort out our work visas, you'll be able to find something" he said. "Do you have anything you'd really like to do?"

"I've got all kinds of ideas floating around," she said. "But nothing definite. I could always find a transporting business and see if they need anyone."

"I can't say for certain, but I get the idea that the States are not as progressive as they could be when it comes to women in the workforce," he said. "So, you may get some opposition there. John told me that Wisconsin is largely heavy industry and dairy, plus there's bound to be other things."

"I don't fancy being a dairy farmer," she thought. "No time off."

"You're right there," he agreed. "I wonder what else they have there?"

"We'll find out soon enough," she said. "How are we getting to the airport tomorrow?"

"Dad's taken the day off, so they're both coming with us to see us off," he replied.

"So, tears and drama?" she asked.

"Probably," he laughed. "But I have a little sympathy, Will's in South Africa, Alex is in Italy, and we're flying off to the States, so they're pretty much on their own, like your folks in South Africa."

"That's true," she agreed. "I'll be nice."

"We do need to stop and the bank in the morning," he said. "I should change the cash I got yesterday for the Land Rover into traveller's cheques."

"Is there anything else last-minute that we need to do?" she asked.

"I don't think so," he said. "We've got tickets, passports, visas, money, bags are packed, our stuff is crated up and on its way, you've got your supply of pills, I can't think of anything else."

Oak Creek

William and Elizabeth did take James and Katrina to Heathrow the next day and saw them checked in at the TWA desk, then said their goodbyes as James and Katrina left through the immigration gate. Travelling first class on TWA was a little different from their first trip nearly two weeks earlier. When they checked in for the flight, James got seats on the left side of the plane so that when they came into Chicago, they might have a view of the Loop. They were seated in row five, seats one and two. On the flight, Katrina discovered that, whereas the vodka was fine, she did not like caviar, but the balance of the meals was excellent and to her taste. Everything was served at the seat from the trolleys and was presented very elegantly. It was a significant step up from the service they had received before. They had flown first class before, on a BOAC flight from London to Lusaka via Entebbe, but all in all, they had to say that the TWA service was better than the BOAC service. But as James commented, there was competition on the London to Chicago route, whereas BOAC had the London to Lusaka route to themselves. That may well have had some impact on the level of service offered. Their route took them north up over Iceland, then ice-covered Greenland, then the vast expanses of northern Canada, until they crossed the border and started down over Michigan.

As they descended into the Chicago O'Hare airport, James was treated to his view of the Loop, which he pointed out to Katrina. They were amazed by the tall buildings clustered along the lakefront and the expressways snaking around the city. On their last trip to Wisconsin, they had been told that it was not Motorway, but Expressway and in many other states Freeway. They had learned that there were also Tollways, Toll Roads and Turnpikes, but were not sure that they really understood the difference, except that Tollway and Toll Road suggested paying money!

Snow had fallen, and the browns of two weeks ago were now partially covered with white. The dark browns of the woods still stood out, but grassy areas were now all white, and most of the roofs of the houses had snow on them. It was a different world. When they landed, they could see piles of snow where it had been pushed off the runways. Obviously, quite a bit had fallen since they had left barely a week before. As James was picking up his hire car in Chicago, he wondered if the roads to Wisconsin had all been ploughed and what the drive would be like.

The drive north was easy enough, once they had cleared the heavy traffic of Chicago. What James had not realised was that the main road north to the Wisconsin State line was in fact a toll road. He had changed some money at the airport, so at least he had the means to pay the tolls. Renting the car had been interesting, as he had no credit cards and had to put up traveller's checks as security. Clearly, if he was going to be travelling for the company a lot, he needed to get a credit card as soon as possible. At least it was sunny, so the drive north was pleasant enough, no falling snow or sleet to deal with, and the road surface was dry, so little chance of ice.

They left the I-94 expressway at College and almost immediately turned south on 13th to find the Ramada Inn. There was snow in the parking lot and it had been ploughed away, probably by the red bus with Ramada Inn emblazoned on its side. The bus was equipped with a plough, and it was reasonable to presume that it had been used to clear the snow. The inn was sandwiched between 13th Avenue and the expressway and was clustered near a Holiday Inn and a Mini Price Motel. They were given a room on the fifth floor, which gave them a view over open ground to the Mini Price Motel and to what looked like a depository for old earth-moving equipment. Behind that and the inn was a railway line, and there were power lines in abundance. That did strike both James and Katrina. Neither of them could recall ever seeing as many power lines in such a small space before. They were more used to the minimal number of power lines of Zambia, particularly when they had lived on a remote mine served by a single line. James was sure that they would see many more differences in the weeks to come.

"Shall we find somewhere to have dinner, *Suikerbossie?*" James asked.

"That would be nice," Katrina agreed. "Does this hotel have a dining room or do we have to go farther afield?"

"They have a dining room," James assured her. "But, should we try somewhere else?"

"Do you have any idea what's near here?" she asked.

"No, but there's a telephone directory here, perhaps we can find somewhere," he thought.

"What about this place, Selen's?" she asked.

"Where is it?" he asked.

"East Layton," she read out. "Is that far from here?"

"No, I don't think so," he replied. "I think from looking at the map that the hire car company gave us, that Layton is the road that runs along the north side of the airport, so maybe fifteen minutes from here."

"Let's try it," she suggested. Selen's was a place that specialised in prime rib, any day of the week. The portions, at least to James and Katrina, were huge, and there were the choices, always the choices, dressings, bread, and even how the meat was cooked, rare, medium or well. By the time they had struggled through the dinner, they had both overeaten and sleep called, so it was a quick drive back to the hotel, a shower, and then collapse into bed and digest the vast meal they had consumed.

Saturday morning, they slept late or at least until seven. The six-hour time change had its effects, as they had discovered before, and they were unable to really sleep late. After breakfast, James suggested a drive around the area. Outside, they discovered that it was colder than it had been when they arrived the day before, and there were light flurries of snow falling. It did not look as if the snowfall would amount to any appreciable accumulation, so James was not concerned about driving. They went south on 13th until they came to Rawson Avenue, a large road that was east-west. James asked Katrina which way, and she suggested west, away from the lake. They crossed over the expressway and kept going west until they came to another major intersection. Another right turn and they were going north. Just after the turn, the road crossed another that cut across it diagonally, and James presumed that if he took that road, it would lead into the centre of Milwaukee. A little farther up the road, Katrina told James that she remembered that there was a shopping mall close by. Sure enough, they came upon the Southridge Mall.

This was their first encounter with an American shopping centre. There were two floors of shops, which were arranged along a gallery that gave access to all the shops from the shelter of the central open space. That made it a pleasant place to be, even in the dead of winter. James and Katrina wandered up and down, window shopping and then discovered the food court. Most of the offerings were in the category of fast food, but they ate anyway, taking in the atmosphere of the place. The biggest challenge was remembering where they had parked. The car park was huge and probably half full, so there were cars everywhere, and after a while, they all began to look the same. Fortunately, James had parked near a lamp standard that had a letter on it, so once they found that, it was just a question of walking up and down the aisles close by until they recognised their car.

They took a leisurely drive back to the hotel and had a brief snowball fight in the car park before going to their room. James had managed to get snow down inside his clothes and was eager to get his wet things off and into something dry. Their room had been cleaned and the bed made up. It was already getting dark, and the sun went down a little before six. With the sunset, what little heating effect there had been from the sun went as well, and the temperature dropped to about five degrees. Cold! At least outside it was cold. In the hotel room, it was warm, even hot, as they had yet to learn how to really regulate the temperature. Katrina just shed most of her clothes and paraded around the room in bra and panties, a circumstance that James heartily approved of. Ensuring that he discharged the static from his body first, he reached for her in one of her passes and tumbled with her onto the bed. From there, things just took their natural course, and the bra and panties soon were on the floor along with James's clothes.

Later, Katrina asked James if he had thought about anything for dinner, and James was considering his reply when the phone rang. It was not the manager relaying complaints about noisy lovemaking, but Tony Whitaker asking if they had eaten yet or had plans to. James admitted that they had yet to eat and had in fact just been considering what to do. Tony suggested that he stop by the hotel, pick them up and take them to a place in Racine, just south of Oak Creek. James put that to Katrina, and she nodded yes. Her only concern was what to wear. James consulted with Tony and relayed the answer, smart casual but not formal, whatever that meant. James and Katrina discussed it and concluded that for James it meant a jacket and tie, and for Katrina a trouser suit with a matching blouse. That way, she was smart enough without worrying about being cold in a dress. Their assumptions had been correct, and Tony and Margaret were similarly attired.

Over dinner, Margaret asked them what they had done that day and where they had been. James was happy to let Katrina give her a blow-by-blow account of the day and only added the odd comment. Margaret asked if Zambia had any shopping malls like Southridge, and both James and Katrina laughed at that. They assured her that there was nothing of that ilk in Zambia and told her that South Africa was only just getting its first malls that would compare with the American malls; the first and most elegant one was Sandton City, which had opened its doors in 1973. There just was not the population base in Zambia to warrant the expense of constructing such a facility, so more traditional shopping was likely to remain for some time. Margaret commented that the Southridge Mall was not that much older; it had only been opened in 1970, as a sister to the Northridge Mall. Tony then got down to more practical matters.

"How did you rent the car at O'Hare?" he asked James.

"We used some traveller's checks as the deposit and will get most of the money back when we return the car," James explained.

"We'll fix that Monday by giving you a company credit card," Tony assured him. "Then I suggest you take the car back, get back as much as you can, then re-rent it using the credit card."

"Thank you," James said. "What do you suggest for a place to live? We can't just live in the hotel?"

"There's a place on Lake Shore Drive right on the north end of Grant Park, which I think puts it right at the south end of Cudahy, that has apartments for rent, you might try there," Tony suggested. "You might want to wait a week or so to get a paycheck stub so that you can show that you're employed."

"Can't Ray just call them?" Margaret asked.

"Sure, that's a great idea," Tony agreed. "You'll also need to set up a bank account. Do you think you'll want your money paid in directly, or do you want a check?"

"Paid in directly," James said. "Are there people who still want checks or cash?"

"You'd be surprised," Tony told him. "I think some of the guys don't want their wives to know how much they're making, so they take cash or a check, which they immediately cash, and then they give their wives housekeeping money. What did you do in Zambia?"

"All the professional staff got their money once a month, by direct deposit," James explained. "The mine paid cash to many of the hourly Zambian workers, but I was never given the option. The only decision I had to make was which bank I wanted the money to be put in."

"What are you guys doing tomorrow?" Tony asked.

"We hadn't really thought about anything yet," James replied.

"Why don't you come on out to the house for lunch?" Tony suggested. "We won't keep you out late in the evening, I'm sure you're still sleeping odd hours because of the time change."

James looked at Katrina, and she nodded slightly. "We'd be delighted," he replied. "What time and where?"

"Well, Katrina's been there before with Margaret, but in case she can't remember all the twists and turns in the road, here's a map," Tony replied, passing over a hand-drawn map as he did so. "Come around eleven. Now we'd better get you back to the hotel before you fall asleep on us."

The excursion to the Whitaker home turned out to be not just a visit to their house for lunch, but, as Tony put it, a meet and greet, so that James and Katrina could meet some other people. There were none from James & Brown; there were instead lawyers, doctors, estate agents, shop owners and even a professional musician. They were all neighbours of the Whitaker's, and Katrina commented to James later that she felt a little like a new prized acquisition being shown off. Men and women split, and the men went downstairs into something magical and mysterious called a rec room, to play pool and watch American football on the television, and the women stayed upstairs and talked about all manner of things. One lady had been to Africa, she had been on a safari in Kenya and was the local expert on all things African, a cynical view that Katrine had until she thought about it and realised that among the people she knew in Africa, she would be the only one who had been to America and would be the local expert on all things American. American football was lost on James, he did not understand the rules, he could not understand why they all seemed to spend more time standing around than actually doing something with the ball, he did not see the need for two squads of men on the same team, that would come on and off the field depending on who had the ball. For him, it had been rugby, which was a much more free-flowing game, and whoever had the ball tried to keep it long enough to score a try, while the others tried hard to take it away and score their own try. Katrina rescued James at about three by saying that she had booked a telephone call with her parents in the Cape. It was not the truth, but she guessed James had had enough of being sociable in a new and strange place. There was only so much that one could take in at one time.

On Monday morning, Katrina dropped James off at the company offices. She had accepted an invitation to lunch with Margaret Whitaker and two other ladies, and they were also going to take her to check out the apartment block in Cudahy. James walked in, and the receptionist directed him to Ray Pierce's office, where there were formalities to be observed and a company identity card to be issued. He provided Ray with all the information he needed to complete the forms required by the INS, the Immigration and Naturalization Service, in order to start the process of getting a Green Card, or Resident Alien status. Ray told him that he would need to get fingerprints taken and gave him a card for himself and one for Katrina, and told him that the local police station would do it for him. There were also forms to fill out to get Social Security numbers that would be used to deduct taxes and Social Security payments from paycheques. Ray also gave him a company credit card and the set of strictures that went with it. The mysteries of expense accounts were then explained, and what was permissible, what was borderline or questionable and what was forbidden. He was cautioned to get receipts for everything, even those items that were small and often overlooked. He was also given a telephone credit card and told that it could be used for personal calls when he was out and about visiting potential customers, as well as for company calls. Ray then suggested that he take the rental car back and re-rent it using the credit card, rather than his own cash.

"You mean go back to the Chicago airport?" James asked.

"No, no need for that," Ray assured him. "Take it to the airport here and turn it in with the people here. They'll be able to take care of it for you. When you've done that, why don't you pick up your wife and get your fingerprints taken at the Oak Creek police department?"

"One small problem," James said. "Katrina has the car at the moment. She had a luncheon engagement with Margaret Whitaker. Would it be acceptable to take care of all these items tomorrow?"

"Of course," Ray agreed. "Why don't you find Tony Whitaker and see if he wants to get you started?"

James remembered his way around the offices and quickly found that of Tony Whitaker.

"James," Tony said. "Good to see you. You ready to get started?"

"Of course," James said. "What do you want me to do?"

"Keen to get going," Tony laughed. "Before we do anything here, let's just meet the rest of the people on this floor. This is Marlys, she looks after me, you now as well, does travel arrangements, types up stuff and keeps track of expenses."

"Nice to meet you, Marlys," James said.

"Nice to meet you," she replied.

"Those guys are the sales correspondents, Mark Lesnewski, does shovels, Tom Nelson, who does drills and Jim Edwards, he looks after draglines," Tony waved at them in turn. "This is Cathy, she's with Robert Andrews, the shovel king, and this is Robert in his lair. Bob, this is my new man, James Martin."

"We met," Robert said. "Glad to have you aboard, James. Make sure I get some of your time, don't spend it all on draglines."

"We won't forget you," Tony promised. "Next door here is Bill Riding, he has drills. Bill, you remember James Martin?"

"Sure do," Bill replied. "Good to have you with us, James. You done much blasting?"

"Quite a bit," James assured him. "But with typically much smaller hole sizes than your drills produce."

"You'll figure out the differences soon enough," Bill said. "You should meet Dan, he's the big seller these days, looks after draglines."

"That's true," Tony agreed. "This is Dan Wells, James Martin."

"Good to see you again, James," Dan said.

"Now out here, you already met Cathy, then we have Jill, who manages Bill and Tom and Helen, who looks after Dan and Jim Edwards. Down that way are Dick West and his people who look after international sales," Tony said, completing the introductions for the people in and around the offices on that floor. "Upstairs are the construction guys, and downstairs is mahogany row where the big wheels hang out."

"Where are the engineers for these product lines?" James asked.

"Two floors up," Tony replied. "Close enough, maybe one day we'll get a bigger building and they can be on the same floor we are, if that's what you were thinking."

"I was actually," James admitted.

"Well, let's get some coffee and I'll fill you in on the projects," Tony suggested.

They got coffee, and Tony then went through the various projects he had on the books. Obviously, the number and type varied with enquiries and requests from the salespeople, but recent activity in the coal mining industry had created quite a backlog. The projects varied from general enquiries for machine sizing to specific use questions regarding actual operation in mines. Tony then showed James where he kept the technical specifications of the machines the company made. There would be little point in designing a solution to a mining problem around machine sizes that the company either did not make or could not quickly modify an existing design that would then meet the needs. Tony then pulled out an organisation chart and pointed out to James who the various field representatives were, with his own editorials on the likelihood of enquiries leading to orders. Within the United States, there were a number of field representatives generally scattered in areas where mining activity was greatest. Outside the United States, the International Sales people were typically located in major cities in those countries with significant mining industries, so Australia, Brazil, Chile, South Africa and were also placed where travel to surrounding countries was convenient, so, Didcot, to cover Europe and North and West Africa and Singapore to cover Malaysia, Indonesia, India and China. James already knew George Murphy, the field man in South Africa, who also covered Zambia, Botswana, Namibia, Zaire, Zimbabwe and other surrounding countries if and when a need arose. Canada was an anomaly because, although it was not part of the United States, it was managed from the US and was not part of the International Sales group. They took a break for lunch, then got back into the particular projects that Tony was working on. By the time five rolled around in the afternoon, James was ready for a break. Just before he left, Tony told him that he should be ready to travel on Wednesday of that week, as he was to go with him to Gillette, Wyoming, to visit with a customer. They would be back on Friday.

James left the office and found Katrina waiting for him outside the offices of James & Brown.

"Have you been waiting long?" he asked.

"Not too long," she assured him. "I've been watching the people leave the office and wondering what they all do."

"So, how was lunch and the flat?" he asked.

"Lunch turned out to be fun," she said. "The ladies were nice and full of questions, it amazes me how little Americans know about Zambia, or even Africa, but then, as I realised yesterday, we know little about the States. The flat is on the fifth floor, fifth in American terms, not British terms, in that big building near the lake at the end of Grant Park. It's got a nice view of the park and the lake, one bedroom, one bathroom and a living cum, kitchen, dining area."

"Should we take it?" he asked.

"I think so," she said. "If they transfer you to the US payroll, then rent won't be an issue. They said we could have it next week, so maybe we could move in over the weekend. We both need to be there to sign the lease, so we should pick a day."

"What do we do for furniture, plates, knives and forks and such?" he asked.

"Maggie introduced me to this store called Kmart," she replied. "It's only huge, man, and it looks like we can get everything we need there, and it's not that dear."

"Is it like OK Bazaars?" he asked.

"I suppose so," she thought. "It's not Selfridges or Harrods, maybe not even Marks and Sparks, more like Woolworths, but we can afford it. What about your day?"

"Well, I met all kinds of people. Tomorrow you and I need to go to the police station to get our fingerprints taken for our Green Cards, and Tony wants me to take a trip with him on Wednesday to Wyoming, we'd be back on Friday," he replied.

"So you're going to go off and leave me in the frozen wastes?" she said.

"What will you do while I'm away?" he asked.

"Stay warm," she said.

"It's only two nights, so I won't be gone long," he promised.

"Are you excited to be going?" she asked.

"Yes," he said. "I wonder what Wyoming is like. I suppose it's colder even than here, do you think I have enough clothes?"

"I suppose it depends on whether or not you go outside," she thought. "How far is it to Wyoming?"

"I don't know," he admitted. "Maybe we're just as bad as the people here; we know little about the US."

"Let's get back to the Ramada and think about dinner," she suggested. "It's supposed to snow a lot again tonight, so I'd rather not be driving the streets."

The visit to the Oak Creek Police Department the next day was interesting; the officer behind the desk was most helpful, and they had their fingerprint cards completed quickly and efficiently. He then gave them some wipes to clean the ink off their fingers and directed them to a bathroom to clean off the rest. That done, James drove them to the airport and the rental car company, turned in the car and then re-rented it using the company credit card. That now gave him more cash back in hand. He then had Katrina drop him off at the company so that she could take the car if she wanted to go somewhere.

"All done?" Tony asked James when he arrived at the office.

"All done," James confirmed. "We had our fingerprints taken, and I've dropped the cards off with the personnel people. I also took your advice and rented the car again using the company card."

"Great, so here is the schedule for Wednesday," Tony said. "Sadly, it's a roundabout way to get to Gillette; we have to fly to Sheridan and drive, so we fly from here to Minneapolis, then to Denver, then switch airlines to Western to fly to Sheridan. Keith Sanders will meet us in Sheridan and drive us to Gillette. We should get there late Wednesday night."

"What do I need to take?" James asked.

"You have a camera?" Tony asked.

"Yes," James replied.

"Take that, take the warmest clothes you've got and boots if you have," Tony suggested.

"There are no flights into Gillette?" James asked.

"Not yet," Tony said. "But at the rate things are going, someone will set up flights there pretty soon, if the airport is equipped for it. If the company plane was available, we'd use that, but the Construction guys have it for the moment for a big deal on a highway project in Florida."

"There's a company plane?" James asked.

"Sure," Tony said. "We just got a new Lear 35, goes like a rocket, a little small inside, but you get there quickly and don't have to mess around waiting in airports for flights and connections."

"Who are we seeing in Gillette?" James asked.

"The coal sub of Magnate Oil, Magnate Coal," Tony explained. "It seems that all kinds are getting into coal these days. We've got AMAX, who you probably know better as a copper company; they bought Ayrshire Collieries back in '69 and have been expanding their coal operations ever since. Atlantic Richfield may be an oil company, but they're starting up a new big coal mine out there. Wyodak has been around forever and was once part of Homestake, and we have Sun Oil starting up their big new mine, then we also have Shell with a coal sub."

"What is Magnate looking for?" James asked.

"Shovels," Tony replied. "The overburden in the Powder River Basin is pretty thin, and the coal seams are thick, so the mining lends itself to shovel and truck operations. We just need to figure how many and what size shovels that they will need to match up with whatever truck fleet they decide upon."

"How long will the mine last?" James asked.

"Reserves are said to be such that a thirty to forty-year life of the mine is quite likely," Tony explained. "These mines are all pretty big, James. There's a ton of coal out there."

"What about bucket wheel excavators like those the Germans use and those in the Victoria brown coal fields in Australia?" James asked.

"So far, the operators have shown no great enthusiasm for bucket wheels," Tony said. "The coal is harder than the lignites the Germans and Aussies are digging up, so shovels and trucks looks better, better for us anyway, it's been a few years since we made a bucket wheel, and we'd probably not be able to compete against the Germans."

"How does the coal get to whoever buys it?" James asked.

"Typically, by train," Tony explained. "They have hundred-car trains, so 10,000 tons per train load. So, one of the first things they'll need to do is build a railroad spur into the mine. That happens to be good for us, because when we ship machines, we usually ship them out by railroad car. Go and see Marlys and gather up the sales packets on our shovels and the spec sheets, and while you're at it, pick up some drill stuff too. Eventually, those guys are going to need to drill and blast, so we might as well start them thinking along those lines now."

"Will the other companies have already been there?" James asked.

"Possibly," Tony thought. "If they haven't been yet, then they will do pretty soon. I gather decisions are expected within a few months."

When James came back with the packets of literature, Tony told him to keep them and remember to take them with him when they left on Wednesday.

That evening, Katrina showed James the road atlas of the United States that she had bought that day, and together they found Gillette. James explained the circuitous route they would have to take to get there, which explained the length of the trip.

"Tony told me today that if the company plane had been available, we could have gone there and back in one day," James said.

"They have a plane?" Katrina asked.

"Apparently," James replied. "It's a Lear Jet."

"Must be nice," she said. "I imagine no waiting around for airlines or connections."

"That's exactly what Tony said," he laughed.

"When will you get to fly on it?" she asked.

"No idea," he said. "What did you do today?"

"I went to Kmart and have a list of what we need to set up house and what it will cost us," she said.

"Is it a lot?" he asked.

"I don't think so," she said. "I've just listed the minimum: plate, cup, knife and fork each, sheets, blankets and such, a simple bed, small kitchen table and chairs, saucepans and the like, the apartment comes with stove and fridge, so we don't have to worry about them."

"Well, as time goes on, we can always add," he said. "We probably won't be throwing any dinner parties for a while. Will you take me to this Kmart when I get back?"

"I will indeed," she promised. "They have this weird thing called a blue light special; as I understand it, when this blue light flashes next to something, the price is reduced."

"We should see if we can guess when they're going to put the things we want on sale," he said.

"My guess is that they discount the stuff that hasn't sold in a while," she suggested. "If they can get rid of it, they probably are happy. One nice thing, the Kmart store is really close to the apartment building."

"So we can pick up everything there we need for now?" he asked.

"We can," she assured him.

"Sounds like a plan. What do you want for dinner?" he asked.

"Well, *ou* man, if I'm going to be on my own for the next two nights, then you should *somma* take me somewhere nice tonight," she said.

After dinner, Katrina modelled a new swimsuit she had bought. The hotel had a pool indoors, and she planned to try it out and get some exercise in by swimming up and down. It was a one-piece suit, designed for swimming, not sunbathing. It was a dark Navy blue with a high neck and only a little cut out of the back. Katrina was looking for comfort, swimming not attracting oglers, not that she was not worth ogling, in James's mind, she was beautiful and worth a second or third look on any day.

Tony picked up James the next day on his way to work, which meant that Katrina could keep the car if she chose to venture out into the snow and ice. Tony told James that they would stop at the office briefly, then go to the airport to catch their flight. At the airport, they checked in for the Northwest Orient flight to Minneapolis and found the gate. The flight on the Northwest Boeing 727 was short enough, flying over snow-covered farmlands, forests and lakes that looked as if they were just frozen sheets of ice, under grey skies all the way. The terrain looked like it was gently rolling, with hills here and there, but nothing that looked like a mountain. In Minneapolis, they were able to find their connecting flight easily enough and set off on another flight, which took longer and, as far as James could tell, just droned on over miles and miles of farmlands, covered in snow. As they approached Denver, the skies cleared, and James was treated to a view of the famed Rocky Mountains, covered in snow. In Denver, they had to change concourses to find the Western Airlines gate, but the walk was short enough. The height of the mountains impressed James. Then he also considered that even the airport at Denver was high up, over 5,000 feet up, higher than any mountain in the whole British Isles. The flight up to Sheridan had them paralleling the mountains for a while, until they trended off to the west, and other smaller ranges came into view. What struck James was the lack of habitation. It had become sparse on the flight out to Denver; now it was even more sparse. Wyoming clearly was not densely populated.

Sheridan was a much smaller airport than Denver or Minneapolis, and their contact, Keith Sanders, was waiting at the gate for them.

"Hey, Keith," Tony said. "Meet James Martin, he's my new sidekick, started on Monday."

"James," Keith said. "I heard you were coming. I gather you were working in the mines until recently."

"I worked at a couple of copper mines in Zambia," James confirmed.

"Hope you brought your winter clothes," Keith said. "It's cold out there."

"How far is it to Gillette?" James asked.

"Just over 100 miles," Keith said. "About an hour and a half or less, depending on where the smokeys are. This new 55 speed limit is ridiculous out here in Wyoming and Montana, that's why I got a FuzzBuster."

"A FuzzBuster?" James asked.

"It's a radar detector, it tells me where they're operating and I get warnings before they can get any kind of lock on me," Keith explained. "Is that your bags?"

"It is," Tony confirmed. "Okay, you ready, James?"

"Ready," James confirmed. They went out to the parking lot and Keith opened up his Chevrolet Suburban for them, Tony in the front and James in the back seat, with their bags all the way in the back. The Suburban was huge, and James noted that it did have four-wheel drive and thought that that was probably a good idea in Wyoming. He also noted behind the back seat that there were boxes with chains in them for when the road conditions got really bad. Judging by the number plates, Keith lived in Colorado, James guessed in Denver, as that would give him a good airport to work from and also not an unduly arduous drive to the new coal mines of Wyoming. The number plates intrigued him; he had seen Illinois and Wisconsin plates now and assumed then that each state had its own.

The drive to Gillette was quick enough, with the aid of Keith's FuzzBuster they exceeded the posted limit of 55 by quite a bit, and James had to agree with Keith, 55 in Wyoming might be good for miles per gallon of fuel, but it would make travel tedious, going across miles and miles of open range lands, covered in snow. In Gillette, they found the motel where they would be staying and checked in.

"Dinner at six?" Keith suggested.

"Fine," Tony agreed. "James?"

"Fine," James agreed. He then went his own way and found his room, which was on the ground floor and was very basic, but did have the usual television and telephone amenities. He then used his new telephone credit card and called Katrina.

"So, what's Wyoming like?" she asked.

"What we saw today, a bit like the Karoo in July, but with more snow," he replied. "Not many people, a few cows, some wild animals, they told me were pronghorn antelope, and not many cars on the road. How was your day?"

"I went for a swim, I did some laundry," she said. "I found the laundromat and learned all about washers and dryers."

"That doesn't sound like much fun," he commented.

"It was a new experience," she said. "I met some interesting people and listened to the gossip. What's the time there?"

"We're only one hour behind you," he said. "We're going to get some dinner soon. Have you had dinner yet?"

"I'll probably set something from room service," she replied. "What's your plan for tomorrow?"

"We're going out to the mine site to take a look around and I suppose get some facts and figures," he explained. "After that, we come back and do everything else in the office and send them a proposal."

"Well, call me when you get back from dinner," she said. "I miss you."

"I miss you too. I'll call after dinner," he promised.

Keith took them to a restaurant that seemed to James to be patronised by men in cowboy hats and their spouses, girlfriends or partners. There was obviously nowhere to hang or store hats, so the best solution was to leave them on. He felt that he and Tony rather stood out in their suits, ties and shoes, whereas everyone else, including Keith, had on boots, and ties were not at all in evidence. The restaurant was warm, unlike the outside, so people lingered, in no hurry to go out and brave the winter chills and winds.

"You've been here before?" Tony asked.

"A few times," Keith said. "Mostly ranchers and now a few miners creeping in. Mining is quite new here, the first big shipments of coal only left here a year ago from the AMAX Belle Ayr mine; they had shipped out some smaller amounts in '72 and '73, but last year ramped it up quite a bit, and expect more to come."

"So, what are we looking at, Keith?" Tony asked. "Overburden thickness, coal seam height, annual tonnage?"

"Well, the coal seam is about seventy feet thick, and the stripping ratios range from a low of 1.5:1 to 3.5:1 before it starts to become non-economic," Keith replied. "Annual production, they're looking to build to about 20 million tons a year in five years."

"So, three 20-yard machines, what's our model number, JB120?" James suggested. "Two for the overburden and one with a larger coal dipper, presuming they start with the least overburden. What about drilling and blasting, should we add a couple of JB512 machines?"

"That'll do for starters," Tony agreed. "Then, when they want to ramp up coal production, another coal machine and as they get into deeper overburden, another one or two more 120s."

"Sounds good," Keith agreed. "I think that's what I heard from my spies about the other guys. We're all in the same ballpark; the limiting factor is the truck fleet and how well they balance the trucks and the shovels and how much standing time the shovels will have waiting for trucks."

"Do you know what trucks they're thinking of?" James asked.

"I heard that Unit Rig has the inside track," Keith replied.

"I like the Unit Rig trucks," Tony commented. "I think the diesel-electric is better than a straight mechanical drive."

"We had them in Zambia," James said. "I remember seeing them at the Nchanga pit."

"You have experience with them?" Keith asked.

"No," James replied. "All the equipment at the pit I ran was much smaller, but then it was a smaller operation than the Nchanga pit."

"So, what's the plan tomorrow?" Tony asked.

"We've a meeting with the mine planning and finance guys at nine," Keith replied. "And we've got lunch lined up with the mine manager at noon."

"Where?" Tony asked.

"Here," Keith said. "There's really nowhere else yet."

"So, what's good to eat here?" Tony asked.

"Steak, baked potatoes and beans," Keith laughed. "Not much green here." A waitress came to their table and beers were ordered all round, and she also took orders for steaks as well, mainly as to how well they would be cooked. When it came, the food was good, plain, nothing elegant, but good. James looked around as he ate. The walls were decorated with cowboy scenes, the occasional stuffed head of an antelope, and even in one corner, a bison. There was a bar that was well patronised, and there was a general level of noise from conversations, no hushed tones there, no whispered asides or raucous laughter or arguments.

James called Katrina after he returned to his room at the motel.

"How was dinner?" she asked.

"Meat and potatoes," he replied. "Lots of cattlemen in cowboy hats, not much on the way of anything green anywhere. What did you have for dinner?"

"I ordered room service, just some chicken," she said. "I miss you."

"I miss you too," he said. "I'll be home the day after tomorrow. It seems that getting out of here in the afternoon and back to Milwaukee is not that easy. Apart from the one-hour time change, there just aren't good flight connections, but we should be back just after lunch the day after tomorrow."

"Can't wait," she said. "Love you, honey."

"Love you, sweetie," he replied. "Sleep well."

Wyoming

James got up bright and early and went to find some breakfast, he had found a table and had just started eating when Tony and Keith joined him.

"So, James," Keith said. "Tell me about yourself."

"There's not much to tell," James replied. "I was working in a copper mine in Zambia until recently and just joined the company."

"Never been to Zambia," Keith said. "I want to go to Africa one day, on safari, but I was thinking of Kenya or Tanzania."

"Zambia's a little different to them," James said. "Kenya and Tanzania are a little more of the plains and savannah, but Zambia is more bush, so the game viewing is different."

"What about South Africa?" Keith asked.

"They have some really good national parks and some private reserves as well," James replied. "Plus, the national parks are cheap compared to some of the catered safaris."

"George Murphy is an old friend of mine, and he's been after me to take a trip there," Keith said.

"You should go," James said. "George can show you around and take you to the Kruger Park and maybe one of the private parks that are close."

"Yeah, it's just the getting there," Keith bemoaned. "It's such a long flight, how is SAA?"

"We've only flown them once internationally," James said. "That was from Jo'burg to London, it was okay, but I'll bet it would be much better if you could fly up front."

"Call George," Tony suggested. "See what he can fix up."

"I'll do that," Keith said. "Now, are we ready to check out and go and see these guys?"

The mine site was only about a fifteen-minute drive from the motel. The short walk to the car had been cold, and the car itself had had barely enough time to even begin to warm up on the drive to the mine.

At the mine, it seemed to James that it was just rolling prairie, but there was infrastructure going in, and James saw a railway line and the beginnings of load-out buildings that would be used to store coal before it was loaded into railway wagons. The offices were in temporary buildings, and he could see the foundations of more permanent offices and workshops already in place. Keith had obviously been before as he led the way to the right office, tramping across well-beaten-down snow.

"Hey, guys," he said as they entered. "This is Tony Whitaker and James Martin, they're our applications folks. They're the ones to talk about what you're going to need. Tony, James, this is Mike Garrison, Bill Munson and Sid Wheeler."

"Hey, guys," Mike said. "Would you like some coffee?"

"Thanks," Tony said. "James?"

"Please," James said, he was chilled from the car ride and the short walk to the offices and wished that he had brought heavier clothes, but the offices were well-heated and he began to thaw out quickly. They got coffee and then gathered around a table on which Mike laid out maps of the property and various sectional diagrams that showed the coal deposit and indicated seam thickness and how much overburden lay over the top of it. The problem was fairly simple; given the production requirements, they could quickly calculate the number of machines that would be required to move the overburden and take away the coal. They had dates when they wanted the various pieces of equipment assembled and ready to operate. James let Tony lead the questions, only adding his own towards the end of the session. His questions were about truck sizes and the best match-up between the shovels and the trucks. Conventional wisdom suggested three to four shovel bucket loads to fill each truck. Mike said that they were thinking of one model of truck with truck pans for either overburden or coal, so that way the maintenance on the basic truck would be simpler, as they would have only one model on site. So, it was an optimisation problem, something big enough for the coal, which might have some excess capacity when it came to the overburden.

James then asked about drilling and blasting, wanting to know how consolidated the overburden was. He suggested a drill size and a hole pattern to start with. He thought about the whole project and suggested a simple economic model that would address all those issues. He and Mike went back and forth for a little while and soon came up with a set of conditions that they could solve for. James thought back to his days in Zambia and silently thanked John Wells, who had been his finance person, for the help he had given in constructing similar models for the mine that James had run.

"That's cool," Mike said. "I really like that, we can modify that as we want and change the conditions for truck costs as we go and for explosive costs. That's really useful, you've done this before, James?"

"I have," James replied. "The mine I ran was much smaller and the orebody much more complex, but the fundamental issues were the same: production requirements, equipment size and costs and running costs. I used a similar model there, and because we were dealing with much smaller equipment, fragmentation was a big driver, both in bucket size and equipment maintenance. In some cases, it was better to go with a tighter pattern and get better fragmentation as the extra costs were more than offset by reduced loading equipment repair and maintenance costs."

"You wouldn't be able to program that for us?" Sid asked.

"We can do that," Bill said. "We can give the logic and the conditions to one of the weenies in Houston, and they can write up the program."

"Thanks, guys," Mike said. "So, how much for your shovels and drills?"

"Why don't we send a proposal?" Keith suggested. "It'll include pricing, delivery issues, assembly requirements and suggestions for parts that you may want to carry on site."

"Okay," Mike agreed. "Can we have that in a month?"

"We can do that," Keith promised.

"It was good to see you again, Keith," Mike said. "Come back and see us when you have a proposal ready. Rudy told us that you're having lunch with him. I'll make sure he knows what we've talked about."

"Thanks, Mike," Keith said. "I'll see you in a month."

"Nice to meet you, Tony, James," Mike said. "Don't let this reprobate lead you astray out here."

"Can we get them a decent proposal in a month?" James asked after they had left the site.

"Sure," Tony said. "There's not much in the way of variable equipment that they're looking for, so it's standard machines, just some with coal dippers and some with rock dippers. We could probably have a proposal back to them in a week, but if they're happy with a month, then we'll take it. I'll make sure it gets back to you, Keith, in plenty of time, so that you can bring it to them. Do you want Bob and Bill to come out and go with you?"

"That'd be good," Keith said. "I'll call the office this afternoon and give them an update and schedule something."

"When are we meeting Rudy for lunch?" Tony asked.

"In about an hour," Keith replied. "Why don't we get some coffee and talk about the meeting we just had?"

"Okay," Tony said. "What's the chances that there's anyone from Bucyrus, P&H or Marion around?"

"We'll see," Keith said. "I know their local reps, so if I see one, I'll let you know."

They went to the same restaurant that they had eaten at the evening before and got a table. It was not busy, so there was no pressure to eat and run, which was good as they had an hour to while away before Rudy joined them.

"Good job back there, James," Tony said. "I like the way you put it together for them, makes a package from us for the shovels and drills look more attractive."

"Given that all the manufacturers have similar models," James said. "Why, if I were them, should I buy ours and not some other machines?"

"Good point," Tony said. "Price will be an issue, so will reliability and service and parts support. These guys are buying a machine for twenty years, so they want to be able to run it around the clock as much as they can, can't afford to have it breaking down too often."

"The AMAX Belle Ayr mine has what kind of machines?" James asked.

"They've got Bucyrus shovels," Keith replied. "And Unit Rig trucks, some with high-capacity bodies for coal hauling."

"Why don't we make trucks?" James asked.

"I think in the past, because the distribution method was different," Tony replied. "Trucks have been typically sold through distributors like our construction equipment line, our mining machine line is sold direct, except for a few overseas sales, when it's more expedient to sell through a local guy, depending on who you have to buy off the get the order."

"We would never be party to anything like bribery," Keith laughed. "But, sometimes a facilitating payment is called for."

"If we did make trucks, would we offer package deals?" James asked.

"Good question," Tony said. "I honestly don't know. On the face of it, it makes sense, but we'd have to have a truck that competed with Unit Rig or WABCO, maybe the smart thing to do would just be to buy one of them."

"Who's out there that makes big trucks?" James asked.

"Well, there's Unit Rig and WABCO, then there's Cat, Euclid, Terex, Dart, Kress, Cline, Rimpull and a few other offshore guys," Tony replied.

"We had Cat, Unit Rig, WABCO, Euclid, Terex, Berliet and BelAZ in Zambia," James said. "Oh, I forgot, International Harvester with their Payhauler, but it was much too small for these mines."

"What did you have?" Keith asked.

"Cat," James said. "We had an almost solely Cat fleet, with a couple of drills from other suppliers. The big selling point for us was the local Caterpillar dealer who had a good infrastructure in parts and service."

"There's Rudy," Keith interrupted. They all waited until Rudy joined them and sat down. "Rudy, this is Tony Whitaker, who leads our application group and James Martin, who's just joined the company after running a mine in Africa."

"Nice to meet you," Rudy said. "Say, James, what kind of mine?"

"A copper mine," James replied. "So, much smaller equipment than you'll need and a different kind of orebody."

"What, a porphyry?" Rudy asked.

"No, a series of intrusions that occurred as lenses," James explained. "The geology was quite unique, and it made mine planning a challenge."

"Not like us," Rudy laughed. "We've got a simple seam of thick coal overlain with a gently increasing overburden. So, no complex mine planning, just planning for the most efficient way to mine the coal."

"You know we met with Mike and the team?" Keith asked.

"Yeah," Rudy said. "He said you'll have a proposal for us in a month. Can we get it sooner? I need to get the guys in Houston up to speed with the latest capital numbers."

"We can do that," Keith promised. "How about two weeks?"

"That should work," Rudy said. "I need equipment prices, parts lists and prices, delivery estimates, and what I need to put them together in terms of crews, cranes and welders, and I need to know how you'll support things long term."

"We can do that," Keith promised.

"Good," Rudy said. "I'm hungry, you guys eaten yet?"

"No," Keith said.

"Okay then," Rudy said. He nodded to the waitress who came over and took orders. "Say, Keith, I heard that you bought a new rifle?"

"I did," Keith confirmed. "I got a Sako thirty-aught-six, bolt action, planning to try it out soon on a black bear in Montana."

"Let me know when you're going," Rudy said. "I might like to tag along and see what I can get. I won the lottery this year and got an elk license. When I go for it, I'll let you know, maybe you'd like to come with me. You hunt Tony?"

"In Wisconsin, in the deer season," Tony said. "I join the million other drunks in blaze orange trying not to get shot by someone else, but usually do manage to get my quota."

"James?" Rudy asked.

"My wife was the hunter in the family when we lived in Zambia," James explained. "She taught me to shoot; she usually went out with a nine-three."

"What make?" Rudy asked.

"Husqvarna," James replied. "It was a nice gun, it shot well, and I got good groups with it, almost as good as Katrina's."

"Did you bring it with you?" Rudy asked.

"No," James said. "Katrina sold it to a friend."

"Pity," Rudy said. "But, my guess is that there would have been a mountain of paperwork to bring it into the country. Good, food's here, let's eat."

Conversation was intermittent while they ate, but generally centred around hunting and fishing, interests that Rudy and Keith obviously shared. James wondered how many decisions were influenced by personal relationships and how much by simple dollars. After lunch, they went their separate ways, Rudy back to his mine and the rest to the drive back to Sheridan. On the drive to Sheridan, Keith and Tony talked about the proposal while James sat in the back and just listened. The people in Oak Creek were going to have some work to do, but then, perhaps it was routine for them, and they already had all that was necessary in various files, and it was just a matter of pulling it all together and typing it up. On the drive, James did notice several pickup trucks that had gun racks behind the seats, with rifles and shotguns in them. That was something new for him, to see weapons so openly displayed. He looked behind him in the Suburban and noted gun racks on one side of the vehicle at the back, and presumed that Keith used them when he went on hunting trips.

At Sheridan, they checked into a hotel for the night. They were too late for any flights back to the Midwest that evening, so they would wait until the morning.

"Dinner at seven?" Keith suggested. "I know a place just down the road, we can walk there from here, maybe ten minutes."

"Sounds good," Tony said. "Let me get rid of this tie and jacket and change into something less formal. James, did you bring any jeans?"

"No," James replied. "I've got some khaki trousers and a light jacket."

"That'll do," Keith said. "Meet you down here at ten of?"

"Fine," Tony said. They went their separate ways to their rooms, and James called Katrina as soon as he had dropped his bag.

"Sweetie," she said. "Where are you tonight?"

"In Sheridan," he said. "We get a flight first thing in the morning and should be back in Milwaukee early afternoon."

"Good," she said. "I'll be at the airport. How was the day?"

"Interesting," he replied. "We had a really technical meeting this morning with the mine planning people, and then lunch with the mine manager, and all he wanted to talk about was hunting. He and Keith, the local salesman, seem to know each other quite well, and I got the impression that they go on hunting trips together."

"Is it cold there?" she asked.

"Bloody cold," he said. "Must be well below freezing, and there's a little snow in the air. Hopefully, it won't mess up the flights tomorrow."

"I hope so, too," she agreed. "You've been away long enough; time to come home."

"I miss you too, lovey," he said. "We're going out to dinner tonight, apparently we're walking there, so hopefully it's not too far, I don't fancy a long walk in this cold."

"Maybe we should look for some warmer clothes for you?" she said.

"That might not be a bad idea," he said. "Does the Kmart shop sell clothes?"

"Clothes, shoes, household goods, furniture, even car parts," she said. "A little like OK Bazaars with hardware and car stuff thrown in."

"Perhaps I'll look at some boots and another coat when I get back," James said. "What are you having for dinner tonight?"

"I'm not sure," she said. "I'll have to go and look at the menu, don't forget this weekend we go and get the flat."

"I hadn't forgotten," he promised. "What time do we have to be there?"

"The lady I talked to said ten," she replied. "Then, we can go shopping at Kmart and buy some essentials. She said we have to pay a month in advance, plus a security deposit that equals another two months. Do we have enough money for that?"

"We do," he said. "But, it won't leave us much for shopping, we'll have to camp out until they pay me."

"We'll manage," she said.

"What did you do today?" he asked.

"I took another swim, mainly to get the stiffness out after yesterday's marathon session," she said. "Then I sat down and made a few notes thinking of a novel, I thought maybe something set in Africa, maybe Zambia, maybe South Africa, or even Botswana."

"Why not invent something about Jan Englebrecht?" he suggested, referring to an ancestor of Katrina's who had walked across the Kalahari desert on an ivory hunting expedition that had gone horribly wrong.

"Maybe I'll do that," she said. "I've got his journal with me, so wouldn't have to invent too much, just take a bit of poetic licence here and there."

"I should go," James said. "Love you, sweetie. I'll talk to you later."

"Love you," she replied.

James joined the others in the lobby of the hotel, and Keith then led the way to the restaurant. He had been right, it was fairly close and they were there in eight minutes, but it was eight minutes in frigid air and James was thankful to get inside away from the icy blasts. It was a cowboy bar complete with a mechanical bull, the first that James had ever seen. Keith got them a table, and they ordered beer and steaks. It seemed to James that there was not much on the menu that was not beef-related, only one or two chicken or pork dishes, and all the vegetables were side orders, except for the baked potato included with each meal. A group of cowboys came into the bar, and it was not long before one of them was on the bull, only to be thrown off after five seconds. As James looked at it, five seconds would seem like an eternity to the man on the machine, and he wondered how long really good riders were able to stay on. Keith provided the answer: eight seconds was the requirement for scores in a rodeo event to count, and while many achieved that, just as many were thrown after only a second or two.

"You fancy a go?" Keith asked.

"I don't think so," James said. "I've little experience of horses and none of bulls, so would have no idea what to do."

"It's simple," Keith said. "You sit on the bull, grab the rope with one hand, then hold on."

"Rather you than me," James said.

"When did you last ride a bull?" Tony asked Keith.

"When I was younger, much, much younger," Keith said. "I had a rodeo scholarship when I was at college, so rode broncs and bulls, got pretty banged up too."

"Where did you go to college?" James asked.

"U of Wyoming," Keith replied. "It's in Laramie. Nice school, I got a degree in mechanical engineering. For me, it was cheap, because we lived in Rawlins, I paid in-state tuition."

"I'm sorry," James said. "I don't understand."

"If you live in a state, you get a cheaper price than someone who comes from another state," Tony explained.

"So, like an overseas student?" James asked.

"That would be a good analogy," Tony agreed.

"Is there a big difference?" James asked.

"Can be," Keith said. "Can be three times as much if you're from out of state. What do they do in England?"

"I suppose it's the same in a way," James said. "For Brits, there's one price, and for overseas students, there's another, higher price. I think that's why some colleges really try and attract overseas students, they get more money that way."

"Same as here," Keith said. "Only it applies to states as well as other countries."

"I saw that the number plates on the cars are different here than in Wisconsin," James said. "Is each state different?"

"Sure," Keith confirmed. "You'll have seen that my Suburban has Colorado plates, because that's where I live. Each state has its own plates, and the fees are different, too. Same with driving licenses, each time you move, you have to get a new one."

"Does that mean you have to take a test each time you move?" James asked.

"Between states, and then usually only the written test," Keith replied.

"There's a written test?" James asked.

"Sure," Tony said. "That plus, for first timers, a road driving test. I think you might have to do both, so get the book for Wisconsin and read it, and you'll be fine."

"What licence are you using now?" Keith asked.

"My Brit licence," James replied. "I had thought of using my Zambian license, but I didn't think the rental car people would accept it."

"Probably have no idea where Zambia is," Keith laughed.

"So, what's your guess, Keith, what are these guys gonna do?" Tony asked.

"It's all going to depend on the final assembled cost of the machines and their, and maybe our, best estimates of operating costs and output," Keith said. "We can expect BE and P&H to be in the ballpark, so in the end, I guess, it's a crap shoot, who they like the best and who they think will be around the longest and give them the best service."

"How did you buy machines, James?" Tony asked.

"We sized the fleet we needed, then we got quotes from a few firms, and then we did our comparison weightings," James replied.

"How did you weight?" Keith asked.

"Local support, delivery time, cost FOB works plus shipping costs, estimated production figures, based on the manufacturer's data, plus a couple of other items," James explained.

"What about technical features?" Tony asked.

"A little," James said. "But overall costs really drove things, plus local support. Zambia is a little remote, even more than here; you can't just drive there, you might be able to rail stuff in, if the border is open, so the local dealer who had the best infrastructure had an edge, and that was the Cat dealer."

"So, ex-works price, delivery and erection costs plus financing costs based on the payment schedules," Keith suggested.

"Probably," Tony agreed. "Pity we don't have the trucks to package with our stuff, think Unit Rig would go for an exclusive partnership?"

"I doubt it," Keith said. "What's in that for them?"

"You're probably right," Tony sighed. "So, we just have to guess what the others are doing and send in our best price. We should check, will they be looking for an IFB or an RFP?"

"I doubt if they'll constrain themselves to an IFB," Keith said. "Who wants to be tied to opening the envelope and reading the numbers, and just taking the low bid? Better to have an RFP, at least then you can discuss, counter and come to a mutually satisfactory deal." Tony had been referring to the niceties of invitations to bid versus requests for proposals. Keith was right, invitations for bid tended to be limiting and, providing the suppliers all met the specifications, then the contract went to the lowest bidder, something that was not always in the best interests of the buyer. Requests for proposal provided more latitude on both parts and usually led to negotiations, leading eventually to a contract.

"Do any of these people work for BE or P&H?" James asked, waving at the others in the restaurant.

"I don't see any of the local reps," Keith said. "But, you never know. Fortunately, it's noisy enough in here that it's hard to hear what's being said at the next table."

"We'll go over things at the office," Tony said. "You're right about being overheard. I once heard a whole sales pitch on the plane, two guys from one of the opposition were going over things before their meeting. Stupid on their part. As it turned out, I didn't need the information, but it might have been different another time."

"So, you guys want another beer?" Keith asked.

When James got back to the hotel, it was quite late, but he called Katrina anyway.

"Hello," Katrina said when she answered the telephone.

"Sorry to call so late," James said. "I've just got back to the hotel."

"What's it like there?" she asked.

"Getting colder," he said. "Cold and snowing, but they assured me that we'll be able to fly in the morning, so I should be home as scheduled."

"Busy day?" she asked.

"Quite," he said. "Then Tony and the local chap took me to this place that was a restaurant, but which also seemed to be the gathering spot for all the local cowboys. I've never seen so many cowboy hats, and for the first time in my life, I actually saw a chap wearing spurs."

"So, that part of Wyoming is mainly ranching?" she asked.

"I think it has been," he said. "But, that's all changing with the coal mines and the cowboys are becoming truck drivers and shovel operators."

"I'll bet the money's better," she thought.

"Probably right," he said. "Did you think any more about your novel?"

"A little," she said. "I like the idea of a book about *Oom* Jan, so I made notes based on his journal, then I had a light dinner, then watched TV until you called just now. I miss you, I wish you were here."

"I miss you," he said. "I'll be home tomorrow. I love you."

"Can't wait, I love you too," she said.

Keith delivered James and Tony to the airport bright and early the following morning and said that he was on his way to visit other potential customers in the north of the state.

"So, James," Tony said, after they had finally boarded their aircraft bound for Denver. "What do you think about our prospects?"

"It seems to me that it's going to be price negotiation no matter what," James thought. "That, and when can we deliver."

"I got that too from the meeting. We may be lucky there," Tony commented. "It all depends on how long a lead time there is for the other guys' machines. My sources tell me that they're pretty booked up, so may have difficulty meeting the delivery dates requested, but all of them have pulled rabbits out of hats before, so we shouldn't bank on that. I called the office yesterday and gave them all the details, so they should be working on the proposal. When we get to Denver, we'll have to hustle; we've only got a forty-five-minute layover."

"Well, at least we got away in time," James said. The flying time to Denver was a fairly short hop of just over one hour. Then they walked over to the Northwest Orient gates and found their flight to Minneapolis. That flight was a little longer, just short of two hours gate to gate, then there was another wait, and finally, the flight to Milwaukee, putting them into the Billy Mitchel Field at one-thirty in the afternoon. It seemed to James that it had been a roundabout way to get there, but there were no non-stop flights from Milwaukee to Sheridan and back. Katrina was there to meet James and went with them to baggage claim to wait for their luggage. When it came, Tony said his farewells and said that he would see James in the office on Monday morning.

"So, you don't have to go to the office this afternoon?" Katrina asked James.

"It doesn't look like it," he replied.

"How was your trip?" she asked.

"Interesting," he said. "The US really is big; we flew over miles and miles of farmland, quite a few big towns, and that was only part of the country. What did you do this morning?"

"I went for a walk," she said. "I drove to Grant Park in South Milwaukee and marched around the park for a while. I enjoyed it, got some fresh air, even if it was a little chilly. I thought about walking near the hotel, but there really isn't anywhere to walk there; everything here is designed around cars."

"I think you'd like Wyoming," he said. "It's big, lots of empty space, not many people and has mountains as well as prairies. Perhaps, not this time of year, but someday we should visit."

"That sounds like fun," she said. "Do you want me to drive?"

"Why not?" he said. "You've been driving around a lot more than me lately, so you probably know your way better than I do."

"I doubt that," she said. "I could never work out how you could go somewhere just once, and be able to go right back there years later."

"I suppose I just remember places," he said.

"I was going to drag you off to our room and ravish you," she said. "But when I left to come and get you, the housekeeper had only just started on our floor, so we'd probably be disturbed."

"We can make up for lost time this evening," he promised.

"We can," she agreed. "That's the one thing about this job that I'm not too keen on, the travelling. I'm sure I'll get used to it in time, and if I'm working, I won't have so much free time on my hands."

"How's your book coming?" he asked.

"I started," she said. "I wonder if I could find an old typewriter that I could use?"

"Maybe tomorrow we can drive around a bit and see what we can find," he suggested. "If they're still cleaning our room, where should we go?"

"By the pool," she suggested. "It's warm, they're aren't too many people, there's places to sit that aren't right by the pool."

That is what they did. Housekeeping had just started on their room, so they went and sat by the pool and talked about Katrina's great opus, or what James said would become her opus.

"My biggest challenge is going to be reading my own handwriting," she lamented. "I should try and find a typewriter soon, or I'll have no idea what I've written so far. At the moment, it's fresh enough that even if I can't read every word. I can guess."

"I was thinking the same thing," he said. "I took all kinds of notes on this trip, and I probably should look through them to make sure I can still read them."

"Do you have them here?" she asked.

"I do," he said.

"Why don't you quickly go through them while we wait for our room?" she suggested. He did that while she looked over her own notes and made corrections or just wrote over them so that she could read them.

For dinner that night, they went to the family Mexican restaurant that they had been introduced to by George Murphy and tried burritos. Both had to admit defeat and concluded that they could probably have ordered just one between them. That was something that they had noticed after arriving in the States: the meal portions in restaurants were, to them at least, huge. Katrina had taken to eating breakfast, then only a light lunch and again a light dinner, when she could; if not, she said that she would probably inflate like a balloon. Over dinner, James gave her a more detailed report on his trip, from the flight out, to the drive to Gillette, then the meetings and lunchtime discussion about hunting.

"What's Denver like?" she asked.

"I only saw what I could from the plane," he replied. "It's high, like Jo'burg, but it's right up against the mountains, so lots of snow."

"I heard it's called the Mile High City," she said.

"So I understand," he said. "But, I suppose you could also call Jo'burg a mile-high city; it must be well over 5,000 feet up."

"Probably nowhere near as cold and snowy as Denver, though," she said.

"Probably not," he agreed. "Are you finished?"

"I'm *dik geëat*," she said, telling James that she was full.

"What time do we need to go and see the people about the flat?" James asked.

"I said we'd be there about ten tomorrow," she said. "So, now, we should go back to the hotel, you've got two nights to make up for."

"That sounds exciting," he laughed.

"It will be," she promised. "It will be."

At ten on the dot the next morning, James and Katrina were at the apartment building and met the manager. She took them up to the fifth floor and showed them the apartment. It looked south over Grant Park, which was still snow-covered and had groves of leafless trees, and to the east was the grey, wintry-looking expanse of Lake Michigan; to the west, they could see houses that made up part of South Milwaukee. The apartment was unfurnished, so they would have to get some furniture and kitchenware, but it did come with a stove and a refrigerator. There was a living, dining space, as well as a separate kitchen area and one bedroom. The manager explained the rent and the included utilities, and mentioned that there was a laundrette on the ground floor as well as other amenities, including bins for rubbish. She also apologised for the fact that the only parking was in the open, there were no garages to be had, so in the winter one's car could be covered in snow, or have ice on the windshield. Well, they had been dealing with that at the hotel and had already purchased a scraper for the ice that came with a brush for the snow. The apartment was heated, which was nice, and with the southerly exposure, it would get whatever winter sun there was. James and Katrina had a brief chat and then told the manager that they would take it. She then led them to her office, and papers were signed. There was the matter of first and last months' rent and the security deposit, but they had come prepared for that and had enough money. They were given the keys and told that they could move in whenever it suited them. The manager pointed out one key that was to their mailbox and showed them where they were and told them that the post office delivered every day, except Sunday, and also pointed out the box for outgoing mail. She told them that parcels would need to be collected from the post office; if they got one, there would be a slip in their mailbox that they should take to the post office.

The drive back to the hotel was short enough, and then they let the front desk know that they would be leaving the following Saturday. That should allow enough time to arrange for either the rental of basic furniture or acquisition of something cheap and cheerful from Kmart. Housekeeping had been in early while they were out, so they shed clothes and tumbled into bed.

"You know if we told someone what our daily life was like, they would think we did nothing but make love," Katrina said.

"They'd probably be jealous," James said. "It's not everyone who has the best-looking person in the hotel to share his bed with."

"Flatterer," she said. "You're just trying to butter me up."

"I was wondering, maybe not butter, that could go rancid, but I wonder if we could find a place that sells things like almond oil?" he said.

"Add that to the list of things we need to look at tomorrow," she said.

"So, we've got furniture, crockery and utensils, typewriter, now almond oil or something similar," he said. "We'll be busy. What's in the yellow pages?" She dug in the drawer and pulled out the directory, and started leafing through it.

"What?" she asked.

"I was just looking at you and thinking how lucky I am," he said.

"You're just randy, that's all," she laughed.

"That too," he agreed. "So, back to business, addresses for furniture?"

She read out three addresses, then moved on to crockery and utensils, then shops that might sell used typewriters and finally a couple of shops that seemed to specialise in lotions, oils and the like.

"What do we do for dinner?" she asked.

"Let's go and see what we can find that is fairly close to the place where we've rented the flat," he suggested.

"Okay," she agreed. They took the car and drove north to College, then east towards the lake.

"We should fill up as well," James suggested. "Look, there's a petrol station over there." He pulled off the road and, after a few minutes of puzzling, worked out where the filler cap was for the car and filled it up. "Petrol's cheap here," he said to Katrina when he got back into the car. "So, now where to eat?"

"There," Katrina said, pointing. "There's an Italian place, let's try that." The restaurant was quite small, but they did get a table right away.

"I was looking at the houses," she said. "They all seem to be fairly small here, not like where Maggie lives, and have you noticed, no fences anywhere?"

"I saw that," he said. "I wonder why? I wonder what they do about dogs?"

"Ask one of the chaps at your office," she suggested.

"I'll do that," he said. "So, what do you fancy to eat?"

"Lasagne, I think," she said. "Plus a Chianti." A waitress came to their table and took their orders. James looked around at the other patrons and decided, rightly or wrongly, that many were of Italian heritage.

He saw someone come in the door and wave at him. It was Tom Nelson from James & Brown. James waved back, and Tom came over to see them.

"Tom," James said. "This is my wife, Katrina. Would you like to join us?"

"Thanks," Tom replied. "This is my wife, Kathy. James just joined us recently," he explained to Kathy. "They moved over from England, but before that, they lived in Africa."

"Oh, where?" Kathy asked.

"We lived in Zambia," James said.

"I'd love to hear about that," she said. "I teach geography at one of the high schools here, and it's hard sometimes to explain to my students that life is not the same everywhere."

"We're finding things different here," Katrina said. "Where we lived before there were no expressways, no shopping malls, no snow."

"So, have you found a place to live yet?" Tom asked.

"We've rented a flat in that big building just down the road by the lake," James said. "Now we need to get furniture and stuff."

"Do you need help transporting anything?" Tom asked.

"Well, we need to buy a bed and a table and some chairs," James said.

"There's a great used furniture store not far from here," Kathy said. "We've picked up a lot of our furniture from there. I could take you there if you like. I imagine you're on a budget."

"We are, so that would be super," Katrina said.

"Plus, we've got a pickup so we could move it to the apartment for you," Kathy added.

"Would you?" Katrina asked. "That would be so nice."

"When do you move in?" Kathy asked.

"We rented the apartment this morning," Katrina said. "We were going to move from the hotel next Saturday, but we could move in as soon as we had somewhere to sleep."

"What are you doing tomorrow?" Kathy asked.

"Nothing planned," Katrina said.

"Where are you staying?" Kathy asked.

"The Ramada that's south of the airport," James said.

"Why don't we swing by at ten tomorrow, and you can follow us to the store, and then we can truck whatever you buy to the apartment?" Kathy offered.

"You're sure?" Katrina asked. "We don't want to take you away from your family on a Sunday."

"We've got no kids," Kathy said. "So, you're not taking us away from anyone."

"We should order," Tom said. He called over the waitress, who took their orders and came back with wine, beer and James's and Katrina's meals.

"Please start," Kathy said. "Don't let it get cold."

83

"So, James, how was Wyoming?" Tom asked.

"Cold," James replied, between mouthfuls. "I don't think I've been in that kind of cold before."

"You mentioned furniture, what about linens, crockery and kitchen utensils?" Kathy asked.

"I was thinking of Kmart," Katrina said.

"That would work," Kathy said. "I doubt that you'd get any better prices anywhere, unless you happened to hit upon a sale."

"This is so nice of you, I can't imagine how we could repay your kindness," Katrina said.

"Come to the school and talk to my students about Zambia," Kathy said. "That would be great."

"I'd be happy to do that," Katrina said. "I've got time on my hands until I get a Green Card and can officially work."

"How can I get a hold of you in the week?" Kathy asked.

"Until we move, the Ramada, after that, I suppose we need to get a telephone number for the apartment," Katrina said.

"That's simple enough," Tom said. "James can call the phone company from the office, and they'll set it up."

"I need to set up a bank account too," James thought.

"Set it up at the Lake Shore bank," Tom suggested. "That's who the company uses for payroll."

"So, have you been with James & Brown long?" Katrina asked Tom.

"Eight years now," he replied. "I like them, they're good to work for."

"Are you from Wisconsin?" Katrina asked.

"We both are," Tom replied. "Both from Green Bay, went to college at Marquette, then got jobs here."

"What did you do in Zambia?" Kathy asked.

"James worked on a couple of mines, and I worked in the family transport business until we sold it, then I sold industrial minerals," Katrina replied.

"Industrial minerals for what?" Kathy asked.

"Glass, paint, toothpaste, tyres, pottery and a few other things," Katrina replied.

"Mention that when you come to the school," Kathy suggested. "I've been trying to impress on my students that geography is not just place names, but rivers, commerce, economies, weather, all interacting together."

"I can try," Katrina agreed. They ate, they talked and parted, confirming the meeting for the morrow.

At the hotel, Katrina told James that she liked Tom and Kathy, perhaps more than some of the other ladies she had met, because they had no pretensions, they were just trying to make their way in the world, and they were willing to lend a helping hand. They bathed and went to bed, anticipating the expedition the next day to look for furniture. It looked like the typewriter and lotions might have to be put off until one day after work. One thing that they had noticed since moving to Wisconsin was that shops stayed open far longer than in Zambia or even for that matter, England.

Shopping

Tom and Kathy were at the Ramada at ten and suggested that James and Katrina follow them. It was about a twenty-minute drive to the used furniture store, and the weather favoured them; it was cold, but the skies were clear, so no snow. Katrina had been half-dreading a run-down place that sold furniture that she would be reluctant to give houseroom, but inside, they were greeted by aisles of beds, tables, sofas and more. It looked as if the store cleaned all the items carefully before putting them out, and the only difference between what they were looking at and what they could have got from Kmart was the fact that it had been used, the signs of which were some scuffing of the finish and a few nicks here and there. It certainly helped with the budget, because they were able to get a bed, a kitchen table and four chairs and a small sofa for what would have been the price of just the bed new. James and Tom loaded everything into the truck, and Kathy suggested that they take it to the apartment, while she and Katrina went to Kmart to buy the linens, a foam mattress, crockery, cutlery and cooking utensils. When Tom and James had taken everything up to the apartment, they could meet up at Kmart to help with everything else.

Katrina took charge of the money and went looking to buy. Starting from scratch meant that they needed sheets, blankets, pillows, and towels, just for the bedroom and bathroom. Then there were plates, knives and forks, and something to cook with. Fortunately, Kmart was well stocked with all those and more, and it was more a question of how much to spend. Fortune smiled and they hit two Blue Light Specials as they were looking and picked up a whole set of crockery, plates, cups, dishes, for a bargain price and a bedding set, sheets, blankets and eiderdown. Finding the right cooking set took a little longer, and Katrina and Kathy looked, pondered and discussed all the various sets that were on display, until Katrina hit upon one that looked adequate and did not seriously deplete the funds. Added to that was a set of kitchen utensils, including the most important item, the corkscrew. The last item on the list was a mattress. Katrina wanted a new one, and although the used furniture store had had mattresses, she just could not bring herself to buy a used one, preferring one that came in a large plastic bag and was brand new. Kathy had to direct her to the right size, because the bed they had bought was a double, but there were mattresses for queen size, king size and twin, so Katrina needed to get the right-sized mattress. James and Tom showed up at the right time, in time to take charge of the mattress and carry it out to the truck. The last thing Katrina bought was a set of glasses, eight water glasses and eight wine glasses.

"Where can we get some wine?" she asked Kathy.

"There's a Kohl's close by," Kathy replied. "We can get it there."

"What's your preference?" Katrina asked.

"Red, if that's okay with you?" Kathy replied.

"Fine," Katrina agreed. "What about Tom?"

"We'll get a six-pack," Kathy said.

At the apartment, Katrina and Kathy found James and Tom busy finishing assembling the bed frame and the kitchen table. There was packing to be disposed of, and James went downstairs to where he had seen a large bin full of rubbish. Katrina put the beer in the refrigerator, then looked on as Tom finished screwing on the last leg of the table. Then James came back from disposing of the rubbish.

"Do you know what we forgot to buy?" she asked James.

"No," he said.

"Coat hangers," she said. "We have a closet with a rail in it, but nothing to hang clothes on. I saw some at Kmart, but didn't think to get any."

"Tomorrow, after work," James suggested. "We can also go looking for typewriters at the same time."

"If you're looking for a typewriter, try Ace Business in West Allis," Kathy suggested. "They've got a good selection and the guys there are helpful."

"I saw them in the Yellow Pages," Katrina said. "Maybe, I'll drop you at the office tomorrow and take a run out there."

"It's easy enough to find," Kathy said. "Take the expressway north and get off at National, then just go west until you see them, they'll be on your right. You'll have to park on the street, but it's never that busy."

"Gosh, thanks," Katrina said.

"So, are you hoarding the wine and the beer?" James asked. "Or can working men get something to drink?"

"Okay, okay," Katrina said. "Kathy, Tom, what would you like?"

"I'll have a glass of wine," Kathy said.

"I'll take a beer," Tom said.

"Cheers," James said, after the wine and beer had been handed around.

"Cheers," the others echoed.

"When we need to buy groceries, is Kohl's the best place?" Katrina asked.

"There or A&P," Kathy said. "I prefer Kohl's, but that's only because it's a local chain, not like A&P."

"A&P?" James asked.

"The Great Atlantic & Pacific Tea Company," Tom explained. "A&P for short."

"I'm hungry," Katrina said.

"Why don't we go and get a pizza?" James suggested. "Tom, Kathy?"

"We should be getting home," Kathy said. "If you need anything else, just let us know."

"Thanks," Katrina said. "I really appreciate the help."

After Tom and Kathy had gone, James and Katrina took stock of their apartment, as they had learned to call it, not a flat. They were not thrilled about the colour of the carpet, but they were in no position to pull it up and replace it. The view from the windows was of Grant Park, Lake Michigan and parts of South Milwaukee. The lake was a dull grey, singularly uninviting; the park was snow-covered where it was grass, with islands of brown leafless trees, except for the few conifers. The small part of South Milwaukee that could be seen presented images of small houses, typically clad with red siding and with dark composite shingle roofing, all very different from their last house, which was a brick-built house with a corrugated iron roof, set among similar houses amid acres of African scrub bush. The furniture they had bought was adequate for what they needed, even if it would never grace the pages of House & Garden.

"Shall we wait until Saturday to move, or come earlier?" James asked Katrina.

"Let's move as soon as the telephone is installed," she suggested.

"I'll call the telephone people tomorrow," he promised. "Could you come to the factory tomorrow at lunchtime, and we'll go to the bank and open a bank account?"

"Good idea," she agreed.

"So, what shall we do for dinner?" James asked.

"Let's just go back to the hotel and eat there," she suggested. "That way, if we have a glass of wine or two, we don't have to worry about driving."

They ate at the Ramada, then watched as snow started to come down lightly at first, then heavily. Katrina was concerned about trying to go anywhere the next day because of the snow, but James was confident that the various authorities would have the roads cleared. In the morning, when he and Katrina went out to the car, the first thing they had to do was sweep off the snow that had accumulated overnight. But, James had been right about the roads, they had been ploughed and salted, and the only issue they could see was, was Katrina going to be able to park at the side of the road at the typewriter shop. At the office, James told Tony that he had bought furniture and such and only needed to get the telephone connected, and then they would vacate the hotel. Tony showed him where to find the number for the telephone people, and they were happy to send someone out to activate the telephone, but wanted an account set up first. That was a palaver because James and Katrina had not been in the country long enough to establish a credit rating, so they did not appear anywhere in any system. Finally, the company did agree to activate the telephone if James sent them some money in advance, which he agreed to do, but that also first meant setting up a bank account. It seemed to be an endless circle of requirements where one item depended upon another, that depended upon another and so on, almost coming back to where he had started.

Tony and James met with Robert Andrews and Bill Riding and told them about the meeting with Magnate Coal. That set the wheels in motion to create a proposal to send out to the company for various shovels and longer-term drills. Next on the docket were requests to go to Minnesota to an iron mine to check on the performance of a shovel that was working there, and to go to Florida to visit a phosphate mine. Tony grinned and told James that he would go to Florida, and James could take the iron ore mine issue in Minnesota. James asked where he would have to go and was told to fly to Hibbing, and he would be met there by the local sales representative.

"I like the idea of an assistant," Tony joked. "That way I can take the sunshine in Florida, while you deal with the cold on the Iron Range."

"I suppose that's understandable," James agreed, ruefully. "What's the issue with the shovel in Minnesota?"

"They say that it's not meeting the output they want," Tony replied. "It could be something wrong with the machine, it could just be the way they're using it, spend a day or so just watching and draw your own conclusions."

"Surely they've already had time and motion types out to check on it?" James asked.

"Not yet," Tony said. "From what Bob told me, if they get time and motion guys from the head office, they'll get billed for them, but they figure we'd do it for free to keep in with them, so why spend the money? They're probably measured on dollars per ton produced, and back charges from the corporate office won't help their numbers, even though the time and motion guys are already paid for. I guess it's a question of whose pocket the money comes from."

"I can understand that," James said. "There was a service bureau in Zambia that did work for the copper companies, but you had to pay an overall fee and special fees for special jobs, so we tried to never use them as they were expensive."

"Fix your travel up with Marlys and let Bob know when you're arriving," Tony suggested. "Bob will take you there and introduce you, then probably leave you to do your studies. Make sure he picks you up at the end of the day."

"Okay," James said. "I'm going to set up a bank account at lunchtime. I don't know how long that'll take, so is it okay if I'm back a few minutes late?"

"Of course," Tony said. "Take all the time you need."

"Can we get access to the computer that the company has?" James asked.

"Why, what do you have in mind?" Tony asked.

"Well, I was wondering after I've gathered data on this shovel, if we could simulate the best use for it?" James asked.

"We can ask," Tony said. "Let me know what you need, and we'll see if we can get it done. Have you done this before?"

"I have," James said. "We had problems in Zambia with production, with availability, so we modelled all kinds of things and were able to improve things a lot. I remember most of what we did, but might need some help with the programming."

"Okay, I'll talk to the computer guys and see if we can get some time and a guy to help you," Tony promised. "What kind of simulation?"

"I was thinking of a Monte Carlo simulation, put in some parameters for loading time, add truck cycle time and how many trucks, then see how production varies with the number of trucks, the cycle times and the wait times, it may be that just one more truck makes all the difference, it may be that six more will make no difference, we'll have to see," James explained. "I did it once underground, but then I used dice to create semi-random numbers. We managed to show them that the production targets just could not be met, even under the best of circumstances. So, they added more trains, changed the targets and got more realistic."

James met Katrina outside the office at noon, and they drove to the bank and met with a manager there. James explained who they were and that they had just moved over from England and wanted to open an account, one to get paid and two to be able to pay rent, telephone, et cetera. The manager knew that they might be coming; he had a close relationship with Ray in Personnel, so had everything ready. James deposited the rest of his traveller's cheques and withdrew enough cash to do some grocery shopping. He also got some temporary cheques to be able to pay bills before cheques arrived with their names on them. James and Katrina settled on a joint account that gave them both access to the money and the ability to each write cheques. The manager cautioned them to be sure to keep the register properly up to date, as there could be confusion in the future. He also told them to come and see him when they were ready to buy a car or a house, and he would be able to help them.

"That was simple enough," Katrina commented to James as they left the bank.

"I suppose they deal with a lot of people from the company, so know we'll get paid," James said. "Let's get some lunch, there's a place just down the road here. So, how did it go at the typewriter shop?"

"We were right about the snow," she said. "It was piled up at the side of the road, so I parked across the street and walked over. I had to climb over the snow pile. The man in the shop was very nice and I bought a second-hand portable Smith Corona, a spare ribbon and some paper."

"That's great," he said. "So, when do we see the masterwork?"

"Some time yet," she laughed. "Is this the place for lunch?"

"It is," he confirmed.

The restaurant, diner, was quite small, but they did get a table for two in a corner by the window. They ordered, and then James told Katrina about his next trip.

"Minnesota, that's just north of here, isn't it?" she asked.

"Next state up," he confirmed. "I gather from what Tony said that it's cold there, which is why he's going to Florida. I can't see why it should take more than one night away. If I leave here early in the morning, then I can get a whole afternoon there, then the next morning and come home that afternoon."

"I suppose we'll have to get used to this," she said. "I think while you're in Minnesota, I'll stay at the hotel and we can move when you come back."

"I should get back to work," he said. "Would you pick me up at five?"

"I'll be outside waiting," she promised.

Marlys gave James his tickets for the next day and the number to call Bob, the local representative. Marlys also told him where he was going to stay, at a small motel not too far from the mine site. James called Bob, and Bob told him that the mining company had been complaining, whining was the actual term he used, that they were not getting the production they had thought possible. Bob's personal opinion was that they were just not using it well, and it spent a lot of time just sitting and waiting. The company did not want to take his word for it and wanted an expert to come and take a look. Bob also said that he thought that what the company really wanted was ammunition to support a request for money for more trucks. James gathered up the specification sheet for the size of shovel that the company had, which would give him a start when calculating what the output should be.

Katrina was waiting for James when he left the office. She had found a convenient place to park across the street, which had actually been cleared of snow.

"What time is your flight tomorrow?" she asked.

"Seven," he replied.

"So, we'd better get up early," she commented. "I went and did some more shopping this afternoon."

"Oh, what did you get?" he asked.

"Some almond oil and a couple of other things," she said. "I was thinking that we could experiment tonight. I went to this place run by two women, it's on Kinnickinnic. They had all sorts there and would let you sample and try."

"We need to have an early dinner then," he said.

"We do," she agreed. "Shall we just eat at the hotel?"

"I think so," he agreed. "Before we get back to the hotel, can we stop at Kmart? I need to buy some boots and heavier socks, and another pair of trousers and a flannel shirt. If I'm going to be out in the cold, I think I'm going to need more clothes."

"You should also look at some thicker gloves," she suggested. They drove to Kmart and wandered around and found boots, a woolly hat, gloves, flannel shirts, heavy trousers and long underwear and an outer jacket that might not grace the boardrooms of the world, but which was certainly warmer than his suit jacket. The long underwear caused a laugh, but as Katrina pointed out, keeping warm was the main thing.

"I never thought when we left Zambia that I'd have to be buying Arctic wear," he said.

"I heard that it can get really hot and humid in the summer, so it looks like we'll need two different wardrobes, winter and summer," she said. "I should get a dolly hat as well, I'm tired of my ears getting cold and aching."

"Get some gloves as well," he suggested.

"I wonder why people settled here?" she pondered.

"I suppose if you come from central Europe or Scandinavia, then it's not much different," he suggested. "Plus, they had shipping on the lakes, then the railways came, then heavy industry started. I'll bet it was a really nice place before there was lots of immigration, I can see fur trappers and Indians."

"Indians there must have been," she agreed. "Look at the place names, then there must have been French, I suppose, traders and fur trappers."

"The Missouri must have had a big impact; you can come by river all the way from the Gulf of Mexico," he added.

"Now that might be interesting one day, to take a riverboat from here all the way down to New Orleans," she suggested.

"I wonder how long that would take?" he said. "Are we all done here? We should pay and go back to the hotel and get some dinner."

They did eat early, then Katrina showed him the typewriter, then the various oils and lotions she had bought.

"Which do you want to try first?" he asked.

"Let's have a shower, then see what comes," she said. Showering did not take long; when there is something else promised, lingering in a shower just does not seem logical. Katrina lay down on the bed, and James poured some of the almond oil onto her back and started to rub it in.

She breathed a big sigh of contentment, then turned over and let him do the front. That led to explorations down the length of her body, and her legs and everything in between. Finally, he used some of the oil on himself, and she guided him in.

"That's wonderful," she said.

"It is," he agreed, wholeheartedly. They made love, slowly, making things last as long as possible, until neither could restrain themselves any longer.

"That was lovely," she said, clinging to him, with her legs wrapped around him, trapping him and holding onto him as long as she could.

"Again?" she asked.

"I think so," he said. "Just give me a few minutes."

"We could always do something while we wait," she said.

"What do you have in mind?" he asked. She rolled them both over and then untangled herself from him and straddled him, moving up his body until she was positioned over his head.

"Get busy," she commanded. He did as requested, and as he did, his erection came again, a fact she discovered when she reached behind her. "Now, let's put this to good use, shall we?" she said. They made love again, with her on top.

"I love you, Katrina," he said, when they were both spent and lying down in each other's arms.

"I love you," she echoed. "Don't stay away in Minnesota too long."

"I won't," he promised. "I'll get done as soon as I can and be home the day after tomorrow."

The alarm sounded at some ungodly hour of the morning the next day, and James and Katrina dragged themselves out of bed. It was still dark out, but it was clear; there were stars visible, and it looked cold. James packed his suitcase quickly, putting in all the extra clothes he had bought. Katrina dropped James at the airport and said that she was going to go back to bed. James did not blame her one bit; it was an early morning. He got the North Central flight to Minneapolis and had a short wait there before getting another flight to Hibbing. As they flew to Hibbing, it seemed to James that it was trees as far as he could see, with the odd lake now and then to break things up. The Hibbing airport was small, much smaller than Milwaukee, so finding Bob was fairly simple; he was the lone person waiting to meet someone.

"Bob?" James asked.

"James," Bob replied. "Thanks for coming. Got your bag?"

"I do," James confirmed.

"You got an early start," Bob commented. "Had breakfast yet?"

"Only some coffee on the plane," James replied.

"Okay, there's a place near here," Bob said. "We can get something there, and I'll tell you what I know."

Breakfast was huge, scrambled eggs, sausage, hash browns, toast and coffee as well. While James ate, Bob talked. He told James about the complaints, he told him what he thought was really going on, and he gave James some insights into the people he would be meeting. The parent company in Cleveland was cutting budgets here and there, looking to shore up their results for the quarter, so they were being very chary with their cash. The mine was performing moderately well, but in Bob's mind, they could do better, but his comments largely fell on deaf ears. He was seen as a salesman who would try and push the sale of a new machine. Breakfast done, Bob drove James to the mine and introduced him to the manager there.

"Sven, this is James Martin. He joined the company recently, he's a mining engineer," Bob explained.

"Where'd you work?" Sven asked.

"Zambia, in a copper mine," James replied.

"Underground?" Sven asked.

"For a while, then an open pit," James replied. "I got to start up a new mine from scratch."

"That must have been interesting," Sven said. "What was your biggest problem?"

"Getting all the new equipment from the docks to the mine site," James said. "We had to haul it all by road."

"What size trucks?" Sven asked.

"Fifty-ton," James replied.

"Did you haul those?" Sven asked.

"No, we put the pans on them and drove them," James said. "We had a police escort and basically took over the road for a while."

"Well, find yourself a place to hang out and watch that shovel of yours and then tell us what you think. Rudy here will take you out into the pit," Sven said.

"Thanks," James said. "What time will you pick me up this afternoon, Bob?"

"Why don't we say about six?" Bob thought. "I got a thermos of coffee here for you and some lunch."

"Okay, I'll see you later, Bob," James said. "Is there somewhere I can change into some warmer clothes?"

"Sure," Sven said. "Rudy'll show you to the change house. You need an extra jacket?"

"That might be nice," James said. Rudy took him to the change house, where James put on his new long underwear, flannel shirt and trousers and boots. Rudy handed him an extra-large jacket that went over his own jacket. Although James felt as if he was overdressed, he guessed that by the time he had spent an hour or two in the pit, he would be heartily glad of the extra clothes.

He went with Rudy, who drove him around the pit explaining what they were doing, then dropped James at a vantage point where he could watch the shovel. James just hoped that it would not start to snow while he was out there; it was going to be a cold enough day. He watched the shovel and the trucks and made notes, timing both the loading operation and the round trips that the trucks would make. There were times when he just sat and waited for something to happen, and there were other times when everything seemed to be jammed up. He was very glad when he saw Rudy come back to collect him.

"Good day?" Rudy asked.

"Cold," James said. "I could do with a hot shower."

"I'll drop you at the office," Rudy said. "Bob's already there."

"Thanks, Rudy," James said. "Could you get me the schedule of routine maintenance done on each of the trucks and the shovel?"

"Sure, I'll have it for you tomorrow morning," Rudy promised.

"What times are the shift changes?" James asked.

"We do six to two, two to ten and ten to six, but there's not much going on ten to six, no production anyway," Rudy explained.

"Thanks," James said.

"Okay, here's Bob, see you tomorrow," Rudy said.

"Good day?" Bob asked.

"Cold," James said. "I could do with a hot shower. I need to get my clothes from the change house."

"We'll get you to the motel and then, after you've warmed up a bit we'll get some dinner," Bob suggested. James found that the motel actually had a bath, so he did not shower, but languished in a hot bath for a good twenty minutes, or until the water started to really cool down. Warmed through, he called Katrina.

"How are you?" she asked.

"I've about warmed up," he said. "I don't know how people can live here, it's so cold."

"Did you pack enough clothes?" she asked.

"I think I had everything on that I brought, and the mine lent me an extra overcoat," he said. "My hands were the worst; it's hard to make notes when it's so cold."

"Well, I'll warm you up when you come home," she promised.

"Anyone who says that the life of an application engineer is glamorous is sadly mistaken," he commented. "How was your day?"

"I went for a swim, then I sat down and started typing. I think I covered ten pages, but now that I read it through, I may just start again," she said. "Have you had dinner yet?"

"No, I'm waiting for Bob to pick me up," James replied. "I'll call you when I get back from dinner. Love you, Sweetie."

"Love you too, stay warm," she said

Bob collected James from the lobby of the hotel and drove them to a place in the woods. It looked like a huge log cabin, with fire burning in the grate and all.

"We're meeting a couple of guys for dinner," Bob explained. "They're with one of the other iron ore companies and are interested in a drill; done much blasting?"

"I have," James confirmed. "Probably not with the size of holes these chaps would use, but I've done my share."

"Great," Bob said. "Okay, here they are, Anders, Pete, this is James Martin, he just joined the company, he comes from a copper mine in Africa."

"Nice to meet you, James," Anders said, and Pete nodded hello. "How big was the copper mine?"

"Not as big as the Nchanga open pit," James said. "We had a fleet of fifty-ton trucks and six-yard front-end loaders and some drills for up to six-inch holes."

"Did you shoot much?" Pete asked.

"Almost everything," James said. "There was a thin layer of soil and soft rock, but it was blast everything else. We used a lot of ANFO with pentolite boosters."

"What about blast sequencing?" Anders asked.

"We used a whole pattern of various millisecond delays," James replied.

"Did you get good results?" Pete asked.

"For the most part," James said. "I went away for a couple of weeks, and when I got back, some higher up had been out and told my stand-in to widen the pattern, and it was a mess; we had to do a ton of secondary blasting. I kept the pattern tight because if I didn't, I paid for it in maintenance costs for my front-end loaders; there was an almost direct relationship between fragmentation and machine availability."

"Could you come out tomorrow and take a look?" Anders asked.

"We can do that," Bob assured them. "It'll be right after lunch, is that okay?"

"That's fine," Anders said. "I hear you're over at Sven's place. How's he doing?"

"I only met him briefly," James said. "I've spent most of my time in the pit watching a shovel truck operation."

"Sven's got his corporate office on his arse about costs," Anders laughed. "He needs something to shoot back at them. So, why did you leave Africa, James?"

"The copper price dropped and mines got shut down," James explained.

"They laid off a bunch?" Pete asked.

"They did," James confirmed. "I was offered a job working for a chap I really did not like, so I elected to take the offer they gave me to terminate my contract early."

"Africa had to be a whole bunch warmer than here," Anders laughed.

"It was," James agreed. "But, it had its challenges."

"I'll bet," Pete said. "So, Bob, did you get your deer last year?"

"I did," Bob said. "I got a great four-point. I got most of the meat processed into sausage, you?"

"I got an eight-point buck right at the beginning of the season," Pete said. "You hunt James?"

"I went out with my wife a few times in Zambia," James said. "She's the hunter in the family. She taught me how to shoot."

"Ever been ice fishing?" Anders asked.

"Ice fishing?" James asked.

"Basically, we cut a hole in the ice on a frozen lake and drop a line in," Bob explained. "Most of us have fishing houses that we tow out onto the ice to stay warm while we're fishing."

"If you tow them out, the ice must be thick," James commented.

"It is," Bob confirmed. "We test the ice thickness, and when it's safe, then we start. You should try it one day."

"We should eat," Anders said. They ate and they talked, about deer, about birds and about fish. It reminded James very much of the dinner he had had in Wyoming. After dinner, Bob dropped him back at the hotel, promising to pick him up at seven the next morning.

James called Katrina and told her about the evening and the dinner.

"They talked about hunting and ice fishing," he told her.

"Ice fishing?" she asked.

"Apparently, they wait until the ice is thick, then cut a hole in it and drop a line in and wait, but they do have little houses that they tow out onto the ice to stay warm," he explained.

"I suppose if you live in the ice and snow for half the year, you find things to do," she said. "So, what's the plan tomorrow?"

"I spend the morning at the one mine, then after lunch, I take a look at another, then come home," he said.

"No change in your flight?" she asked.

"None," he confirmed.

"Okay, I'll be at the airport to pick you up," she promised.

"What did you have for dinner tonight?" he asked.

"I just had some tomato soup and a grilled cheese sandwich," she said. "It was enough."

"I miss you, *Suikerbossie*," he said.

"I miss you too," she replied. "I love you, be home tomorrow."

"I will, I love you," he replied.

James had time for an early breakfast before Bob came to pick him up at seven. He had decided to wear his warm clothes, so had no need to use the change house. Bob gave him more coffee and dropped him off with Rudy and promised to be back at noon. Rudy took James back out to his vantage point, gave him screeds of information about truck and shovel availability and maintenance schedules, and left him to his observations. James set himself up and settled down to watch again. He made notes about times, and his mind wandered as he thought about Katrina. He thought about the first date they had had and the thrill of being with her. He thought that he was really blessed to be able to spend his life with her. His mind was wandering so much that he almost missed a couple of passes that the shovel made, so he had to bring himself back to the present and concentrate. Time actually passed fairly quickly, and it seemed that almost no time had elapsed before Rudy came to pick him up. He saw Sven briefly and promised to have a report to him in a couple of days. He said that he would send it to Bob, who could bring it out to him. Bob arrived just before noon, and they went to lunch, then drove off to the other mine. Anders saw them arrive and took them out into the pit, and they got out of the truck and looked around.

"The drills that you already have, what kind of penetration rates do you get?" James asked.

"It depends," Anders replied. "With the jet drill, we get about 20 feet an hour; with that rotary over there, we get about 55 feet per hour."

"What bucket size do your shovels have?" James asked.

"Ten cubic yards," Anders said.

"Much secondary blasting?" James asked.

"Some," Anders said. "More than I'd like."

"We'll send you a proposal and some suggestions about a pattern to start with, but you'll have to adjust based on results," James said.

"Thanks for coming out," Anders said. "We'll look for your proposal."

"Thanks for showing us around," Bob said. "I'll come out to see you when I hear from James."

"Okay, James, I'll run you out to the airport," Bob said. "You'll have a little wait, is that okay?"

"It's fine," James said. "I can start writing up my notes. Does Anders really want another drill?"

"I think they do," Bob confirmed. "They've got to replace those old jet drills with something more efficient. Thanks for coming up. When do you think you'll have something that I can take to Sven?"

"Next week, I would think, unless I get sent off somewhere else," James said.

"Okay, James, I'll see you," Bob said as they pulled up outside the airport. Bob waved goodbye, and James went to check in and was offered a seat on an earlier flight to Minneapolis. That he took, it might mean a longer wait there, but at least it was a bigger airport to wander around in. It seemed to James that the taxi times at both ends added up to more time than the actual flight, so they were in Minneapolis at the gate in about fifty minutes, with all the messing about on taxiways. In Minneapolis, James marvelled at the number of places there were flights to, from Hibbing, where he had just come from, to Seattle, to Denver, to Los Angeles, Chicago, and even places in the south. It seemed it was the main airport for Northwest Orient and North Central. When he got his flight to Milwaukee, it was only a little longer than the flight from Hibbing, so he was in Milwaukee just after five.

Katrina was there to meet him at the gate, looking glamorous in new sunglasses.

"You got new sunglasses," James said, after he had kissed her, and they started walking to the baggage area.

"The glare of the sun off the snow was beginning to bother me," she said. "So, I went and found a cheap pair of glasses."

"They might be cheap, but they make you look like a film star," he said.

"You're just saying that," she said.

"No, really," he said.

"How was your trip?" she asked.

"Cold," he said. "I don't think I've ever been so cold."

"Well, we'll get some early dinner, then we can have a bath and I'll see what I can do to warm you up," she suggested.

"I like the sound of that," he said. "There's my bag. How was your day?"

"I took a swim, then rewrote the stuff I did yesterday. These people came up to me while I was typing and started talking to me in Spanish; they seemed to think I might be Mexican," she said.

"Probably because you're not lily white," he thought. "Do you want to drive?"

"Get in and I'll drive," she confirmed. There had been no more snow, so the roads were now quite dry. It was still cold, but as James noted to Katrina, not as cold as northern Minnesota.

"So, what's Minnesota like?" she asked.

"Trees, as far as I could see, there were trees, then there are lakes, tons of them, not much in the way of mountains, I'd say rolling hills like here, iron ore mines, big ones," he replied. "I only saw Minneapolis from the air, so can't say much about it, except that it's a pretty big town, the airport is bigger and busier than Milwaukee. Here we've got German and Polish immigrants; there, it sounded like Scandinavian immigrants. It was cold, colder than here, snow and ice everywhere, snow piled up on the sides of the roads, snow pushed up into piles in the car parks."

"So, if we visit, go in the summer?" she asked.

"I think so," he agreed. "Or maybe late spring, I get the feeling that summer could be hot and oppressive."

"Okay, here we are," she said as they arrived at the hotel. "Let's get an early dinner, then see what we can do about warming you up."

"I need to get out of all these extra clothes," he said. "I'm sweltering."

"So the long underwear came in useful?" she asked.

"It did," he confirmed. "I must have been the only idiot standing around in the cold, while everyone else was sitting in the cabs of their trucks or machines. I should have really rented a car and driven it out to the place, but thinking about that, that wouldn't have worked, as there was nowhere to park and be safe."

"Will they want you to go back?" she asked.

"I hope not," he said. "I can see why Tony went to Florida; the coldest day there can't be anywhere near the cold of northern Minnesota."

"Okay, you strip off and take a shower, then we'll get some dinner and then get down to the serious business of warming you up," she said.

New Mexico

"Good trip?" Tony asked James the next day.

"Cold," James said. "I'd no idea it could be so cold."

"Northern Minnesota is one of the coldest spots in the US," Tony said. "Almost as cold as much of Canada. So, did you get what we need?"

"I did," James confirmed. "I got about twelve hours of readings at the mine, then Bob asked me to go to another mine and look at their drilling, they could probably use a JB514. What should we do, send them a proposal?"

"Let's talk to Bill and then he can decide," Tony said.

"They also asked for some suggestions as to patterns," James said. "I sketched up a pattern on the plane on the way back, and we could include that if you want."

"Might be a good idea," Tony said. "How did you decide the pattern?"

"I looked at what they have now, with a rotary drill, and then factored in the bucket size of the shovel and came up with a starting number that I told them they should adjust based upon the blasting results and the fragmentation they get and the amount of secondary blasting they will accept," James explained.

"Sounds good," Tony said. "I talked to the computer types and they have a guy who can talk to you after lunch today. So, for now, let's go and see Bill and tell him that he may have a drill prospect."

Bill was happy to hear about possible interest in a new drill and asked James to write up a call report. He said that he should also call Bob in Minnesota and talk to him to see how serious the mine was. James went back to the office he shared with Tony and started on his reports, first the drill prospect, which was the easiest to deal with, it was just a straightforward sales lead. The other, the shovel performance he decided could wait until he had seen the computer programmer. He knew what he wanted and thought that it would not take long to write up a simple program to reduce the data he had collected and to produce some simulations based on changing the number of trucks available. Marlys

105

took care of typing up the sales report; there was a standard format, so all James had to do was provide information. That took until lunchtime, and Tony asked him to go with him as they were meeting with a customer. The customer was from a mining company in Brazil and was interested in a dragline for a coal mine. James knew that Brazil had iron ore in abundance, but was not familiar with their coal reserves and where they were. Fortunately, the mining executive, Renato Vargas, spoke English because neither Tony nor James spoke Portuguese. Dick West was the principal contact, and he did most of the talking. Tony and James just listened, and they learned that this was a preliminary enquiry, as the mine was still in the early planning stages. Tony made an aside to James that Renato was probably making the rounds of all the equipment suppliers to gather information and get a sense of who might be the easiest to work with. The project was in the state of Rio Grande do Sul, which James learned was in the extreme south of Brazil and an important wine-growing area, as well as having much of the coal reserves of Brazil. Based on the sketchy information that Renato provided, Tony suggested a size of machine, and Dick gave him a budgetary price, ex works from Wisconsin, and told him that ocean freight and erection would have to be added to that.

After lunch, James met with the computer programmer, Herb White, and explained what he wanted. Between them, they sketched out a flow chart and agreed upon the sets of conditions that James wanted to solve for, and James provided all the data he had collected. Herb promised to have output for him the next day. Jobs like this were typically run overnight so as not to interfere with the main functions of the computer, which were engineering analysis and accounting. Herb was happy to have something different to look at; it was not the dry numbers of the accounting department, nor the data-driven finite element analysis of the design engineers; it was a straightforward simulation of what could occur if the mix of shovels to trucks was changed. James remembered having to bribe computer people in Zambia to get time to run similar things there, but in Wisconsin, that turned out to be unnecessary. By the time he was done, it was time to

106

go home, so he went back to his office and found that Tony had already left, going out to dinner with Renato and Dick.

Katrina was in her usual spot, waiting for him.
"Have you been waiting long?" he asked.
"No," she said. "I've just arrived. There's a lot of people who work here."
"I suppose there are," he agreed. "So, nice day?"
"Lazy," she laughed. "I did type a few more pages, then I took another swim. I got a call from Kathy, she asked me if I could go to go to her school tomorrow and talk to her students, What do I wear?"
"Something conservative," he suggested. "Don't want to stimulate the hormones of the teenagers too much."
"What about my brown jacket and trousers?" she asked.
"That should be fine," he thought. "When should we move?"
"I thought Saturday," she said. "We'll need to do some grocery shopping. Oh, I almost forgot we have a phone now, I went there this afternoon and the phone chappie came. The phone is on the wall, and we have a number."
"Have you thought about what you're going to say tomorrow?" he asked.
"A little," she said. "I thought we'd make some notes while we have dinner. I wonder if anyone will ask what we ate in Zambia."
"Tell them you ate locusts and caterpillars," he laughed.
"Well, I did eat locusts when I was small," she said. "Gibson used to cook them up with butter, and I ate them with him. I never tried the woolly caterpillars, though, even though he said they were good."
They spent some time over and after dinner making notes and went to bed satisfied that Katrina had enough material for the talk.

It must have gone off well because when she collected James from his office the next day, she was all smiles.
"It went well?" he asked.
"It did," she said. "Kathy had a big map of Africa, so it was easy to show where Zambia is and where Kitwe and Mkushi are."

"What kind of questions did you get?" he asked.

"Why was I so light, not black? What did we eat, what did we wear, what kind of house did we live in, not too much about the economy, but there were a few questions about lions and tigers?" she replied. "What about you?"

"I got all my reports and stuff done and sent off," he said.

"No travels planned?" she asked.

"Nothing in the immediate offing," he said. "It looks like a week or two's worth of office work, just answering queries from the chaps in the field."

"Great, it will be nice to have you home with me," she said. "We're invited out to dinner. Dorothy West called and asked if we'd like to go with them to a place in Mequon. I had to look that up, it's north of Milwaukee."

"What time?" James asked.

"She said that they'd pick us up at six-thirty," she replied.

"Do I have to wear a suit?" he asked.

"She didn't say anything about what to wear, so play it safe, go with a blazer and grey trousers," she suggested.

Dinner with the Wests turned out to be dinner with the Wests and a couple from Australia who were touring the States. They were in the wine business and had a large vineyard and winery in South Australia. Most of their product was exported to England, but they were trying to get some relationships built in the States to broaden their market. Katrina told them about her dad's venture into Hannepoort grapes, and they told her that they were familiar with the wine. That led to a lot of discussion about vines, trellising, harvests, which was actually a nice change from shovels, trucks and drills.

James and Katrina moved on Saturday. They packed all their clothes, said goodbye to the people at the hotel and went to their apartment.

"So, now we need some groceries," Katrina said. "Kohl's?"

"Why not?" he agreed. "Do you suppose it's that much different to A&P?"

"I suppose it's personal preference," she thought. "So, what do we need at Kohl's?"

"We should make a list," he suggested.

List in hand, they went to Kohl's and bought groceries, enough for a week. The weather turned ugly and snow fell fast, so that when they went out to their car with the groceries, they had to sweep it all off to be able to see anything.

"So, what shall we have for lunch?" Katrina asked.

"Something hot and easy," James suggested.

"Soup it is," she said. "I wonder how much snow we'll get. When does it actually stop snowing?"

"I asked Tony and he said that it can snow as late as the end of May, but usually by April it's done," James replied.

"That's another month at least yet," she said. "I wonder if we shouldn't take up some kind of winter sport?"

"I heard that there are some small ski hills in Wisconsin, but I saw a chap in the park the other day and he was just shuffling along on skis," James commented.

"I wonder if that was cross-country skiing?" she suggested.

"Of course," he said. "I wonder how much the skis cost?"

"There's got to be a shop somewhere that sells that kind of stuff," she said. "Let's look in the Yellow Pages when we get home."

"Herman's Sporting Goods," James read out of the Yellow Pages. "They seem to be the place that has everything."

"Shall we go and have a look tomorrow?" Katrina asked.

"Let's," he agreed. "If you organise the soup, I'll set the table. I think I'll move it a little so that we can look out of the window while we eat. Look at the snow, it's really coming down. I wonder how much we'll get?"

"Inches by the look of it," she thought. "I never thought that I'd see so much snow. The only snow I'd really seen before we came here was on the tops of the Witteberge when we went to see my folks."

"We had snow in England," he said. "But this much only very rarely, I wonder if the lake has any effect?"

"I wonder if sometime we should get a TV?" she asked.

"Sometime," he said. "I wonder how much they are, I should ask if there's anything like a TV Licence here."

"Okay, soup's ready," she said. "Grab some rolls there, would you?"

"So, you still glad we came, even with the snow and the cold?" he asked, between mouthfuls.

"I am," she said. "It's new and different, and we've got the summer to look forward to. There's so much to explore here; it's a really big country. When do you get your first holiday?"

"Not until next year," he said. "But, there are some long weekends with public holidays."

"When's the first?" she asked.

"Memorial Day, the 26th of May," he replied.

"Okay, I'll plan something for that weekend, Kathy said something about Door County, which, looking at the atlas, is a peninsular sticking out into Lake Michigan past Green Bay," she said. "I'll see if I can find us a cheap hotel there for a couple of nights."

"What shall we do this afternoon?" he asked.

"Well, we could make the bed," she suggested. "Then we could try it out."

"I like the sound of that," he said. "I'll wash up quickly, and then I'll help you with the bed."

After the bed was made, they had a quick bath, then went to try it out.

"Can anyone see in through the window?" Katrina asked.

"Not unless they've got a really powerful telescope," James replied. "We're up on the fifth floor, so unless we actually stand by the window, no one's going to see us."

"Good," she said. "Now, where were we?"

"I think you were about to show me a good time," he suggested.

"I thought you were supposed to be the one showing me a good time," she retorted. Their badinage went on for about another thirty seconds, then it was lost to kissing and lovemaking.

"Again?" she asked, after about half an hour past the first climax.

"Again," he said. "I love you, *Suikerbossie.*"

"I love you, *my wellustig ou bok*," she replied.

"*Wellustig?*" he asked.

"Lecherous," she explained.

"It's hard not to be lecherous when you're near me," he said. "I love being with you and that you're here with me."

"Come closer and show me that you really care," she invited. James did as asked, and they whiled away the afternoon, alternately making love and then just enjoying the closeness that a loved one brings.

"I suppose we should think about dinner," she finally said. "Are you hungry?"

"Not really," he said.

"Well, I am," she said. "And you should be after all the energy you've used up."

"What shall we do?" he asked. "Cook or eat out?"

"Let's see if we can brave the weather and find a place that sells pizza," she suggested. "I have a fancy for pizza."

"Pizza it is," he said. "Let go of me, and I'll see what I can find in the Yellow Pages. You know that Italian place we went to the other day had pizza on the menu, should we try there?"

"Why not?" she said. "It's close enough that we could walk."

"Okay," he agreed. "Dress warmly."

"I will," she said.

Their walk took them over snow piled up at the sides of the road and through newly fallen snow. It was only a short walk, but by the time they reached the restaurant, they both sported white caps from the falling snow. The restaurant had a vestibule, so they were able to shake off the worst of the snow before they went in and stamped their boots to get rid of more.

"You're back," the waitress said. "You were here just the other day."

"We were," James confirmed. "We just moved into an apartment close by."

"Oh, you've moved into the tower?" she asked. "You didn't walk over, did you?"

"We thought we would," James said.

"You must be cold," she said. "I'm Vittoria. What can I get you?"

"A couple of Chiantis would be fine," he said.

"And to eat, here's the menu, take your time," Vittoria said. James opened the menu and found the page that featured pizza. It was almost a create-it-yourself feature. You told them what you wanted, and it was put together on the spot and then baked.

"I wonder what happens when all this snow melts?" James thought, setting aside the menu for a minute.

"I'll bet it's a mess," Katrina said. "But I suppose most of it will melt away and drain into the lake."

"What about all the salt they chuck on the roads?" he asked.

"Pollutes the lake, I suppose," she said. "I wonder if the salt levels are even measurable; it's a huge lake."

"I suppose over time it will build up," he said. "I imagine they've been using salt on the roads for ages."

"It seems to me that the worst problem is going to be snow that melts then freezes again at night," she added.

"Think of all the ice on the roads then, no wonder they chuck so much salt around," he said. Vittoria brought them glasses of Chianti, huge glasses, with probably half a pint in each. They ordered their pizza, then sat back and relaxed after their busy day.

"I hope we can walk home after this," Katrina said. "Cheers."

"Cheers," James echoed.

"Do you remember any of the Italian words we picked up from the folks at the Mkushi mine?" she asked.

"Not really," he said. "I didn't spend much time with them, and all the ones I talked to spoke English."

"This is a busy place," she commented. "But it also looks like people eat early here; there's been a few leave since we arrived, and no one has come in after us."

"Here you go, folks," Vittoria said, placing a huge platter in front of them with the pizza on it, already sliced into wedges.

"That's huge," James said.

"Take home what you don't eat, Dearie," Vittoria said.

"Really?" Katrina asked.

"Sure," Vittoria confirmed. "Enjoy."

James and Katrina both helped themselves to slices of the pizza and fell to eating with gusto.

"This is good," James said.

"It is, isn't it?" Katrina agreed.

Sunday meant a trip to Herman's Sporting Goods and an introduction to cross-country skiing. Unlike much of the downhill skiing equipment offered, the cross-country skis were relatively inexpensive.

"Should we buy some?" James asked.

"How much do we have in the bank?" Katrina asked.

"We've enough," he said. "The question is, will we use them?"

"I'd like to try," she said. "Do we need any special clothes?" James asked and learned that the shoes were special because they locked into the skis, but apart from that, nothing special was required, unless they wanted to spend money. The salesman did suggest good gloves and hats that covered the ears. They already had them, so it was the skis, poles and shoes. The skis were different lengths, longer for James as he was heavier. They also learned about waxing the bottom of the skis and bought some wax, as with most sports, spending was only limited by personal discipline, so they bought the essentials and nothing else. Other clothing items might follow in time, but neither saw any point in lashing out on things that did not need to try out the sport. Back home at their apartment, they dressed for the outdoors and then took the skis downstairs to the park and tried them out. It was a funny motion, almost like taking long strides; both of them fell a few times, to great laughter. Getting back up was interesting. James finally worked out that if he lay on his back and grabbed the tips of the skis, he could rock back and forth until he rolled over onto his knees. From there, it was fairly easy to stand back up. Both James and Katrina discovered that they had worn too much in the way of clothing; something light that kept out the wind would probably be better, but they decided that, for the moment, they would live with the clothes they had and not rush out and buy whole new wardrobes.

"That was fun," Katrina said later as they were drinking tea and looking out onto the snowy expanse of the park.

"At least doing that, we won't be snowed in for the whole winter," James said. "You haven't been able to swim since we moved. I wonder if there's anywhere close where they have a pool?"

"I noticed a YMCA not far from here," she said. "I wonder if it's just for young men, or if it's open to the public and if they have a pool?"

"If they do, it'll be an indoor pool," he said. "Outdoor pools here can't get much use for months, like the one downstairs."

"I wonder how thick the ice is?" she said. "Maybe you could go ice fishing on it."

"And catch what?" he laughed. "An old boot or two?"

"I'll go and see if the YMCA takes the public," she said. "Now, we should think about dinner. We have that pizza that we brought home last night, shall I just stick it in the oven and heat it up?"

"Better than letting it go to waste," he said.

"So, James, what did you do over the weekend?" Tony asked him the next day.

"We moved into the apartment and tried out cross-country skiing," James replied.

"Great, so ready for another trip?" Tony asked.

"Where to?" James asked.

"New Mexico," Tony said. "There's a couple of coal mines out there right on the Arizona, New Mexico state line, and there's a new one looking to open up. We need to go and check it out. We'll leave next Monday and be back Wednesday."

"Do you know what size machine they're looking for?" James asked.

"We're supposed to tell them," Tony said. "We'll go and take a look and get some information on the deposit and recommend a bucket size and boom length."

114

"Do you have a rule of thumb for dragline production?" James asked.

"About 250,000 cubic yards per yard of bucket per year," Tony replied. "That's assuming a sixty-second cycle and mechanical and electrical availability of 85% and utilisation of 85%. So, there are some other enquiries that we should answer, two in Kentucky and one in Illinois. Those we can do from the office, they sent enough information in, and they're just looking for rough order of magnitude numbers. They may get serious at some point; we'll see. Here, take a look at these two; they're both in Kentucky and pretty similar."

James got to work and calculated what kind of production would be required, and then sized the machine to match it. He asked Tony why they could not create a computer program that would come up with the solution, and Tony waffled a bit, then disclosed that David Brooks, the company vice president of sales, believed that customers liked the hand-drawn diagrams.

"Don't the engineers have some kind of plotter?" James asked.

"I think they do," Tony said. "Let's see." He made a quick telephone call and then told James that, indeed, the engineering department had, in fact, a couple of plotters.

"Could we use them?" James asked.

"I suppose so," Tony said. "What do you suggest?"

"Get the programmers to help us write a program that calculates all this stuff and then plots out a casting diagram that shows bench heights, boom lengths and such," James suggested.

"Why don't you see what you can do?" Tony said. "Then we'll run it by a customer or two and see what they say."

James set to and did the calculations for one of the enquiries that had come in, and then wrote out roughly how a program could be written to do what he had just done. That all done, he went off to find Herb, who had helped him before. The program was very simple and was promised by the end of the day, including the interface with the plotter to get a diagram. James gave Herb the data that he had and said that he would not bother him for output until the next day. James then asked Marlys to get him a box of index cards and started to make up a card for each of the mines he had been to, noting what equipment was at each operation. He also found in back issues of the various industry journals and magazines that occasionally there was a write-up of a mine, and that usually listed what they had on-site. So, he started to build a database of mines and equipment, noting how much was from J&B and how much from the other manufacturers. He did note that certain companies seemed to have preferences for specific manufacturers and wondered if that was merely happenstance or an actual preference. Of interest was the match-up of sizes of shovels and trucks, all generally falling into the same pattern, but with a few odd outliers.

The rest of the week, James stayed busy, responding to enquiries from the field salesmen, no women, he noted, all men. He thought back to what he had been told in England and started to make notes of the enquiries and add his guess of weighting to them, which he would modify as things progressed, or not. Herb had plots and numbers for him, so he, with the approval of Tony, sent them off to the field salesman in Kentucky. Katrina investigated the YMCA and discovered that over time, the Young Men's Christian Association had in fact changed a lot, and it was now more of a general support organisation for the community and did offer memberships for people to use their exercise facilities, which included the swimming pool. The membership fee was not outrageous, so she signed them up for a family plan that allowed both of them to go as often as they liked and use whatever was there. The Y, as she learned it was commonly referred to, was within walking distance of the apartment along College Avenue. So, on the days when the sun shone, she walked to go for her swim, but on the days when snow fell or it was just too cold, she drove. Katrina also patronised the laundry facilities in the apartment building and stocked on quarter coins to run the machines, washers and dryers. Those were the most convenient things, the dryers. In the cold weather, it would be hard to dry things, unless they were hung around the apartment, whereas for a few quarters, they could tumble around inside a machine and come out dry. Driving was still an adventure at times, if it snowed, or it thawed and froze, and there was ice on the roads. Taking James to the office in the morning sometimes took a while as the going was slow because of the road conditions.

The time came for James to go to New Mexico, and he packed his warm clothes and boots, and Katrina dropped him at the Milwaukee airport.

"I'll call you tonight," he promised as he said goodbye.

"Where are you staying tonight?" she asked.

"A place called Gallup," he replied.

"Go well," she said.

"I will, love you," he replied. He found Tony by the check-in desk of North Central, and he checked in his bags to Albuquerque, via Chicago. The first leg might be North Central, but from Chicago, it was the Golden Fantail of Continental. The flight to Chicago was short enough, and then they went hunting for the Continental gate. The Albuquerque flight was a Boeing 727 and was a little more elegant than the Convair that North Central flew. At least it had a real First Class cabin, and the service was excellent. On the flight out, James asked Tony about the place they were going to and who the company was.

"The site is on a Reservation," Tony explained. "K&L Mining have a concession for forty years to mine coal there, they'll pay a royalty to the Tribal Council and probably have some agreement as to how many members of the tribe they'll employ."

"Are there other mines out there?" James asked.

"Pittsburgh and Midway have a mine there, and there's another at Black Mesa and another at Kayenta," Tony replied. "It's pretty remote, so they have to put in all their own infrastructure, but for a mine life of at least forty years, that's doable."

"We're flying into Albuquerque, what's that like?" James asked.

"Desert town," Tony said. "The Rio Grande runs through it, but it's pretty dry; you could see a lot of cowboy boots and hats."

Tony was right. When they landed at Albuquerque, James was struck by the number of people sporting cowboy hats and boots. They were met by Charlie Evans, the salesman whose territory included Arizona and

117

New Mexico. He had driven up the day before, from Phoenix, where he lived and would be driving them back part of the way he had come. Charlie had another Chevrolet Suburban, as Keith did in Wyoming. Tony and James loaded their bags into the back, and they set off to drive west on I-40 towards Gallup.

"I thought we'd stop for lunch at Grants," Charlie suggested. "Then we'll meet the K&L guys in Gallup, and tomorrow early we'll drive out to the mine site."

"How far is it to Gallup?" James asked.

"About 140 miles," Charlie replied. "The mine site is about fifty miles from Gallup on the Reservation."

"Whose reservation?" James asked.

"Navajo," Charlie replied.

"Is it large?" James asked.

"Huge," Charlie replied. "It's mostly in Arizona, but it extends into Utah, Colorado and New Mexico."

"Is most of your business copper?" James asked.

"Most," Charlie confirmed. "Between the copper mines of Arizona and New Mexico, there's usually quite a bit going on; the coal is pretty new, and most of it is up in this part of the world. Tony told me that you used to work in a copper mine."

"I did," James confirmed. "I worked underground for a while, then in an open pit that I helped start up."

"Why'd you leave?" Charlie asked.

"The price of copper dropped, and the mine economics just didn't work, so they mothballed the place and laid us all off. I was offered another job, but it was working for a chap I really didn't like, so took the offer they gave me and left," James explained.

"We've seen the effects of that price drop here, too," Charlie said. "Most of the mines have cut back a bit. Say, we're about here, let's grab some lunch and then we'll go on to Gallup."

"Sorry to change the subject, but is this a lava flow we're passing through?" James asked.

"It is," Charlie confirmed. "There were ancient volcanoes near here, and you see the flows and the remnants of volcanic plugs, like Shiprock.

There are also uranium mines in Grants, but they're underground mines, no sales there for us."

The restaurant in Grants was basic, probably typical of many such places in the American West, a cowboy motif, serving Southwestern cuisine, which James learned meant chillis.

"Who are we going to meet?" Tony asked, after they had ordered lunch and were sitting drinking coffee, waiting for the food to arrive.

"George Simpson, he's the project manager, and Bob Berg, he's the mining engineer," Charlie replied. "They're both pretty good guys."

"Do they have production levels set already?" Tony asked.

"They do," Charlie said. "They'll start out slow, then as they get the railroad spur in, they'll ramp up production."

"I'm presuming that they'll need shovels and drills as well as draglines," Tony commented.

"They will," Charlie agreed. "The big ticket item will be the dragline, so they'll probably spend most time talking about that. They've been to the P&M mine and to Kayenta, so they've got a pretty good idea of what they're looking at."

"Is the deposit simple?" James asked.

"I guess so," Charlie said. "They start out with about eighty feet of overburden, and then it grows as the coal seam dips."

"How long before they're into rehandling the overburden?" James asked.

"You'd have to tell them that," Charlie said.

"It's going to be a matter of how big a machine they get," Tony said. "Smaller bucket, longer boom, less rehandling, so it's the economic trade-off of machine size versus production costs."

"And if they do some pre-stripping with smaller equipment?" James asked.

"Again, economics," Tony said. "Maybe you could look at that and see if there's something we could suggest."

"I will," James promised.

"Here you go, guys," the waitress said as she brought out their food.

They were back on the road to Gallup soon enough, running through miles of open range land dotted with sagebrush and the occasional stand of trees that signalled the presence of water. There were patches of snow, lingering in shaded spots, mostly under the trees and bushes. It looked like an interesting country, but not very inviting. Charlie left the freeway at Gallup and went to the hotel where they would be staying. It was built in the Southwest style with adobe walls. They got rooms and then repaired to the bar to await the people from K&L. James looked around and noticed that a great many of the patrons were probably Navajo or one of the other tribes.

"Is Gallup in the Reservation?" he asked Charlie.

"No," Charlie replied. "The Navajo Reservation starts about ten miles north of here, and to the south, there's the Zuni. Here's George and Bob."

"Charlie," George said. "How you doing?"

"Fine, thanks, George. This is Tony Whitaker and James Martin, both from Oak Creek; they're our application guys."

"Tony, James," George said. "This is Bob Berg, he's our mining engineer. Charlie said that you guys are both mining engineers, where'd you go?"

"I went to Penn State," Tony replied.

"I went to the Royal School of Mines in London," James replied.

"Both good schools," Bob remarked. "I went to Colorado."

"I'm an oil guy," George added. "I went to Texas A&M and then worked in the oil fields for years, before K&L decided to get into mining, so I'm going to manage the overall project and let Bob get on with the mining."

"Can we get you guys a beer?" Charlie asked.

"Great idea," George said. "So, looking forward to the spin out into the range lands tomorrow?"

"We are," Tony said.

"We've got a site office there," George said. "We got maps, drill cores, and mine plans out there."

"What sort of production are you looking at?" Tony asked.

"We're looking for about four million tons in the first five years, growing to six million thereafter," George replied.

"How steeply dipping is the coal seam?" James asked.

"Not too steep," Bob replied. "About two feet in a thousand."

"Does the ground rise or fall?" James asked.

"It varies," Bob said. "Probably about a fifty-foot variation over the deposit, sort of gently rolling hills, no mesas or other distinctive features."

"Do you get much rain?" James asked.

"About two inches a year, most of it falling in July and August, some light snow in the winter months, but nothing like Wyoming or Utah," Bob replied.

"There are some other mines nearby. What equipment do they have?" James asked. Between Tony, Bob and Charlie, they came up with a reasonable list of the main items of machinery that each mine had, but James wanted to know a little more: how many trucks and of what size, how many bulldozers, how many graders. No one could answer all those questions, but Charlie promised to see if he could gather up all the information in the next month or so.

"James used to work in a copper mine in Zambia in Africa," Charlie commented. "He told us earlier that he had the job of starting up a new pit."

"What did you use?" Bob asked.

"Mainly a Cat fleet with fifty-ton trucks and front-end loaders," James explained. "We did a lot of drilling and blasting, but with much smaller holes than you'll use. Fragmentation was a big issue for us as it related directly to maintenance costs of the front-end loaders."

"Did you ever get to see the Nchanga mine?" Bob asked.

"I did," James confirmed. "It was a little bigger than the pit I ran."

"Don't they use a bucket wheel there?" Bob asked.

"They've got one," James said. "They use it to pre-strip soft materials before they have to start drilling."

"Is it any good?" Bob asked.

"Depends who you talk to," James replied. "Some of the operations people there would be happy to see the back of it, others quite like it. I think the biggest issue they have is keeping the conveyors that run around the pit running properly."

"Could we use something similar?" Bob asked.

"You could," James agreed. "But, you'd have more flexibility if you went with scrapers or shovels and trucks to knock down the hills to give the dragline a uniform digging depth."

"We should talk a bit more about that when we're out there tomorrow," Bob said.

"Are there any draglines in Zambia?" George asked.

"There's one at Maamba Collieries," James replied. "A Bucyrus-Erie 1260."

"You guys hungry?" Charlie asked.

"I could eat," George said.

James called Katrina after dinner.

"How's New Mexico?" she asked.

"Dry, a little snow here and there, but not much, lots of open space," he replied.

"What did you do today?" she asked.

"We drove out here from Albuquerque, then met with a couple of the mine people and tomorrow morning we drive out to the mine site," he replied. "What was your day like?"

"Quiet," she said. "I went for a swim this morning, then after lunch, I tried out the skis again, I typed a bit more of my book, then grabbed something for dinner. So, any hunting stories today?"

"No, it was all business, all very technical," he said.

"You'll be home Wednesday?" she asked.

"I will," he said. "Tomorrow out to the mine site, then drive back to Albuquerque in the afternoon and get the first flight to Chicago in the morning, we should be back in Milwaukee at about one-thirty."

"I'll be there," she said. "Do you have to go to the office?"

"I doubt it," he said. "But you never know, I'll check tomorrow and let you know."

"I miss you," she said.

"I miss you, I love you, Suikerbossie," he replied.

"Love you," she said. "Sleep well!"

The drive out to the mine site in the morning did not take long, and they were shown the lay of the land and then geological maps and mine plans. James took copious notes and some photographs. It was chilly at the site, but then they were up at almost 7,000 feet. The skies were clear, crystal clear in the cool air, and there was a little frost on the ground that crunched as they walked about. James saw four aircraft passing overhead, probably bound for the East Coast or somewhere in the Midwest. There were some pronghorn antelope that looked them over, then ran off into the distance. It seemed almost a shame to think about the development that was going to happen and the disturbance, not only of the ground, but the serenity of the place. George pointed out where the railway would come and where the trains would be loaded. Bob showed them where they planned the first mine to be. James could imagine it, but it was still going to be a huge undertaking to get everything to the site and in operation. It was a much bigger task than he had had in Zambia, but then he did not have to get a railway line built or have a power line laid on. George talked about the workforce they would have to find and train, something James could relate to, having done a similar thing in Zambia. When Tony was satisfied that they had all that they would need, they took their leave of George and Bob and left to drive back to Albuquerque.

They made Albuquerque in time to get an afternoon flight back to Chicago, which would get them into Milwaukee at about eight-thirty that night. That sounded like a much better plan than staying an extra night. James called Katrina and gave her the new arrival time, and she promised to be at the airport to meet him.

"So, what do you think?" Tony asked when they were on the plane and winging their way back to Chicago.

"It's interesting, I think we should suggest a shovel to go with the drill and dragline, strip off the humps and bumps and let the dragline just operate with no rehandling," James replied.

"Can you gin up some economic numbers?" Tony asked.

"I should be able to," James said.

"Great," Tony said. "Are you enjoying the job?"

"It's been really interesting," James said. "I've learned a lot and seen a lot already."

"Well, you're doing just great," Tony said.

"Katrina, how are you?" Tony asked when they arrived in Milwaukee.

"I'm fine, thank you," she replied. "Did you have a good trip?"

"We did," Tony confirmed. "James did a great job. So, James, see you bright and early tomorrow?"

"I'll be there," James said. He went with Katrina, and she drove them home.

"Did you get some dinner?" she asked.

"On the plane," he said. "And you?"

"I got myself something light," she said. "I'm glad you came home early."

"So am I," he said. "I'd rather spend the night with you than in some strange hotel."

"Is New Mexico a nice place?" she asked.

"I think so," he said. "Rather like living in the Karoo. Lots of sheep and cows and open range lands."

"Okay, we're here," she said as they pulled into the parking area of the apartment building. "Come on, it's cold out here."

In the apartment, James kissed her hello properly and pulled her close to him.

"I miss you when I go away," he said. "I wish there were some way you could come with me."

"I'd probably be in the way," she said. "You wouldn't keep your attention on the job, your mind would be wandering, like it is now."

"I was just thinking how lucky I am to have married you," he said.

"And you were also thinking about how to get me into bed," she said, poking him in the chest with her finger.

"That too," he admitted.

"Well, come on then," she said. "Bath and bed, then you can show me how much you missed me."

Appalachia

James spent the next couple of days refining his thoughts about the mining options and running all kinds of calculations. He really did need to work out how to get it all included in a computer program that would make life so much easier. He had a program that would do the calculations for the dragline, but he needed to expand upon that and add in the various options for including other mining methods, like those they had discussed in New Mexico. He took his data to Herb and got a run for just the dragline, and it enabled him to pick the size of machine, with the bucket capacity and boom length to suit. To add the other mining methods would require much more programming, but first, he would have to work out just what the calculations would be; it was no good asking Herb to write something without telling him in detail what was wanted. By the end of the third day, he had a reasonable flow diagram of the decisions, and for each branch, he could then create the mathematics that would be required. He was tired but content when he went home.

"James," Katrina said when he got home. "I'm a little worried about this bloke that's been hanging around the Y watching me swim."

"Did you talk to the staff?" he asked.

"I did, but what if he follows me home?" she asked.

"Should I come with you?" he asked.

"That would be nice, but I want to be able to go on my own; I shouldn't have to worry about some weird bloke," she said.

"I wonder if there's something we could get you, so if he does try and follow you, you can discourage him?" James thought.

"What, like a gun?" she asked.

"Probably not," he said. "But maybe something else, let me see what I can come up with and don't go to the Y for the next couple of days."

"I won't," she promised. "I'll just ski in the park instead. Oh, I noticed when I was skiing the other day that the snow's melting slowly. There are bits of grass showing now."

"Do you feel like cooking, or shall we go out and get something to eat?" he asked.

"Let's go to our Italian place," she suggested. "I think drive tonight, it's sleeting out."

"Back again?" Vittoria asked.

"We are," James replied.

"What can I get you tonight?" Vittoria asked.

"A glass of Chianti each and some lasagna, only one order of lasagna, we'll share if that's okay?" Katrina replied.

"Sure thing, Honey," Vittoria said. She left and was back quickly with the wine and promised to have the lasagna in about ten minutes.

"You've been busy," Katrina said to James as they sipped their wine.

"I've been trying to make life easier," he laughed. "If I can work out how to do it, I think we could use the company computer to do a lot of the work for us."

"I'm sure that if there's a way, you'll come up with it," she said. "Are you enjoying the job?"

"I am," he replied. "It's different, not like running a mine, more like going to college again."

"Well, so far you've been to Wyoming, Minnesota and New Mexico, where next?" she asked.

"I've no idea," he said. "I answered some enquiries from Kentucky last week, and I know that Tony answered at least one from Illinois."

"I like the sound of New Mexico," she said. "Not too many people and wide open spaces. Are there many mines there?"

"They've got copper mines," he said. "Although we went to Gallup, the mine site is actually in Arizona, so all the new coal mines are in Arizona; they do have uranium mines, but I think they're all underground."

"Here you go, folks," Vittoria said, interrupting their conversation as she put a plate of lasagna in front of them, then she gave them an extra empty plate. Katrina halved the dish and pushed some onto the other plate, and gave it to James. It was still a large serving, quite enough for each of them.

"Eat up," Katrina said.

"I like this," James joked. "No washing up."

"You're not going to get away with that for too long," she said. "Tomorrow, I'm cooking and you're washing up."

"Look at the stuff that's coming down out there," he said. "It's changed from sleet to snow. Does it ever stop snowing here?"

"Memorial Day, which is in late May," she said. "At least that's what Kathy told me."

James mentioned to Tony the next day that Katrina was concerned about a man who seemed to be showing an unwanted interest in her.

"Get some Mace," Tony said. "It'll make the creepiest of creeps leave her alone."

"Where would I get that?" James asked.

"Any gun shop, just tell them that you're concerned about your wife being followed," Tony said.

"I'll check on that," James said. "Did we hear back from the people in Minnesota about their shovel performance?"

"Yeah, Bob told me that they've ordered up six more trucks," Tony said. "Oh, and the other guys just ordered a new drill."

"So, my visits were worthwhile?" James asked.

"Absolutely," Tony said. "Have you got anything yet that we can send to Charlie to talk to the K&L guys?"

"I do," James said. "I've got this whole report that you could send."

"Okay, write up a transmittal letter and have Marlys send it off with the report attached," Tony said.

"You don't want to look at it first?" James asked.

"I should," Tony said. "You have it handy?"

James handed him a copy, and Tony read through it, then read it again and finally handed it back to James.

"Looks good," he said. "I might change a few words, but that would just be me; the mathematics and sizes all work out, so go for it."

"Really?" James asked.

"Sure," Tony said. "I doubt that they'll get anything better, or even as good, from the other guys, so it gives us a leg up."

"Tony suggested we get some Mace to fend off anyone following you," James told Katrina that evening.

"It may not be necessary," she said. "I drove to Kohl's today to get some groceries and went by the Y and saw the bloke being taken off in a police car, so I stopped and went in and talked to the pool person, and she told me that he had been ogling a couple of the teenagers and their swimming coach had got concerned and called the cops. It turned out that he was wanted for all kinds of things, not only in Wisconsin, but also in Illinois."

"That's good to hear," James said, relieved. "I wonder, though, if it might not be a bad idea to get some Mace?"

"What, just to carry in case?" she asked.

"You never know," he said. "I wonder what Mace is?"

"Don't know," she said. "I made dinner, so set the table, would you?"

"What else happened today?" he asked a few minutes later as they were eating.

"We got a letter from my folks," she said. "They said they're doing well, picking grapes and getting ready to press."

"I wonder when we'll be able to get to go and see them again?" he said.

"Probably not for a while," she thought. "You'd need to get some time off, and when we do our first trip should be something for us, maybe a trip out west to Yellowstone or something like that."

"I wonder how much snow they get there?" he said.

"Probably lots," she thought. "But, I would think that June would be a good time to go, school holidays haven't started, so some people, but not millions."

"We should probably look at buying a car soon," he said. "We can still use the hire car, but at some point, they're not going to want to continue paying for that."

"What should we buy?" she asked.

"I think it's going to be very much a question of what we can afford," he replied. "Maybe this weekend we'll take a look and see what's available and how much."

"Where should I look for a second-hand car?" James asked Tony the next day.

"Try Car King in West Allis," Tony suggested. "You don't need to buy a car just yet; keep driving the rental and expense it."

"You're sure?" James asked.

"Sure," Tony assured him. "Wait until the snow's all gone and the salt is all gone too, then buy."

"How much do they cost?" James asked.

"How long's a piece of string?" Tony said.

"So, it depends on what we want?" James said.

"There you go," Tony said. "You want a Cadillac, it's going to cost more than a cheap Chevy. Say, John Williams from the UK is here, and he stuck his head in earlier and asked if you and Katrina wanted to join him for dinner tonight."

"Where is he?" James asked.

"Downstairs in Mahogany Row," Tony said. "Go down and see him."

"James," John said as James walked past the various offices where the chief executives of the company sat. It had the feel of hallowed ground, and James felt as if he should be tiptoeing through. "How are you? How are you settling in? Have they kept you busy?" John asked.

"I'm fine, thanks," James replied. "We found a flat we can afford, and I've been busy, so no complaints."

"Say, why don't you and your wife come and have dinner with me tonight? I'm at the Pfister, come around six, I'm still on UK time," John said.

"Thank you," James replied. "That's kind of you."

"Not kind, just checking up on you," John laughed. "See you at six."

James went back upstairs and called Katrina, and told her that they were invited out that evening and not to cook. That made her happy. Her only concern was what to wear. James suggested the blue trousers and jacket that she had; it was elegant, it was formal enough for almost any occasion.

"John, this is my wife, Katrina," James said, making the introduction when they met with him in the bar of the Pfister.

"Nice to finally meet you," John said. "James never brought you over to Didcot, so you met Howard, but no one else. How do you like it here?"

"It's very different," she replied. "I've never seen so much snow in my life. All I've seen before was some on the tops of mountains in South Africa."

"Well, you get used to it," John said. "Find something to do that gets you outdoors."

"We took up cross-country skiing," she said. "That gets us out, when it's not too cold and snowy."

"How is your move going?" James asked John.

"We've picked Dick West to go over and replace me," John replied. "Keep that under your hat for a day or two; we should announce that and a whole raft of other changes next Monday."

"What are you going to do?" James asked.

"Well, I'm taking over from Dave Brooks; he's retiring at the end of the month, so I'm coming over earlier than we planned," John said. "We're going to set up a management development program, and I want you to be in that."

"What would that entail?" James asked.

"We'll give you some different assignments in the next few years. If you want to take it, we'll pay for the Executive MBA program and you'll be assigned a mentor," John explained. "We've not really done anything about developing our people at any level; it's all been very haphazard, so we're making things more formal."

"Who would be included in this development program?" James asked.

"We've picked out the first twenty," John said. "We've got some salespeople, engineers, manufacturing, accounting, parts and service. I think we've covered the gamut."

"You said I'd be assigned a mentor, do you know who that would be?" James asked.

"There are two of you who have been assigned to Hank Miller, you and Bill Evans from manufacturing, I get three, one from accounting, one from engineering and one from personnel, we've made it quite formal, you meet with your mentor once a month and review things, it's a big commitment for us, one of the reasons David is bailing out early, he didn't want any part of it, felt it was a waste of time," John elaborated.

"So, was it deliberate not to assign a mentor in the area I was currently working? I've never even met Hank Miller; he seems so remote as the president," James asked.

"Very," John said. "We want the management to learn who's in the company, and we want the people in the program to see things from a different point of view. We've decided to invest quite a bit in this, so most of you will be in the MBA program, that is, if you want to be?"

"That sounds like a great opportunity," James said. "What's Hank Miller like? I know next to nothing about him."

"He's a finance guy, got an accounting degree, then worked in public accounting for a couple of years before joining us. He's spent most of his career here in finance and accounting and is the first to say that we need people with a broader view of the company," John replied. "Hank may seem remote, but he's actually not; he's very personable, but will expect you to tell him how things are, not what you think he would like to hear."

"How does one get selected for the program?" James asked.

"You have a sponsor," John explained. "I'm your sponsor, and that's based on reports from Tony and others that you've dealt with. So, Katrina, what did you do before you met James?"

"I worked for a while in the family business, we transported heavy equipment, like mining machinery and sugar mills," she replied. "Then, after James and I moved to the small mine, I sold industrial minerals."

"That sounds like fun," John said. "Any idea of what you might like to do here?"

"Not really," she said. "When I get authorisation to work, then I'll start looking seriously for something."

"If you need any help, let me know," John said.

"Thank you," she said.

"Let's go and get something to eat," John suggested.

"What do you think about this MBA program?" James asked Katrina later when they were in bed together.

"I think take whatever they offer," she said. "Maybe I'll sign up for a degree too, I never had the chance in Zambia, I went straight to work after school."

"Any ideas about what you might study?" he asked.

"I'm thinking about business," she said. "I'm sure that you could help me. I wonder if they do a part-time course, or if I'd have to sign up for three or four years full-time?"

"Are you sure that you don't want to do something completely different, like art, biology or zoology?" he asked.

"I hadn't thought about that," she said. "I should widen my horizons a bit, maybe even psychology, then I'd understand a little better what goes on in that head of yours."

"I don't think you want to dig too far into that," he laughed. "You'd discover that I've a one-track mind."

"I knew that already," she said. "Not that I'm complaining."

The big announcement came on Monday, and as John had said, there were many changes. David Brooks was leaving, John took over from him, Dick West was destined for England, to be replaced by George Murphy, and so on and so on. The various members of the group selected for management development were also separately contacted, and times were set for them to meet with their respective mentors. James found Bill Evans and suggested lunch before they met with Hank Miller.

"Bill," James said. "I'm new here. What can you tell me about Miller?"

"Not a whole lot," Bill said. "I know he's a finance guy, really into the numbers, but as a person, no idea. Are you going to sign on for the MBA program?"

"Yes," James said. "The last company I worked for had a management program, but it seemed to me that the head office in London picked people that they knew, or had been to the right schools, or were in some other way connected. I was never sure how much the local operations management influenced who made it to the list, so when they told me here that they would fund the MBA program, I decided it was too good to turn down."

"What's your background?" Bill asked.

"I got a degree in mining engineering and then worked in a couple of copper mines, you?" James asked.

"Got a degree in mechanical engineering and went to work here in the machine shop," Bill replied.

"John William told me that you had to be sponsored for this program," James said. "He's my sponsor, who's yours?"

"Gene Thompson," Bill replied. "He's a pretty good guy, takes an interest and doesn't yell and scream too much. So, do you suppose there's anything we should do before we meet with Miller?"

"Read the last annual report and maybe the last quarterly report," James suggested. "Who would have copies of them?"

"The annual report we can just pick up by the front desk," Bill said. "The quarterly, maybe ask Roy Pierce if he has a copy."

"This is actually quite interesting," James commented to Katrina that evening, as he read through the reports.

"May I?" she asked.

"Of course," he said, handing over the documents to her.

"You're right," she said, after a few minutes of reading. "This company's got loads of cash on its balance sheet."

"Probably from the way the contracts and the payment instalments are put together," he said. "Oh, I was asked today if I'd go to Kentucky next week to look at some mines there."

"Where?" she asked.

"No idea," he said. "All I know is that I would fly into Lexington and the local man will meet me there."

"How long will you be gone?" she asked.

"I was told that I'd leave on Tuesday and be back Friday morning," he replied. "I don't know much about Kentucky, apart from race horses, Daniel Boone and moonshiners."

"I wonder if they have snow there?" she said.

"Maybe not as much as here," he thought. "I've noticed that a lot here has melted too; there's a lot more green in the park now."

"I saw that," she said. "When do you meet with the Bwana Mkubwa?"

"Tomorrow at ten," he replied.

"Nervous?" she asked.

"A little," James said. "I've never met him, to that matter I don't know that I've ever met a president of a company."

"They're no different to you," she assured him. "Just lived longer and have a fancier title. What's the other chap like?"

"Bill's okay," James said. "I quite like him, he's never met Miller either. This is a big change for the company, Tony told me that they've never done anything like this before."

"Wear your best suit tomorrow," she said. "You need to look your best when you're talking to the boss."

"James, Bill, come in," Hank Miller, the Chief Executive Officer and Chairman of James & Brown, said the next day when they reported to his office at ten. "Coffee?"

"Thank you," James said, echoed by Bill.

"So, tell me about yourselves, Bill?" Hank asked. Bill gave a quick summary of his education and career to date, then James had his turn. Then Hank asked questions, questions that seemed to probe into their natures, their curiosity, their willingness to learn and what they thought they might get out of the development program and if there was a job or an assignment that they would really like. Hank then told them that he expected them to be transferred to different jobs after a year or so, moving around so that they would get a better overall understanding of the company. That led to questions about education and training; there were probably jobs that required a professional qualification, so moving them into those slots would not work. Hank told them that they had considered that, and in those areas where they might lack the education to do the job effectively, they would be assigned to a mentor who would guide them through the process. James had been in the position before of training a man who had then been placed over him, and wondered how James & Brown would deal with that. Hank told them that there were details yet to be worked out and that he and the rest of the management team would be looking at those very situations. The meeting lasted until noon, at which time they were each given assignments that took them out of their normal jobs and were dismissed with the instruction to be back in a month, ready to talk about their progress.

"Well, that wasn't so bad," James commented to Bill as they left the hallowed halls.

"No, he's an okay guy," Bill agreed. "When do we sign up at the college?"

"Next week, Friday," James said. "I've got a trip to Kentucky next week, but I should be back before lunch. What can you tell me about the costing of parts?"

"A little," Bill said. "If you've got a few minutes, then I'll show you how we put together work orders for parts and how we assign costs to them. What can you tell me about the market for our machines?"

"I'll put together some numbers for you," James promised. "Maybe tomorrow we could meet for lunch and I go over them with you."

"So, how was the meeting with the Bwana Mkubwa today?" Katrina asked James.

"He's actually quite nice," James replied. "He gave us each a project, and I'll have to rely on Bill for information, and I promised to help him."

"I've been looking into courses at the college here," she said. "I'm thinking of finance as a degree."

"That would be super, when would you start?" he asked.

"I think this autumn when the new academic year begins," she said. "What I need to do before then is get copies of my school certificates."

"I wonder what they'll make of a Rhodesian certificate?" he said.

"Probably ask me if I can speak English," she laughed.

"How is the novel coming?" he asked.

"I did some more today, trying to imagine from his journal what it was actually like trekking through the Kalahari, not knowing where it might lead and who or what you might meet," she said.

"When you finish it, do you think you'd like to get it published?" he asked.

"That would be nice, but I wonder how I'd do that?" she said.

"I'm sure we can find out," he assured her.

"I can probably get quite a few pages written while you're off traipsing around Kentucky," she said. "It helps with the loneliness."

"Do you have any regrets that we came?" he asked.

"No," she said, quite firmly. "This is a job that is worth it, and I look to the future and know that you won't always be flitting around, so some inconvenience and hardship now will lead to better things to come."

"Call me when you can," Katrina told James as she saw him off at the airport at the start of his trip to Kentucky.

"I will," he promised. "I love you."

"Love you, go well," she replied. James boarded his plane, just a short hop to Chicago on North Central, before getting the next flight to Lexington on Eastern Airlines. In Lexington, James saw a man holding up a James & Brown brochure.

"Hal Sanders?" James asked.

"You're James Martin?" Hal asked in reply.

"I am," James confirmed.

"Got your bag? Great, we'll go," Hal said. "It's quite a drive to Hazard, about two hours, so we'll get lunch there. We'll meet the company guys for lunch, then go out to the site. We might want to find a place to change clothes. Did you bring boots with you?"

"I did," James confirmed. "Boots, jeans and a light jacket."

"We'll stop at a diner I know on the way, have a cup of coffee and let you change clothes," Hal said. "It could be muddy where we're going, and I doubt that any of the mine guys will have suits and ties."

"What kind of coal mines are these we're going to?" James asked.

"They're mountain top and contour mines," Hal explained. "Mountain top is just that, strip the top off a mountain and expose the coal seam, contour mining, follow the contours around the mountain and expose the seam of coal, then also use augers to take out under the mountain."

"Where do you live?" James asked.

"I live in Evansville," Hal said. "So, I drove up to Lexington yesterday."

"This is quite different to Wyoming or New Mexico," James said after they had been driving for almost an hour. "Lots of trees, lots of hills, when does a hill become a mountain?"

"Don't rightly know," Hal admitted. "Here the folks would call them hills and hollers, but on the maps, you'll see mountains, more down towards the Virginia line."

"Coal has been mined here for a long time?" James asked.

"Long time," Hal confirmed. "Lots of underground mines, some old strip mines, and now more and more strip mines."

"This is part of Appalachia, isn't it?" James asked.

"Sure is," Hal confirmed. "Appalachia runs down from Pennsylvania to Alabama, but what is normally associated with Appalachia is along the Virginia, Kentucky, and Tennessee borders."

"Are all the moonshining stories true?" James asked.

"There are plenty of guys up in the hollers stilling," Hal confirmed. "There are times we get mistaken for revenuers and get shot at."

"Revenuers?" James asked.

"The government," Hal explained. "The guys that are supposed to find and break up the stills."

It was lunchtime by the time they got to Hazard, and Hal obviously knew where he was going, because he drove straight to the restaurant.

"Hey, guys," he said as he and James went in.

"Hey, Hal," a man replied.

"James, this is Larry, Bob, Tom and Jed," Hal said. "Guys, this is James, he's one of our mining engineers."

"Good to see you, James, so Hal, how's things?" Larry asked.

"Fair," Hal said. "I've been busy in western Kentucky and Indiana."

"You been out to these parts before, James," Larry asked.

"No, first time," James said.

"Well, ya'll are in for a treat," Larry said. "We'll take a run-up to the site after lunch and drive around some high walls."

"Been down a coal mine before?" Bob asked.

137

"I've been down a couple of underground mines and some surface mines," James confirmed. "I worked underground in a copper mine for a while, then an open pit."

"Where'd you do that?" Jed asked.

"In Zambia," James said.

"So any whites in the mine?" Jed asked.

"Mostly the management and engineering," James said. "Nearly all the workforce was local."

"How many?" Jed asked.

"I think all told in the underground mine we had about 12,000, between the mine, the concentrator and the smelter," James replied.

"Holy shit, that's huge, that's more than twice as many people who live here," Jed said.

"What about your surface mine?" Bob asked.

"About 400 all told," James said. "That includes the mine, the mill and all the maintenance staff."

"Close to town?" Tom asked.

"The closest town of any size was about a hundred miles away," James replied. "Our biggest issues were with electricity supply and water."

"Well, we're not quite that remote," Larry said. "We'll have issues, but nothing we can't handle. Let's get some lunch, then we'll drive on up to the site."

The drive up to the mine site was through forests, then onto cleared land where James could see what looked like an extremely wide road following the contour of the hill. He could see the coal seam, and it looked like it had been worked already, because there were big holes in it, like someone had drilled holes. Those were the signs of the auger mining, a segmented auger driven into the coal seam under the hill that pulled the coal out into waiting trucks. They drove further on, and the overburden above the coal seam increased.

"Here's where we need to start taking off more material," Larry said. "We need something bigger than the front-end loader we've been using."

"I can see that," James said. "What sort of production are you looking for?" Larry gave him some numbers, and they talked about shovels and trucks, and drills to match. They drove farther on, and Larry pointed to a different site.

"Here we want to strip the top off the mountain," he said. "I've got some sections here that show the depths to the seam across the top."

James studied the map and the sections and made his own guess as to what would be required, then told Larry that he would run some numbers and confirm his suggestions. James looked over the terrain and noted that it was rolling hills, some higher than others, and the hills seemed to go on forever. In the far distance, there were a few taller peaks, almost lost in the bluish haze that covered everything. James asked about weather delays and lost time and learned that the risk of snow was fairly low; they did lose a few days a year to rain, but for the most part, there were few constraints on the mining.

They all returned to the town, and James promised to have numbers to Hal within a few days, so that he could pass them on to Larry and his team. Hal and James found their hotel and checked in, then met in the bar.

"So, what do you think?" Hal asked James.

"I have to admit having problems a few times understanding Larry, Tom and Jed," James said. "But I have enough to put something together for you. Do they have the funds to buy machines?"

"They do, or can get it," Hal assured him. "Larry might sound a bit like a hillbilly, but he's pretty astute when it comes to finance."

"I could almost see Jed as a moonshiner," James commented.

"I don't think you'd be far wrong," Hal laughed.

"Do we see someone else tomorrow?" James asked.

"Boone Coal," Hal replied. "They're back aways, between here and Lexington. They're looking at mountaintop removal, bigger project than the one Larry's looking at. Just hope it doesn't rain, or it'll be miserable getting up there."

"How long have you been doing this?" James asked.

"Fifteen years now," Hal said. "Before that, I was with a dealer who sold smaller machines. It's gotten really busy since the Arab oil embargo, and now coal is king and people can't invest enough."

"What states do you cover?" James asked.

"Illinois, Indiana, Kentucky, Tennessee, and the western ends of Virginia and West Virginia," Hal enumerated.

"So, you're busy?" James asked.

"Very, we saw K&L today, we see Boone tomorrow, you sent me some stuff for three other prospects in the last couple of weeks, and I've got two more meetings with guys later this week when I get back home," Hal said. "Still, better than the bread line. My grandpappy was on the bread line in the Depression. He left Hazard and moved to Evansville for whatever work he could find."

"So, your family is from Hazard?" James asked.

"They were," Hal confirmed. "But I keep quiet about it, never sure if my family had some kind of feud with the families of the guys I'm dealing with."

"Does that still go on?" James asked.

"Not seriously," Hal said. "But why muddy the waters?"

"Why indeed?" James echoed. "Is tomorrow like today, tramping around mine sites?"

"I think not even," Hal said. "From what they told me, they haven't really cleared the site yet, so boots and jeans. Ready for dinner?"

James called Katrina after dinner and related his experiences of the day.

"What's it like there?" she asked.

"Warmer than New Mexico," he said. "Not as high up, a mountain here is less than 2,000 feet, where we were in New Mexico was almost at 7,000 feet. Here, lots of trees, lots of hills and hollows, hollers as I've heard them referred to all day. I could see moonshiners thriving here. There's poverty, there are small coal mines all over the place, there are railway lines all over leading to mine tipples, as they call them. If I were black, I wouldn't want to be here after dark, maybe not even in the daytime. I got the impression that they'd not be made at all welcome."

"So, you and I shouldn't go there?" she asked.

"We would probably be fine," he said. "They'd probably think you were southern European, Italian or Spanish."

"What about tomorrow?" she asked.

"More of the same," he said. "We go to another mine site that's between here and Lexington."

"What's Hazard like?" she asked.

"Small town," he said. "Probably saw boom and bust a few times with coal, there's a river here and a railway, I saw some signs on the outskirts that were disturbing, I'm not sure of the people here, they're probably nice enough, but I get the feeling that if we weren't with local miners, we'd be looked at askance. It's very nice from a scenery point of view, hills, trees, and mountain mist. But apart from coal, no industry that I've seen, so dependent on agriculture, maybe some tobacco and small holdings. I gathered from the local rep here that it was difficult to get to until the railway came, so isolated with not much contact with the rest of the country."

"Where will you stay tomorrow night?" she asked.

"Hal said that we'd stay in Lexington, then I could get an early flight out in the morning," James replied. "When we get to Lexington, I'll check to see if there's a flight out in the evening that I could get."

"That would be super," she said.

"What did you do today?" he asked.

"I went for a swim, then battered away at the typewriter," she replied. "I've got fifty pages done so far, I might need some help with some sketch maps to include."

"Let's look at what you need when I get home," he said. "I'll see you soon, I love you."

"Love you, Honey, sleep well," she replied.

"All set?" Hal asked the next morning, after they had had breakfast.

"All set," James confirmed. "How far to Boone Coal?"

"Maybe half an hour," Hal said. "It's not too far, and the weather looks good, so no rain to contend with. We drive back towards Lexington aways, then take off into the hills; they've got a site office set up near the proposed mine. You married?"

"Married, yes, kids no," James replied.

"Where'd you get married?" Hal asked.

"In Zambia," James said. Hal looked at him sideways, obviously trying to frame the question that was in his mind. He must have decided to just let it go, because he asked nothing further, but pointed out old coal mines and relics of past tipples. They came to a turn off, and there was a sign that pointed to Boone Coal. They drove up the winding road, that twisted and turned among the hills, past rocky outcrops, streams and trees, always trees. The mine office was a temporary building set in a cleared area, with parking for perhaps a dozen cars. Hal pulled up, and they both went into the office.

"Hal," a man said. "Ya'll come in now."

"Howdy, Bruno," Hal said. "This is James Martin, he's one of our mining engineers."

"How do, James," Bruno said. "That's Andy, Floyd, Gerry and Pete," he added, going around the room. "What do you want to do first, take a look at the site or the plans?"

"James?" Hal asked.

"Could we look at the plans quickly, then go and see the site and then come back and look at the plans again?" James asked.

"Sure thing," Bruno said. "This is a topo map of the general area, and this is a geology map of the same area. Here we've marked the boundary of the property, and here our proposed mine." James looked at the four maps and plans and took in the general features of the land.

"You'll be stripping overburden here and dumping where?" he asked.

"Here and here," Bruno replied, pointing to areas on the mine plan.

"How many seams are you dealing with?" James asked.

"Just the one, but it's a big one," Bruno said. "It's about twelve feet thick on average, with not much variation, so we don't have to worry about two and three-foot seams and the shales that would lie between them."

"And reserves that would last how long?" James asked.

"Thirty years at the production rates we're looking at," Bruno said.

"Where would the power come from?" James asked.

"There's a 230kv line down by the highway," Bruno said. "We'd put a transformer in down there and run a line up here."

"Could we take a look at the site?" James asked.

"Sure, we'll be back soon, guys," Bruno said to his team. Hal and James went with Bruno, and they climbed into an ancient Chevrolet Blazer. James quickly saw why they were using an old vehicle, the road, such as it was, wound up through the hills, at times it ran up a stream bed and when they finally topped out at the peak of the mountain, they had cut back the trees just enough to allow passage of the Blazer, with only a little scraping of the sides. The view from the top was spectacular; they could see for miles, over range after range of rolling hills, with hollows still filled with morning mist and a forest that seemed to go on forever.

"Okay," Bruno said. "Over there will be the first cut, the main road up will be down there, and the first dump will be over there."

James looked over the wooded mountains and tried to imagine what the mine would look like. It was easier to see it as a series of sections through the hill, stripping off the overburden and exposing the coal below.

"How will you get the coal down to the main road?" James asked.

"We'll have semis that we'll run up and down the mountain to a tipple that we'll put in by the railroad," Bruno explained. "We did think about a conveyor or a ropeway, but we decided to go with the trucks, more flexibility that way."

"And to load the coal trucks?" James asked.

"We've decided on front-end loaders, we'll match them to the truck body size, what we need from you is a dragline, drills and shovels," Bruno said.

"You want some coffee?" Bruno asked when they returned to the offices.

"Please," James said, and Hal nodded yes as well.

"These are the coal production numbers we're looking at," Bruno said. "Then these are the overburden numbers that we'll need to drill, shoot and remove. You can see here the plan."

"I see," James said. In his mind, he could see the top they had just been to and how Boone Coal planned to remove it all and expose the coal seam below. In many ways it was a far easier mining problem than the copper mine he had run, which was a series of lenses that were not connected and which meant that simply stripping away the overburden meant the unnecessary removal of waste material, which cost money. Bruno and his team had a contiguous seam of coal that ran under the entire mountain top, so the easiest way to get it all, was remove the top of the mountain and take all the coal out. Using an underground mine that went into the side of the mountain as an adit could be done, but a good proportion of the coal would have to be left to shore up the workings so that the whole lot did not collapse onto the people working in the mine. One of the things that did intrigue him was that Pete was the engineer assigned to sort out the reclamation of the site, so that as they went they could grade the land and plant grasses and other vegetation both to hold the land so that rain did not cause problems and so that the mine did not leave a huge scar on the landscape that would remain for decades to come. That was one of the negatives about mining; there were scars left, whether it was spoil heaps or large holes in the ground.

"Have you enough?" Hal asked James.

"I do, thanks, Bruno," James said.

"When can we have something back?" Bruno asked.

"I'll have numbers and suggestions to Hal by late next week," James said.

"I'll run out and see you as soon as I get them," Hal promised.

"Okay," Bruno said. "Have a nice day."

"Thanks, Bruno," Hal said. He and James left and drove back to the main road.

"How long to get to Lexington?" James asked.

"Maybe an hour and a half," Hal said. "You want to see if you can get an earlier flight?"

"If possible," James said.

"Let's stop at that diner over there and see if they have a phone," Hal suggested. They did that, and James called the office and talked to Marlys, and she suggested that he call her back in an hour or so. That would put them almost into Lexington, so Hal suggested that they go straight to the airport and call from there to see if James could go on a flight that day.

"What's your view on the Boone Coal project?" James asked Hal.

"It's a go," Hal said. "They're a sub of Magnate Oil."

"Another one?" James asked. "They've got Magnate Coal in Wyoming."

"I guess so," Hal said. "Anyways, Bruno is a Magnate Oil guy and the rest have been hired for this project."

"Is it unusual to have a reclamation engineer as part of the team?" James asked.

"That's a new one on me," Hal admitted. "I guess that with new rules and with publicity about old mine sites, acid water runoff, and the usual state things are left, then reputable companies will start to step up to the plate and do the right thing, probably cost less if you plan for it right from the beginning, rather than trying to go back and fix it later."

"In Zambia, we had dumps regulations, but the government has yet to even think about reclaiming old mine sites, ponds and dumps. The dumps regulations came out after the Aberfan disaster when the coal mine tip ran away and took out the school," James said. "I wonder if we'd think about making an offer to Magnate Oil to give them a better price if we combined the machine requirements for Magnate Coal and Boone Coal?"

"Ask when you get back," Hal suggested. "But, I'll bet it would be too complicated for the accountants at Magnate Oil, having to divide up a purchase between two subs, and how much input would Magnate Coal and Boone Coal have in the decision? My guess is that Bruno would baulk at that, and so would the guy in Wyoming."

"You're probably right," James said. "Bruno and his team have a lot of work to do; they'll have to build roads up to the site to start with, and the roads will have to be fairly good to take the weight of the machine sections as they're shipped in to be erected."

"They do," Hal agreed. "But, I guess it's worth it to them. Say, would you be available in a couple of weeks to look at a project near Evansville, you just fly into there, then we drive over the river into Kentucky and look at a mine there?"

"I don't see why not," James said. "I'll check with Tony when I get back."

"Great," Hal said. "Okay, we're here. Why don't you find a phone and call Oak Creek and check on your flights?"

James called Marlys and was told that he was indeed on a flight that afternoon, leaving at three and getting into Chicago an hour and a half later, but with the time change, at three-thirty local time, and then he could get a flight to Milwaukee at five. James went back and told Hal about his flight changes, and Hal came in with him, saw him checked in, then they grabbed something to eat quickly before James's flight. The last thing James did before boarding his flight was to call Katrina and let her know that he was arriving that afternoon.

Milwaukee was actually bathed in sunshine when James landed. Katrina was at the gate to meet him.

"Lovely to have you back early," she said, giving him a hug and a kiss.

"I was lucky that we finished early and was back in time to Lexington to get a flight," he said. "You look lovely."

"It's such a nice day, I thought I'd leave the heavy winter stuff and try something more summery," she said. She had on a light blue shirt dress that did indeed look as if it were for the summer.

"It's new, isn't it?" he asked.

"I got it at Kmart," she said. "This and the sandals, they're getting all the spring and summer clothes in now. Is that your bag?"

"It is," he confirmed. He picked up his bag and they walked out to the car park and found the car.

"See, how much the snow is melting," she said, pointing to the pile at the edge of the car park. It was a good foot lower than it had been less than a week ago. "This warm spell's not going to last," she bemoaned. "The forecast that I heard on the car radio is for a cold front to come through tomorrow morning, and the temperatures will drop back down below freezing again."

"I suppose we should enjoy it while it lasts," he said. "Do you want to drive?"

"No, you can drive us home," she said.

At home, Katrina took off the dress and paraded around the room in only her bra and panties. The afternoon sun was streaming in their window, and it was quite hot in the room. James thought that a good idea and went and took a quick shower to wash off the dust and dirt of travel, and came back parading through the room with no clothes.

"I see you've missed me," she laughed, taking off her bra and panties. "There you are all ready, well come here and show me how much you missed me."

"I did miss you, I do each time to go on a trip," he said.

"I hope we never get tired of one another," she said.

"Maybe the secret is to not let things become humdrum," he said.

"Perhaps we should a couple of times a week try something completely different."

"I thought we'd tried just about every way possible," she giggled.

"I'm sure there's always something new," he said.

"You're right," she agreed dreamily.

"I wonder what the people at James & Brown would say if they knew what a randy old goat you really are?" she said later as they both sat on the bed, cross-legged, facing one another.

"They'd probably be jealous that I've got such a beautiful wife, who is also randy and attacks me at every opportunity," he said.

"I'll show you all about attacking you," she said, pushing him down onto the bed.

"I surrender," he said.

"Of course you'll surrender," she said. "You just want to have your way with me."

"I thought I was the one being ravished," he laughed.

"So, did you see any Kentuckians that piqued your libido?" she asked.

"Not one," he said.

"I'll bet," she said. "There had to be some hillbilly girls in tight shorts and torn shirts that you fancied."

"Not one," he protested. "I'm yours, only yours, and it's only you that I love and lust after."

"So, we'll see," she said. They tumbled around on the bed until they could both no longer contain their climaxes, and afterwards they clung to each other, happy to be back together, happy to have each other and happy that they both enjoyed making love as much as they did. After a while, Katrina untangled herself from James and trotted off to the kitchen.

"I cooked dinner," she said. "I put it in the oven before I came to pick you up. If you'd set the table, we could eat. Don't bother with getting dressed, it's warm enough."

"I'm not sure I could eat with the distraction of you," he said.

"Yes, you could," she said. "Just imagine me sitting in my underwear."

"So, now I'm supposed to fantasise about you with more clothes on," he laughed.

"Why not?" she said. "I was thinking that you could do something for me after dinner."

"What?" he asked.

"I bought a sketch pad and some pencils," she said. "Will you pose for me?"

"Of course, what do you want me to do?" he asked.

"Just stand like Michelangelo's David," she said.

James posed while Katrina sketched. He discovered that it was quite tiring just standing there, trying to maintain the pose, while she drew. After an hour, he pleaded for a break.

"You can take a break, you deserve it," she said. "What do you think?"

"That's really good," he said.

"You're not just saying that?" she asked.

"No, genuine man, that's only good," he said, and it was; she had quickly sketched him and had captured details that he was surprised about.

"Do you want to try?" she asked, handing him the sketch pad and the pencils.

"Okay," he agreed. "Why don't you lie on the bed, like the Maja, and I'll try?" Katrina stacked pillows and lay down, hands behind her head and smiled at him. He sketched for some forty minutes, then showed Katrina the results.

"Not bad," she said. "Not bad at all. I think mine's better though."

"You're right," he agreed. "I'd argue, but I have to admit that yours is better."

"I might just do some more in the next weeks," she said. "We've no television, so something for me to do while you're studying."

Pittsburgh

James worked hard for the next few weeks, writing up his reports on his mine visits, attending the first classes of the Executive MBA program and collecting information about the cost structures that governed the manufacture of their machines. He essentially traded information with Bill, cost elements for market types and sizes. In the evenings, Katrina continued with her sketching and with practice, she improved. The weather warmed up, cooled down in a sort of yoyo cycle, but with a general trend of the minimum temperatures slowly moving up, so each cold snap was not quite as cold as the last.

"Do you have your next meeting with the Bwana Mkubwa tomorrow?" Katrina asked James.

"I do," he said. "I think I'm as ready as I can be, and I'm sure that Bill is, I've been feeding him all kinds of information and showing him how mining methods change the demand."

"Well, I'm sure you'll wow the *ou*," she said.

"We'll see," James laughed. "I'm not sure he'd be too keen about being called an *ou*."

"As long as he doesn't know, it won't bother him," she laughed. "What are you going to wear?"

"Best suit, white shirt, tie, black shoes, polished," he replied.

"Sounds good, but I'd better inspect before you go off tomorrow," she said.

James was duly inspected the following morning and passed muster. He went to the office and kept himself busy until just before ten, then he made his way downstairs to the office of Hank Miller. Bill joined him and they waited for the boss to call them in, which he did at ten on the dot.

"Morning, James, Bill, coffee?" Hank asked.

"Yes, please," James said.

"Yes, please," Bill echoed.

"Lou, could you get us all some coffee, please," Hank asked his secretary. "So, how have you both been doing?"

"Bill," James suggested.

"Right," Bill said. He then talked briefly about how work was and about the market information he had obtained and what the classes for the EMBA program had been. Then it was James's turn.

"Okay, that's good," Hank said. "Next, I'd like you both to take a trip before next month to Pittsburgh and tour the Construction Machinery plant there and come back and tell me what you saw. So, tell me what the balance sheet in the 10-Q tells you."

"James," Bill said.

"Right," James said. He then talked about the balance sheet, what it represented and what was not included.

"What's your view of the off-balance sheet items?" Hank asked.

"I think they could get you into trouble unless we know what and why is not being shown on the balance sheet," James said. "Our subsidiary in Brazil is not wholly-owned, so we don't record their assets and liabilities as ours, but what if their liabilities become a problem, then we're on the hook as the majority owner with some explaining to do and potentially some expenses to incur?"

"Off-balance sheet items can be tricky," Hank agreed. He then launched into a fairly long explanation of what would possibly be considered as an off-balance sheet item and the rationale behind the decision. It was interesting for both James and Bill to hear some of the thinking behind how the numbers were presented to the shareholders.

"Sorry to have bored you with accounting niceties," Hank finally said. "I'll see you in a month and am looking forward to hearing about the Pittsburgh plant."

"That was interesting," Bill said to James when they left. "I'd no idea that accounting was such a subjective art."

"I suppose it fits with the joke that when you ask your accountant what the numbers are, he asks you what do you want them to be," James commented. "So, when do we go to Pittsburgh?"

"Check your schedule and I'll check mine," Bill said. "I'd go sooner rather than later, don't like leaving things to the last minute."

"I'll do that," James promised. "I have a trip to Pennsylvania next week. What if we just add the Pittsburgh trip to the end of that?"

"Sounds good, give me the details and I'll tell my boss that I'm taking off for a couple of days," Bill said. "He won't be happy, but he can argue with the big boss. Say, do you and your wife fancy coming out with us on Friday for a fish fry?"

"That would be great," James said. "Where?"

"What about the Packing House?" Bill asked.

"Would six be fine?" James asked.

"That'd be fine," Bill confirmed. "What do you think Miller is looking for in a report on Pittsburgh?"

"If I were him, I'd be looking to see if we just say that everything is great, or if we come back and suggest changes that reduce the time it takes to make the machines and reduce the amount of inventory we carry, less time and less stuff is less money tied up," James suggested.

"Okay, we should get together before we go and draw up some kind of process flow and see how far off we are," Bill suggested.

"I went through the factory in Didcot, and the machines must be about the same. I'll see how much of that I can remember and put something together. I might even contact the chief engineer there and ask him if he'd send us something," James added.

"Okay, well, let me know your travel schedule and otherwise, see you Friday at the Packing House," Bill said.

"So, did you wow the Bwana Mkubwa today?" Katrina asked James when he got home that evening.

"I'm not sure," James said. "But I did get him expounding about the niceties of accounting, which took up most of the time. It was actually quite interesting and useful. How was your day?"

"I typed, I sketched, I went for a swim," she said. "I tried sketching trees today, so went out and braved the chill in the park for a while, what do you think?"

"These could go in a textbook," he said. "They're really good."

"You're just saying that," she said.

"No, really," he assured her. "They are good."

"What else happened today?" she asked.

"We're asked out to a fish fry on Friday with Bill Evans and his wife," James said.

"Oh, our Green Cards arrived," she said. "And we've also got Social Security Numbers, so I suppose that if I wanted to work, I could do so."

"I'm surprised they came that quickly," he said. "I expected months and months of waiting."

"It's funny," she said. "The Green Cards are more blue than green, and they've been laminated in plastic, but the Social Security Card is just a scruffy piece of thin cardboard, and they even tell you not to laminate it. They also say not to lose them."

"I would imagine that that would be a pain to sort out," he said. "I suppose that means that we can travel outside the US now, and come back without worrying about visas."

"That's what the blurb on the back says," she told him. "That and that if you're over 18, you're supposed to carry it with you at all times."

"I can just see someone stopping us and saying, papers please, like in the films about Russia or Nazi Germany," he joked.

"I'll bet we never get asked for the card, except at the border," she said.

"I'm not taking that bet," he said.

James and Katrina went to the Packing House on Friday, and James saw Bill, who waved him over.

"James, this is Amanda," he said, making the introduction.

"Nice to meet you," James said. "This is Katrina."

"Bill told me that you're from Africa," Amanda said. "How are you liking it here?"

"It's cold and there's more snow than I've ever seen," Katrina replied. "But I like it here better than England; England was crowded, here at least there seems to be a little more room. Are you from here?"

"No," Amanda said. "We're both from Idaho."

"Idaho, that's a long way west, isn't it?" Katrina asked.

153

"Between Washington and Oregon on the west and Montana and Wyoming on the east," Amanda replied. "We both grew up in Boise, then came here for a job."

"Do you work as well?" Katrina asked.

"I'm a gate agent," Amanda replied. "A fancy title for someone who takes your boarding pass when you get on a plane."

"I'll have to look out for you," James said.

"Have you settled in, found grocery stores, doctors, dentists?" Amanda asked.

"We should probably get ourselves a dentist," James said. "We haven't really thought about doctors and dentists yet."

"The practice we go to is very nice," Amanda said. "I'll give you their number, I can also give you the name of a family doctor and who my gynaecologist is."

"Thank you," Katrina said.

"Howdy folks," a waitress said. "What can I get you?"

"I'd like a Pabst," Amanda said. "Katrina?"

"The same, please," she said.

"I'll take a Miller," Bill said.

"Pabst for me," James said.

"You all here for the fish fry?" the waitress asked.

"We are," Bill confirmed.

"Okay, I'll get your beers, then I'll be back with the fish," she added.

"So, what do you guys have planned for the weekend?" Bill asked.

"We're going to buy a car," James said. "We've been to a couple of places to look, and tomorrow we'll actually buy one."

"Any preferences?" Bill asked.

"Not really," James said. "Something we can afford mainly."

"We got our Green Cards today," Katrina said. "So, now I could work as well, but I'm not sure what I could do here."

"What did you do in Zambia?" Amanda asked.

"My Dad owned a transport business," Katrina said. "So, I worked in that, we moved things like bulldozers and other heavy machinery, then my Dad sold up and moved to South Africa and James and I moved to

154

a small mine in the bush, and I sold industrial minerals. I never went to uni, so was thinking of getting a degree here."

"So, you can drive big rigs?" Amanda asked.

"If big rigs are large transporters, then yes," Katrina replied. "I used to do the estimating and the scheduling, and sometimes I drove if we were short-handed."

"What was the biggest thing you moved?" Amanda asked.

"I'm not sure," Katrina said. "Probably some machines that went to the Nchanga copper mine."

"What kind of trucks did you use?" Bill asked.

"We had some old ex-army Thorneycroft," Katrina said. "But then we got Oshkosh, they were assembled in South Africa, and the local Caterpillar dealer sold them."

"That sounds more interesting than dealing with whining flyers whose flights have been delayed or cancelled," Amanda said.

"Oh, we had our share of whiners," Katrina laughed. "Sometimes it took longer than expected to deliver stuff, then the whining began."

"You should talk to James & Brown, we have a traffic department that manages the transport of machines and parts going out for delivery," Bill said. "George Whitehead is the guy to talk to. I'll get his number and give it to James."

"Shouldn't I go to personnel and ask them if there are jobs?" Katrina asked.

"You can talk to them in time," Bill said. "First, though, you need to talk to George. If he wants to hire you, then personnel will just go along with what he says. A lot of our stuff goes out by rail. Did you ever deal with a railroad?"

"Quite a lot," Katrina said. "We worked with Zambian Railways, and before the border was closed, we dealt with Rhodesian Railways and, by extension, South African Railways. We even moved a locomotive once, it had crashed, so we went in with cranes and removed it and took it back to the railway shops for repair."

"I know this sounds silly, but did they have schools in Zambia?" Amanda asked.

"Not so silly as you might think," Katrina said. "We had schools, primary and secondary and a university in Lusaka and technical colleges on the Copper Belt, but I went away to boarding school in Rhodesia."

"What was that like?" Amanda asked.

"I liked it," Katrina said. "It was hard at first, but I soon got used to it and made friends there. I would go home for the long breaks and spend the short breaks with a friend in Rhodesia."

"How did you get there? Did your folks drive you there?" Amanda asked.

"Only the first time," Katrina said. "After that, I went on the school train, it used to come and collect all the kids who were going to school in Rhodesia and bring us back, two days and a night, or two nights and a day, depending on which way we were going."

"So you slept on the train?" Amanda asked.

"Slept, ate, they would make up the beds in the compartments. There was a dining car on the train, and they served meals there; looking back, it was very nice," Katrina replied.

"Okay, folks, here you go," the waitress said, interrupting things and bringing the plates of food. "Enjoy, can I get you anything else, another beer?"

"Please," Bill said. "You guys?" There were nods all around, so another round of beers was delivered.

The car-buying experience was new and different for James and Katrina. They went to a second-hand car dealer and looked around.

"Can I help you folks?" a salesman, whose name tag said that he was Bob, asked.

"We're interested in that Subaru," James said.

"Nice little car," Bob said. "Good gas mileage, good in the snow."

"Can we take it for a test drive?" James asked.

"Sure thing," Bob said. "Let me just get the keys." He left and was back almost immediately with the keys. He offered them to James, who gave them to Katrina. She started the car up, then waited until James and Bob were seated, then took off.

"Turn right out of the lot," Bob said. "Drives nicely, doesn't it?"

"It does," Katrina confirmed. "I see it's got four-wheel drive. How does that work?"

"Normally it's a front-wheel drive, but that extra lever there pulls in the back wheels," Bob said in explanation. "If you just pull over there, you can try it."

"I see," Katrina said. "Easy enough."

"You driven many cars?" Bob asked.

"Quite a few," Katrina said. "But I've got almost as many hours in an Oshkosh truck. I like this, James. We should take it."

"Okay," James said. "So, the price is $950. We've got the cash."

"You guys are not from here, are you?" Bob said.

"No," James confirmed.

"Well, I like you guys, so I'm going to tell you how it's done. There's the price, you look at it and counter with $500, I grab my heart and gasp and ask if you're trying to ruin me, then I come back with $850, you move up a little and so on until we agree on $750," Bob said.

"And you do this even with new cars?" James asked.

"Especially new cars," Bob confirmed. "If you look at the stickers on new cars, you'll see Manufacturer's Suggested Retail Price. That's the thing, it's a suggested price and right now the big four can't sell cars for love or money, so they're all willing to offer all kinds of incentives and rebates. They just built too many cars and not enough people are buying, the prices went up too fast, which is why we're doing great business."

"Thanks for the help, Bob," Katrina said. "You've been very kind."

"Shall we go and write up the sale?" Bob asked. They filled out papers, paid money and left with their new car, well, not exactly new, but in good enough condition. On their way home, they dropped off the hire car and got the last paperwork to turn in to James & Brown.

Katrina did not have to call George Whitehead; he called her with the news that their belongings had arrived from England. They arranged delivery, then Katrina took the plunge and explained that she had been in the transport and heavy haulage business in Zambia, and did he have any jobs? George suggested that she go to his office and talk to him; he told her when and where.

"I've got an interview tomorrow," she told James when he came home that evening. "George Whitehead called to tell me that our stuff has arrived from England, and we arranged delivery, then I just asked him if he had a job."

"What did he say?" James asked.

"Basically, did I know anything about transporting stuff," she said. "I told him about our business in Zambia, and he suggested that I go and talk to him tomorrow at eleven."

"If you get done before noon, let me know and we'll get some lunch somewhere," James said. "Our stuff took long enough to come, I can't believe it's been on the water the whole time, it must have been sitting somewhere."

"Probably customs," she said. "I doubt that they're much different here than in Zambia, make you sit and wait. When are you and Bill going to Pittsburgh?"

"The day after tomorrow," he replied. "I'm supposed to meet the local chap, Howard, there, and we're going to a mine site a little to the south and east of Pittsburgh, then I'll meet up with Bill and we'll take a look at the factory there, be back on Friday."

"How are your classes going with the MBA?" she asked.

"No complaints so far," he said. "We're going through business analysis now, and all the stuff that John Wells helped me with is coming in really handy."

"How many of you finally signed up?" she asked.

"Nine, seven from here and two from Pittsburgh," he replied. "I've no idea why the others in the management program didn't sign up, the company's paying, so why not?"

"What do I wear today for my interview?" Katrina asked James.

"I would wear trousers, because if I were George I'd take you out into the shop and ask you how you would ship things," James suggested.

"So, closed-in shoes as well?" she said.

"I would," James confirmed. "You'll do just fine; they'd be silly not to hire you."

"You're just saying that because we're married," she protested.

"No," he said. "Your dad told me that you were really good at looking at a job and estimating what size loads and such. They might have more issues here with axle loading and oversized loads, no cutting off bridge railings here."

"Probably not," she laughed. "Okay, Honey, if I'm done by noon, I'll call you and we can go to lunch."

James was busy in his office when George and Katrina appeared at the door.

"Katrina," he said. "You're done?"

"I am," she confirmed. "George was nice enough to show me where you hide away."

"You're a lucky guy," George said. "Katrina is very accomplished."

"Thank you for showing me the way, George," Katrina said. "I'll see you on Monday."

"When you get here on Monday, go straight to Personnel; they'll sign you up, get you a badge and all that, and then we'll talk about what we need you to do," George said. "Nice to meet you, James."

"So, you got a job?" James asked Katrina after George had gone.

"I did," she confirmed. "I think he was a little sceptical at first, but we talked, then we took a tour and he asked me about weights of things and what I'd put them on, after that it was easy."

"So, shall we go and get some lunch?" he said.

"Let's," she said. "Where's Tony?"

"He's on a trip to Australia," James explained. "He gets the fancy trips and I get all the rest."

"I can't believe I got the job already," she said when they were seated in a local diner. "Can you believe it, they're going to pay me $1,000 a month, it would be more if I had a degree. Plus, there's the pension, health care, all that stuff, just no sales bonus."

"What are you actually going to do?" he asked.

"As I understand it, work with the railway, sorry, railroad companies and trucking companies to schedule the delivery of parts to warehouses and mine sites," she said. "There's another bloke who deals with all the raw materials that come in, and another who schedules the shipping of the various bits of new machines to the mine sites. I get to look at parts going all over the US and to Australia, South Africa and so on, so deal with shipping lines as well."

"Are you still going to sign up for a degree?" he asked.

"I may," she said. "I'll look and see if they have one in the evenings that I could do."

"Well, congratulations," he said.

"Oh, there was a funny bit too," she said. "He asked me if I was in any part African. Apparently, they can claim me as an African American on their reports they have to do on the hiring of minorities."

"How much African are you?" James asked.

"Counting on both sides of the family, one-eighth," she said. "There was Motshaba on Dad's side and Modjaji on Mom's side, one Bushman and one Bapedi. So, he said they can get credit for me being a woman and of African descent."

"I never thought of that," he said. "We should eat up, I have to get back to work."

"You'll be back on Friday?" Katrina asked when she dropped James off at the airport.

"I'll be back on Friday," he confirmed. "What are you going to do today?"

"I thought I'd shop around for some clothes to wear when I start work," she said. "I want a couple of changes of clothes that are comfortable to wear in the office and that will also work in the warehouse and on the factory floor, and I need some shoes as well."

"I'll call you tonight," he promised. "Love you, *hlala kahle*."

"Love you, *hamba kahle*," she replied.

James boarded his plane, which was just a short hop to Chicago, and there he found his Allegheny flight to Pittsburgh. In Pittsburgh, he found Howard brandishing a James & Brown brochure.

160

"Howard?" James said. "James Martin."

"Good to meet you, James," Howard replied. "Got your bag, let's go."

"Who are we going to see?" James asked.

"Penny Coal, they're a sub of Penny Oil," Howard said. "They're looking at a project in the hills to the south of here, my guess is something like an eighty-yard machine with a long boom."

"Will they need drills and shovels as well?" James asked.

"Probably," Howard said. "We're late to this project; the Bucyrus and Marion guys have already been here more than two weeks ago."

"Do you think that Penny Coal has already made their decision?" James asked.

"Wouldn't surprise me," Howard complained. "But, we've got to show the flag, show willing and put in our offer."

"How high would you rate our chances here?" James asked.

"Ten, fifteen per cent, pretty low odds," Howard said. "I hate to waste your time and mine, but I suppose it's a live one and we can't ignore it."

They drove for about an hour and then pulled into a site office.

"Morning, gents," Howard said as they entered the office.

"Morning, Howard," one of them said.

"Chuck, this is James Martin, one of our mining engineers," Howard said, by way of introduction.

"Okay, let's get to it," Chuck said. "Time's a-wasting. This is our deposit; you can see it's a group of non-contiguous seams running from here to here. We're thinking of an 80-yard dragline with a 360-foot boom."

"If time is of the essence, why not just use shovels and trucks? You'd be in production about a year earlier, you'd have more flexibility, you wouldn't lose as much time when you had to tram the shovels between coal exposures?" James asked.

"How would we set the mine up?" Chuck asked. James sketched a mine plan and suggested a shovel size and indicated where the haul roads would go.

"Your initial investment would be lower, you'd gain a year in revenue, so if you discounted everything back to present values, you might not have the lowest operating costs per year, but I think when you factored in the initial investment, your internal rate of return would be better," James added. He noticed that the others had crowded around, and he was getting nods of agreement from two of them and looks of bewilderment from two others.

"You sure you're a mining engineer, not a finance guy?" Chuck asked.

"Sometimes it's the same thing," James said.

"You've done this before?" one of the others asked.

"Not in a coal mine, but in a copper mine," James said. "I started up a new mine that was a series of unconnected lenses and that demanded flexibility. This seems to me to be a similar problem."

"You know, Chuck, this would work," one of the others said.

"Yes, but the operating costs are lower with the dragline," Chuck said.

"Maybe," was the reply. "But think what a year's worth of production a year earlier would be worth to us."

"We'll need to run some numbers," Chuck said. "Howard, get us a proposal for the shovels and drills. Can you do that by next week?"

"Sure," Howard said.

"Let's take a quick run out and look at the site," Chuck suggested. He took James and Howard, and they drove out to the hills. It reminded James a little of the site he had seen in Kentucky, but then that perhaps was not surprising; they were in the beginnings of the Appalachian mountain chain, so the terrain reflected that. Chuck pointed out the area that would be mined and expounded on the geology of the formations. There was little to see in the way of workings, so it was all imagination, trying to visualise where things would be and what the mine would look like.

"Seen enough?" Chuck asked.

"Thank you," James said.

"Great," Howard said.

"Great, then if you'll excuse us, we've got some rethinking to do," Chuck said.

They drove back to the office, and Howard and James left. "That was a short meeting," James said.

"You've got them thinking," Howard said. "We might get something out of this yet. How did you come up with that?"

"As I said, I've been through it before," James replied. "I spent hours running scenarios and doing discounted value calculations. If Chuck presents those kinds of numbers and ideas to his corporate finance people, they'll understand."

"He jumped at the lower initial investment," Howard commented. "It does mean a possibly smaller sale for us."

"But if we were dealing with probabilities of ten to fifteen per cent and if we've pushed that up to more than twenty-five per cent, we may get a sale after all," James suggested.

"Good thinking," Howard said. "Let's get back to Pittsburgh and call Oak Creek."

"I think we should ask for pricing for the size dragline Chuck talked about, just to be on the safe side," James suggested.

"We'll do that," Howard agreed.

Howard had an office in a small annexe of the company factory in Pittsburgh, so James was already at his next port of call.

"Thanks for coming out, James," Howard said after they had finished with their telephone calls. "Can I run you back to the airport?"

"No thanks, Howard," James said. "I have a visit set up here tomorrow to go through the factory, so am staying at a Holiday Inn close by."

"I'll run you over there," Howard offered. They drove to the Holiday Inn, and while James was checking in, Bill came in.

"Bill, hi, this is Howard Hill, he's our local man based here," James said. "Howard, this is Bill Evans, he's one of our manufacturing people from Oak Creek."

"Howard," Bill said. "You done for the day, James?"

"We are," James replied. "Howard, are you free for dinner?"

"Sorry, got another appointment," Howard said. "I'll see you again James. Good to meet you, Bill."

"Seems a nice enough guy," Bill remarked after Howard had gone.

"He is, but a little doom and gloom," James said. "We came late to the prospect, but he didn't explain why the Bucyrus and Marion people had already been a couple of weeks ago, and we're just hearing about the project now. Why don't we drop our stuff in our rooms and meet back in the bar in fifteen minutes?"

"So, what do we do tomorrow?" Bill asked.

"I'd start at the shipping dock and work backwards," James suggested.

"I like that idea," Bill said. "If we think in terms of a sale, then what the customer is interested in is the finished machine; he doesn't care about inventories of gears or steel."

"From shipping, what's next, the assembly floor?" James asked. "Oh, before I forget, I got these notes from the Didcot factory; they show a flow chart of things through their factory."

"How did you get this so quickly?" Bill asked, unfolding the large chart that James had.

"One of the accountants from there was coming over for meetings in Oak Creek, so he hand-carried it over for me," James explained. "When you make stuff, how much is acceptable right away and how much has to be adjusted or reworked to make it usable?"

"We get some," Bill said. "Probable more than we should, so if it's not to print, then it sits and waits for a review and decision by engineering, and that's just work-in-progress dollars sitting around, and a delay in the assembly of the machine."

"I was reading some stuff about Japan and Toyota right after the War, and I read that because they were short of materials, they only made something when they needed it, so didn't build to stock, but built to order. I know we're largely build-to-order, do we do any build-to-stock?"

"Very little," Bill said. "We won't release work orders unless it's for a machine that is sold."

"I wonder if they do the same here in Pittsburgh, or if they build for stock?" James pondered.

"My guess is that any build-for-stock orders are not for our stock, but to sit on a dealer's lot," Bill suggested.

"So, for the most part, we do, in Toyota terms, pull through rather than push manufacturing?" James asked.

"I think so," Bill said. "But I think that's by default rather than design, the machines are just too big and expensive to build just for the sake of it."

"Who takes us around the factory tomorrow?" James asked.

"Ron Edwards, he's the manager here," Bill said. "I met him a couple of times last year. In fact, he's going to come and have breakfast with us tomorrow, probably wants to be sure that we give the boss a good report on the factory here."

"I've always wondered about how far parts and bits travel while they're being made," James commented. "If we took a gear set from one of the machines, it would be interesting to see where it went, how far it travelled."

"My bet is a few miles," Bill said. "If you start with bar stock or a forging or casting, then it goes to a machine shop to clean it up before starting to cut teeth, then it goes to gear cutting, then it goes to deburring, then to heat treat, then to stores, before assembly. I'll bet it goes to stores between each operation, but I may be wrong there."

"Well, we'll see tomorrow," James said. "I saw a place just down the road that advertises ribs. I've not tried them yet. What do you think?"

"Great idea," Bill said. "Meet you in the lobby in five?"

"How's Pittsburgh?" Katrina asked James when he called that night.

"Warm and humid," he said. "There're rivers here too, two of them combine to become the Ohio. It's a city with lots of hills, and lots of old heavy manufacturing works."

"What was the mine site like?" she asked.

"Pretty, in the hills, nothing there yet, just a couple of prefab offices," he replied. "We may or may not get something out of it, I'd rate our chances as twenty-five to thirty per cent, we'll see."

"Is Bill there?" she asked.

"He arrived just as I was checking in," James said. "So, we just went to this place where they serve barbecue ribs, we should see if we can find somewhere in Milwaukee that sells ribs. How was your day?"

"I did some clothes shopping," she said. "I bought some trousers that I can wash, don't have to be dry cleaned. I bought some blouses and pullovers, and a light jacket, and I got myself some light boots that I won't mind getting grubby. I'm looking forward to starting on Monday and to seeing where all the parts go."

"I can bring home a brochure that shows where the parts warehouses are and where the international offices and warehouses are," he said.

"That would be super," she said. "When are you due in tomorrow?"

"About six," he said. "Let's see, I'm on a North Central that arrives in Milwaukee at six-ten."

"I'll be there," she said. "I miss you."

"I miss you, I love you," he said.

"Love you too, sleep well," she said.

"James, this is Ron Edwards," Bill said the next morning when James went to get breakfast.

"James," Ron said. "Bill tells me that you're not a manufacturing guy."

"Right," James confirmed. "My management experience was all running mines, both underground and surface."

"So, a lot of scheduling and assigning resources?" Ron asked.

"That's about it," James said. "I had men and equipment and a job to do; the trick was to best use what I had."

"It's pretty much the same here," Ron said. "I've got men and machines and jobs to do, the trick is to schedule the work efficiently so it can get done as quickly as possible with the least amount of disruptions."

"I was wondering, James, did you ever get what we would call re-work?" Bill asked.

"Secondary blasting," James said. "If your first blast didn't go well, you were left with a load of large rocks, too big to be loaded into the trucks, so we had to blast again using a different technique. It was a pain to do, it took time, a lot of work and delayed things."

"Was there a cost implication if you over-blasted the first time?" Ron asked.

"There was," James confirmed. "Our biggest costs were explosives, tyres, fuel and labour; it was a balancing issue to use enough but not too much to skew the costs. We did find a direct correlation between good fragmentation and maintenance costs of our loaders, so my tendency was to use enough bang to get good fragmentation because that kept the availability of my loaders in the 90 per cent range, if I didn't, it was down in the 70s."

"Well, what do you guys want to do today?" Ron asked.

"Could we start at the shipping dock and work backwards?" Bill asked.

"Sure, we could do that," Ron said. "What if we pick whatever is in the shipping dock and then go back through the plant, tracing a similar machine?"

"That'd be great," Bill said.

Ron took them to the factory, and after equipping them with hard hats and checking that they had safety boots, led the way to the shipping dock.

"Okay, this is a JB202, a dragline that's on its way to Florida," he said. "You can see that the boom and counterweight are shipped separately, so all that's on this truck is the main part of the machine. So, let's go back and see what's on the assembly floor. Okay, there's another 202, it's going out as a crane, but it's essentially the same machine."

"How long does it take from receipt of order to shipping?" James asked.

"A month," Ron said. "That's from receipt of order to out the door."

"Do you ever rush orders from customers who have to have it today?" James asked.

"Sometimes," Ron said. "But usually sales then canvases the dealers and finds a machine in one of their yards, and they arrange the sale and shipping."

"If we track back from the assembly floor, where do the major components come from?" Bill asked.

"We've got a gear shop, a boom shop, a mainframe shop and a few others," Ron said. "Where to from here?"

"Let's follow the mainframe back," James suggested.

"That takes us to the foundry as the mainframes for the 202s are cast," Ron explained. He led them to another building that smelled of molten metal and sand, and was hot and noisy as the electric arc furnaces melted another crucible of steel. "That's a melt for a 204, should be pouring just now." They moved aside and watched as a crane hook was moved into place, and the crucible was picked up and then poured into a mould. "It'll sit for a while to cool, then we'll clean it up, then machine the surfaces that need finishing, then it'll go to the assembly floor."

"How is cost tracked in this?" James asked.

"Because the machines are standard configurations, each component group has a cost, so as the machine is configured, we aggregate those costs, then we regularly look at the costs for each shop and check to see that we're close or if the costs need adjusting," Ron explained.

"Do the parts have standard costs?" James asked.

"They do, any scrap or re-work is an adder that comes as part of the overhead," Ron said.

"Could we go back to the assembly floor and follow up on a different set of parts?" James asked.

"Sure thing," Ron said. "What about the gear shop?"

"Great," Bill said. They trooped back to the assembly floor and then took a different route to a factory filled with gear-cutting machines. James was fascinated to watch the machines chew into the steel as if it were just soft wood, and from a large blank, a gear emerge with teeth cut precisely.

"How many parts are in the 202?" James asked.

"If we take the engine as one part, then 5,350, give or take, depending on the options that are purchased," Ron replied.

"How do you know how many parts to stock?" James asked.

"We estimate the number of machines that will be sold in the year, then compare that to the sales forecast and make our plans," Ron said.

"I remember my dad telling me about something called the two-bin system at the Spitfire factory," James said. "Essentially, they had parts in two bins; when one was empty, they went to the second and also asked for the first bin to be refilled."

"That's an interesting idea," Ron said. "I might look into where we could use that. That would probably work really well on the assembly floor for fasteners."

"Where is the bodywork for all these machines made?" Bill asked.

"We've a body shop in an annexe, along with a paint shop," Ron said. "We've also got a separate shop for honing out hydraulic cylinders and putting those systems together, mainly to keep contamination out."

"We buy engine packages for these machines, don't we?" James asked.

"We do, we get them from Cummins," Ron said. "We've used Cat, Detroit Diesel and Ruston Hornsby in the past."

"If I were to take a casting for a gear, how many feet would it travel before it was installed?" Bill asked.

"Never looked at that," Ron said. "It might be interesting to see just how far bits travel around the factory and if there's a better way to lay things out."

"I imagine that with some of your machines, forges and furnaces, that is not always the easiest thing to do?" James asked.

"You're right about that," Ron said. "Moving the forge and the furnaces would take a lot and cost a lot. So, what next?" Bill suggested the stores, and there they saw completed and purchased parts waiting to be installed into machines. They also walked out to the raw material yard where there were racks of steel plates, bars, angles and tubes, all of which would get turned into parts in the coming weeks and months. To James, it was fascinating, a completely different business from extracting minerals from the ground.

"So, you guys want some lunch?" Ron asked.

"Thanks," Bill said. "That would be great."

"Do you have a map of the factory site that we could have?" James asked.

"Sure, I'll get you one right after lunch," Ron promised. He took them to the factory cafeteria, and they got lunch and then sat and talked.

"So, how are two guys getting on in this management program?" Ron asked.

"It's been really interesting so far," Bill said. "We've got Hank Miller as our mentor; it's a bit intimidating."

"I guess that could be," Ron sympathised.

"The two that you have from here, what do they report back?" James asked.

"They've learned a lot and have been asking me all kinds of questions, mainly about finance and accounting. I've had to pull in the plant controller a few times to explain stuff," Ron said.

"Do you have a view as to whether or not it's worthwhile?" James asked.

"I think it is," Ron said. "We've never really helped our people broaden their outlook, so we just dump them in a new job, and it's sink or swim; some succeed, some don't."

"Where you worked before, did they have something like this, James?" Bill asked.

"They did, local reviews were supposed to be passed up to London, who would then decide who was high potential. I had to work for one of the anointed ones once, but he got fired for playing around," James said. "I was also told once that because I worked in production in the mine that I was B stream, the A stream people all worked in accounting and finance."

"Someone was either very brutally honest or very cynical," Ron said.

"I think a bit of both," James said. "I often thought that we had a top-heavy management structure with too many layers, but I was so far down my opinion didn't matter."

"Well, you've got the ear of the CEO, so it's up to us to use it," Ron said. "You guys done?"

"Thanks," Bill said.

"Okay, let's go and get you a factory plan and whatever flow charts we have," Ron said.

"Do you have numbers on scrap and re-work?" Bill asked.

"Sure, I'll get you those, too. Will you send me the numbers for Oak Creek?" Ron asked. "Okay, here's a map of the place, and here's flow charts for castings, gear elements and forgings."

"Thanks, I'll send you the numbers for scrap and rework for Oak Creek as soon as we get back," Bill promised. "Any final thoughts?"

"Maybe one," Ron said. "As long as a work order is open, it'll collect costs, so get parts through the process as quickly as possible and do it right the first time; otherwise, it's going to just collect more and more costs."

"If you looked at the theoretical process times, how does that compare with actual times?" James asked.

"You mean how much time does it spend just sitting around waiting for something to happen?" Ron asked. "Good question, I'll have my IEs take a look at that and get back to you. So, I'm going to have Rita here run you guys back out to the airport. If you need anything else, call, and I'll see what I can do."

"Thank you," James said. "We really appreciate the time you've given us."

"So, what do you think?" Bill asked James as they flew back to Chicago.

"I was thinking about the scrap and re-work, what causes that?" James asked.

"Parts don't meet print," Bill said.

"So, what kind of tolerance is called for?" James asked.

"Depends on the part, but many about two to five thousandths," Bill replied.

"And what are the machines capable of?" James asked.

"About that," Bill said.

"What's the coefficient of thermal expansion of the steels we use?" James asked.

"Ah, I see," Bill said. "We're probably just creating issues."

"If we got machines that could give us a result of two-tenths, how much would that help?" James asked.

"A lot," Bill said.

"I'll bet if we did an internal rate of return calculation on a new machine that would reduce re-work costs by half, it would be well worth the investment," James suggested. "And if we reduced re-work, then we'd reduce the amount of work in process that would reduce inventory and free up cash."

"I like that," Bill said. "We should put something together in the next week or so, send it out to Ron for him to look at, then present it to Hank Miller."

"I picked up a drawing in the shop and then I read the plate on the machine tool, and as the tolerances were the same, it struck me that it was going to be hit or miss to get a good part, and on a really hot or cold day that was going to be even more hit or miss," James said.

"I thought you didn't know anything about manufacturing," Bill said.

"I don't, I just read something about how Toyota really pushed quality and how their products are far better than Ford or GM," James said. "If we get machines that will produce an order of magnitude better product than is called for, then we can go after the next problem and so on. The result will be lower costs. Because scrap and re-work is an overhead, there's no real incentive for the factory floor to fix the problems."

"You're treading on dangerous ground there," Bill laughed. "We in manufacturing haven't taken the time to work out how and where the scrap and re-work is really coming from, it's always been a fact of life."

"Yes, but if you could reduce or even eliminate it, you'd be money ahead," James suggested. "When I got rid of secondary blasting, I had some ratios that had been sacred, go up, but my overall costs came down. I took a lot of grief from the operations management about my powder factors, the amount of explosive I used per ton of ore, but the finance people came to my rescue and pointed out that my system costs were significantly down."

"You're right," Bill said. "We tend to look at ratios that we're used to seeing and not a bigger picture of overall costs; we should play with that a bit."

"Can you get me some numbers on what new machine tools would cost?" James asked.

"Sure," Bill said. "We're looking at a new lathe, a new gear hobber and a new mill. I'll have numbers for you on Monday."

"Okay, we're almost here. How long is the layover?" James asked.

"Ninety minutes," Bill said. "I'm looking forward to getting home. I don't know how you can stand to travel as much as you do."

"It has its drawbacks," James admitted. "But some rewards too. I've already been to five states."

"You're back," Katrina said when she met them at the gate in Milwaukee. "Did you have a good trip?"

"It was interesting," James replied.

"It was," Bill confirmed. "If you'll excuse me, I'm going to go and find Amanda, she's working afternoons this week."

"So, what was the factory like?" she asked.

"Very similar to Didcot," he said. "Smaller machines than in Oak Creek, and most of them go out fully assembled. They're the kind of machines you used to transport in Zambia."

"I decided that we'd eat out tonight," she said, as they walked out to their car. "So, we're going to our Italian place."

"Sounds great," he said. "You know, it struck me that when we're both working, then I should take a turn cooking."

"Good idea," she agreed. "You take a week and I'll take a week, and whoever doesn't cook, washes up."

"Agreed," he said. "It's not too long to Memorial Day, are we set for our trip to Door County?"

"We are," she said. "I got us a rather nice-looking inn in Fish Creek."

"I'm looking forward to that," he said.

"You're just looking forward to a roll in the hay," she laughed.

"It's spring," he said. "There's no hay, but maybe a romp in the woods, if there are any."

"I gather that that's what Door County is famous for, trees and woods," she said,

"Oh, I thought you meant romps in the woods," he laughed.

"You wish it were so," she laughed. "We'll see."

Door County

"Are you ready?" James asked Katrina for the second time as he waited for her to get ready for her first day at work.

"I'll be there just now," she said. James pondered that and recalled when just now meant two hours, but it could also mean two minutes; he would have preferred to hear, now now, which actually meant now. This just now must have meant two minutes because she came out of the bedroom, dressed and ready to go. The weather was slowly warming up, so a light coat was all that was needed; no longer was there a need for furs, mittens, goloshes and scarves. They left their flat, apartment, and took the lift down to the ground floor and walked out to their car. There had been no snow for a few weeks, so they were spared the task of brushing off the snow, and the temperatures had stayed above freezing for the past week, so no ice to scrape off the windscreen.

"Do you want to drive?" James asked.

"No, you drive," she said. The trip did not take long, and they parked in the employee car park and James walked Katrina into the offices and took her to the personnel office, where she would sign on to the company and get her number and badge.

"I'll call you around noon," she said. "I may be busy, you may be, but if not, we can have lunch together."

James went back to his office and found some notes on his desk with machine tool prices. Bill must have been in early to get them some quickly. James wrote up his report on the visit to Penny Coal, then did some rough calculations as to investment and return. He talked to Robert Andrews and Bill Riding about the mine and the machines that it might call for. He explained to them why he thought that shovels and trucks were a more viable option for the mine and also told them that Howard rated their chances of getting the order as fairly low. Still, an enquiry is an enquiry, and they had to respond, so Mark and Tom were detailed off to put together the proposals for the shovels and drills. Apart from the basic description of the machines and the prices, there were also estimated delivery dates, with the caveat that they might change depending on when the order would be placed and what other business had come in in the interim. James then looked at his notes from the visit to the Pittsburgh factory and started to put together a proposition to acquire new machine tools that would replace the old with more capable machines. He made an estimate of what that would mean in terms of less re-work and scrap and reduced work-in-process inventory, then did a cash flow calculation. As far as he could see, the numbers made sense, so he took his work out to the shop and gave a copy to Bill to review.

Katrina called him just before noon and told him that she could eat with him and that she would meet him in the company cafeteria. James had just sat down with his lunch when she came in, got hers and joined him.

"So, how was the first morning?" he asked.

"Busy," she said. "I met with Ray Pierce and did all the paperwork, the tax stuff and who my dependent is if I die. I got my badge, and then Ray took me to George's office. George told me what I would be doing and then suggested that I go and meet with the parts people. That was interesting, some of the parts can be small enough to go in the mail, but some take a whole low loader. I suggested to George that I actually sit in the parts department. If I'm going to be doing all their shipping, it makes sense to me to be there."

"What do the parts people think about you working there?" James asked.

"I think they're just happy to have someone looking after them," she said. "I just need to find out now where our parts warehouses are and where many of the mines are, as some parts will go directly there. Then I need to check on the shipping companies, the trucking companies and the railways to see who has the best rates and times."

"So, you'll be busy?" he asked.

"I think so," she said. "This afternoon, I'm going the spend time with George learning who the shippers are and who the contacts are."

"Will you be ready to go home at five?" he asked.

"Probably more than ready," she laughed.

"Hey, guys," a voice said. It was Tom Nelson.

"Hi Tom," James said. "Please join us. Katrina was just telling me about her first day here."

"You joined us?" Tom asked.

"I talked myself into a job in traffic," she replied. "I get parts, so am learning where the warehouses are and who the shippers are."

"So, if we have a customer who needs a part in a hurry, I know who to call," Tom joked.

"How's Kathy?" Katrina asked.

"Busy, the school year is beginning to wind down, and she's looking forward to the summer break," Tom replied.

"I should get back," Katrina said. "Say hello to Kathy for me, Tom."

"I will," he promised. "So, James, tell me about Penny Coal."

"Howard was pretty pessimistic going in; it seems we were last to get to them, but it struck me that they had been almost trapped into the accepted way of thinking that they had to use a dragline. It seemed to me that they could get up and running much faster if they took a different approach. The numbers also look better, even if the operating costs with the dragline will be lower, the upfront investment drives the discounted cash flow," James explained.

"You might have to explain that all again," Tom warned. "Dan Wells is not happy that you steered them away from a dragline."

"Thanks for the warning," James said.

Dan Wells called James into his office later that afternoon.

"What's this I hear about you not recommending a dragline for the Penny Coal mine?" Dan asked.

"We were last to visit and Howard put our chances at ten to fifteen per cent," James said. "Then I looked at the deposit, and although you could do it with a dragline, it would be a complex operation; it struck me that they would be better off using a different mining method, plus the numbers work out."

"If you take that approach, the numbers will always work out better for shovels and trucks," Dan commented.

"I don't think so," James said. "There are many operations where the most logical mining method is with a dragline, where the operating cost per cubic yard of overburden removed is low enough to balance the initial investment. The problem with the Penny Coal mine was that there was no way to optimise the use of the dragline to its full potential."

"Okay, maybe this time, but before you go telling people to use shovels and trucks instead of a dragline, check with me first," Dan said.

"Okay," James said. "Did you hear anything back from the K&L mine?"

"Sure did, we're in final negotiations now for a 280 and for a couple of drills and a shovel," Dan replied. "Oh, and we heard from Boone Coal as well. I'm going out there tomorrow to negotiate. Remember to check with me first before you go recommending shovels instead of draglines."

"I will," James said. He was on his way back to his office when Robert Andrews called him into his office.

"Just wanted to thank you for the lead with Penny Coal, looks like a good solution to me," Robert said.

"Dan didn't think so," James commented.

"No, he wouldn't," Robert said. "But, don't worry about it, your job is to call the mining methods as you see them. Sometimes our field guys get fixated on things and seem to think that Powder River Basin coal is shovels, Midwest coal is draglines or stripping shovels, and Appalachian coal must be a dragline. You and I know that that's not always the case. So, don't worry about Dan, he's plenty to think about."

James left the office at five and met Katrina, who was also on her way out. They drove home, and James remembered that he had promised to cook dinner. While he busied himself in the kitchen, Katrina perched on a stool by the counter that separated the kitchen from the dining area and told him about the rest of her day. She had been introduced to the various shipping companies that they used and had actually scheduled some loads to be taken far and wide. There was a bit of a backlog in the parts department, so she was determined to clean that up as quickly as possible.

"So how was your afternoon?" she asked.

"Oh, I got a scolding for not recommending a dragline for the project in Pennsylvania," he said. "Then I got praise for doing it, two blokes with different views of the world and different goals."

"Will that affect you in any way?" she asked.

"I wouldn't think so," he said. "They told me when I started that I should call things as I see them, so I did."

"What did Tony say?" she asked.

"He's not back from Australia yet; he gets in tomorrow," James said.

"Any idea what he'll say?" she asked.

"Not a clue," he said. "But if he looks at the deposit, he should come up with the same solution that I did."

"Do they want you to recommend machines just because?" she asked.

"I don't think so," he said. "Maybe I'll see if John Williams has any advice. Anyway, are you ready to eat?"

"I am," she said.

"So, now you're working and are no longer a kept woman, are you going to madly resist my charms?" James teased after dinner.

"I could resist your charms well before I started work," she stated. "But I rather like you, so am amenable to your advances, no matter what and when."

"I was asking Marlys about Door County today," he said. "She told me that it's the kind of place that people go for romantic weekends."

"They do, do they?" Katrina laughed. "So, how do you plan to sweep me off my feet?"

"That would be telling," he said, grinning. "You said that we're staying in an inn. Do you know anything else about it?"

"It's on a cherry farm, not too far from the lake shore, but then looking at the map, nothing in Door County is far from the lake," she replied. "They said they had eight rooms available and asked me which one we wanted. I told them the honeymoon one."

"Oh, do they think we're just married then?" he asked.

"I didn't say yes or no," she said.

"How long a drive is it?" he asked.

"Amanda told me about three hours, so perhaps we should leave straight from work?" she suggested.

"That's a good idea," he said. "I'll make sure the petrol tank is full, so that we don't have to stop on the way too often."

"They say they have a bath in the room," she said. "I hope it's big enough for two."

"I'm sure we'll manage," he said. "So, talking about baths, shall we?"

"You just want to get me into bed," she teased.

"Of course," he said. "It's because you're so desirable."

"That's just lust talking," she laughed.

The next two weeks seemed to James to be interminable. Tony came back from Australia, listened to Dan's complaints, then reviewed the report that James had written and agreed with his assessment. Ron Edwards had only some minor changes to the financial justification that James and Bill had put together to buy new machine tools, and when the issue was presented to Hank Miller, he listened, asked questions then said that he would be following up with Ron. More queries came in about machines, and James had a full calendar for June, with trips scheduled for Utah, Wyoming, again, Montana and Colorado. Katrina got busier and busier and took on not only parts, but some of the purchased items that needed shipping in. She was delighted with her first paycheque and went lingerie shopping to celebrate. When the Friday before Memorial Day came, James made sure to fill the car with petrol at lunchtime, so that when he and Katrina left, early at four, not five, they started out immediately on their trek north.

"So, where to?" James asked as they pulled out of the car park.

"Through Milwaukee, then head for Port Washington," she instructed.

"Then where?" he asked.

"Sheboygan," she said, reading from the map.

"Traffic's already busy," he said. "I suppose lots of people are going away for the weekend."

"I went and bought some new undies," she said. "Especially for this trip, very revealing."

"You shouldn't distract me," he laughed. "Just the visions of you in revealing undies are enough to make me lose my concentration."

"Well, hang on to the wheel," she said. "They're lacy and almost see-through, I like them and I'm sure you will too."

"I'm sure I will," he agreed heartily.

"Where did you go?" he asked.

"I found this speciality shop," she said. "So, while you were busy with one of your classes, Amanda and I went shopping."

"So, Bill's in for a treat too?" he said.

"Definitely," she said.

They passed Port Washington, Sheboygan, Manitowoc and came to Green Bay. There, James filled the petrol tank as he had no idea how many petrol stations there might be scattered along the peninsula. From Green Bay, they drove to Sturgeon Bay and across the bridge. Well, not across the bridge immediately, as they had to wait while the bridge opened to allow a boat to pass.

"That's interesting," Katrina said as she studied the map while they waited for the boat to pass. "This waterway actually cuts all the way across, so the next bit of Door County is an island. Looking at the map here, it looks like a canal was cut through the last bit to connect the two lake shores."

"I'll bet this place could be cold and damp in the winter," he said. "It's a pity it's so cloudy, I'll bet it's pretty here when the sun shines."

"At least it's not too cold," she said. "It must be in the seventies."

"Look, the boat's gone and the bridge is going back down," he said. "I'm glad it's just cloudy and that we don't have rain, that would have been a miserable drive in the rain."

"Well, summer is almost here," she said. "Now, where, you need the road to Egg Harbor and Fish Creek, left here. I hope there aren't too many other people at this inn."

"Well, we can always keep to ourselves," he said. "I'm sure we can find something to do."

"We need to get out of the bedroom for at least part of the day," she said. "So, after breakfast, we'll explore a little, then we can find lunch somewhere, maybe even find somewhere quiet and have a roll in the hay, but maybe it's not warm enough for that."

"Okay, we're getting closer," Katrina said. "Take the next right, then the first left after that, and look for the sign for the Porte Inn."
"I see it," James said. "It looks nice, very rustic, looks like a big red barn."
"Howdy folks," a lady said as they pulled up to the front door. "If you'd like to park over there, then we'll get you settled in."
"Hello again," Katrina said when they went into the inn. "We have a booking, it's under the name of Martin."
"Yes, here we are," the lady said. "I'm Marie, by the way, we've put you in room three, at the top of the stairs to the right, dinner's in half an hour. Do you need help with your bags?"
"No, thank you," James said. "We can manage." He carried the bag that they had up the stairs and followed Katrina, who had the key. She opened the room, and it was rather charming. It looked out over the orchards, and there were myriads of trees in blossom. There was a huge four-poster bed and a big bath with claw feet.
"The bath is plenty big," Katrina commented.
"Plenty," James agreed. "Is the bed comfortable?"
"Feels nice," she said. "I'd like to change clothes before dinner. Why don't you run us a bath, and we can wash off the travel grime?"
"I'll do that," he said. He ran a bath while Katrina unpacked and hung clothes in the wardrobe that was in the room. "Bath's ready," he said. They actually bathed; normally, their bathing would lead to more, but there was dinner to go to, so other activities were put off until later. James watched Katrina dress, and he saw what she meant by the almost see-through lacy underwear.
"I like those," he said.
"I thought you might," she said. "You're such a lecherous *ou*, these would appeal to your baser nature. I've got more, so fashion show later."
"Look forward to that," he said. "What do I wear for dinner?"
"Khaki trousers, white shirt and your tweed jacket," she said. "I doubt that this is a formal place, but you never know."

"What are you going to wear?" he asked.

"I thought I'd just go as I am," she laughed.

"Probably give them all heart attacks and ideas," he laughed.

"No, I thought the tweed skirt with a light pullover, with the black sandals," she suggested.

"That sounds nice," he said. "Take a shawl with you in case it's cool down there."

"Howdy again, folks," Marie said when they went downstairs. "The dining room is just through there, take any seats."

James and Katrina went in, and there were two tables, each set for nine people. One table was already full, or at least it had eight seated at it. So they sat at the other. Two other people came in, looked around and sat down with them.

"Hi, I'm Mel, this is Melanie," he said.

"I'm James, this is Katrina," James replied.

"Where are you folks from?" Mel asked.

"We live in Cudahy," James said.

"But you're not from there, where do you originally hail from?" Mel pressed.

"I'm from England and Katrina is from Zambia," James replied.

"Is that Northern Rhodesia?" Melanie asked.

"It was," Katrina confirmed. "It became Zambia upon independence in 1964."

"What brings you to Wisconsin?" Melanie asked.

"A job," James explained. "I work for an equipment company, and you?"

"I'm a paediatrician and Mel's an anthropologist," Melanie replied. "Do you have kids?"

"No," James said. "No plans for children."

"They'll come in time," Melanie said. "Do you work too, Katrina?"

"I do," Katrina confirmed. "I'm in the traffic department of the company. I arrange railroad cars and trucks to deliver parts."

"What brings you to Door County?" Mel asked.

"We thought we'd like a weekend away, and people at work told us that Door County was really nice," Katrina replied.

"I'll bet that it's nothing like the Rhodesias," Mel said.

"No," Katrina agreed. "There are some parts of the Cape in South Africa that are somewhat similar, with the orchards, but in Zambia, nothing like this."

"Howdy folks, I'm Sven, the other half of the inn," a man said. "I'll be joining you for dinner."

"Is this all of us?" Melanie asked.

"Ja," Sven said. "We're not full, so I get the light load. Dinner tonight is boeuf bourguignon, followed by an apple tart, beef from a farm up the road and apples from here. Let's see, Mel and Mel are old friends, you must be the Martins, James and Katrina from Cudahy?"

"We are," James confirmed.

"What did you do in Africa?" Melanie asked.

"I worked in a copper mine and Katrina worked in her dad's transport business," James replied.

"So, now you're in Wisconsin," Sven said.

"Does it get cold here in the winter?" James asked.

"It can, it can," Sven replied. "We've got the lake on both sides, so we get lake effect snow a lot, and there're no hills to moderate the winds, so it can be brutal, but the rest of the year makes up for that."

"When we came up, we had to stop at the bridge for a boat and looking at the map, it looks like someone dug a canal, making this an island," James said. "Why was that done?"

"Back in the 1890s, the president of the Chicago and North Western Railway decided to dig the canal so that ships going to Green Bay could avoid the Porte de Morts Straits that are at the top of the peninsula. The canal was eventually handed over to the government, and the Corps of Engineers now maintains it. It's 125 feet wide and now is 20 feet deep, but when it was first dug, it was only six feet deep," Sven explained. "There was already the deep inlet at Sturgeon Bay, so the bit that had to be dug was not very long, only 1.3 miles, not like the Panama or Suez. So now we have three bridges that connect us to the rest of the world. There was a fourth bridge, a railroad bridge, but that was taken out a couple of years ago after the railroad had shut down."

"I remember that bridge," Mel said. "Wasn't it originally built as a road bridge?"

"It was a toll bridge, then the railroad added to it, and it was a road-rail bridge," Sven explained.

"I thought that in the States it was all railroads, how is it the Chicago and North Western was a railway company?" James asked.

"Don't rightly know," Sven admitted. "It's also the only railroad that runs trains on what we call left-handed operation. The story goes that when they added a second track, they ran things opposite so folks could wait in the heated depot. Did they have railroads where you lived?"

"There is a line that runs from Kitwe down across the Zambezi at Victoria Falls to Rhodesia, then to Bulawayo, where it connects to the rest of their system. You can get a train from there to Cape Town. Going the other way, the line runs through the Congo to Angola and Lobito Bay, and we have a new line that the Chinese have built from Dar es Salaam," James replied.

"How far is it from this town, Kitwe, to Cape Town?" Melanie asked.

"I would guess at about 2,400 miles by rail," James replied. "The shortest route by car is a little over 2,000 miles, but the railways wander around a bit."

"That's a long way," Sven said. "You've driven it?"

"When I first went to work, I took the boat to Cape Town and drove up," James said. "And Katrina and her family did it a few times. I see you grow cherries here, and you told us that you have apples. Do you have any others?"

"Some plums and we're trying some grapes and we keep sheep, mainly to keep the grass down in the orchards," Sven explained. "Okay, here's the beef, bon appétit!"

Dinner was marked by relative quiet, which probably spoke to the food and how good it was. Conversation resumed over coffee.

"What's the biggest difference between here and where you were before?" Melanie asked Katrina.

"The snow and ice," Katrina replied. "In May and June, we could get frost overnight, but by ten, the temperatures were back up in the eighties and the skies clear. Also, the freeways and the shopping malls, we had no freeways and only a few big shops, but no malls."

"What did you do for doctors?" Melanie asked.

"The mines had their own hospitals and the doctors that worked there, the government had hospitals, and there were a few doctors that were in practice for themselves," Katrina replied.

"So, medical care was good?" Melanie asked.

"I wouldn't say that," Katrina said. "If you work for one of the big mines, then there is reasonable medical care; in the bigger towns, there are the government hospitals, but in the rural areas, there might be a clinic within 20 to 50 miles."

"What about pediatric care?" Melanie asked.

"A friend of mine told me that we reduced the infant mortality rate, but then we had malnutrition problems when the children got to be two or three," Katrina replied.

"So, what were the big problems?" Melanie asked.

"I suppose malaria, sickle cell anæmia, accidents, malnutrition, and all the other things that come with living in the tropics," Katrina said. "I would think that from a doctor's point of view, that it would be a fascinating, if at times very frustrating, place to work."

"I think we've asked these good people enough questions," Mel said. "They're here for a weekend away."

"So, what's your plan tomorrow?" Sven asked.

"We thought we'd take a look at the rest of the peninsula," James said. "It really is very nice here."

"We like it," Sven said. "If you'll excuse me, breakfast is at seven until nine, so any time you're ready, come on down."

"It's been a while since I've been interrogated," Katrina laughed that night when they were in their room later.

"She did have a lot of questions," James agreed. "So, you have boasted earlier about a fashion show, do I get to see it?"

"Let's have a bath first," she suggested. "Then you can make yourself comfortable, and I'll show you what I bought."

185

"So, what's first?" he asked after they had bathed and he was reclining on the bed, propped up with pillows.

"The red," she said. She came out of the bathroom in a red lace bra and panties that were almost there. She did her walk and pirouette, then went back for the next item. In all, she had four changes, and it seemed to James that each was more revealing than the last.

"Which do you like the best?" she asked.

"I think the black," he said.

"You would," she laughed. "I like these, but I don't think I'll be wearing them for work, too delicate for everyday wear. So, are you ready to show me how much you appreciate the great sacrifices I made for you?"

"Any time," he said.

"I smell coffee," Katrina said the next morning. "Be a dear and go down and get some for me?"

"Of course," James said. He quickly put some clothes on and went down and found the coffee. He poured two cups and took them back upstairs.

"Many people about?" she asked.

"Not that I saw," he said. "I peeked in the dining room, and no one was eating breakfast yet. Let's see, it's just before seven, so early yet."

"What shall we do today?" she asked as she sipped her coffee.

"I think take the tour," he said. "We could go north and look at the ferry terminal, then run down the other side of the peninsula and, perhaps, have lunch in Sturgeon Bay, then come back here."

"That sounds like a plan," she agreed. "What's the weather look like?"

He opened the curtains and looked out. "Cloudy, high clouds, so probably no rain, but also no sun."

"Well, we can't have everything," she said. "Do you think it's cold out there?"

"Let me check," he said. He opened the window wider and reached out. "Doesn't feel too bad," he said. "Certainly not freezing."

"Let me get dressed and we'll go down and see what's for breakfast," she suggested.

186

"Wear something warmish, it's not seventy degrees out there," he warned.

"I'm thinking of trousers and a pullover," she said. "And no sandals today, I think takkies today.

"Howdy folks," Sven said as they went to the dining room and noticed that the tables were set up differently, no family-style dining at breakfast, but tables set for two and four. "You're the first here, so take your pick."

"What about here?" Katrina said. "We can sit out and look at the cherry blossoms."

"So, what'll it be?" Sven asked. "We can do you omelettes, scrambled, over easy, or no eggs, just muffins and fruit."

"I think an omelette, please," Katrina said.

"So, tomato, western, plain?" Sven asked.

"Let's try western omelettes," Katrina said. "And could we get some tea?"

"Sure, coming right up, you want hash browns with the omelette, toast, white, wheat, rye?"

"Yes, please on the hash browns and wheat toast please," Katrina replied. When Sven had gone, she commented to James that she still could not get used to the choices, so many choices for everything.

"I know," he agreed. "I got offered grits when I was in Kentucky. I'm not sure what grits actually are."

"Here you go, folks, tea, you want cream with that?" Sven asked.

"Yes, please," James replied. "Maybe one day I should try rye toast just to see what it's like."

"Don't get too adventurous," she laughed.

"Western omelettes," Marie announced as she came through from the kitchen. "Sven has your toast and jellies, more tea?"

"Thank you, that would be nice," James said. The omelettes were huge; one would have probably sufficed for the two of them, but they ate them anyway and enjoyed every last bite. Other people drifted in, two families of four and the Mels that they had met the night before. James nodded good morning to them and then looked to see what jams and jellies they had been offered for their toast. There was strawberry, grape, raspberry, plum, boysenberry and plain honey. James elected to go for the raspberry. It was quite delicious. Breakfast was a noisy meal as it seemed everyone had something to say.

"Get you anything else?" Sven asked.

"No, thank you," James said. "That was great. Any idea what the weather will do today?"

"Supposed to have some sun this afternoon," Sven said. "We'll see. You'll be back for dinner?"

"We will," James confirmed.

Door County lived up to its billing as a scenic destination. It was rural, farming, orchards, woods, with scattered houses and small communities. James and Katrina drove north from Egg Harbor to Fish Creek.

"Look," James said as they drove into Fish Creek. "There's an island out there."

"The map says that it's Chambers Island," Karina said.

"I wonder if anyone lives there?" he said.

"I'll bet it can get pretty isolated in the winter," she thought.

"Where next?" he asked.

"Ephraim," she read off.

"Ephraim," he repeated. "That's a funny name to find in the middle of Wisconsin. Have you noticed how so much of this land is divided into neat rectangles?"

"I suppose if you're laying out a community and there's not hundreds of years of history of agriculture, then why not, easy to plough if it's all straight lines," she said.

"I wonder if there were Indians here before white men showed up?" he pondered.

"Probably," she said. "There are so many place names in Wisconsin that can only be Indian names, why not be here as well? Look, the sun's beginning to show."

"So, perhaps the forecasters were right," he said. "Where next?"

"Sister Bay," she said. "Then Ellison Bay then we go over to the pier where the ferry runs from."

"Shall we see if there's a coffee shop somewhere?" he suggested.

"Good idea," she agreed. "I'm surprised at how hilly it is, not really big hills, but a fair amount of up and down. Look, there's a café over there, let's try that for coffee."

"Morning folks," a lady said when they went into the café. "Sit anywhere and I'll be right with you."

"I suppose this is what you'd call rustic decor," Katrina commented to James as they sat themselves at a table by a window.

"Goes with all the trees," he said. "I'll bet it's really pretty in the autumn."

"Okay, folks, name's Lila, what can I get you?" the waitress asked.

"Coffee, please?" Katrina said.

"You want cappuccino, American coffee, espresso?" Lila asked.

"I think cappuccino," Katrina replied.

"How about some pie, we've got apple, peach, plum cherry?" Lila asked.

"James?" Katrina asked.

"I think cherry," he said.

"Same for me," Katrina added.

"Okay, that's two cappuccinos and two cherry pies," Lila confirmed. "Be right out."

She was back quickly enough with the slices of pie. Looking at them, both James and Katrina thought that they could have been satisfied with just one slice between the two of them. They were still getting used to the portions that were served in America, generally much larger than in Zambia, South Africa or England. Lila came again, this time with the coffee.

"Enjoy," she said. "Can I get you anything else?"

"No, thank you," James said. Lila left and they tried their coffees, and approved. The cherry pie was next, and it was also approved of. The café might be small, but the food was good.

"So, how are you enjoying the new job?" James asked Katrina.

"I'm having fun," she said. "I've even got a business card. I've learned a lot, I've shipped parts all over the place, I made friends on the phone with parts managers all over the country."

"Will it be enough in the longer term?" he asked.

"I don't know," she said. "It's enough for me now because it's new and there's a lot to learn, but I couldn't do it for twenty years, any more than you could be an application engineer for twenty years. You'll want to look at something that gives you new challenges, I know you."

"You're right," he laughed. "But the company must realise that as well, otherwise, why have a management development program?"

"How do you think that's going?" she asked.

"As far as I can judge, well," he said. "Miller gave us our next project, Bill and I are to look at the dealer network we use to sell our smaller machines."

"What, like Wilfred Watson is to Caterpillar in Kitwe?" she asked.

"That's right," he said. "Wilfred Watson deals with all the Caterpillar equipment that comes into Zambia, and they provide parts and service as well. So, Bill and I have to look at who we use and why."

"I'm glad we got the chance to move to the US," she said. "There's opportunities here for us, and I'm sure that in a while we'll be able to afford a house."

"I've never owned a house," he said. "In Zambia, it was mine houses, I know your folks owned their house. Did they have a mortgage on it?"

"No, they were lucky, Dad built in largely himself, so after they bought the land, we lived in a shack for a while until the house was built," she replied. "But I suppose if we buy a house, we'd have to take out a mortgage. I wonder how you do that?"

"I suppose the first person we might talk to is the bank manager, I'm sure he can tell us how to go about it," James said.

"Well, maybe we're getting a little ahead of ourselves here; we don't even have enough saved up for a down payment yet," she laughed.

"No, but with both of us working, we should be able to save a bit," he said.

"Can I get you folks anything else?" Lila asked.

"No, thank you," James said.

"I'll take that, whenever you're ready," Lila said, indicating the bill.

"Here you are," James said, proffering some cash.

"Be right back with your change," Lila said.

"So, where to now?" James asked Katrina as they left the café.

"Let's go and look at the ferry terminal," she said. They drove through the rest of Sister Bay, then Ephraim and Ellison Bay, then the road turned east and ran across the peninsula.

"It's not much to look at, is it?" she commented as they pulled up to the ferry terminal.

"Well, I suppose it's only a short ride," he said. "There's a ticket booth over there with a timetable, let's park and take a wander around."

"Look, there's a ferry coming in," she said. They watched it arrive and cars and one lorry drive off, then the waiting cars were driven on. She counted fourteen cars loaded on, and it looked like there was space for a few more.

"It's got a funny name," she commented to James. "Eyrarbakki sounds almost Scandinavian."

"When the ferry's gone, let's see if the man in the ticket booth can tell us anything about it," he suggested. When the ferry had gone, they asked the man in the booth, and he told them that the name was that of a village in Iceland, which was where some of the settlers of Washington Island came from. He also told them that the trip took about half an hour and the schedule changed a lot between summer and winter, driven by the tourist traffic. Curiosity satisfied, they retraced their steps and started down the other side of the peninsula towards Sturgeon Bay. That proved interesting as they had to backtrack a few times as they discovered that roads were dead-ended by bays.

"The map says that there's a big lake just up here, Kangaroo Lake. I wonder how it got its name?" she said. "I'll ask Sven tonight."

"We're almost in Sturgeon Bay," James said as they approached the town. "We should look for somewhere for lunch."

"Drive around the town a bit and we'll see if anything takes our fancy," she suggested.

"What about that place?" he asked, pointing to a small restaurant.

"Let's try it," she agreed. They parked and went in and looked at the menu; it seemed that fish was a speciality, so they decided to try.

"Table for two?" a man asked.

"Yes, please," James said. They were led to a table by a window and given menus.

"Helena will be your server today," the man said.

"Howdy folks," Helena said, bringing glasses of water that she set on the table. "Can I get you folks something to drink?"

"Do you have a white wine?" Katrina asked.

"We've got a house white," Helena said.

"Thank you, we'll try a glass each," James said.

"Take your time with the menu, I'll be back with your wines," Helena promised. She was back quickly with two glasses of wine and table mats that advertised the restaurant. "I'll give you a few minutes and be back for your orders."

"Cheers," James said, raising his glass.

"Cheers," Katrina echoed. "Not bad, quite drinkable, what do you have a fancy for?"

"I think I'll try the trout," he said.

"I'm going to try the perch," she said.

Helena came back, and they gave her their orders. There was the usual list of preparations, side dishes and sauces to go through, but they were becoming used to the seemingly endless lists of options and knew how to politely shut it off and ask for what they wanted.

"I wonder what it's like living in such a close community?" James said.

"Probably a lot like living in Kitwe, most people know who you are and what your business is," she thought. "The big difference is tourists by the ton in the summer and autumn and peace and quiet in the winter, but as we said before, I'll bet that winters here could be brutal."

"Some of the blokes at work were talking about summer cottages by lakes or up here," James said. "I wonder what it's like having a summer cottage, you probably have to do all kinds of things to get it ready for the winter, or you'd be dealing with frozen pipes and all sorts of problems."

"Didn't you tell me about ice fishing after your trip to Minnesota?" she asked.

"I did," he confirmed. "I wonder if the big lake freezes over enough to do that, or if you have to go and find a smaller lake?"

"If Lake Michigan freezes up, then it must be bloody cold," she said.

"It must freeze up at times, because Bill told me that the Coast Guard has an icebreaker stationed in Milwaukee," he said.

"I would never have thought that you'd need an ice breaker on an inland lake," she said.

"Okay, folks, here you go," Helena said, bringing out their plates of fish and all the accoutrements that went with them. "Enjoy, anything else I can get you, another glass of wine?"

"Thank you, we will," James said.

"I'll probably go to sleep in the car on the way back to the hotel," Katrina said. "A large lunch and two glasses of wine, certain recipe for sleep." They ate, and the fish was good, well prepared and in a generous portion. They sat, ate and talked, in no hurry to leave, and Helena assured them that there was no need to hurry; they were not that busy.

"So, should we head back?" James asked Katrina after they had finished their coffee.

"Let's do that," she said. "I rather fancy a sundowner on the porch they have at the hotel."

"We've just had lunch," he protested.

"Yes, but when it gets to five or six, I rather fancy a sundowner looking out onto the orchards," she said.

"Okay, you have the map, where to?" he asked.

"Left, look for the road signs that say B, that will take us along the lakefront all the way to Egg Harbor," she instructed.

"The water doesn't look very inviting," he commented as they drove along the lakefront.

"It looks downright cold," she said. "Should we find somewhere to pull over and see?"

"Okay, what about just up ahead there?" he suggested. They parked and walked the short distance to the lake and tested the waters. James was right, the water was cold, not quite freezing, but probably not too many degrees above.

"It's a little too cold to go swimming," he said.

"A little?" she said. "It'd have to warm up a lot before I got in."

"So, if you have a boat up here, don't fall in," he commented.

"Don't indeed," she agreed. "At least in Lake Kariba, if you fell in, you wouldn't freeze to death."

"No, you'd only be worried about the crocodiles," he said. "Shall we go on?"

"You're back," Sven said when they arrived at the hotel.

"We are," James said. "We were wondering, why is Kangaroo Lake called that?"

"The story is that it's the shape of the lake, supposed to look like a kangaroo," Sven replied. "Don't see it myself, but others swear to it. It's a funny lake, very shallow, no more than six feet anywhere."

"That is shallow," James agreed. "Oh, we also saw an island off Fish Creek. Does anyone live there?"

"Chambers Island," Sven said. "Private island, only landowners and guests, there's no power there, there's a small landing strip and a jetty, but it's pretty much stay away. So, ready for an afternoon drink on the porch?"

"That was the idea," Katrina said.

"Go and get a seat, and I'll bring a wine list if that's what you want, or I've got a pretty good selection of beers and can always make you up a mixed drink, any preferences?" Sven asked.

"Bring us a wine list, if you would please," James replied. He and Katrina went out onto the porch and sat at a table that looked out onto the orchard and the sheep grazing between the trees.

"Here you go," Sven said. "It'll be just you and the Mels tonight, the others left today."

"The Mels, as you call them, are regular visitors?" James asked.

"Pretty much every three months, summer and winter," Sven replied.

"You're open in the winter?" Katrina asked.

"Only weekends," he replied. "People come to cross-country ski and just get away from the city."

"Melanie said that Mel is an anthropologist," James said.

"Teaches at UW in Milwaukee, Melanie has her own paediatric practice," Sven explained.

"How many acres of trees do you have?" Katrina asked.

"We've got 250 acres in all, most under apples and cherries, plus a few plums," Sven said. "The biggest challenge is getting pickers in the Fall."

"I can imagine," Katrina said. "The sheep don't bother the trees?"

"No, sheep are fine, they're grazers. One of my neighbours tried goats, but they're browsers and ate the bark right off the trees and killed a few before he figured out what was happening. In the winter, I have to feed the sheep, but I've also got fifty acres under hay just for that."

"You must be really busy," James said.

"I've got my son doing the farm work," Sven said. "He and I share the profits; I provide the land and the trees, he does the working. Okay, I'd better go and get things rolling in the kitchen. I'll be back in a few for your drinks orders."

"So, what'll be folks?" Sven asked when he came back with some olives and almonds.

"You've got a nice-looking Chablis here," James said. "Could we try that?"

"Sure thing," Sven said. "I'll be right back with some glasses and an ice bucket."

Sven left, and Mel and Melanie came out onto the porch.

"Good evening, would you mind if we joined you?" Mel asked.

"Please," James said, rising and indicating a chair for Melanie.

"Did you have a nice day?" Melanie asked.

"We did," Katrina said. "We went and looked at the ferry terminal, then went south to Sturgeon Bay for lunch and had to backtrack a few times as we went down dead-end roads, and you?"

"We took the ferry to Washington Island. We have a friend who lives there," Melanie replied.

"I hope that I don't offend, but tell me, Katrina, is there African in your heritage anywhere?" Mel asked.

"There is," Katrina confirmed. "On both sides, back to my great-great-grandparents."

"I thought so," Mel said. "There are features that you have that could only come from that. Do you mind telling me which groups?"

"On my dad's side, Motshaba, a Bushman and my mum's side, Modjaji, a Bapedi, which is one of the northern South African tribes," Katrina explained.

"Fascinating," Mel said. "If I were you, I wouldn't broadcast that around Milwaukee too much. You may have noticed that in South Milwaukee and Oak Creek, there are almost no blacks."

"I think people I meet think I'm part southern European," Katrina said. "Either Portuguese, Spanish or Italian."

"That would make sense," Mel said. "The rest of your family is classic Afrikaner, probably a lot of Huguenot, mixed with Dutch, am I right?"

"You are," Katrina confirmed.

"And James, straight English?" Mel asked.

"That's the family story," James confirmed. "Whatever English means, after all the invasions and mixing."

"That's true," Mel nodded. "I teach a class or two at UW and am always fascinated by the fact that people are trying to separate humanity into races as though they were different species, when in fact, apart from facial features, skin tone and few other environmentally driven adaptations, we are the same, one species."

"I've got your wine here," Sven said, bringing out a bottle, two glasses and an ice bucket. "Mel, Melanie, the usual?"

"The usual," Melanie confirmed.

"So, James, Katrina, back to Milwaukee tomorrow?" Mel asked.

"We do," James confirmed. "We have to be back at work on Tuesday. We thought we'd leave after breakfast and wander our way back through Green Bay, Appleton, Oshkosh and Fond du Lac. Katrina wants to see Oshkosh; she used to drive a big Oshkosh low loader when we lived in Zambia."

"Oshkosh is famous for their big trucks," Mel agreed. "It's also the home of OshKosh B'Gosh, which is a famous children's clothing line and for the annual fly-in of the Experimental Aircraft Association."

"We presumed that Oshkosh was an Indian name," Katrina said.

"We call the first peoples Native Americans now," Mel said. "The term Indian is rather falling out of favour, particularly as we have nothing to do with India. But you're right, Oshkosh was the name of a chief at one point, and the town was named after him."

"Are you both from Wisconsin originally?" James asked.

"Melanie is, and I'm from Iowa," Mel replied. "We met at college in Madison. How did you two meet?"

"There was a boat club in Kitwe, and I went there a couple of times and met Katrina's parents, then eventually met her," James replied.

"And you've been together for how long?" Melanie asked.

"Five years," James said. "We got married right at the end of the rains in 1970."

"Well, you've certainly packed a lot into those five years," Melanie commented.

"We've been lucky," James said.

"You make your own luck," Melanie said. "Sven, are you out here to tell us it's dinner time?"

"I am," Sven confirmed. "If you'd all like to come in now, we'll serve dinner."

"I wonder if all Americans ask as many questions as the Mels?" James mused that night after dinner.

"We're new to them, we're different, so we're a curiosity," Katrina said. "It's probably not every day that they meet someone from Zambia."

"You're right," he agreed. "But at least they had an idea of where it is."

"True," she said. "Not many people do. So, tomorrow, after Green Bay, Appleton and lunch in Oshkosh?"

"Sounds good," he said. "I wonder where the Oshkosh factory is?"

"I'm sure we can find it," she said. "Are you ready for a bath?"

"I am," he said. "I'll go and run it."

"I'm ready for my bed tonight, being sociable is tiring," she laughed.

"At least you don't have to be sociable all the time," he said. "Imagine being in something like the hotel or airline business."

"No way, man," she said. "I'd be a pilot but not a stewardess, having to deal with passengers all the time."

"Bath is ready," he said.

"I'll be right there," she said. "Move up a bit, you're taking up far too much room." James moved, and she climbed in, and mutual washing led to lovemaking that was repeated in bed later, for both of them a great way to end the day.

Learjet

James and Katrina found the Oshkosh factory and drove around its perimeter, trying to spot what kind of vehicles were there. There were quite a few, all big heavy lorries of one type or another, most of them drab green, which probably meant that they were destined for the military. They ate lunch in Oshkosh by the river that bisected the town. They were back in Cudahy by five that evening, wanting to be home and off the roads before the masses all returned from their long weekend getaways. They had enjoyed their weekend away, but were happy to be home, happy not to have to be sociable and answer questions. Katrina cooked dinner, but only something very light as they both felt that they had done nothing but eat for the past two days or so.

"So, James, ready for your next trip?" Tony asked when James arrived at the office the next day.

"Of course," James said.

"I'd like you to go to Salt Lake City, Kennecott is talking more machines, so go and have a look and tell me what you think," Tony instructed. "Then, go on to Rock Springs and look at a prospect for a dragline there."

"Rock Springs?" James asked.

"Wyoming," Tony said. "Take the company plane, it'll be easier than trying to get to Rock Springs any other way. Fly out to Salt Lake and meet with Ben Bragg, and when you're done there, fly over to Rock Springs and meet up with Keith."

"What do I have to do to get the company plane?" James asked.

"We keep it at Mitchell Field at an FBO on Layton," Tony said.

"An FBO?" James asked.

"Fixed Base Operator," Tony explained. "A place where corporate jets are usually kept and serviced. Be there at eight tomorrow morning, that'll put you into Salt Lake before lunch, you can do Kennecott and fly on to Rock Springs later that afternoon. Do Rock Springs on Thursday morning, then come home that night."

"And all I have to do is show up?" James asked.

"They know you're coming," Tony said.

"You're not going?" James asked.

"No, I've got some stuff to do in Indiana," Tony said.

"I get to use the company plane tomorrow," James told Katrina that afternoon when they were driving home.

"I know," she said. "I'm coming with you. While you go and talk to the mine, I'm going to visit the local parts warehouse, then I'll just tag along when you go to Wyoming."

"That's wonderful," he said. "Tony told me to be at the place on Layton at eight tomorrow morning. I suppose we can just leave the car there."

"What kind of plane is it?" she asked.

"I didn't ask that," he said. "I've never been on a corporate jet before. I wonder what they're like?"

"I wonder," she echoed. "I suppose, as I'm visiting a parts warehouse and a mine site with you, I should just take trousers and boots."

"You might want to add a blouse or shirt to that," he laughed. "Showing up in just trousers and boots might be too much for some."

"I'm sure they'd all be as happy as anything if they're all as lecherous as you," she said.

"Is the local parts manager going to meet you at the Salt Lake City airport?" he asked.

"So I understand," she said. "We fly in and go to a place called Atlantic, and he'll meet me there. George already told him that we'd be landing at ten in the morning local time."

"I suppose that means that the flying time is about three hours because there's a one-hour time change between here and there," he said.

"I'm looking forward to this," she said. "It'll be fun, and I get to see you do your stuff."

"Don't expect too much," he cautioned. "I may just ask questions."

"Where do we stay in Rock Springs?" she asked.

"Marlys put me, us, in the Outback Inn there," he said. "We'll see what that's like when we get there. I'm meeting the field rep for Wyoming, a chap by the name of Keith."

"He's the hunter, isn't he?" she asked.

"He's certainly one of them," James confirmed.

"Let's go and eat out tonight at the Mexican place," she suggested. "Then we can go home and pack."

The trip from their flat to the hangar on Layton Avenue only took a few minutes, so they were there at about seven-thirty the next morning.

"James Martin, Katrina Martin?" a man asked.

"We are," James confirmed.

"I'm Bill, your pilot today. Is that your bags, do you need to use the bathroom?" he said. Both James and Katrina thought that a good idea, so found the respective bathrooms. They rejoined Bill in the lobby of the building, and he led them out to a plane. It looked tiny to James, much smaller than a commercial jet. They climbed up into it and saw six very comfortable-looking seats. Two at the back and four in the middle, arranged in pairs facing one another.

"Pick any seats you want," Bill said. "This is Chuck, he's the copilot today. We'll just close up and go, we figure wheels up at fifteen before the hour, puts us into Salt Lake at nine thirty-eight."

"We can just go?" James asked.

"Sure, you're aboard, your baggage is stowed, we're gassed up, we can go," Bill said. "We'll take off and then turn to the west and climb to about 40,000 feet, then head on out to Salt Lake."

"I like this way to fly," Katrina said as she sat down in one of the seats and fastened her seat belt. "Fancy being able to come and go as you please?"

"Not bad," James said.

"If you'll just review the safety card here," Bill said, coming back to talk to them. He pointed out the exits, where the oxygen masks were, where the life jackets were and how to open the door in the event of an emergency. Then he went back to the cockpit, sat down, and they started to move. They could see through the cockpit door and watch things happening as they went. James looked at Katrina, and she just grinned at him, a big, wide grin, full of absolute delight. They saw that they had turned onto the runway and then heard the engines wind up, and they were on their way. They left the ground in a remarkably short time and climbed out, making odd turns as they did, until they levelled out and the engines throttled back to cruise. Bill came back briefly and offered them breakfast and coffee. He showed them where it all was and how to pull open the tables and left them to it. James served up the coffee and the breakfasts, and he and Katrina sat and ate, looked out of the window and marvelled at their fortune. James picked up the safety card again and read that they were, in fact, flying in a Learjet 35. He looked around, and the cabin was comfortable enough, but not tall enough for him to stand upright. There were the six seats and the two pilots, and he supposed that somewhere behind them there was space for luggage, but he had not seen Bill stow it, so was not certain where it was.

"This is super," Katrina said. "We're up here, way above all the other planes, and it's just us."

"Welcome to the corporate world," he said. "I don't suppose we'll get to do this very often."

"You're probably right, but we've done it at least once," she said.

"I suppose I should look at the information that I was sent about the places I'm going to," James said. He pulled out papers from his case and started to go through them. He noticed that Katrina had her own stack of paper, which looked to him like a computer printout.

"Where's the Angel Mining Company operation?" she asked him.

"I think it's in Montana, not too far from Butte," he replied. "What do you have there?"

"This is a list of all the machines that the company has shipped in the past thirty years and who they sold to," she explained. "I'm trying to get a sense of how many machines and of what type are in the areas covered by each parts warehouse."

"I have a lot of information at the office about what equipment each mine has, so we should compare notes and maybe mark them on a map for you," he suggested. "Do you know if there is a similar printout of all the parts that have shipped and for what machines?"

"I'm looking into that," she said. "It would be interesting to know, say, if the main bearing on the hoist drum of a shovel fails frequently, then we could ask why?"

"You could probably eventually get to mean time to failure," he said.

"What's that?" she asked.

"If you have enough information, you may be able to predict that the bearing is 90% likely to fail after 2,325 hours," he explained. "If you could do that, then you could make sure that there was a spare on hand at the warehouse. Even better, not from a sale of parts point of view, but for the mining company, you could get the engineers to look at why it fails and do some redesign."

"Oh, like the turbochargers on those trucks you had at Mkushi, they all failed after so many hours until they came out with a redesign of the oil line?" she asked,

"Just like that," he. confirmed.

"Interesting," she said. "I wonder if I come up with anything, if anyone will listen?"

"That's a good question," he said. "I suppose it would come down to how much an engineering change would cost and how much we sell in parts and how much we value goodwill."

"So, not so straightforward?" she asked.

"No, but no reason not to do it anyway, at least you would know what parts to expect to ship to which warehouse," he said.

The plane droned on, and they finally heard the engines throttle back more and felt it start to descend.

"We'll be landing in fifteen minutes," Bill said. "We'll be landing to the north, so if you look out on the left, you'll see the Kennecott mine."

"Do you want to sit over here?" James asked Katrina. "Then you'll be able to see the mine as well." She moved and strapped herself in. The plane made its twists and turns, and they flew lower and lower until, on the left, they saw the mine. They were past it quickly enough and soon on the ground, at nine thirty-eight. There were a few minutes of taxi time, and then they pulled up at the Atlantic base. Bill opened the door and dropped down the stairs. As they left the plane, Katrina was delighted to see a red carpet leading to the building. She looked around, and the skyline to the east was dominated by mountains, snow-capped mountains, which she learned from Bill were the Wasatch Mountains, and to the west, there were distant hills and probably more mountains, but not as dominating as the Wasatch. The skies were blue, clear as a bell, with not even a hint of a cloud. James joined her, and they walked into the building and were met by two men.

"Mrs Martin?" one said. "I've talked to you on the phone enough. You must be James Martin. I'm Gus Bergquist, I'm the local parts manager. This is Ben Bragg, our local field rep."

"Mr Martin, do you have a departure time?" Bill asked.

"Ben?" James asked.

"Let's say three," Ben said. "That'll give us plenty of time at the mine. Is that okay with you, Gus?"

"Fine by me," Gus said.

"So, three then, Bill," James confirmed. They then split up and went their separate ways.

Ben drove James out to the mine and called in at their offices.

"Charlie, this is James Martin, one of our application engineers," Ben said, making the introduction.

"James," Charlie said. "Been in a copper mine before?"

"I worked for the Kasalia Consolidated Copper Mines in Zambia," James replied. "I worked underground for a while, then started up a new open pit, nothing like the size of this one."

"What did you use?" Charlie asked.

"Front-end loaders and fifty-ton trucks," James said. "I got to visit Nchanga a few times, and their equipment was probably more your size."

"Okay," Charlie said. "Why don't we take a drive around in the pit, and we'll talk about what we need?" He led the way to a pickup truck, and they got aboard and went off into the pit. The pit was big, even bigger than the Nchanga mine in Zambia. It struck James that most of the shovels at the mine came from Marion and Harnischfeger, no James & Brown in evidence. He wondered if the mine management would even consider another supplier in the mix, with a couple of Bucyrus machines along with the Marion and Harnischfeger machines; they already had three suppliers to deal with. But then, he supposed that was also true of the truck fleet, with WABCO, Dart, Unit Rig and Euclid. Still, it was instructive to listen to Charlie, his complaints, his praises, few though they were and all the problems that faced the production manager of a truly giant mine. Charlie talked about the drilling and the issues there and pointed out the drills that they already had. Even though the price of copper was still down, he had to plan for the future, and the deeper they went, the more overburden had to be taken out to ensure a safe working pit. Unlike an underground mine where you could get to the ore a number of ways, in an open pit the only way was to take all the material above the ore off and that meant out to the sides as well, because you could not have a pit with straight sides going down, that led to collapse, so the pits eventually got to look like upside down cones.

"What are you looking for?" James asked.

"Bigger shovels and bigger trucks," Charlie said. "As we go deeper, our economics are changing, and we need to drive operating costs down, so cost per ton of overburden removed could use a drop."

"You're happy with the drills you have?" James asked.

"We'll probably need another," Charlie said. "Shoot us out a proposal with shovel sizes and prices and drill prices, plus delivery dates."

"What size trucks are you looking to move to?" James asked.

"Most of the fleet right now is 65 and 85 ton; we'd like to move up to 150 ton, so match your shovels accordingly," Charlie replied.

"Are you going to change your bench width?" James asked.

"We'll have to in a few spots," Charlie said. "We're concerned about slope stability; we don't want a Chuquicamata here." Charlie was referring to a massive slope failure at a big copper mine in Chile that had happened in 1969 and had essentially created a whole new science of slope stability and geotechnical monitoring.

"How soon do you need numbers?" Ben asked.

"Couple of weeks should be fine," Charlie said. "We're only at the budget stage right now, we'll refine our needs as we firm up the mine plan and then look to the investment. But we need real numbers, not a sky-high budget number."

"We'll do that," Ben promised.

"So, how many trucks are you looking to acquire?" James asked.

"Somewhere in the order of fifty," Charlie said.

"And the truck cycle time to the dump is how long?" James asked.

"Forty-five minutes, give or take," Charlie said. That number was useful because it gave James a sense of how many shovels they would be looking at. "Seen all you need to see?"

"I have, thank you," James said. "Ben?"

"Good to go," Ben said.

"Okay, I'll run you guys back up to the office and look for your numbers in a couple of weeks," Charlie said. He drove back up, and Ben thanked him for his time, and then Ben and James left.

"What do you think?" James asked Ben as they drove back towards Salt Lake City.

"Bidding war," Ben said. "We'll give them a price for say, three shovels, and three drills, they'll get prices from the other guys, then it's a bidding war."

"It's a fairly large order," James commented.

"Sure is," Ben said. "I'd really like the truck order, pity we don't own Unit Rig, we could put a hell of a package together."

"I would presume that none of the truck companies will commit to a shovel manufacturer," James commented. "This is not like putting a front-end loader and truck package together."

"You're right there," Ben said. "Want to get some lunch?"

"That would be great," James said. "What other customers do you cover?"

"I've got the copper and gold mines in Nevada," Ben replied. "I get to do a lot of driving."

"What else is in Utah?" James asked.

"There's a phosphate property over in Uintah County, there's the usual stone quarries, none of which are big enough for an electric shovel, there are prospects all over, there's copper down in Lisbon Valley that I think will one day lead to a bigger mine. There's more in Nevada than Utah," Ben replied. "So, what do you fancy to eat?"

"What's good in Utah?" James asked.

"Beef, lamb," Ben replied. "I'm not a big lamb fan, but I do like a nice rack of lamb."

"Fine with me," James said. "You pick the place." Ben considered for a minute, then set off with a purpose, making his turns left and right until they came to a restaurant in the centre of the town.

"Lamb's Grill," Ben said. "Been here since about 1919, I think."

"Gentlemen," a hostess said when they entered. "Table for two?"

"That'd be great," Ben said. She led them to a table and offered them menus. James noted that there was no wine list.

"What's the situation with Utah and alcohol?" he asked Ben.

"Can't serve it unless you're a private club, but you can buy a club membership for only a few bucks, but it's still a pain to work around," Ben explained. "For me, it's lunchtime now, so I'm not that bothered, but in the evenings I do like something with my dinner."

"Do you like living here?" James asked.

"All in all, I do," Ben said. "The church influence is strong, but the weather's nice, I like to ski in the winter, it's not too crowded, and I get on fine with my neighbours who are all in the church."

"Gentlemen, sorry to interrupt, I'm Amber and I'll be your server today," a young lady said. "What can I bring you?"

"James," Ben asked.

"I'll try the rack of lamb," he said. "And do you have something like a lemonade?"

"We do," she confirmed. "Sir?"

"The same for me," Ben said. She left and came back quickly with the lemonades, then disappeared again, presumably to place the order with the kitchen.

"Your wife works for the company, too?" Ben asked.

"She does," James confirmed. "Her family used to have a heavy haulage business in Zambia, so she talked to George Whitehead and got a job in traffic. He gave her parts shipments, so she's getting to know what goes where. She was telling me the other day that she's probably got as many hours driving an Oshkosh low loader as a car. We took a trip last weekend and actually drove by the Oshkosh factory. We couldn't go and ask for a tour because it was closed for the holiday."

"I gather that you're going from here to Rock Springs," Ben said.

"We are," James confirmed. "There's a coal mine there that needs a dragline."

"It's a different formation from the Powder River Basin," Ben said. "But there's been coal mining there for years. Rock Springs is on the railroad, but it's a desolate place, not like here."

"Excuse me, gentlemen," Amber said. "Your lamb." She put the plates in front of them, and James was again taken aback at the size of the portions. Amber left them to it, and they attacked the lamb. It was good; it was easy to see why it had a good reputation.

"Do they raise sheep in Utah?" James asked.

"We do," Ben said. "We've got some pretty big flocks, mostly looked after by Basque shepherds who stay with the flocks."

James and Ben ate their lunch, then talked about the mines that Ben called on in Nevada, most of which were cutting back because of the dip in copper prices. Utah had some coal, but most of it came from underground mines, so there was no great market there for James & Brown. James asked Ben if he could put together a list of all the equipment from the various mines, no matter who the manufacturer was. He was looking for patterns in buying, if there were any, and what combinations of machines seemed to be the most popular. Ben agreed to do that and gave him, then and there, a list of the equipment at the Bingham Canyon mine and at two of the Nevada mines. Ben wanted to hear a little about James's experience in Zambia, so James related to him the start-up of the open pit he worked at and what equipment they had there. At two-thirty, Ben suggested that they go to the airport and see if Katrina was done as well.

"Thanks for coming, James," Ben said as he said goodbye. "Will you let the guys in Oak Creek know what I need?"

"I will, as soon as I get back," James promised. James went into the building and saw Bill.

"You set?" Bill asked.

"I am," James replied. "I don't know about Katrina. How long a flight is it to Rock Springs?"

"About forty-five minutes, essentially up and down," Bill said. "I've no idea how long it would take to get there commercially; you'd probably have to go through Denver and backtrack."

"Have you been to Rock Springs before?" James asked.

"Once," Bill said. "It's not exactly a tourist spot. This may be Mrs Martin now." James looked out, and indeed it was Katrina. She came in with Gus.

"Thanks for coming out, Katrina," Gus said.

"If you need anything, call," Katrina said.

"I will, nice to meet you, James, enjoy Rock Springs," Gus said.

"Thanks," James said.

"All set?" Bill asked,

"We can go?" James asked.

"Whenever you're ready," Bill said. "We don't have to wait for anyone."

They walked out to the plane and climbed aboard, and took their seats. Bill went through the safety briefing again, then closed up and went forward to the cockpit.

"This is a short flight," James said to Katrina. "Bill told me forty-five minutes, so I suppose up and back down. How was your day?"

"Fascinating," she said. "But I'm not sure why we have a warehouse here. There's only really the Bingham Canyon mine, and we have nothing there. Where we do have machines is in Nevada."

"Is this the closest big airport and railway station?" James asked.

"It could be," she said. "I'd have to study a map and see where the mines are and where the airports and railways are. Utah is well served with rail, road and air, whereas where I understand the mines to be, there is little in the way of rail or air, so it may be best to site the warehouse here and send everything out by truck. Gus also took me to lunch at a small place not too far from the warehouse. How was your day?"

"We had a tour of the mine and looked at machines, and they told us what they need. Ben doesn't hold out much hope," James replied. "They are going to get larger trucks, which will mean larger shovels, so we'll see."

"I got to see the mine," she said. "Gus took me to a lookout point and we watched the mine for a bit and saw what was going on. It's big, even bigger than Nchanga."

"It's big and going to get bigger," James said. "Okay, I think we're about to take off." They did indeed take off, and they climbed out, then turned to the east and went over the Wasatch Mountains towards Wyoming. They essentially followed the I-80 freeway, past Evanston, then started down to Rock Springs. Bill had been right; it had been an up-and-down flight, that actually only took forty minutes.

On the ground, they were met by a representative of the fixed-based operator who took James and Katrina to a small building where they could wait until their luggage was unloaded. They were joined by Keith Sanders.

"Hey, James, nice to see you again," he said.

"Good afternoon, Keith, this is my wife, Katrina, she works for traffic in Oak Creek and came out to see the parts warehouse in Salt Lake City," James explained.

"Nice to meet you, Katrina," Keith said. They were joined by Bill, who came in with their luggage.

"Do you have an estimate for departure tomorrow, Mr Martin?" Bill asked.

"Keith?" James asked.

"I'd plan for two," Keith replied. "The mine site is about forty miles east of here, and our meeting with them is at ten, so out, visit, back, it'll be well after lunch."

"Do you want us to provide something?" Bill asked.

"Might be best," Keith suggested. "No point in driving right by here to go back to Rock Springs just to get a late lunch."

"Okay, so we'll plan for wheels up at two tomorrow afternoon," Bill said. "We'll be here from one on."

"Thank you," James said.

"You guys got a car?" Keith asked Bill.

"We're set," Bill assured him.

Keith drove James and Katrina into Rock Springs. The terrain looked dry, very like what James had seen in New Mexico. Hills, but not mountains, sage brush, a few antelope here and there, and blue skies. When they actually got to Rock Springs, it struck James as a small town that probably owed its existence to the historical mining of coal for steam locomotives, because the Union Pacific line ran through the town. There were not many hotels or motels in Rock Springs, so they took what was available, the Outlaw Inn. It was an interesting-looking building, and inside was just as interesting, and the hotel boasted a swimming pool, which the staff claimed was the first in Wyoming. Keith suggested that they take their luggage to their room and then meet him in the Open Range Bar.

"Are you going to change?" James asked Katrina.

"I think I might," she said. "I don't need to be clomping around in my safety boots. I think I'll have a quick shower and then we can go down and have a drink." She went off to the bathroom and showered quickly to wash off the grime and dust of the day, then James showered while she dressed. Ready, they went to the bar and found Keith.

"Hey, guys, what can I get you?" he asked.

"What kind of beer do they serve here?" James asked.

"They've got most things, try a Coors, it's from Colorado, so almost a local beer," Keith suggested.

"I will," James said. "Katrina?"

"Same for me," she added.

"So, Katrina, James told me that you used to go hunting in Africa," Keith said. "What did you get?"

"I would go with my dad," she said. "We shot mainly kudu or impala, sometimes an eland, but there's a lot of eating on an eland."

"You never went trophy hunting?" Keith asked.

"No, we went for the pot," she said.

"I think James said you used a Husqvarna nine three," Keith said. "Did you like it?"

"I did," she replied. "I could get consistent groups with it, and it shot well over iron sights."

"You didn't use telescopic sights?" Keith asked.

"No, a lot of bush shooting was snap shooting, so you had to get good with iron sights," she explained.

"Did you bring it with you?" Keith asked.

"No, we sold it before we left Zambia," she replied.

"Pity," Keith said. "Well, if you ever fancy coming out here for deer, let me know. So, James, what did you do today?"

"I went to Bingham Canyon," James replied. "They're looking to go up in truck size, so are looking at bigger shovels."

"And you, Katrina?" Keith asked.

"I spent time with Gus Bergquist, and we talked about parts and shipments, then we took a look at Bingham Canyon from the lookout," she replied.

"Did you want to come with us tomorrow?" Keith asked.

"Only if I won't be in the way," she replied.

"You won't be," he assured her. "We're going to have dinner tonight with Dean Jones, he's the project manager, you can ask him about what kinds of parts he's thinking about keeping on site."

"What are they looking at?" James asked.

"They want us to tell them," Keith said. "We'll take a look at some plans and the site, then you can do your stuff and figure out bucket size and boom length."

"Do you know if the deposit is a simple one?" James asked.

"I think so," Keith said. "But Dean can tell you that. Here he is now. Dean, hi, this is James Martin, one of our application engineers, and this is Katrina Martin, who works with our parts people."

"Hey, guys," Dean said. "You two married?"

"We are," James confirmed.

"You're not from here," Dean said. "Where do you guys come from?"

"We moved here from Zambia recently," James replied.

"Not much coal mining there," Dean commented.

"There's Maamba Collieries, but you're right, that's about it," James said.

"How do they mine?" Dean asked.

"They've got a dragline there," James replied.

"You've been there?" Dean asked.

"We both have," James replied. "I went just to look, and Katrina has been there delivering large equipment; her family used to own a heavy transport business in Zambia, so moved a lot of mining equipment."

"Is Zambia heavy jungle?" Dean asked.

"No, in many ways it looks very similar to here, except a lot more trees," James replied. "There are rolling hills, scrub bush, but no snow or ice. In the Zambezi Valley, the vegetation is more lush. There are issues with access, there's one rail line, and the roads are not always that good. There's limited power, most of which comes from hydro plants."

"So, it has its challenges," Dean said. "Ours are similar, but we do have the benefit of a good railroad line and a good highway and power is not a problem. The winters can be harsh, so operations have to account for that. Getting people is sometimes a challenge; you'll have already seen that Rock Springs is a pretty small town."

"So, what can we get you, Dean?" Keith asked.

"I'll take a Coors," Dean replied. Keith signalled to the waitress and she came and took the order.

"So, Dean, what do you have in the way of coal here?" Keith asked.

"With the current reserves, a mine life of thirty years," Dean said. "But, we're looking at an adjacent property that might extend the life another ten years at least."

"Where will the coal go?" Katrina asked.

"We're putting in a power station right here," Dean said. "Cheaper to ship electrons than railroad cars of coal."

"Is the deposit simple or complex?" James asked.

"Pretty simple," Dean replied. "Single seam of coal overlain with fairly uniform overburden, not much of a dip to the strata. No rivers to contend with, and as far as we can tell, no aquifers that we're going to break into. Say, I'm hungry, should we eat?"

They took a break from coal mine discussions and moved to the dining room, where the same waitress presented them with menus. James noted that it was largely beef, but they did have a pork dish and a chicken dish. He elected to go with chicken, but Katrina stuck with beef. Over dinner, the conversation turned to fishing. Dean was an avid fly fisherman and liked to go into the mountains and try his luck in the mountain lakes and rivers for trout.

"You done much fishing, James?" Dean asked.

"Some," James replied. "Katrina's done more than me."

"What did you fish for?" Dean asked.

"Bream, tiger fish, pike and a few others," she replied. "Mostly with spinners."

"So, no fly fishing?" Dean asked.

"I went a couple of times with my dad to the mountains in the east of Rhodesia," she replied.

"Well, if you ever fancy some good fly fishing, go onto the Arapaho res and try there," Dean suggested. "You'll need to buy a fishing license, but it won't cost you much. The best spots are a hike in, maybe two days, or one really long one, and the terrain's pretty tough, but it's worth it."

"How far are the mountains from here?" James asked.

"About an hour north," Dean said. "But to get your fishing licence, you have to go to Lander, so about 120 miles, say just under two hours."

"Is there much snow there?" James asked.

"In the winter, covered in the stuff, but in the summer, it's a great place, away from people, quiet with great fishing," Dean replied.

"Who do we see tomorrow?" Keith asked, dragging the conversation back to the purpose of the trip.

"Simon Davies, he's the mining engineer," Dean replied. "He's one of your countrymen, James."

"I knew a Simon Davies at college," James said. "I wonder if it's the same one?"

"Excuse me," the waitress said. "Is there anything else I can get you?"

"I'm good," Dean said.

"No, thank you," Katrina said.

"Okay then, I'll just take this whenever you're ready," the waitress said, placing the bill on the table. Keith picked it up and said that he would take care of it.

"So, James, see you tomorrow," Dean said. "Katrina, you coming as well?"

214

"I will," she said. "I'd be interested to know what kinds of spare parts you plan to carry."

"Okay, I'll get Roger Evans, he's the mechanical engineer, to talk to you about that," Dean said. "We're on for ten, right?"

"We'll be there," Keith promised.

"Okay, see you guys tomorrow," Dean said.

"So today it was fishing, not hunting," Katrina commented to James when they went to bed.

"I wonder if they'll ever be one who talks about something completely different?" James said.

"Probably not," she thought. "It's nice being able to travel with you, to see what you do and not to be alone at night."

"It is, isn't it?" he agreed.

"So now we can tell our grandchildren, if we ever have any, that we had it away in a motel in Wyoming," she said.

"Not once, but twice," he said.

"Oh, so you're ready again, are you?" she asked.

"I am," he said. They made love again, tenderly, enjoying every moment of the intimacy, and then dropping off to sleep in each other's arms.

The alarm went off at seven, giving them ample time to shower and dress before breakfast. When they went to the dining room, Keith was already there, making notes about something.

"Sleep well?" he asked.

"We did," James assured him.

"Just setting up your next trip, James," Keith said. "Dan Wells wants you to go with him to a big new operation in Montana; you'd fly into Sheridan, and I'd pick you up there."

"Do you know when?" James asked.

"He's talking week after next," Keith said. "You guys fancy some breakfast?"

"That would be a good idea," James said. "You said yesterday that we may not get lunch until later."

"Those guys all take their own lunches out there," Keith said. "Right now it's just trailers with the temporary offices."

"How long will it be before the mine starts operations?" Katrina asked.

"Well, if they order machines now, delivery starts in say three to six months, then another six months at least to put it all together, then they can start digging, so maybe coal production in two years if they get everything right," Keith replied.

"Where will people live?" James asked.

"You saw that trailer park when we came into town, well, that's probably going to grow a little until people start looking at permanent housing," Keith said. "There'll be a swarm of people while construction is going on, then it'll drop back a bit to just the operations staff."

"When do we need to leave to drive out to the mine?" James asked.

"About nine should be fine," Keith said. "We'll get there in plenty of time. So, you guys should eat, and then we can get going."

The drive out to the mine site retraced some of the route they had taken the day before from the airport into town. Then they continued east until they left the interstate and took a side road, then another smaller side road until they came to some trailers that made up the offices. They were there a few minutes before ten and were offered coffee while they waited for a meeting to end.

"Hey, guys," Dean said. "Come on in."

"James," a voice said.

"Hi, Simon," James said. "I never expected to see you here."

"When did you leave Zambia?" Simon asked.

"Late last year," James replied. "They mothballed my mine and offered me a job working for a real wanker."

"Well, fancy seeing you here," Simon said.

"So, you two do know each other?" Dean asked.

"We do," Simon confirmed. "We were at college together."

"Okay, well, Simon, why don't you walk us through the project and what we have?" Dean said. Simon did just that. He pulled out maps, plans and drawings and talked about the deposit, the coal seam, the overburden, the production levels they were looking for and the issues

216

that they foresaw. James looked at it, and it all looked fairly straightforward.

"Would you like to see the site?" Dean asked. "Simon can run you out there, and Katrina, if you wanted to talk about parts and service, Roger can walk you through all that."

They went their separate ways, James and Keith with Simon and Katrina with Roger.

"So, when did you get married?" Simon asked James.

"Five years ago in Zambia," James replied. "Katrina's family ran a transport business, moving mining equipment and other heavy stuff. She talked herself into a job here with our traffic department, which ships machines and parts. You?"

"Got married in Queensland," Simon said. "The company had a mine there, and they offered me the chance to transfer here and work on this start-up."

"So, you guys were really at college together?" Keith asked.

"We were," James confirmed. "There were thirty-three of us in our class, and we scattered to the four winds when we graduated. I went to Zambia and Simon to Oz, others went to South Africa, Canada, Ghana, Malaysia, Turkey, the Congo and a few other places."

"Nobody stayed in England?" Keith asked.

"A couple did," Simon said. "But opportunities were limited; it was either the National Coal Board, or a few other places, tin, iron ore, or sand and gravel operations. I was never a big fan of underground coal mines, which was most of the Coal Board."

"I didn't fancy them either," James agreed. "Plus the Coal Board always seemed to me to be too bureaucratic, and it was heavily unionised with a militant union, or at least that was my impression."

"Isn't this a big change from Queensland?" Keith asked.

"A lot bloody colder," Simon laughed. "We get some snow in Oz, but it never gets as cold as it does here. Okay, this is where we'd start, the first cut would be right over there."

"It looks pretty bleak," James said. He and Keith looked out over the land, and it was some low hills, grass covered with some sagebrush and a few straggly trees.

"I thought we'd pre-strip some of the hills and leave the dragline with a pretty uniform cutting depth," Simon said. "That way we can cut back on rehandling and just run the thing."

"Makes sense," James agreed. "Do you have an idea of size?"

"You're supposed to tell us that," Simon laughed. "But, don't tell Dean I told you this, my suggestion is a 60 cubic yard bucket on 330 feet of boom."

"I would agree," James said. "Based on those sections you showed us and the production rates you're talking about. We'll confirm that with the proposal we send out to you. What about coal loading?"

"We're going to use bottom dump trailers, 100-ton capacity, with maybe a Cat front end," Simon replied.

"Okay, so we'll size a shovel for that," James said. "Are you planning to blast all this, too?"

"We'll have to," Simon said. "We're thinking of twelve-inch holes loaded with ANFO, pattern to be decided, shoot us something on that if you have anything. I'm sure that you've come across other operations in similar conditions. Let me know what they do."

"I'll do that," James promised.

"How do you like the job?" Simon asked.

"It's been interesting," James said. "I've frozen my arse off watching a shovel for a day at an iron mine near Hibbing, I've looked at a new mine in Arizona, another couple in Kentucky and one in Pennsylvania, and I gather from Keith that it's Montana next."

"So, you get around a bit?" Simon asked.

"I do," James confirmed. "Before we came here, I was at Bingham Canyon, I hadn't appreciated just how big that place is."

"I've not had the chance to go there," Simon said.

"Take a drive one weekend," Keith suggested. "There's a public viewpoint that you can drive up to, it gives you a good overview of the mine."

"I might just do that," Simon thought. "You know, one thing that was really new to me was snow fences."

"Snow fences?" James asked.

"In order to stop the highway drifting over, we put up tall fences upwind of the road, the fences slow the wind down and the snow drops before it gets to the highway," Keith explained. "Between here and Evanston, there are some pretty impressive snow fences."

"You're right," Simon agreed. "The first time I saw them was in the summer, and I wondered what lunatic built part of a fence that tall in the middle of nowhere, then when the snow came, I understood."

"Should we get back to the office?" Keith asked.

"Probably should," Simon agreed. "Have you seen enough, James?"

"I have, thanks," James said.

At the office, Dean offered coffee and then asked when he might expect a proposal.

"We'll have numbers back to you in two weeks," Keith promised. "I'll bring them out myself."

"That'll be fine," Dean said. "We need numbers for draglines, for coal loading shovels and for drills."

"We can do that," Keith replied.

"Katrina's going to talk to the parts folks that you have and get us prices on recommended parts that we should carry, and also tell us what you're going to place at your own warehouses," Dean added. "Roger has his ideas, but we'd like to hear what other folks are doing and what your experience has been."

"Is there anything else you'd like to talk about?" Keith asked.

"No, I think that about covers it," Dean replied. "Thanks for coming out, and we'll look for your proposals."

"Thanks for talking to us," Keith said. "I'll be back in a couple of weeks with all the proposals."

"Okay, see you then," Dean said. That struck James as a polite note of dismissal, so they all left.

"So, what do you think?" Keith asked as they drove back towards the airport.

"The mine seems straightforward enough," James replied. "It's like all of them, send me numbers, then I'll negotiate. Do you know if the other suppliers have been out yet?"

"One has," Keith said. "The Marion guys were here last week. I saw the local guy in Rock Springs."

"Do the personal relationships mean anything?" James asked.

"They can do," Keith said. "When it comes to weighting how the company thinks we'll support them, if they know you, then they're likely to give you more weighting than someone they don't know. How did you do with Roger Evans, Katrina?"

"I think at first he was being very condescending, but I asked him a question or two and he got serious after that," she replied. "I have his list of parts he sees as potential issues. The question for us is, are those parts truly an issue, and if they are, do we carry them in Salt Lake City, or do they carry them here?"

"You'll have to talk to the parts guys about that," Keith said.

"I will," she said. "I'm looking through past shipments now and who they went to, so there must be information somewhere about what fails and when."

"So, what do you think of Wyoming?" Keith asked her.

"I think it would be nice to visit when it's a little warmer," she said. "I'm not sure I could deal with the cold."

"You get used to it," Keith assured her. "I grew up with it, so I'm not sure I could handle heat all the time. Okay, we're here, let's see if Bill and Chuck are ready for you."

They were indeed ready, so James handed over their bags to be stowed, then he and Katrina paid visits to the bathrooms and were ready to go.

"Thanks for coming, James, nice to meet you, Katrina," Keith said. "I'll look for the proposals from Oak Creek in the next week or so."

"I'll follow up with everyone when we get back," James promised.

"Okay, see you week after next in Sheridan," Keith said. "Are you tagging along on that trip, Katrina?"

"I doubt it," she said. "I think the only reason I got to come this time was that James was coming on his own. If there are others going to Montana, I doubt that they'd want me along."

"Probably right," Keith said. "Okay, well, have a good flight."

"Thanks, Keith, I'll see you soon," James said, then he and Katrina walked out to the plane, where Bill was waiting.

"All set?" he asked.

"We are," James confirmed.

"Okay, we'll take off out of here and head east, flight time should be two hours and twenty-nine minutes," Bill said. "We've got lunch. aboard, so as soon as we're up at 39,000, we'll get it served."

"Thank you," James said. Bill went through the safety procedures again and pointed out where everything was. Then he went forward, and they started out. Chuck was doing the flying this time, so Bill had the co-pilot duties. They taxied out onto the runway and took off, to the west, James noted, which meant that they did a long climbing turn to bring them back to an easterly heading. When they were up at altitude, Bill came back and served drinks and lunch. The bar was open, he said, so they could help themselves to whatever was there.

"How did you enjoy your trip?" James asked Katrina when Bill had gone back to the cockpit.

"It was super," she said. "I like this bit, riding in your own plane above all the regular traffic and being able to come and go as you please. The mine visits were interesting, even though there wasn't much to see today."

"Was Roger really condescending?" James asked.

"He was at first," she said. "But then I asked him what he thought the mean time to failure was on the gears. I think he wondered if I knew what that meant, so I put it in other terms for him. After that, he was fine. Thank you for explaining that on the way out here, it really helped a lot."

"What does George expect from you, a trip report?" James asked.

"I would presume to," she said. "I'll give him one anyway, with a copy to Gus, do I need to send a copy to Fred Brock, the parts manager?"

"I'd ask George that," James suggested. "Fancy another drink?"

"Who's driving, you or me?" she asked.

"I'll drive," he volunteered.

"In that case, yes," she said. James poured her another glass of wine, and they sat and looked out of the windows at the world going by.

"Look, there's a plane down below us going the other way," James said, pointing it out.

"I see," she said. "Who is it?"

"I can't tell from here," he said. "It's gone."

"There's another one," she said. "It's going the same way we are, are we going faster?"

"It looks like it," he said. "Very slightly, we'll probably be running parallel for a while." They did indeed fly along on the same general heading, with the now-identified Continental Airlines flight, veering slightly to the south of them, which suggested to James that it was headed to Chicago. Eventually, they lost sight of it and started down on their descent to land at the Milwaukee airport.

"Thank you," James said to Bill and Chuck when they left them to drive home.

"Any time," Bill said. "Drive safely."

"I will," James assured him. The drive home was short, and there was some traffic as the rush hour was now well underway. At the apartment building, they collected their mail, then went upstairs to unpack and think about dinner.

"That was fun," Katrina said. "I'm glad I got to do it at least this once."

"It is the way to travel," he agreed. "But, something tells me that trips in the company plane are going to be few and far between. There must be a lot of demand for them, and I wonder who decides where it goes and who gets to ride on it?"

"I suppose every puts in a request and then someone has to decide. I would guess that in the event of competing requests, the one that has the highest potential for the biggest sale would be the winner," she said.

"That's far too logical," he laughed. "I might just ask Tony how it's managed and who has the ultimate say."

Montana

James briefed Tony on his visits and what he had seen and learned. They created the range diagrams for the draglines in Rock Springs and came up with a bucket size of 60 cubic yards and a boom length of 330 feet, as Simon had suggested. The mine would actually need two machines to get to the production targets that they had set, so Dan Wells would be happy. Then they sized the shovels and drills, and then made the rounds of the three product managers, telling them what the needs of the two mines were. All three were happy, not just Dan, so by the time lunch time came, there was a flurry of activity as papers were gathered, proposals drafted and calculations made of the costs and therefore the prices. James then got himself ready for his next meeting with Hank Miller. He and Bill had gathered information on the dealer network that the company used to sell its construction machinery line. There were successful dealers and some that were just in the doldrums. Whether or not that was a function of the activity in the territory that they covered, or the dealer itself, was a matter for further investigation. It looked to James and Bill as if at least two of the dealers just did not produce the sales that would be expected with the activity in their area. There was enough road construction, building and other works that the demand should be there.

James met Bill at the door to mahogany row, and they went in together. They were kept waiting a few minutes, then were surprised when Hank Miller came out and suggested that they go to lunch.

"So, what can you tell me about our dealers?" he asked as they sat down for lunch in the small room that was used for entertaining customers and other dignitaries. James and Bill looked at one another, and Bill indicated that James should make their report.

"It seems to us that there are a few dealers who are not performing as one would expect," James said. "In their territories, there is activity, but we're not seeing the expected sales. That may be a function of the type of dealer we have. If the customer is a major construction company with, for example, a sewer line contract with a city, then there will almost certainly be penalty clauses for delays, so any issues with the machines will need to be addressed quickly and efficiently. To do that, the dealer needs to be a reasonable size and have the service personnel that may be required. Two of our current dealers fall short in that area. On the other hand, if the customer is essentially a one-man company, then lack of service will not weigh so heavily as the cost of the machine."

"So, it comes down to decision drivers on the part of the customer?" Hank asked.

"That's how we see it," James agreed.

"I see," Hank said. "For those dealers who are not performing, should we find new ones or find a way to help them improve?"

"That may depend on what other dealers of machinery there are in the territory and whether or not they would take us on as a supplier," James thought. "If the other possible dealers already represent another supplier, then what would be their incentive to change?"

"So, do we need to increase levels of service to the dealers?" Hank asked.

"That would depend on what we mean by level of service," James said. "If they want to be able to respond to any breakdown, then they'll need a huge inventory of spare parts, which may not be possible given the inventory they would have to carry and the cost to them, or to us if we place it out with them as consignment inventory."

"So, perhaps we need a mechanism to rapidly fill parts orders?" Hank suggested.

"That may be a solution," James agreed. "We have a choice there, to pull parts from the production of new machines, or to know what the likelihood of part failure is and carry at least enough to cover the time it would take to replenish stocks."

"You've thought about this," Hank commented.

"We've discussed it a lot," James said.

"Have you shared your ideas with Fred Burns yet?" Hank asked.

"No," James admitted. "We're concerned lest he think we're intruding on his bailiwick."

"You may be right," Hank said. "So, tell me, James, you were in Salt Lake City recently. Is that the right place for a parts depot?"

"It may be," James replied. "It has good air, rail and road access and is halfway between the mines of Nevada and those of western Wyoming. My first thought was that it had few customers, but that was because I was only looking at Bingham Canyon, but there are other mines to the east and west, so now I think it's actually not in a bad place."

"What about our dealer in South Africa? What do you know about them?" Hank asked.

"I dealt with our local man in South Africa who also handled Rhodesia and Zambia, but I never had much dealings with our distributor there," James said. "Most of my dealings were with the Caterpillar dealer."

"Should the dealers in places like South Africa handle mining machines as well as construction machines?" Hank asked.

"I think we would be better served keeping our own subsidiary for mining machines," James replied. "It would need to be a really big company to take on mining machines as well as construction machines."

"What's your view, Bill?" Hank asked. "You've been very quiet."

"I confess that a lot of this is new to me," Bill replied. "I've been learning as we've investigated, and I would concur with what James has said."

"Well, I'll be talking to Fred soon, so perhaps your next project is to look at how we use steel plate, are we getting the best yield from the plate we buy?" Hank asked. "I know that's more in your area of expertise, Bill, so I'm looking to you to see if we can improve our usage, cut down on waste and not buy as much plate."

"We'll take a look," Bill said.

"So, how are the MBA classes going?" Hank asked.

"Very well," Bill said. "It's been instructive and we're both keeping up with the assignments."

"Good," Hank said. "We're investing quite a lot in this program, so we're looking for results at some time."

"How was your session with the Bwana Mkubwa?" Katrina asked James that evening.

"Fine, I think," James said. "He keeps us on our toes with different areas to look at each month. It's almost a better program than the MBA."

"Is it unusual?" she asked.

"Very," James said. "If a company does have a development plan for its managers, that usually just means they'll move you around to gain experience in different areas. I've never heard of a company that has mentors like this and where the mentors are so involved."

"Are the other mentors as involved as Miller?" she asked.

"From what I've heard, yes," he replied. "I've heard a few bitches and complaints about having to dig into things, and from a few managers complaining about us investigating their fiefdoms and raising questions."

"So, Kasalia wouldn't have done this?" she asked.

"If they had even put me into the development program, then they'd have given me a couple of assignments at different mines, but I think always in production," he replied. "I doubt that they would have even thought about anything else."

"Why didn't they put you into the program?" she asked.

"I don't know," he admitted. "It may be that they were waiting to see if I would be worth taking on as permanent employee and not on contract, or it just may be that the reviews they sent back to London weren't that impressive, so they'd written me off, or classed me as B stream, as one manager told me once, or I pushed back too much and asked too many questions and wasn't subservient enough, who knows?"

"I can see them being put off when you came back at them," she said. "You do have a tendency to not tolerate mediocrity well and are not shy about pointing it out."

"Am I that bad?" he asked.

"I don't think so," she said. "But I can see others being intimidated and not wanting to have you around."

"So, enough about me, how are you doing? What did George say about your trip?" he asked.

"He listened, then gave me a whole pile of reports and suggested that I start going through them and analysing parts sales, what, where and when," she said. "So, I may have talked myself into a lot of work."

"You should talk to Herb, the programmer that I go to," James suggested. "I'm sure he could write you a program to do all that and then just run it and look at the results."

"Do you think so?" she asked.

"I do," he said. "Why don't I take you to meet Herb, and you can tell him what you need and see what it would take to get it?"

"That would be only *lekker*," she said. "So, it's your turn to cook. Did you have anything planned?"

"I do," he said. "I'll start on it, you pour us a glass of something each, and I'll get busy."

"What else do we have to do?" Katrina asked James as they lay in bed later that night.

"What do you mean?" he asked.

"Well, we got our Green Cards, we got new Wisconsin Driving Licenses, we've got a place to live, and a car, what else? We've signed up with doctors, dentists and opticians?" she asked.

"I suppose save up to buy a house," he said. "I don't really want to rent forever."

"What about credit cards?" she asked. "You've got the company cards for travel, but what about our own? This whole country seems to run on credit cards."

"It does, doesn't it," he agreed. "Maybe go and buy something at a place like Sears and see if they'll give you a card."

"I might try that," she said. "What if I try and buy us a record player and put it on tick?"

"Try it and see," he said. "Get one in your name, then I'll see if I can get added to your account. I'm prepared to bet that they'll want to set it up as my account, with you as an added name."

"We'll see," she said. "I'm going to get one in my name, after all, I've got a job, maybe we should set up separate bank accounts as well as a joint account, then when I try to apply for a credit card, I can pay for things out of my bank account."

"Let's do that," he said. "I'm sure Mr Winter at the bank would be happy to do that."

"Okay," she said. "You pay rent and telephone bills, car insurance and all that stuff, and I'll pay for groceries and other household things."

"Good idea," he said. "We'll need to make sure that we both know what's what, though, so no secrets."

"I agree," she said. "Good, that's done, now what?"

"I'm sure we can think of something," he said.

"Ah, so that's it," she laughed. "What if I said I was too tired?"

"Are you?" he asked. "Have you been doing too much at work?"

"I'm fine," she assured him. "But you didn't answer my question."

"Oh," he said. "Then we'd go to sleep."

"Come here," she said. They cuddled close, and one thing did lead to another, culminating in a round of lovemaking that did leave them both tired and sleepy.

James did introduce Katrina to Herb, and she described what she needed. Herb saw no particular challenge and said that he would have a program written by the next day, then they could run the data that the company already had and see what came out. James met with Dan Wells, Tony and John Williams, and they planned out the strategy for the meeting in Montana. Apparently, they placed a high probability on securing orders for equipment for that mine, so were leaving nothing to chance and taking a whole team. James was given the task of producing range diagrams for a variety of overburden depths and then sizing the machines to fit. They were going to go prepared to recommend a machine size at the meeting. James thought about things and asked Tony if the company would spring for one of the Texas Instruments SR-52 programmable calculators. He was sure that he could write a program for it that would solve for bucket size and boom length, which would then let him work out solutions while they were meeting. Tony liked that idea and told James to buy one and expense it. James asked him if he was sure; the calculator did cost $395, so it was not a cheap item. Tony assured him that it was fine and to go ahead. James bought one and then spent a couple of days learning what it would do, then creating the formulae he wanted to solve for to determine the machine size. He tried a number of cases and both ran his program and did the calculations manually, and came up with the same answers each time, which should not have surprised him, as he had written the equations. One other thing he did was have Herb print out for him diagrams for a range of overburden depths, from as little as 50 feet to as much as 200 feet, every 25 feet, with all the double handling that that would require for deeper overburden. Those diagrams he stuck in a folder and put them in his briefcase, he could then carry them whenever he went out on a sales call.

Katrina went to Sears to buy a record player, and they did indeed ask her if she wanted a credit card. There was a bit of an argument because they wanted her husband to sign things, but she insisted that the card would be hers, that she would pay the bills and that the name on the card would be hers. Sears, probably most of America, was still having a difficult time treating women as equals. When Katrina told James about her experiences, he wondered what they would do with single women or widows. Anyway, she now had a credit card and they now had a record player, so could play the few records they had brought with them from Zambia.

"When are you off to Montana?" Katrina asked James the following Monday.
"Tomorrow morning at seven," he replied. "It's another company jet trip, here to Sheridan and back, all in the same day."
"When will you be back?" she asked.
"At about six, I think," he said. "Tony said something about the flight time out being two hours and forty minutes, but that the return would only be about two hours, so I suppose the winds must make a big difference."

"So, I'll drop you at the airport tomorrow, and I'll come and collect you when you get back," she promised.

"Thanks," he said. "I wonder what the trip will be like with all the bigwigs?"

"I'm sure they'll be fine," she said. "John Williams seems to me to be a really nice man, who's the other one?"

"Dan Wells, he's the one who didn't like me steering a customer away from draglines," he replied.

"Will that happen this time?" she asked.

"Unlikely," he said. "From the little I did hear, this mine seems to be just right for draglines."

"I like that you'll be back the same day," she commented.

"I think that's the real benefit of a company plane," he said. "You can go to the places that are not so easy to get to without having to change planes and stay overnight somewhere. We probably could have done the Salt Lake City and Rock Springs trip in one day, too. How are your parts shipments going?"

"I've got all the backlog cleared, and now we're shipping as soon as we get the orders, if we have the parts," she replied. "The thing I'm working on now is seeing if we can get the parts in stock, but that's a money issue. We can't afford to stock everything, so I've tried to do a better job of finding out what we have where, so we can take parts from one depot and ship to another if we have to."

"You'll be running the parts department next," he laughed.

"I doubt that," she said. "But it's interesting. I'm just the shipping clerk who gets things moved from A to B. Now, I don't feel like cooking tonight, so where shall we go?"

"Let's just go to our Italian place across the road," he suggested. "We can walk, the weather's nice now, it's getting quite warm, and have you noticed how much lighter it's staying in the evenings now?"

"I had noticed that, maybe now it's lighter, we could take a walk in the park after work," she suggested.

"Good idea," he agreed. "So, shall we walk over to the Italian place?"

"I'll see you later tonight," James said to Katrina when she dropped him off at the airport the next morning. He went into the building and paid one last visit to the bathroom before joining the others.

"Gentlemen," Bill said. "We're ready if you are?"

"Let's go," John Williams said. They walked out to the plane, and James hung back while the others boarded. America might be democratic, but there were still hierarchies to be observed, and he was the lowest-ranking member of the quartet. When he boarded, he took the seat indicated by Tony, opposite John Williams, facing aft. Bill came back and ran through the safety briefing, then went forward and started up the engines. They taxied out and had to wait a few minutes for a North Central plane to take off, then they were off and on their way.

"So, who do we see today?" John asked Dan.

"Peter Keene, he's the president of Keene Construction, they're getting into mining now," Dan replied.

"I've met him a couple of times," John said. "I think both times when we were negotiating big sales of equipment for a highway job and a dam job, nice guy."

"Keith will pick us up in Sheridan and drive us out to the site, which is just over the state line in Montana," Dan said. "Keith has been working with Roger Mason, he's the project manager, and Walt Stewart, he's the mining engineer. I expect Peter Keene to meet with us, then he'll probably hand things over to Roger Mason, but we'll see."

"What are they expecting today?" John asked.

"Not really sure," Dan admitted. "But I'd be ready for anything; they may string things out for the next month or so with long negotiations, or Peter Keene may just say how much and strike a deal today."

"Do you have delivery dates?" John asked.

"I got those yesterday afternoon," Dan said. "This is the latest build schedule." He pulled out a big chart that had calendar weeks across the top and a list of machines below with bars across, showing when they were going to be built.

"If we have to, who can we slip to accommodate Keene?" John asked.

"These two," Dan said, pointing to two machines on the list. "We'd get some complaint, but I don't think they're ready for deliveries anyway;

these guys haven't even started on their railroad spur yet, and these guys are still fighting a permit issue."

"We should call them and test the waters; they may welcome a slip in deliveries," John suggested.

"We can do that," Dan agreed.

"Okay, now what did Bill and Chuck put aboard for breakfast?" John asked. "James, why don't you see what there is and hand it out?"

James did as requested and discovered one of the duties of being the low person on the totem pole on the plane, he got to be the server of coffee and breakfast, and he rather fancied that he would be the barman on the return trip. Breakfast was not bad, as good as anyone might get on a commercial flight. James served all the others, then got his own and sat down to eat.

"So, was that your wife who dropped you off?" Dan asked.

"It was," James confirmed.

"Where did you find her? She's a knock out?" Dan asked.

"We met in Zambia," James replied. "Her family had a transport business there; they moved a lot of mining equipment."

"So, how's the MBA program going, James?" John asked.

"Busy," James said. "Working around the travel has been an issue a couple of times, but I'm managing. So far, the classes haven't been that hard."

"How about your sessions with Hank Miller?" Tony asked.

"He's keeping us busy," James said. "We've looked at all kinds of things; this month's project is to look at plate utilisation in the factory."

"So, John, is this development program worth it?" Dan asked.

"We think so," John said. "We'd like a pool of talent available to use wherever we want, and the board thinks it would be better to have guys who have seen a broad view of the company when we're next looking for a CEO. It's a long-term view, but it's already paying off."

"How?" Dan asked.

"You've no idea what's been turned up by having smart guys ask a lot of questions," John replied. "We've all been a little too complacent in our jobs, and different eyes see different things. So, we've put new tools into

Pittsburgh and we're already seeing big drops in scrap and rework, the numbers tell us that those tools will pay for themselves in less than two years."

"Well, before we make changes in draglines, I want someone to talk to me," Dan stated.

"The people making the changes are the managers of those departments," John said. "They see what has been presented and make their own decisions, and until now, we've not had a bum idea."

"Landing in fifteen minutes," Bill announced. They made the last twists and turns and landed in Sheridan and taxied over to the fixed base operator there. James was closest to the door, so exited first, then stood aside and waited for the others. He noted another company jet, this one a little bigger than the Learjet.

Wyoming might not be the Big Sky Country that Montana advertised, but it might as well have been. The skies were clear, cloudless and vivid blue. To the south and west, there were mountains, not snow-capped, but grey in the distance. Keith was there to meet them in his Suburban.

"Hi, John, Dan, Tony, James, good flight?" Keith asked.

"Any flight you walk away from is a good flight," John joked.

"What time do you want wheels up, Mr Williams?" Bill asked.

"I'd plan for three," John replied.

"Fine," Bill said.

"Okay then," John said. "How far to the mine site, Keith?"

"It's only about twenty miles," Keith replied. "It's literally just over the state line." They loaded up into the suburban, John in the front with Keith and the others in the back. Fortunately, the suburban is a huge machine, and even three abreast was not a squash. Keith drove out of the airport but did not take the freeway. He explained that the exit that they would have to take was just the other side of the town and would entail some doubling back, so it was easier to just use the regular roads.

"Peter Keene arrived about an hour ago," Keith told them. "That was his plane parked next to ours. It's a Gulfstream, very fancy."

"Did anyone else come with him?" John asked.

"Three other guys," Keith said. "Don't know who they are, but they looked like accountants to me."

"What do accountants look like?" Tony asked.

"You know, dark suits, serious looking, buttoned down shirts, could also be lawyers, I suppose," Keith said. "Anyway, we'll find out when we get there. Oh, I just heard from the guys in Oak Creek, the Rock Springs project is a go, and they want to negotiate terms, price and delivery. We've been selected, so now need to finish up. Apparently, they called early this morning, while you were on your way here."

"So, what did you say we could slip in the schedule, Dan?" John asked.

"We'll have a take a serious look with manufacturing tomorrow and see what we can do," Dan said.

"It was quick," Keith said. "James and I were only out there the other day, and they made their decision already; that has to be a record. Maybe your pal Simon tipped the balance, James?"

"What do you mean?" Dan asked.

"Seems one of James's classmates is the mining engineer out there," Keith explained.

"What did they finally settle on?" James asked.

"Two 260 draglines, two 512 drills and two 120 shovels," Keith replied. "Nice order, the whole package. They also want to talk to parts about what parts to stock and what parts we'll carry in Salt Lake. The nice thing about that site is that the railroad spur can go in at any time. They want to go to Oak Creek next Monday for negotiations."

"We'll be ready," John said. "Any problems, Dan?"

"No, none," Dan replied. "I'll get with engineering and manufacturing tomorrow and firm up what slots are open."

"The guys in Oak Creek told me that Bob and Bill are already putting things together for the shovels and drills," Keith said. "Okay, we're here."

There were the usual temporary offices, but these were a little larger than the ones James had been in recently in Rock Springs. They all went in and were greeted by a man, who introduced himself as Roger Mason.

"Come in," he said. "We're all in the conference room, coffee anyone?"

"That would be nice," John said.

"John," another man said. "Great to see you again."

"How are you doing, Pete?" John asked, so James assumed that this must be Peter Keene, the owner of the company.

"John and I go way back," Peter explained to Roger. "We used to do deals together until he went off to England. You back now, John?"

"I am," John said. "Happy to be back, England was fine for a while, but I'm happy to be back. Pete, this is Dan Wells, he's the product manager for draglines, these are Tony Whitaker and James Martin, our mining engineers, and this is Keith Sanders, he's our man in Denver."

"Okay," Peter said. "You met Roger, this is Walt Stewart, he's our mining engineer, this is Jeff White, our engineer, Norris Green, my contracts guy, Bob Jensen, my finance guy and William Vincent, my banker. Okay, Roger, tell us what we've got here."

"Well, gents," Roger said. "We've got some 500 million tons of coal in two seams, we're looking to pull 10 million tons a year out of here, overburden depth starts at 50 feet and slowly climbs to 100 feet in about year twenty, parting is only ten feet, so we figure that we'll pull that out with a large backhoe." He went on to describe the deposit, and James busily entered numbers into his calculator and then showed the results to Tony.

"So, what do you think, Tony?" John asked.

Tony launched into an explanation of mining methods and then told them what size machines the company would recommend for the conditions they set. There was a little back and forth between Tony and Walt, mainly about assumptions made for availability and utilisation of the machines. Once they had agreed upon numbers, James reran his formula and gave Tony the results. Walt nodded his agreement, and then Tony, James, and Walt. Jeff and Keith were excused while the others got down to the serious business of talking about how much and when.

"You guys fancy a drive around the site?" Walt asked.

"That'd be great," Tony said. Walt led the way to a large pickup truck that had two rows of seats. He and Jeff got in the front, and the others the back. They drove out through the site, rolling hills that one day would be stripped bare. James wondered if this mine had a reclamation engineer assigned to the project or not, and if the rolling hills would ever have grass upon them again.

"What are your thoughts?" Keith asked Walt.

"You've got the deal if the price is right and the delivery is right," he said. "Pete Keene likes you guys, I guess he's had good experiences in the past with you."

"When does the railroad spur get put in?" Keith asked.

"We've started that already," Jeff said. "We take off from the main line just a little east and north of Sheridan and basically come straight north, as much as the terrain will allow."

"So, by the time we're ready to deliver, you'll have the spur in place?" Keith asked.

"Sure will," Jeff said.

"Say, what was it you guys were working on back there?" Walt asked.

"We've got all the basic calculations programmed onto a TI," Tony explained. "We just have to select the mining method, then plug in numbers."

"Can I get a look when we get back to the office?" Walt asked.

"Sure," Tony said. "We'll show you what we have."

"You seen enough?" Walt asked.

"Thanks," Tony said. "This will be a nice operation once it gets going."

"How many days might you lose a year to snow and ice?" James asked.

"Not many in the pit," Walt said. "The biggest issue will be getting people to work; we may have to plough the roads and sand them. I'm not sure the county has all the resources they'd need to keep them open."

"Will the mine be a big employer?" James asked.

"Big as far as this county goes," Walt confirmed. "Round here it's mostly ranching and some farming."

"You guys ready for lunch?" Jeff asked when they got back to the offices.

236

"Sure are," Tony said.

"Well, dig in," Jeff invited.

"We won't wait for the others?" Tony asked.

"I'd say that they'd already got theirs," Jeff said. "So, we can dig in."

"John Williams said that you and James are mining engineers, where'd you study?" Walt asked.

"I went to Penn State," Tony replied. "And James went to the school of mines in London, you?"

"Colorado," Walt said. "James, you're obviously not from here. Where did you work before?"

"I worked on a copper mine in Zambia," James replied. "I worked for a while underground, then started up a new open pit, but with much smaller equipment than we're talking about here."

"What happened?" Walt asked.

"The price of copper dropped, and the mine was mothballed, and I had the choice of working underground again for someone I didn't really like, or taking an early out on my contract," James explained.

"Looks like you made the smart choice," Walt said.

"I think so," James agreed.

They chatted about the mine, about where everyone planned to live, and it seemed that Sheridan was the favourite as it was only twenty miles away and did boast some amenities. They talked about the shift from major construction projects to mining, and Jeff and Walt both wondered how Peter Keene would deal with a project that had no definite end. Walt wanted to know who else was buying machines and what the backlog looked like, and when they might expect delivery of their machines. Tony and Keith both hedged on that and said that it was up for negotiation. James had seen the master schedule earlier and understood what they meant. There were customers and projects that might be either more flexible than others or less desirable and would thus get delayed. He was sure that there was language in the contract that let that happen. They also chatted about the programs that James had written for the TI calculator and went over the diagrams and logic that led to the equations. Walt wanted a copy, but Tony was hesitant and said that he would look into it and let him know. At two, the door of the conference room opened, and the meeting had apparently ended. Judging by the smiles and handshakes, it had concluded to the satisfaction of all.

"Thanks for coming, John," Peter said. "We'll look for the first carload in six months."

"It will be here," John promised.

"Okay," Peter said. "Come out and go fly fishing with me one day."

"I might just do that," John said. "Thanks for the order, we'll get back to Oak Creek and put the wheels in motion."

"Great, see you all," Peter said. "Excuse me, Walt, Jeff, if you've got a minute."

"Well, that went better than I expected," Dan said as Keith drove them back to the airport. "I didn't really expect them to place an order today."

"I've dealt with Peter before," John said. "If he puts his mind to it, then he'll just do it. I'm glad we brought a sample contract with us. So, now we have to get hold of Amcoal and Kentucky Blue and figure out how to slip them in the schedule to further out. It may cost us a little, but maybe not, if they're both having issues, they may welcome a delay, particularly if we slip the due dates on progress payments. Let me know how you get on with them, Dan."

"I will," Dan promised.

"So, what did we agree to?" Keith asked.

"Two 280 draglines, two 512 drills and two 140 shovels, and they're going to take a look at our biggest backhoe for parting removal," Dan replied. "There may be another dragline up for grabs in the future as well. Peter Keene was talking about a higher production rate, by I guess that hinges on a contract with a power company for a station not yet built."

"Pretty good week," Keith said.

"I'd say," Tony agreed. "Four draglines and the rest, that's a lot, I just hope we can build them in a reasonable time."

"We'll talk to the shop tomorrow morning and go over the master schedule again and see how things stand," John said. "So, James, what do you think?"

"About what?" James asked.

"What did Walt and Jeff have to say?" John asked.

"They both agreed on the machine sizes, but they both wondered if Peter Keene would make the adjustment from large construction contracts that have an end date, to running a mine that may have a projected life, but it's far beyond their normal time lines," James replied.

"Good point," John agreed. "I think Peter will be okay, but he might get bored with the mine; he likes new and different challenges. He's given his own company the contract to put in the railroad spur, and it's well on its way. He's also going to build all the infrastructure himself, no outside contractors at all. So, for the next two to three years, he'll have plenty to think about. So, James, what was it you were working on in the meeting? Where did you get the numbers you showed Tony?"

"I put together the various mining methods that are possible and created equations for each of them, then programmed them into the new calculator we have, then I could put their conditions in and get the answers," James explained.

"You check this out, Tony?" Dan asked.

"I did," Tony confirmed. "We ran a whole set of possibilities in the office, I ran them the way we've done it in the past, and James ran them on his gadget, then we compared results, they were the same, because the equations we're using are the same, it's just a whole lot quicker now. We look at the production figures, which tell us how much they have to expose in a year, which then tells us how much overburden we have to move. We look at the depths and figure out if it's simple casting, or if it's rehandling based on boom length and machine size and so on."

"Why haven't we done this before?" John asked.

"The calculator just came out this year," James replied. "Before, we would have had to run a program on our mainframe."

"We figured this would give us more information in the field," Tony said. "We could come up with a bunch of options and give them to the customer; the only thing we can't do right now is print out a range diagram."

"Will that follow?" John asked.

"I don't think so, at least not for a while," James replied. "TI is talking about a printer, but that would just be for numbers. We can get range diagrams printed for us now in Oak Creek, but they're usually done overnight when the demands on the mainframe are down a bit."

"I suppose the accountants get first dibs," Dan said. "When we get back, are you going to print out the range diagram for this?"

"We are," Tony confirmed. "We'll send a copy out to Keith, who can hand it to Walt. There was a request from Walt to get the programs that we have. Should we give them to them?"

"I don't think so," John said. "He'll probably pass it on to anyone who asks, so I wouldn't."

"Okay," Tony said. "We'll hide behind the company lawyers."

"Okay, guys, we're here," Keith said.

"Gentlemen," Bill said. "If you'd like to use the bathroom before we go, it's inside on the right." James thought that was a good idea, even though the return flight was only two hours.

"Let's get aboard and go home," John said. James waited until the rest had boarded, then took his seat. Bill went through his usual safety briefing, and then they were off. In the air and at a cruising altitude, John instructed James to be barman and hand around what everyone wanted.

"Here's to a nice order," Dan said. "So, are you ready to lose some money, Tony?"

"You're on," Tony replied. He fished in one of the compartments and pulled out some playing cards and dealt ten out to himself and Dan.

"What are you playing?" James asked.

"Gin rummy," Tony explained to James. "Three or four of a kind or runs of three or more of a suit, first one out wins, loser counts pips, and we add up the score. High score loses and pays."

"Did you hear anything else from Jeff and Walt?" John asked.

"Jeff wants to talk to someone about spare parts," James replied. "He also wants information on electricity supply that he should plan for; he's going to be in charge of putting the lines in, and he wants to know what voltage he should get the power company to provide."

"I'll take care of that," Dan said. "Hey, I was collecting those."

"So, what's the name of the game?" Tony asked.

"You're out already?" Dan asked in disgust. "You caught me with 52. Deal again and we'll see about that."

"I gather from Hank that you're doing fine," John commented to James. "I think he's surprised that guys other than accounting understand discounted cash flow analyses."

"We ran a lot of them when we started up the mine in Zambia," James said. "We had to do them all with a manual calculator; this TI would have helped a lot."

"James, get me another, will you?" Tony asked. "I'm on a roll here, taking Dan's money." James did his barman thing, serving drinks all round. He had to admit that even though he had to do all the serving, it was still a far better way to travel than by commercial carrier. To be able to come and go, pretty much at will, was really nice.

"We're starting down now," Bill told them. "We'll be on the ground in twenty minutes." They were twenty minutes to the dot. There were a few minutes spent taxiing, and then they were home. James left first and stood and waited while the others deplaned.

"Okay, so see you all tomorrow," John said. "Good job, everyone."

James walked out and saw Katrina waiting.

"Hi, Lovey," he said as he got into the car. "Have you been waiting long?"

"No," she said. "I called the people here and they gave me an estimated landing time, so I arrived only a couple of minutes ago. Good trip?"

"It was," he said. "We picked up another order for some machines. I didn't expect that. I thought we'd go make our presentation, then there would be a month or two of back and forth, and then, perhaps, there would be an order. But we made our pitch, then Tony and I left the room and left the bigwigs to it and by two they had a deal."

"So, I suppose a celebration is in order?" she suggested.

241

"Let's go and park the car at home, then walk across to the Italian place, then we can walk home," he suggested.

"Oh, trying to get me drunk, are you?" she laughed.

"Not really," he said. "But if we walk over, then we don't have to worry about drinking and driving."

"No, just staggering home," she said. "It's nice that you're back already, the same day that you left, I like that. It's better than being left alone for a night or two."

"I understand," he sympathised. "I'd rather be home with you than out in some motel somewhere."

"Hi folks, you're here again?" Vittoria said as they entered the Italian restaurant.

"We are," James confirmed. "We decided that we were too lazy to cook."

"So, what'll it be tonight?" Vittoria asked. "Chianti and what?"

"Chianti is good," Katrina said. "Perhaps tonight the saltimbocca."

"Good choice, but if I might suggest a change, go with the Sangiovese instead of the Chianti," Vittoria said.

"Okay, we'll try that," Katrina agreed.

"I like her," James said as Vittoria left to place their orders.

"I think she's part of the family," Katrina said. "If you look at her and the older lady that we see sometimes, there's a definite family resemblance."

"So, what did you do today?" he asked.

"I shipped parts off to Australia," she said. "Some by air, which was expensive and a couple of bigger bits by sea."

"Are you still enjoying the job?" he asked.

"I am," she said. "I got to negotiate a contract with a trucking company for routes to the west. George is happy with what I'm doing, even Fred Brock is happy, he liked the report I wrote about my trip to Salt Lake City, and I think he's looking to his managers and salesmen for more information. I gather he's also got a group looking into past sales of parts to see what sold when and where."

"Did you make any enemies with your report?" she asked.

242

"I don't think so," she said. "They had a reporting format already, but had just been lax in following it."

"Here we go, folks," Vittoria said, placing two plates in front of them and two giant glasses of wine. "Enjoy."

"Yesterday was a good day," Tony commented to James the next day. "Things are looking pretty good right now. The Boone Coal guys just placed an order, so did Penny Coal. We're still waiting to hear from the Magnate Coal guys, and the crew from Rock Springs is back again to finalise an agreement."

"Can we build all those machines?" James asked.

"We can build them," Tony confirmed. "The bigger question is, can we build them in the time frame that they're all looking at. The guys who just want shovels and drills are probably okay, but the master schedule for draglines is getting full and open slots are now getting out there."

"I need to go and see Bill about plate cutting," James said.

"Go," Tony said. "There's nothing on our plate that needs handling today."

"Thanks," James said. He left and went and found Bill poring over a copy of the master schedule.

"Hey, James," he said. "This is going to be a bitch, trying to get all these machines out of here. So, any thoughts about plate cutting?"

"I was talking to Katrina and she asked me if we nest parts on a plate," James replied. "Apparently, dressmakers do it all the time to save fabric, and they have a worse problem than we do, because some patterns call for pieces to be cut on a bias; we don't have that problem, the steel is the same in all directions. I was wondering if there isn't a computer program out there that would do that?"

"I had the same thought," Bill said. "If we got a small DEC machine and the right program, we could build up nesting layouts and save plate."

"How much wastage would we have to reduce to pay for the computer?" James asked.

"At the rate we go through plate, about one or two per cent," Bill said. "There's a lot of money in steel plate."

"So, what do we do?" James asked.

"We could just make our report to Hank Miller, or we could try and expense a DEC as a controller for a plate cutter and then use the extra capacity in the computer to do the layouts and nesting," Bill suggested.

"I like that idea," James said. "How do you do that?"

"We need a new controller for one of the plate-cutting machines, so we just buy the DEC as the controller and bootleg the rest," Bill said.

"Have you looked at nesting software?" James asked.

"I have," Bill said. "There isn't much out there. We'd have to get a CAD terminal and just start putting shapes in and spinning them around to get the best fit. The hard part's going to be programming the cutting head, but I can do that."

"What do I need to do?" James asked.

"You could write it up for Miller and do the financials," Bill suggested. "I'll give you some numbers for wastage, DEC cost and a terminal cost."

"I'll do that," James said.

The heat of Summer

A month or two went by, and it got hot. Summer had arrived, and the contrast to the cold and ice of the winter was startling. Katrina took to wandering around the flat in nothing at all, something that James heartily approved of and did likewise. They were both fortunate that the offices were air-conditioned, but James felt sorry for the men who worked in the factory, in the heat of the place, exacerbated in some areas by the furnaces, in others by the welding torches and flame-cutting machines. His trips to the field were uniformly hot, whether it be to North Dakota or Alabama, the only real difference being the humidity that was really high in the south. He now understood what a continental climate was and appreciated just how much large lakes and the seas moderated temperatures. After the flurry of activity and trips in the Spring, his travels had slackened off to perhaps two or three a month, something that both he and Katrina were very glad of. Separation was difficult for them, particularly because they had no family anywhere close. Their house fund was growing slowly, and the two salaries really helped and allowed them to put away an amount each month. The view of the park was now very different, with all the trees in full foliage; in fact, much of what they had been able to see in the winter was now obscured. There was a scare one day when they first heard about a tornado warning. A tornado had formed west of the Milwaukee area and was moving towards the city, but it petered out before it struck anything. There were some thunderstorms, though, and the rain sheeted down, drowning those poor souls who had decided to go into the park and practice golf swings.
"I'm not so keen about these tornadoes," Katrina commented to James.
"Nor me," he agreed. "I thought they ran in a belt across Oklahoma and Kansas, but it seems they can pop up almost anywhere."
"Look at the rain coming down," she said. "It almost reminds me of a good storm in Kitwe."
"Almost," he said. "I still don't think I've ever seen rain as hard as I saw in Zambia."
"I can't get over how hot it is, almost like October at home," she said.

"Yes, but this has been going on for a month now, and they told me at work that it will only start to get nice again in September," he said.

"When do you start back with your classes?" she asked.

"Early September," he said. "You haven't done any sketching lately."

"No, maybe I'll do some now. Are you ready to pose?" she asked.

"Of course," he said. "How would you like me?"

"I'll be kind to you," she said. "Sit on that chair facing me. I'll just get my pad and some pencils." She sketched, and James sat and fidgeted a little, but not enough to create problems. Then she pulled up her chair closer and did a sketch just of his hand, then his face.

"Okay," she said. "I think that's enough for today. What do you think?"

"You're really good," he said. "These are good, you know, have you ever thought about painting?"

"Not really," she said. "Maybe when we buy a house, I'll see if we can set aside a place to paint that I won't have to keep cleaning up."

"If this rain stops, I vote we go for a picnic tomorrow," he said.

"That would be nice, where?" she asked.

"Looking at the map, there's a nice-looking park in Franklin," he said. "Let's try there."

"I wonder if there will be many mosquitoes?" she asked.

"We'll find out," he said. "I did get some repellent the other day for my trip to Alabama, so I'll take it with us."

"What a pretty day," Katrina said the next morning when they got up. "Skies are blue, the rain has gone, it looks like a lovely day."

"Do you remember when we went out for a picnic by Kamfinsa?" he asked.

"That was fun," she said. "Even when it rained. I remember standing in the rain without a stitch on, and I remember that that was when we first made love."

"As I remember, we made love in the rain standing up against the car," he said.

"We did," she confirmed. "It was the third time that day, first me sitting in your lap, second us lying on the towel, and the third in the pouring rain, leaning up against the Land Rover."

246

"Something tells me that that won't really be possible today," he said. "There are just too many people around here."

"I wonder how far you'd have to go to be able to strip off in the woods and not be disturbed?" she pondered.

"I'll bet there are places in Wyoming," he said. "It looked pretty sparsely populated to me."

"That's a long way to go for a roll in the hay," she laughed. "There have to be places a lot closer."

"Maybe I'll discreetly ask around," he suggested.

"Better be really discreet," she said. "Or we'll be at it when someone else shows up. Let's put some lunch together and then drive out to this park and see what that's like."

"I wonder how crowded it'll be?" he said.

"Judging by the park here on a Sunday afternoon, there'll be plenty of people there," she said.

Whitnall Park was not particularly busy, which surprised both James and Katrina, because it truly was a nice park. They found a place to park and then carried their picnic basket and blanket to a secluded spot among the trees.

"This is rather nice," James commented to Katrina.

"It is," she agreed. "But I don't think shenanigans are in order; there aren't that many people about, but there's enough."

"Pity," he said.

"Pity," she agreed. "I'm surprised there aren't more mosquitoes. I thought I saw a lake as we drove in."

"Maybe they've got someone else to bother," he said. "So, when we get our holidays, where do you want to go?"

"I don't know," she said. "It's such a big country, I wouldn't know where to start. I liked the look of Utah when we went to Salt Lake City. I like the idea of hiking in the mountains in Wyoming; we've no idea what the northern part of Wisconsin looks like, except Door County, and there's so much more."

"Did you ever think we'd end up in the States?" he asked.

247

"No," she said. "It was something that never even crossed my mind, all the people I knew that left Zambia, went to England, South Africa or Australia, I don't know anyone that came here. What about you?"

"The US, no," he said. "I was offered jobs in Australia and Canada as well as Zambia, but the US never seemed an option. I'm glad we came. I get the feeling that life here will be what we make it."

"We need to do some clothes shopping before winter," she said. "We survived the last winter, but I think we could do with some warmer clothes."

"I wonder how far south you'd have to go to get away with one set of clothes?" he thought. "I'm sure that in southern California you'd only need summer clothes, no snow boots and hats and gloves there. What do you want for Christmas?"

"That's months away," she protested. "I don't know, I'd have to think about it, or maybe you could just surprise me."

"I'll have to save up and see what I can get," he said.

"What about you? What do you want for Christmas?" she asked.

"You wrapped in a big red ribbon," he replied.

"You've got a one-track mind," she laughed. "I'll see what I can do. Now, should we eat?"

"I'm hungry," he said. "What did we bring?"

"Chicken, some salad, a bottle of Chablis, some apples and a few other things. Why don't you open the wine?" she suggested.

"Should we do that? I saw a sign when we came in that said no alcohol allowed," he asked.

"Pour out what's in that flask and empty the bottle into it, then get rid of the bottle," she suggested. James did that; he opened the bottle and decanted the contents into the flask, then went off and found a bin where he disposed of the bottle.

"Okay?" she asked when he returned.

"Gone," he said. "I found a bin and no people around, and in the bin were quite a few empty beer bottles."

"So, not everyone follows the rules," she commented. "Cheers, eat up."

The picnic was a great success, just lazing in the shade of the trees, enjoying the day and the company. They saw four other people, who walked by with quick waves and went on, intent on their own day.

James commented to Katrina that he suspected that the two couples were looking for secluded spots as well.

"That was fun," James said when they arrived home late afternoon.

"Is there any of that wine left?" Katrina asked.

"There is," he said.

"Pour us each a glass, would you?" she asked. He did, and they toasted one another. "I'm hot," she said, and then proceeded to strip down to only her underwear.

"You've got some new undies," he commented.

"Do you like them?' she said, standing up and pirouetting for him.

"Very nice," he said. "Did you go to that shop again?"

"I did, when you were away last," she said. "I like the idea of basic black, it sends messages."

"It does," he agreed. He reached for her, and she came and sat on his lap. "This bra is a front close, what little there is of it."

"Are you complaining?" she asked.

"No, not at all," he said.

"I think you need to get rid of those clothes too," she said.

"I can't do that with you here," he said. "Could you stand up just for a minute?"

"A minute," she said. "I'm timing you. Well, thirty seconds, I'm not sure if that's a record."

"What about you?" he asked.

"You'll have to work to get my brookies off," she laughed. He picked her up and carried her into the bedroom and put her down on the bed, and then pulled down her pants.

"So, that's the idea, is it?" she asked. "Carry me off and ravish me."

"That sounds like a really good idea," he laughed. "Are you ready to be ravished?"

"I am," she said. "I've been fantasising all afternoon."

"What is your fantasy?" he asked. She told him in lurid detail what she would like, and he was more than happy to oblige. Their lovemaking continued off and on until the sun started to go down. Even for them, it was a marathon session and left them both sated, satisfied, exhausted and deliriously happy.

"James, I'd like you to go out to California and do some time studies on a shovel there," Tony said when James returned to work. "The user is complaining that he's not getting the production he expected."
"Do they have enough trucks?" James asked.
"Don't know," Tony said. "All I know is that the company is telling us that he should get more out of the machine than he is."
"Where is the site?" James asked.
"Fly into San Francisco or San Jose and drive from there, I gather it's about 140 miles," Tony replied. "You'd better find a place to stay for a couple of nights. Spend a whole day out there, record what you see and come back and write it up."
"Like the iron ore mine?" James asked.
"Just like that," Tony agreed. "Only this time take a hat and sun lotion, it'll be hot out there."
"What are they actually doing?" James asked.
"It's a major construction site," Tony explained. "They've got a 118 shovel there."
"Who's the contractor?" James asked.
"Harvey Thomas, your contact is a Jake Romero," Tony replied.
"When do I need to go?" James asked.
"Go out on Wednesday, spend Thursday watching the shovel and come home Friday," Tony said.

"I'm being sent to California," James said to Katrina as they drove home that afternoon. "I leave on Wednesday and come home on Friday."
"No company jet this time?" she asked.
"Sadly, no," he said. "I have to fly into San Francisco and drive from there, Tony told me that the site is about 140 miles from the airport."
"What do you have to do there?" she asked.
"Basically, watch a machine for a whole day, then write up a report that says whether or not they're getting the expected production," he replied.

"Sounds like it will be a long day," she said. "Take a hat with you."

"I will," he said. "Tony told me that it could be hot."

"When's your flight on Wednesday?" she asked.

"I leave here at eight, so if you'd drop me on your way to work, that would be super," he said.

"And what time will you get back?" she asked.

"Four in the afternoon," he said. "I can take a taxi from the airport and start dinner, if you like."

"Good idea," she said. "Where are you going to stay?"

"One night in a place called Sonora and one night by the airport in San Francisco," he said.

"Take care," she said.

"I will," he promised.

James flew to Chicago on Wednesday, then picked up an American Airlines flight to San Francisco. The plane was a McDonnell Douglas DC-10, not quite as large as the Boeing Jumbo jet, but big enough. The route took them over farmlands, more farmlands, then the Rockies, passing over Denver. James was surprised at the pockets of snow that still clung to the north slopes of some of the mountains, but then, as he thought about it, with elevations of about 14,000 feet, that was to be expected. Beyond Denver, the Rockies stretched out quite a long way, and once past them, they flew over the deserts of Utah and Nevada. The contrast between the intense agriculture of the Midwest, east of the Rockies and the wide open spaces of Utah and Nevada, west of the Rockies, was striking, from greens to browns, from town after town to the occasional town. Next, they flew over the Sierra Nevada range of mountains, which James knew from geology classes included active volcanoes. Once over the Sierra range, they started down into the Bay Area and flew over the bay itself. James was fascinated by the ponds in the bay that were fantastic colours, and he realised that he was looking at salt evaporation ponds. Saltwater from the sea in the bay was trapped in ponds and then left to evaporate, leaving the salt behind. The colours were an effect of salinity, as the concentration changed, so did the colour, all due to algae in the water. Once on the ground, James got his car and a map and started out for Sonora. That meant first crossing the bay, which he did on the long San Mateo bridge, just south of the airport. He had not realised until he got to the other side that it was a toll bridge and had to fish out money to pay his way. After that, it was a series of freeways until he reached Manteca, then he was on State Highways. Ahead of him as he headed east were the foothills of the Sierra Nevada Mountains; he crossed the Central Valley, then started to climb slowly and steadily. Before going into Sonora to find his hotel, he first found the construction site and went to talk to them.

"Good afternoon," James greeted a young lady as he went into the site office. "I'm looking for a Jake Romero."

"Jake, some guy's here to see you," she called out. A man appeared from around a corner.

"I'm Jake," he said. "What can I do for you?"

"I'm James Martin from James & Brown," James replied. "I believe you were expecting me."

"I thought you were coming tomorrow?" Jake asked.

"I will be here tomorrow," James said. "I just wanted to find the site and introduce myself."

"Okay, well, let me drive you out there, then tomorrow you can go straight out," Jake suggested. James went with him, and they drove out to the construction site where a shovel was busy loading a truck.

"I figure you could park here and do your thing," Jake suggested. "I'll probably swing by a couple of times in the day. What time will you start?"

"What time do you start?" James asked.

"We run seven to four," Jake said. "Then a smaller shift from four to midnight, you should be able to get enough with the seven to four."

"I'll be here at seven," James said.

"Okay, I'll make sure the guy on the gate knows you're coming," Jake said. "Bring your own lunch and plenty to drink."

"I will," James said.

"Okay, well, come straight out here tomorrow, no need to stop at the office," Jake said. "Here's a hard hat for you, as I said, park over there, you won't be in the way. When you're done in the afternoon, stop by and see me before you leave."

"I will," James said.

James drove to Sonora and found a shop that sold vacuum flasks and bought himself one. He would fill it with coffee the next day. He also found a delicatessen that advertised that it opened at six in the morning. So he could pick up something for lunch as he drove out to the site the next day. His hotel was an older hotel and catered to the many tourists that came to the area for the gold mining history and to go on to the Yosemite National Park. It was hot, in the high nineties, and dry. James wondered if they ever got any appreciable rain there; it looked so dry. He thought about that for a little while, then called Katrina to tell her about his trip.

"So, what's California like?" she asked.

"This bit is hot and dry," he replied. "It's in the foothills of the Sierra Nevada Mountains, site of the gold rush."

"So, 49ers," she said.

"Yes, but reading the stuff in the hotel, the rush actually started in 1848 and reached its peak in 1849, which is why Clementine had a 49er for a father," he said. "It's a really pretty part of the country, the foothills leading to the mountains, lots of pine trees and not many people if you discount the tourists, but also not a lot to keep people employed."

"What about San Francisco?" she asked.

"I didn't go near," he said. "The airport is to the south of the city, and when I drove out here I took a bridge across the bay that is even farther south, so San Francisco will have to wait for another time."

"What are you going to do tomorrow?" she asked.

"Get some breakfast at a small place I saw here that opens at six, then take a packed lunch and go and spend the day at the site," he replied. "When I'm done, I'll drive back into the Bay Area and stay by the airport and catch a morning flight back to Chicago."

"What's the hotel like?" she asked.

"Old and fairly small," he said. "I think most of the other guests are tourists, apparently it's not that far to the Yosemite National Park."

"I've heard of that," she said. "I wonder one day if we should visit?"

"I hear that the US has some amazing parks, so we might want to pick out those we would like to visit. What did you do today?" he asked.

"Thought about you and got distracted at work," she laughed. "I almost sent a part to Australia instead of Brazil, but caught myself in time. Did you think of me?"

"I did," he said. "On the plane, in the car driving over here and just now before I called you."

"I miss you," she said. "It's lonely without you."

"It is," he agreed. "I wish you were here. I'll be home on Friday, as soon as I can get there."

"Have you eaten yet?" she asked.

"No," he said. "I was going to call you first, then eat."

"Love you," she said. "Talk to you tomorrow."

"Love you," he echoed. "Sleep well."

The delicatessen was open at six, and James got himself breakfast and a lunch to take with him, and they also graciously filled his flask for him. Fortified, he drove to the site and was waved in by the man at the gate. He parked where Jake had indicated and sat down to await activity. It seemed they got off to a slow start because the shovel crew did not arrive until seven-fifteen, and the first truck not until seven-forty. After that, there was an intermittent stream of trucks that came and went, with a fair amount of time when the shovel was just sitting waiting. Jake drove by at nine and said good morning, then sped off to some errand somewhere. James made notes, took times and watched. He had some morning coffee, then later lunch and made more notes. He was very glad that he had not only brought a hat, but also his clothes that he used to wear when he worked in Zambia. Standing around in the heat in a suit would have been unbearable. At four, the crew that was on all packed up and left and out of curiosity, James waited until the next shift turned up, which they finally did at four-thirty. He then left and stopped at the office briefly to say goodbye to Jake and promised to have a report for him by the next week. To him, there were a number of issues that Jake might or might not wish to hear. There were not enough trucks to keep the shovel busy, and there was a lot of lost time at the beginning of each shift. As he drove west back to the San Francisco airport, James put aside thoughts about the shovel and wondered if there were any flights that went overnight to Chicago. When he got back to the airport, he dropped off his car and then went and talked to a ticket agent. He could indeed get a flight that night, leaving just after midnight, that would put him into Chicago just after six. That sounded to James like a good idea, so he changed his ticket, cancelled the hotel and then called Katrina.

"I'll be home early," he told her.
"Why, how?" she asked.
"I'm taking a flight late tonight that gets into Chicago just after six," he explained. "The lady at the ticket counter told me that it's called the red eye, I suppose because there's not much chance of sleep."
"So, what time will you get to Milwaukee?" she asked.
"About seven-thirty," he said. "I'll take a taxi to the office, and we can have lunch together."
"Just don't go falling asleep in your soup," she laughed. "I'm so happy you're coming back early, I'll make it worth your while."
"Promises, promises," he laughed.
"So, what are you going to do before your flight?" she asked.
"Find myself something to eat and people watch," he said.
"Just don't fall asleep and miss the plane," she cautioned.
"I'll try not to," he said. "I suppose the flight isn't really long enough to sleep properly, but maybe I'll manage a nap."
"Call me when you get to Chicago," she said.
"It'll be really early," he reminded her.
"Doesn't matter, call anyway," she said.
"I'll do that, love you, sweetie," he said.
"Love you too," she replied.

James wandered around the San Francisco airport and found a place to eat. Then he just wandered the halls, down passageways that led to clusters of gates, back to the main rotunda, and back out to more gates. It was a much larger and busier airport than Milwaukee, and there were many more airlines flying in and out, some of them new to him. PSA and AirCal flew in California only, but there were also Western, Braniff, Hughes Airwest and a few others. There were also international flights, and he watched a Japan Airlines flight leave, bound for Tokyo. In plenty of time, he made his way back to the American Airlines gates and waited there. In time, the flight was boarded and closed up. There was little traffic at the time of night, so the taxi time was short, and then they were off. James had someone sitting next to him, an elderly man who introduced himself as Graham Brant, a banker from Chicago, a name that rang a bell for James for some reason. James introduced himself as an engineer for James & Brown, and Brant noted that he was actually one of the company's external directors and wanted to know what James had been doing in California. James gave him a quick answer in general terms, just saying that he had been there to check on the performance of one of their machines. Brant asked him where he had been previously, and James gave him a quick résumé of his career to date, which sounded very sparse. Satisfied for the moment, Brant excused himself and buried himself under a blanket and drifted off to sleep. James tried to do likewise, but his mind was full of ideas for his report and comments that he was trying to decide whether to make or not. Criticising one's customers has its drawbacks, and James wondered if further orders from the company were likely or not. If there were no further orders forthcoming, then perhaps he could be a little less circumspect and a little more candid. The problem lay with Jake, as far as James could see, he just did not organise his people well, or the workplace, or the maintenance intervals for the trucks, which all led to standing time for the shovel and less-than-expected production. The question was, do you tell your client that he is the problem?

"Excuse me, Sir," a flight attendant said, shaking James by the shoulder. "Would you like coffee or tea before we land?"
"Tea, please," James replied, realising that he must have fallen asleep at some point in the journey.

256

"So, back to the office?" Brant asked.

"I need to go and write up my report on my trip and do the analysis for the customer," James replied.

"Perhaps I'll run into you next week when I'm in Oak Creek for the board meeting," Brant suggested.

"I'm sure you will be too busy," James said.

"Do you have a business card?" Brant asked. James fished in his pockets, then he and Brant exchanged cards. James read on the card he had been given, Graham Brant, Chairman and Chief Executive Officer, North Chicago Bank, the address being on Michigan Avenue in Chicago.

"So, James Martin, Application Engineer," Brant read out. "What next for you?"

"That's rather up to the company," James parried. "The company has a development program that I am a part of."

"That's a good thing," Brant said. "Too many times companies need to make changes and then they cast around for someone competent to do the job, and they discover that they in fact did little to foster any development, so they often have to go outside."

"I have to say that it's been challenging," James commented. "We are given assignments and are expected to report back on anything from dealer networks to process flow in the factories."

"Good, good," Brant said. "Who's your mentor?"

"Hank Miller," James replied.

"Oh," Brant said. "I wondered who Hank would take on, just you or someone else as well?"

"Myself and Bill Evans, he's one of the manufacturing engineers," James replied.

"Good, we've touched down, I like a good touchdown, one that you can walk away from," Brant said. "I was a bomber pilot in the War, and touching down was always a good thing. Good to meet you, James. Perhaps I will see you in Oak Creek?"

"Nice to meet you, Sir," James replied.

The North Central flight was on time, so James landed at seven-thirty in Milwaukee. He saw Katrina there to meet him.

"Hi, lovey," he said. "I didn't expect you to come and meet me."

"I wanted to," she said. "We'll just get your bag, and we can be at the office by eight. Good flight?"

"As the chap next to me said when we landed, we landed and walked away, so it was good," James commented.

"There's your bag, let's go," she said. They walked out to the car and drove to the office, where they parted ways, promising to meet for lunch.

"So, James," Tony said when James walked into the office. "I didn't expect to see you today."

"I took the red eye from San Francisco," James explained. "I've just now landed."

"So, how was the trip?" Tony asked.

"Well, I've got all kinds of numbers, but the problem comes down to one man, Jake Romero, he's the manager, and he's just not doing a good job, but how do I tell him that nicely?" James asked.

"Maybe just write up the numbers and what they tell us, and then send them out to this Romero guy and see if he figures out that he's the problem," Tony suggested. "No need to tell him that he's an idiot, even if he is."

"I'll do that, and I'll show you the cover letter before I send it out," James said. "Do we do much business with Harvey Thomas?"

"Once in a blue moon," Tony said. "They're a big construction contractor, jobs like highways, bridges, dams, so once in a while they need a big machine, so they buy a shovel or a small dragline. You don't have to sugarcoat the numbers, but let's just send a transmittal letter that says, here are the numbers, and suggest things like truck maintenance times that better fit with an overall schedule, talk a bit about the work area and how our experience has been that if you organise it like this, you'll get better results and so on."

"I met one of the outside directors on the plane," James said.

"Which one?" Tony asked.

"Graham Brant," James replied.

"Right, he's the banker," Tony said. "I've never met him, but he's supposed to be one of the sharper ones."

"What do you mean?" James asked.

"You get to be a director based on who you know," Tony said. "Sometimes that doesn't mean that you're that bright, just that you play golf with the right guy. You put me on your board and I'll put you on our board, we'll both collect our director's fees and be happy."

"Is it that bad?" James asked.

"Not all the time," Tony said. "But more often than you'd think."

"I should get these numbers done before I forget what I was looking at," James said.

"How does this sound?" James asked, giving Tony a draft cover letter just before lunch.

"Let me look at it and I'll tell you what I think later this afternoon," Tony suggested.

"I'm going to lunch now. Is there anything that needs doing right away?" James asked.

"No, go," Tony said. "I'm meeting with Dan for lunch."

James went and found Katrina in the company cafeteria, and they got their lunches and sat down in a corner.

"How was your morning?" he asked.

"Busy," she said. "Yours?"

"I tried to write a tactful letter," James said. "I gave it to Tony to review. How do you tell a chap that the problems he's having are largely of his own making?"

"Tactfully, as you said," she laughed. "That must be hard for you. When it comes to work, you've never been one to shy away from telling things as they are."

"I know," he said. "I think sometimes to my own detriment."

"How are you feeling?" she asked.

"I'm drooping a bit," he admitted. "Somehow I don't think I'll be out of my bed long tonight."

"Well, I'm sure we can do something to make you relax and sleep well," she promised.

"Could you get off a little earlier today?" he asked.

"I'll talk to George," she said. "If I can, I'll call you and let you know."

"Thanks," he said. "I don't know that I'll stay that awake and alert until five. I have to say I'm not that keen on these red-eye flights. You get there quickly enough, but you're hardly all there the next day."

"Well, I for one am happy that you came back early," she said. "We'll go home, get an early dinner, then go to bed early."

"This letter looks fine," Tony said when James went back to the office after lunch. "Let's read it through again on Monday, then send it out, copy to Bob and to Martin Brooks in California."

"I'll do that," James said. "Any objections if I leave a little early?"

"No, go home whenever you're ready," Tony said. The telephone rang and Tony answered it, then gave it to James.

"Hi, honey," Katrina said. "Why don't we leave at three? I talked to George and he's happy for me to go off early."

"That would be super," he said. "I'll see you by the car at three."

"Okay," Tony said. "Now, the week after next, I'd like you to go to Colorado, there's an outfit looking to start up a mine near Craig. Fly into Hayden on Rocky Mountain Airways, and Keith will meet you at the airport."

"When should I leave?" James asked.

"Go out on Tuesday and come back Thursday," Tony suggested.

"What are they looking for?" James asked.

"Keith said draglines," Tony replied. "Take a look and tell us what you think. Don't worry about Dan; if the best solution is shovels, then that's what it is. I'm off to Brazil next week, so you'll have to hold the fort."

"I'll try and manage," James said.

"You'll do just fine," Tony assured him.

James met Katrina by the car and they drove home, stopping at Kohl's on the way to do some grocery shopping. Once in their flat, apartment, as James was trying to remind himself regularly, Katrina shed clothes as it was a stifling afternoon.

"It's going to rain," she predicted. "Look at the sky over there, it's black, looks horrible."

"It doesn't look happy, does it?" he agreed.

"So, glass of wine?" she asked.

"Please," he said. "I'm waking up again now."

"So, I went to see the gynaecologist," she said. "And, she asked me how long I had been on the pill. I told her six years now. She wanted to talk about the long-term effects of being on the pill and asked me if we had considered anything else. I told her that we hadn't, but were open to suggestions."

"What other options do we have?" he asked.

"Well, there's the classics, there's effies, IUDs, interruption, tubes tied and vasectomies," she replied. "Going through all the options and the risks, the effectiveness and long-term health issues, the safest bet is for you to have a vasectomy, which brings up the issue of children, do we want any?"

"My views haven't changed," he said. "I still don't have any real desire for kids, you?"

"I don't either," she said. "The gyney suggested a urology chap who would do the vasectomy. We'd have to go and see him and probably talk about whether or not we both want this, then the procedure itself, then what happens afterwards."

"We should do that, what do I do, call and make an appointment?" he asked.

"That's what she said," Katrina confirmed. "I thought after work on Monday, would that be fine?"

"What's the chap's name?" James asked. Katrina handed him a card, and James called the number, and the office was still open, so he made an appointment for them both to go and talk to the urologist on Monday.

"Good, that's done," she said. "Look, it's starting to rain; it looks as if it's coming down in buckets over there, and it's moving this way. Let me fix something for dinner, then we can eat and watch the rain."

The thunderstorm was impressive, and they even lost power for a while, but it was restored within the hour, so it was no great inconvenience. James started to really droop, so Katrina took them both off for a bath and bed, then they made love. That put James out, and he slept.

"So, are we ready?" Katrina asked James when they left work on Monday.

"Ready," he said. They drove to the doctor's office and were only kept waiting a short while until they were called into his office.

"Afternoon," Doctor Hawks said. "I gather you're here to talk about a vasectomy?"

"We are," James confirmed.

"Have you talked about this, about children?" the doctor asked.

"We have," they both replied.

"You understand that there is only a minimal chance that the procedure can be reversed?" the doctor asked.

"We do," James said. The doctor then discussed at length the process, the risks, the after-effects, what James might experience, and what to look out for in case there were complications.

"Does that still sound reasonable?" the doctor asked.

"It does," James replied.

"When were you thinking of having it done?" the doctor asked.

"I was wondering if Friday after work would be possible?" James asked.

"I can do that," the doctor said. "If you're here at five-thirty, then you'll be out of here by six-thirty at the latest."

"What do I need to do post the operation? How long before we can engage in sexual activities again, and when do I need to come back for a follow-up?" James asked.

"Here is some literature that describes the procedure, what you need to do afterwards and what you might experience," the doctor said. "Basically, rest for a couple of days, use an ice pack, no exertion for a week to ten days, no sex for ten days, if there are no complications, come back in three months for a follow-up, by which time you should have had at least twenty ejaculations to clean out the system. When you come back, we'll need a fresh sperm sample, less than two hours old. Make sure that during the next three months, you use a birth control method. After your test comes back negative, you can stop what you're using now."

"That sounds straightforward enough," James commented. "Are there any issues with flying soon after the procedure?"

"When?" the doctor asked.

"The Tuesday after," James replied.

"If there are no complications, that should be fine," the doctor said. "Any of the complications listed here, call and definitely don't fly. Have you any other questions?"

"No, I think you've answered them all," James said.

"Fine, then we'll see you on Friday," the doctor said. "If for some reason you change your mind between now and then, call us as soon as you can."

"We will," Katrina assured him. "Thank you for your time, Doctor. We'll see you on Friday."

"That was straightforward enough," James commented to Katrina as they drove home.

"You're sure about this?" she asked.

"I am," he confirmed. "We, neither of us, want children. You staying on the pill has its risks, and I don't really fancy all the other possibilities, so this is the best and safest option. Once I've had the snip, then after three months you can go off the pill and we still won't have to worry about being spontaneous."

"I like this," she said. "I'm glad we talked about it, and I'm happy that you're happy with it. So, no sex for ten days, how will you survive?"

"I'll manage," he laughed. "A couple of those days I'll be in Colorado, so it won't be that long, and I can chase you around the kitchen."

"I nearly laughed when he said twenty times," she said. "By my count, it was five times just over this last weekend."

"It was?" he asked.

"It was," she confirmed. "Friday night, Saturday morning, Saturday night, Sunday lunchtime and Sunday night," she enumerated. "If people knew, they would say that we're at it all the time."

"Is it too much?' he asked.

"No, I love it," she said. "So, did you get your letter sent off, the tactful one?"

"I did," he said. "We made a couple of minor changes, nothing much really, then I added the analysis of the times, we left him to draw his own conclusions."

"Will he be happy?" she asked.

"I doubt it," James said. "No one likes to hear that they're making a mess of things, no matter how nicely it's put. Whether or not he does anything differently is up to him."

Friday, the big day, came, and Katrina drove James to the doctor's office. She sat in the waiting room until he came out, with a prescription that needed filling for pain medicines. They stopped at their local pharmacy on the way home and collected the pills and an ice pack. James was very glad of the pills on Friday night, but by Saturday night the discomfort was wearing off, and by Sunday he no longer needed any medicines. As far as he could tell, things had gone well and there were no complications, so there was no need to postpone his trip.

Katrina dropped him at the airport on her way to work, and he caught the North Central flight to Chicago, then a Continental flight to Denver. The plane was a DC-10 and was very plush, at least in First Class. James had a window seat as he liked to see what they were flying over, and what he saw were farmlands and more farmlands.

"May I get you breakfast, Sir?" a flight attendant asked.

"Thank you," James said.

"I like Continental," the lady said who was seated next to him. "They do a good job. Where are you from? You're not from Chicago?"

"From England by way of Central Africa," he replied.

"Ah, I thought I detected an accent," she said. "I can always pick out a fellow Brit."

"I always thought that it was others who had the accents," James joked.

"Perhaps when you're in England, that's true," she said. "But here, we're the ones with an accent, so what do you do, Mister?" She left the question hanging, giving him the opportunity to name himself.

"James Martin, I work for a construction and mining machinery company," James replied. "And you?"

"Jane Logan, I edit a fashion magazine," she replied.

"What, something like Vogue?" he asked.

"Very like," Jane confirmed. "I edit FemStyle."

"I've seen it on the shelves," James said.

"Ah, but have you read it?" she asked.

"I confess not," he said. "My wife has her ideas about fashion, and I have to say that I like her choices and her sense of style."

"Is your wife English too?" she asked.

"No, she's from South Africa, raised in Zambia," James replied. "When we lived in Zambia, there were few opportunities to get dressed up; most of the time we dressed for work or for the bush."

"So you spent a lot of time in the bush?" she asked.

"As much as we could," he replied.

"We're going to do a feature on African safaris and what to wear, any advice?" she asked.

"For the bush itself, clothes should be neutral, lightweight fabrics, cotton is good, I would keep the accessories to a minimum, so no fancy dangling earrings or flashy belts, for dinner in the evening, anything goes, largely driven by luggage allowances on the airlines and charters. Small charter planes tend to have fairly limited space and weight restrictions, so pack light, unless your safari starts at a major airport like Nairobi or Lusaka. Most camps and lodges have laundry services, so clothes should be easily washable."

"What did your wife wear when you went out on safari?" Jane asked.

"Katrina would typically wear shorts and a shirt, light boots, a hat and sunglasses, for the mornings, a light jacket as well, it can get cold overnight in the winter months," he replied.

"Did you go on organised safaris?" Jane asked.

"No, we drove ourselves and camped," he said. "Katrina was quite at home in the bush."

"You weren't afraid of being out in the bush on your own camping?" Jane asked.

"No," he said. "I had faith in Katrina, and we did take a gun, not that we ever had to use it."

"What about cameras and binoculars?" Jane asked.

"We have both, and I think take the best you can afford, for many people they will only go once, so make it something to remember," he said.

"Do you have a trip that you really remember?" she asked.

"We took a trip across the Zambezi once to Botswana," he replied, smiling. "That was definitely a trip to remember."

"Romantic was it?" she asked.

"It was," he said, colouring a little.

"Where would you recommend?" she asked.

"I think it would depend on the experience you want," he said. "If you just want to see tons of animals, then Kenya or Tanzania would be good, for a little different experience, then Zambia or Botswana, for a budget trip, then the South African national parks, like Kruger, are hard to beat."

"If I wanted more information, could I call you?" she asked.

"Of course," he said. "Here's my card, and here's Katrina's. She might be better able to answer questions about what to wear."

"Here's my card, and here's the latest copy of FemStyle," Jane said. "I'll call you one day with a quiz to see if you actually opened it."

"Do you live in Chicago?" he asked.

"No, Los Angeles," she said. "It's either there or New York, and I prefer warm to cold."

"We moved to Wisconsin in the winter," he said. "I had no idea it could get so cold."

"Any regrets?" she asked.

"None," he said. "We've only been here since February, and it's all been so new and different."

"And, where are you off to now?" she asked.

"Craig, Colorado," he said. "I have to look at a prospective coal mine there."

"My trips to Colorado are mostly to the ski resorts," she said. "Do you ski?"

"We tried cross-country skiing this winter just for something to do while the ground is covered in snow," he said. "Downhill skiing, never."

"If you ever come to LA, call me," she said. "I'll treat you to lunch."

"Thank you," he said. "I don't seem to get to the normal places; I get sent to the hinterlands, so when I'll get to LA, I've no idea."

"No matter," she said. "When you know you're going to come out, call me and if I'm in town, I'll treat you to lunch, or dinner, or even breakfast."

"If you could put up your tray tables, we're almost on the ground," the flight attendant said, interrupting their conversation.

On the ground, James said his goodbyes to Jane Logan and went off to find Rocky Mountain Airways. They were located in a different part of the airport, used by the smaller commuter lines. James looked out and saw a small propeller aircraft and watched the pilot and copilot load the bags. Once boarded, he was interested to learn from the safety briefing that if anyone had trouble breathing, then there were oxygen lines that could be pulled up and used. They took off and spiralled up to cross over a pass and then spiralled back down into a small town, where they stopped for about ten minutes before repeating the process again into Hayden. Keith was there to meet him, and after stowing his bag, they drove off to Craig.

"Who do we see here?" James asked.

"Tim Sullivan, he's the owner of Colorado Carbon," Keith said. "He's got a lease on a chunk of property south of here that he wants to mine."

"And he's got the funding to do it?" James asked.

"Filthy rich," Keith said. "Made his money in car dealerships, now he wants to branch out."

"Anyone else?" James asked.

"Yeah, a guy by the name of Bob Yellan he's the project manager and Pete Baird he's the mining engineer; they seem to know what they're about. We'll find out tomorrow. We're having dinner with Sullivan tonight in Steamboat, about forty miles east of here."

"Why so far?" James asked.

"He's got a lodge there," Keith said. "I've been there before, massive place, reeks of money, place where the rich and famous hang out. We're invited to dinner, so probably should wear a tie."

"How did you meet Sullivan?" James asked.

"Peter Keene made the introduction," Keith explained. "Seems that Sullivan and Keene go way back, so Sullivan called Keene and asked him where he should start."

"Why doesn't Sullivan just contract with Keene to run the mine for him?" James asked.

"Good question," Keith said. "Maybe we'll ask him tonight."

Keith was right, the lodge was indeed huge, it was built of logs and had a very rustic feel about it, but rustic tempered with luxury. There were rooms to rent, and James picked up a brochure and was shocked by the prices; he and Katrina would not be staying there anytime in the near future, if ever. There was a large dining room with windows that ran high up to the vaulted roof, giving an amazing view of the mountains. Keith gave their names to the maître d'hôtel, who led them to a table set upon a dais at the back of the restaurant. The dais raised the table up so that they could look over the heads of other diners and see the mountains clearly. They were seated, and after the maître d'hôtel had left, they looked around at the room, the view and the people.

"This chap Sullivan owns this place?" James asked Keith.

"He does," Keith confirmed. "And a ski resort and a couple of hotels in Aspen, a car dealership, a hardware store, two restaurants in Denver and an air charter business, guy's loaded."

"Why does he want to get into mining?" James asked.

"It's the latest thing that's hot," Keith commented wryly. "If it's hot, then Sullivan wants to be in on it. Here he comes now."

"Keith," Sullivan said. "Great to see you again."

"Tim, this is James Martin, he's one of our mining engineers and helps us with applications and machine sizing and selection," Keith said.

"James, good to meet you," Tim said.

"Nice to meet you, Mr Sullivan," James replied.

"Name's Tim," Sullivan said. "So, you been to Colorado before?"

"No, this is my first visit," James replied.

"Love your accent, you from Australia?" Tim asked.

"No, from England by way of Central Africa," James replied.

"Oh, was it there that you did your mining?" Tim asked.

"It was," James confirmed. "I worked for a copper mining company, I spent time underground and started up a new surface mine."

"Where?" Tim asked.

"In Zambia," James replied.

"I'm looking at picking up a safari lodge in Kenya, should I look at Zambia?" Tim asked.

"The customer experience would be different," James replied. "In Kenya, there's probably more chance to see large numbers of animals, because the Serengeti is more open; in Zambia, the Kafue and Luangwa parks have more brush and trees, so you have to go looking."

"Maybe I'll pick up the Kenya place then check out Zambia," Tim said.

"If you do that, then also take a look at Botswana," James suggested. "They don't have much yet that's developed, but the game there is amazing, particularly around the Okavango Delta."

"I'll remember that," Tim said. "So, coal mining, is it hard, does it pay, will it last?"

"If you have a contract to supply a power station, then it will last," James said. "Electricity demand is not going to go down. It pays if your operating costs are about a third of your sell price; other money has to go to royalties, financing costs and overheads. Is it hard? Well, it can be, but if you plan properly, it can be managed easily enough."

"Why did you leave Zambia?" Tim asked.

"Copper is sold on the commodity markets, not on long-term supply contracts," James replied. "The market prices dropped, so the company cut back and mothballed the mine I ran. They gave me two choices: work for a chap I really didn't like, or get paid out of my contract early. I took the money option."

"And now you're here," Tim said. "Well, I've got a supply contract to deliver two million tons a year for thirty years to a small power station. I've also got an option on another two million tons, so I guess I'm in business. How do we keep operating costs down?"

"You pick the right mining method, you manage the equipment you have well and maintain things properly so that your availability is high, you organise the work so there's not a lot of standing time," James suggested. "Or, you could contract someone to do it for you."

"I could," Tim agreed. "But, I don't like sharing the profits."

"That's a matter of negotiation," James commented.

"You want the job?" Tim joked. "You'll meet Yellan tomorrow. Tell me if he can do the job. So, what do you guys want to eat? Henri, bring us some menus."

It looked like it would be a long evening, so James excused himself and quickly called Katrina to tell her that he was still out to dinner and did not expect to be back at his hotel until very late. It was indeed a late evening, and the night was short as they were up at seven the next morning for meetings with Yellan and Baird. The project was actually fairly straight forward and they left just after lunch to drive back to Denver. Their route back to Denver took them almost four hours, driving through the mountains, then down the long slope into Denver itself. Keith dropped James at his hotel and left to go home. The Brown Palace was a fixture in Denver and had a rich history, but James was more interested in calling Katrina, then eating and sleeping before his return flight the next day.

"Good trip?" Katrina asked when she collected him from the airport the next day.

"I think so," he said. "I'm not sure why Keith wanted me to go; it was simple enough."

"Maybe the people at the mine just needed to hear things from someone not in direct sales?" she suggested. "I got a call from that lady you told me about, the editor of FemStyle."

"Were you able to help her?" he asked.

"I'm not sure," she said. "I told her what I would wear, what I took along that I never used, and what I wished I had taken. She asked if she could send me some pictures to comment on, and she even offered to pay me a consulting fee."

"That was nice of her," James said. "You know, we should take a holiday to the west one day, Colorado is spectacular, mountains everywhere, and big ones at that."

"We should make a list," she said. "I'm almost afraid that the list will be so long we'll never be able to see everything on it. The US is so big and so different, it would be hard to see it all."

Autumn, or is it Fall?

Life settled into more of a routine. James and Katrina were getting used to the United States and the differences. They learned that as far as cars, automobiles, were concerned, boots were trunks, bonnets were hoods, punctures were flats and in other usage that rubbers were not things used to erase pencil marks, but to prevent pregnancy, that had been a red-faced moment for James, but it had been handled with humour by Marlys, who had come across the same situation before. The United States and Britain might both speak English, but there were differences that at times could be embarrassing. The weather started to cool down, and the days drew in, and they saw the trees in the park start to turn, from green to red, yellow, and even brown. James was back at the college in the evenings, and he and Bill were also working on the next project for Hank Miller, this time, inventory management. That meant working with accountants and manufacturing people to understand the niceties of raw materials, work in progress and finished goods. Bill showed James how work orders on the shop floor accumulated labour hours, which added direct costs, that, coupled with the original cost of the raw material, and the overhead numbers for each shop, gave value to the parts. It took a while for James to understand where the overhead numbers came from, but with the help of one of the accountants, he grasped the niceties of it all. Katrina was asked if she would move to the Parts Department, and George encouraged her to go. It would be a step up for her, and she had already shown herself to be quite capable of doing the job. She kept track of what parts they had in stock, and fulfilled orders as they came in, then ordered the replacement either from an outside supplier or from the factory. The only drawback was that the Parts Department was located in its own building, some two miles from the main offices. That meant fewer shared lunches and, at times, complicated trips to the airport.

The demand for James's time slackened off a little, almost as though the mining companies had decided that they had started enough projects for the year and would now wait until 1976 to start looking at more. That was not quite true, but there had been a definite slowing down of enquiries, not that that affected the backlog and the production schedule at all. In the manufacturing arm of the company, it was still full steam ahead. Bill had contributed to improvements by acquiring a DEC computer and tying it to one of the flame cutting machines, but also to a CAD terminal. He had improved plate usage by over five percentage points, which paid for the new equipment in three months, and when shown the numbers, the manufacturing manager had ordered more equipment and instituted nesting programs across all the plate cutting. Hank Miller was pleased with the improvements in plate usage and the reduction in spending. He had also taken to discussing the quarterly and annual reports with James and Bill, pointing out what was disclosed, what could be inferred and what was omitted from them. He asked them to study the annual reports of their competitors and to tell him what might be learned from them. That, James discovered, was fascinating, to read what was said and to delve into the numbers and form an opinion as to the health of the company. He had had some classes at university that covered finance and accounting, but they had not gone into the depth of analysis that Hank was looking for. James was still surprised at the lengths the company was going to to develop people. It seemed so unusual and at times hard to believe.

The reason for the study of annual reports became clear when Hank Miller told James and Bill that at the next board meeting, he wanted them to give a presentation on the competitors. The presentation should be about an hour in length, and they should be ready for questions. Hank also wanted to see the presentation before they gave it; he wanted no surprises. That put James and Bill into mild panics; the presentation would take some time to put together, and they still had their regular jobs to do. They had a couple of months to put everything together and be ready to present at the next meeting to be held in mid-November, so they sat down together and drew up a plan of action and divided up the tasks. One of the first things they had to decide on was who the competitors were. For mining equipment, it was fairly straightforward, but should they also include the British, French, German, Japanese and Russians? For the construction equipment, the field was much wider with a plethora of companies from large to small. The first thing James did was look for issues of trade magazines that dealt with the market as a whole and who the players were, at least according to the journals. He sorted through all the bits of information that he gathered and came up with a list of major competitors that they would examine thoroughly and minor competitors that would get a much more cursory review. He and Bill did wonder if the company might be looking at acquiring one or more of their competitors to enhance their position in the market, but they dismissed that idea, arguing that if the company was looking to acquire, then surely they would engage one of the big firms that dealt with mergers and acquisitions, not rely upon the analysis of two people from within the company who could hardly be described as experts.

James took some of his work home and talked about it with Katrina. She volunteered to help him, and they went through the annual reports of several companies together.

"This is interesting," she commented. "I never saw much like this in Zambia; company reports there were skimpy at best."

"I think there's a lot more disclosure in the US than in most countries," he said. "I'm tempted to go back and get old Kasalia annual reports and see what they say about things and how they portray the cutbacks."

"Where do you get all this stuff?" she asked.

"It's public information," he said. "Because all these companies are on the stock market, they have to disclose results for investors and possible future investors. Anyway, enough of this for now. How are you doing?"

"I'm enjoying my new job," she said. "It keeps me busy, I've got maps on the wall of the office with the depots marked and all the mines marked, Herb runs analyses for me and keeps things up to date."

"Have you noticed that the days are getting shorter?" he asked.

"I suppose winter is coming," she said. "We should take a look at our winter clothes and see that we have enough."

"I wonder when the first frost will come. I'd better get a new scraper for the car and some new washer fluid that has the de-icing stuff in it?" he said.

"One of the girls at work told me that the first frost is usually around the middle of October," Katrina said.

"When you think about it, it warms up and cools down really quickly; it goes from cold and ice in April to sweltering in May and June, then I suppose it will go from hot to cold just as quickly now," he said.

"That's true, but think about it, in Zambia it can go from freezing to eighty degrees from six in the morning to ten," she reminded him.

"Let's go out and eat," he suggested.

"Where to?" she asked.

"It's Friday, so fish fry at the Packing House?" he suggested.

"I'll get my coat, you know, I just thought about that, it is cooling down, a week or so ago I wouldn't have even thought about a coat," she said.

The Packing House was busy, but they were able to be seated and ordered beer and the fish fry. James looked around and saw John Williams come in. James was surprised to see him; he had imagined that John would live and dine in a more affluent neighbourhood. John waved and came over to say hello.

"James, Katrina, allow me to introduce my wife, Roberta, Bobby, these young people moved here from Zambia," he said.

"Nice to meet you, Mrs Williams," James said. "Have you eaten?"

"Not yet," John said.

"Would you like to join us?" Katrina asked.

"That would be lovely," Roberta said. The waitress came scurrying back and brought more menus and then hovered.

"What do you suggest?" Roberta asked.

"We come here for the Friday fish fry," Katrina replied.

"That sounds good," Roberta said. "We'll take the fish and two beers, please."

"It'll be right out," the waitress promised.

"What did you do in Zambia?" Roberta asked.

"James worked for one of the mines, and I worked in the family transport business," Katrina replied.

"And how have you found living here?" Roberta asked.

"It's been different," Katrina said. "We had to adapt to the winter, then we had the heat of summer, but there are shopping malls that we didn't have in Zambia, motorways, driving on the other side of the road, all kinds of little things."

"I know what you mean," Roberta said. "When we moved to England, it was amazing how small everything was, as you said, driving on the other side of the road, getting used to the different English accents. I did like it though, I made friends, we travelled around England and Scotland, I took up horse riding, and I lived like a county lady. How did you two meet?"

"We met at the boat club that we had in Kitwe," James replied. "I met Katrina's parents before I met her."

"I met John at college," Roberta said. "He was there studying engineering, and I was there as a chemistry major. You should come to the house, we'd love to have you over."

"Thank you," Katrina said.

"Where are you living now?" Roberta asked.

"We have a flat, an apartment, in the tower that's by the lake in Cudahy," Katrina replied.

"No children?" Roberta asked.

"We decided that we didn't want children," Katrina said.

"Good for you," Roberta said. "I'll bet you've been getting lots of questions and comments about that. We decided no kids, and you wouldn't believe the stories, the comments, the pity, all because we had no kids."

"Were you able to continue with chemistry?" James asked.

"I did," Roberta said. "While John slaved away at James & Brown, I did my doctorate, and when we were in England, I did some post-doctoral work at Oxford."

"I'm still trying to get my degree," Katrina said. "I signed up as an external student at UW Milwaukee and am wading slowly through a finance degree."

"What was education like in Zambia?" Roberta asked.

"I went away to school in Rhodesia, but we did have a new high school in Kitwe, and the University of Zambia was established in 1966, after a lot of back and forth that had been going on since before the War," Katrina explained. "I got out of high school and went straight to work; in retrospect, I probably should have gone to university, either to Lusaka or to Cape Town or somewhere else in South Africa."

"And you, James?" Roberta asked.

"I went to university in London, to Imperial, and went straight from there to Zambia to work," he replied.

"Here you go, folks," the waitress said, bringing the fish fries and the beers. There was general silence for a while as meals were eaten. Then the conversation resumed.

"Do you have family in England, Katrina?" Roberta asked.

"No, all my family live in South Africa," Katrina replied. "My dad sold the business and left Zambia and bought a vineyard in the Cape and now makes wine."

"And you, James?" Roberta asked.

"My folks live in England, but my brother and his wife live in South Africa, and my sister and her husband live in Italy," James replied.

"So, you are scattered to the four winds," Roberta said. "What are you doing tomorrow?"

"We've nothing planned," Katrina said.

"Come on over to the house," Roberta invited. "I'd like to hear more about Zambia; there won't be others there, so you won't be on display."

"On display?" Katrina asked.

"I remember when we first went to England, we made some friends and each time we went to their house, there were always others there, and I felt like a new acquisition on display," Roberta laughed. "Look, here are our favourite Americans."

"We should give them directions," John suggested.

"Do you have a pen?" Roberta asked. "No, well, I'll get one from the waitress." A pen was acquired along with some paper, and Roberta wrote out directions to their house.

"Come at about ten," she suggested. "Stay for lunch, stay for tea."

"Thank you, we wouldn't want to impose," Katrina said.

"No imposition," Roberta assured her.

"She seems really nice," Katrina commented to James when they were in the bath later that night.

"She does," he agreed. "I liked her comment about being on display."

"That was funny, but true," Katrina agreed. "Thinking about it, it's Mr and Dr. Williams, but she doesn't remind you every five minutes that she's in fact Doctor Williams, I like that."

"I wonder what kind of chemistry she's involved in?" he said.

"I'll ask her tomorrow," Katrina said. "I wonder how old they are?"

"Well, John told me that he'd worked for James & Brown for twenty years, so he's probably at least forty, maybe even a little older. I heard somewhere that he'd be in the army for a couple of years too, so let's say forty-five," James thought.

"So, she's about the same age, so I'd say pretty good shape for forty-five," Katrina commented. "I wonder if they're sitting in the bath dissecting us?"

"I doubt it, most Americans shower," James said. "Do we take anything with us tomorrow?"

"Let's stop at the bottle store and pick up a nice bottle of wine," she suggested. "Now, have you finished with your hand wandering?"

"I was just exploring," he said.

"If you want to do that, we should go to bed," she said.

"What do we wear?" James asked Katrina the next day. "We're going to the boss's house, so we have to dress up?"

"I don't think so," she replied. "When we saw them last night, it was jeans and plaid shirts for both of them, so I think we'll be fine with jeans today."

"Okay," he said. "I'll just get dressed, then we can go."

"Give me five minutes and I'll be ready," she said.

"This house is not that easy to spot," James said as they drove out, guided by the directions that Roberta had given them.

"Pretty fancy neighbourhood," Katrina commented. "Big houses, set back in the trees, no riff raff here."

"Maybe we're the riff raff," he joked.

"In some people's books, I'm sure we are," she said. "That's it over there." They drove through some large gates and into the driveway, and John came out.

"Hi, come on in," he said. "Bobby's just thinking about making some tea. She picked up the tea habit while we lived in Didcot. I'm a coffee man myself."

"Hi, guys," Roberta said as John led them into the house and into the kitchen. James and Katrina looked about them, and the house was huge; it seemed to them to be far too large for just two people.

"Tea or coffee?" John asked.

"Tea, please," Katrina said.

"Same for me," James added. Roberta served up tea and offered milk and sugar and some biscuits, cookies, she reminded herself.

"James, come and see my latest venture," John said. He led the way to the garage, which was big enough for four cars. There were two fairly new cars and an older-looking Jeep.

"What year is it?" James asked.

"1944," John said. "I picked it up in Germany and had it shipped over, and have been rebuilding it."

"It looks really nice, have you got it to run yet?" James asked.

"I have," John said. "I borrowed a truck and took it out to the Milwaukee Mile and tested it. I've got the engine and the running gear all nicely done; now it's the body and the seats. Keeps me busy for hours. I'm glad you guys came over, Bobby's having a tough time making new friends, she gets frustrated with conversations about grandchildren and houses, and she's not a big fan of academia, so it's hard for her to find someone to talk to."

"What kind of chemistry does she specialise in?" James asked.

"Polymers," John replied. "The kind of polymers that end up in textiles and other fabrics and fibres."

"I'm not sure either one of us could talk intelligently about that," James said. "I had no real chemistry after high school, and I doubt that Katrina did either."

"Bobby doesn't want to talk about polymers; she's more interested in world affairs, what's going on in South Africa, where we might go on safari, all sorts of things," John said. "Fancy a run down the road?"

"What, just take the Jeep out and drive up and down the road?" James asked.

"Why not," John said. "The Bill here are pretty relaxed and don't come here unless someone calls something in. If we get stopped, we rely on the guy's interest to focus on the Jeep, not that it doesn't have a licence."

"Where did you two disappear off to?" Roberta asked when they finally got back to the house.

"We just went for a little drive around," John said.

"You need to get that Jeep licensed," Roberta said. "One day, the cops will catch you."

"I know," John said. "I've got it to the stage that I can get a licence for it now, so I'll do that in the next week or two."

"Well, now you're back, you can cook something on the grill outside," Roberta suggested.

"Come, James," John said. "We've got our marching orders, the grill's just out the back here."

"Where did you go to college?" James asked, as they basted the steaks with beer.

"University of Colorado in Boulder," John replied. "I majored in mechanical engineering, and as you know, Bobby was a chemist. I grew up in Durango, and Bobby is from Pueblo. I miss the mountains at times. It's not completely flat here, but there aren't any mountains."

"I was in Colorado in the summer," James said. "I imagine that there can be a lot of snow there when winter comes."

"Tons of it," John said. "The snowpack is good for the water; without the snowpack, there'd be little in the Colorado River. Do you ski?"

"Katrina and I tried cross-country skiing this winter, but neither of us has even tried downhill skiing," James replied.

"We've got my family home in Durango, we should go out there in the winter and teach you to ski," John offered.

"I think we'll eat out," Roberta announced as she came outside to check on things. "It's warm enough, I'll just get knives and forks, James, red wine or white?"

"Red, please," he replied. They were joined by Katrina, who came out armed with knives, forks and plates, and then by Roberta, who brought glasses and a bottle of wine.

"Katrina's been telling me all kinds of things about Zambia," Roberta said. "Did you know John that she used to sell industrial minerals?"

"James never mentioned that," John said. "Okay, steaks are ready, let's eat."

"Cheers," Roberta said, offering a toast after she had passed around glasses of wine.

"Cheers," the others echoed.

"I was telling James, and he and Katrina should come out to Durango in the winter," John said.

"That would be great," Roberta said. "You'll love it there, Katrina, it's peaceful, away from the ski resort, there's tons of snow, we could teach you to ski, you don't ski, do you?"

"Only cross country," Katrina said.

"We can do that too," Roberta said. "It'd be fun having someone to share it with."

"We noticed that this house has a wall around it, but none of the others do," James said. "Why is that?"

"There has been a house here for a long time," John said. "This is actually the third house. When the first one was built, they walled the property, and the wall was grandfathered in when they created the city ordinances, so today it's the only one in the whole neighbourhood that is fenced."

Lunch over, they sat and just chatted about all manner of things until Roberta announced that it was time for tea. Roberta served tea, but then she added sherry.

"I shouldn't," James said. "I'll need to stay awake to drive home."

"Stay the night," Roberta said. "We've got three spare bedrooms."

"We wouldn't want to put you to any inconvenience," Katrina said.

"Nonsense," Roberta said. "We'll put you in the room with the bath, I know Brits prefer a bath to a shower, after tea, we'll make up the bed and dig out some towels."

"Are you sure?" James asked.

"Of course," Roberta said. "It'll be fun. We don't have guests often, to be frank, I'm not that bowled over by those I've met so far. We've no family to visit, so having someone here is a treat. James, tell me about working in a mine." James told her a little about his experiences working both underground and in the open pit. She was fascinated by it all and asked what James thought were really good questions. James noted that John just sat and watched her, and he got a real sense of affection between the two. They were happy together. After tea, Katrina went with Roberta to make up the bed and find towels and such.

"I'm glad you stayed," John said. "Bobby's just delighted, she's really taken to Katrina, I can tell, staying over made her weekend."

"It seems such a small thing to make her happy," James commented.

"Don't get me wrong," John said. "We're happy, really happy, but this is something extra."

"I think we've been adopted," Katrina said to James when they drove home on Sunday afternoon. "Bobby told me that you're John's protégé and he's just delighted with your work. Bobby's like an aunt that I never had, I feel I could talk to her about anything."

"John said that she really was happy to have us stay the night," James said.

"She told me that," Katrina said. "She's not at all snobby about being Doctor Williams, did you see that they have an indoor pool?"

"I didn't see that," he admitted.

"Bobby told me the next time we go, to take swimsuits and a change of clothes to spend the night," Katrina said.

"What did you two talk about?" James asked.

"All sorts," she replied. "Zambia, school in Rhodesia, the transport business, hunting, trips to the bush, bathing together."

"You told her we bath together?" James asked.

"She asked me what one thing we did that drew us closer, and I told her we bathed together," Katrina said. "She thought that that was a really good idea. Apparently, the one thing they do together that draws them closer is they dance. I told her that you have two left feet and not much in the way of a sense of rhythm, so that was out for us."

"I wonder how this will change our relationship at work?" James said.

"Probably not much," she said. "Bobby said that John's very good at leaving work at work. What was the jeep like?"

"Fun to drive," he replied. "John's done a great job of restoring it, and it runs as if it were new. He just needs to finish up the body work and get it painted."

"Ready for your next trip?" Tony asked James when he went to the office on Monday.

"Where to?" James asked.

"Merry Olde," Tony said. "They've asked for an application guy to go and look at a coal mine somewhere in the north of England."

"You don't want to go?" James asked.

"No, I'm headed back to Brazil to look at a bauxite property," Tony said. "Fly to Rio, then upcountry somewhere, pretty girls, caipirinhas and the good life."

"When do I go?" James asked.

"They want you to be there next Tuesday, not tomorrow, next week, so leave Sunday, get there Monday and find your way to Newcastle. You can come home any time you're ready," Tony said. "You can meet one of our local guys from Didcot there. Looks like everyone's going out of town, Dan and John are headed to Australia on Thursday of this week, Bob's going to Arizona, and Bill's going as well."

"I should talk to Marlys about flights and send a telex to Didcot asking for details about where to stay," James thought.

"Do that," Tony said.

"I'm going to England next week," James told Katrina as they drove home. "I need to leave on Sunday and will probably be back Friday."

"Are you going to see your folks?" she asked.

"That's why I'll be back Friday," he said. "I'm going to stop and see them for one night before I come home. Tony's on his way to Brazil, again, John and Dan are headed for Australia this week, it'll be an empty office."

"It'll be a lonely flat here too," she said. "What will you do? Call me at the office?"

"That would be best," he said. "There's an eight-hour time change, so I'll call you at about eight in the evening there, that'll be noon here."

"Okay," she said. "What time's your flight on Sunday?"

"At two," he replied. "Here to Chicago, then overnight to London, I'll pick up a hire car in London and drive to Newcastle and meet the local chap there."

"Enjoy your trip," Katrina told James when she dropped him at the airport on Sunday. "I'm going to drive over to Bobby's and stay there until Friday when you come home."

"It was nice of her to ask you to stay," he said.

"I think it's as much for her as me," she said. "She told me that she gets lonely too when John travels. This way we can be miserable together."

"Enjoy yourself," he said.

"I'll enjoy the pool," she said. "Get some exercise in."

"Love you, Suikerbossie," he said. "I'll call you tomorrow from the hotel in Newcastle."

"Love you, sweetie, go well," she said. James took his bag and checked in for his flight, and then sat and waited. In Chicago, he had a longer wait, but eventually the flight was called and he boarded. The flight to London was shorter than usual, and they were on the ground early. And much to everyone's surprise, they were able to get a gate straight away and not have to wait on a taxiway somewhere. James collected his bag and got his hire car. Then he consulted a map to see how best to get to Newcastle. There was no easy way; it was either into London and back out on the A1 or go around London and pick up the A1 on the north side of the town. As they were early, the traffic into London was still light, so James elected to go into the centre of London and back out

284

again. That still took time, but as he was working his way north, he was running against the traffic. He stopped for lunch near Doncaster and was in Newcastle, actually in Morpeth, by three in the afternoon, in time to miss the rain that had just moved into the area. His local contact, Terry Wilcox, had left him a message, so James called his room and they arranged to meet in the bar.

"James, how do," Terry asked.

"Fine, thanks, Terry, and you?" James replied.

"Champion," Terry said. "So, what can I get in?"

"Newcastle Brown, please," James said.

"So, ready for tomorrow?" Terry asked when he returned with the beers.

"I am," James said. "Who do we see?"

"We're going to meet Will Beaumont and Mike Edwards, they're with the company, they want to know how big a dragline they should get," Terry replied.

"Is this rain going to last?" James asked.

"They say it should be blown out by tomorrow morning. We'll see," Terry said. "But most of our time tomorrow will be in their offices; there's not much to see on the site yet."

"Have the Bucyrus, Marion, Page and Ransomes chaps been yet?" James asked.

"Ransomes, yes, and I think Bucyrus, but I haven't seen hide nor hair of the Marion or Page reps," Terry said.

"The project is a go?" James asked.

"Definitely," Terry assured him. "The only question is who gets the order; local support is important to them, so my betting is it's down to us, Bucyrus and Ransomes."

"Will the fact that Ransomes will build it in Ipswich make any difference?" James asked.

"I don't think so," Terry said. "In the end, it will be best price and delivery. How do you like living in the States?"

"It's different," James said. "We went in February, I had no idea what cold was like until then, the summer was hot and humid, it's a big country, and I've been to twelve states already. The people seem nice enough, you get the impression that everything really is bigger and better in America."

"How's John Williams doing? We were sorry to see him go," Terry asked.

"He's doing fine. I went on a sales trip with him to Montana, and we came away with an order for two draglines," James said.

"That'd be John," Terry said. "Drink up, there's a pub down the road that does an amazing steak and kidney, I thought we'd eat there."

"How's England?" Katrina asked when James called her later.

"Wet and dismal," he said. "How are you?"

"I'm fine," she replied. "I'm busy, which is good."

"How's Bobby?" he asked.

"It's only *lekker* man," she said. "I had dinner cooked for me and breakfast, I got to swim in the pool, it almost makes up for you not being here, almost, but not completely. You're still going to see your folks?" she asked.

"I am," he confirmed. "When I'm done here, then I'll drive south and check on them."

"I'm sorry, Lovey, I have to go, I have to answer a call from Salt Lake about some parts, call me tomorrow, love you," she said.

"Love you, stay well," he said.

"James, this is Will Beaumont and Mike Edwards," Terry said, making the introductions when they went to the mining company offices. "James is the application engineer I was telling you about."

"How do, James," Will said. "Did you bring the rain with you?"

"Not guilty," he replied. "It was fine when I drove up from London, the rain didn't start until I got here."

"Well, let's get started," Will said. He produced maps, plans, drawings and sections that showed the coal deposit, and then talked about production levels. To James, it looked straightforward enough for the first ten to fifteen years; after that, there would be some complications as the overburden depth increased. They talked for some time about various ways of dealing with the increase and the cost implications of each. James suggested that they start with a dragline that would fit conditions up to the fifteen-year mark, and then what kind of equipment to add after that that would keep the dragline working at its optimum conditions. He also drew up a table of likely investments and then ran some calculations that showed each option and what the costs would be. They broke for lunch and started back again afterwards. When they finally finished for the day, James recommended a boom length and bucket size for a dragline and also suggested equipment to add in year fifteen. Will was happy; he had the basics to add to the financial plan. All that remained now was for them to formally request a quote for the machine size that James had suggested. James and Terry left and went back to their hotel.

"Are you busy today?" James asked Katrina when he called her later.

"Not so busy today," she said. "How was your day?"

"Interesting," he said. "We'll see if anything comes of it. Tomorrow I'll drive south and stay with the folks, on Thursday I'll see if they need me to do anything, then I'll come home on Friday."

"I'll be at the airport," she promised. "I miss you."

"I miss you too," he echoed.

"Staying with Bobby is fun, but she's not you," Katrina bemoaned.

"Did you get to use the pool again?" he asked.

"I did," she said. "I was swimming and Bobby came in to swim as well, and she just stripped off and jumped in, no swimsuit, nothing."

"Well, I suppose if it's your pool in your house, then you can do what you like, can you see into the pool from outside?" he asked.

"No, it's in a pool house and it's screened from the outside by a hedge and a wall," she said. "I suppose if you climbed the wall, you could peek in, but it's a pretty high wall. I've learned a lot about polymers in the last couple of days, it's fascinating, I'd no idea there were so many and each with their own use. Are you sure you can't come home on Thursday?"

"I'll check," he promised. "That might work. I'll call the airline and see what I can do."

"That would be great," she said.

"I'll leave here early, early tomorrow morning and be at my folks' house by lunch time, then I'll have the rest of the day and the next morning, so yes, I think I'll just do that," he said. "So, I'll see you Thursday."

"Thursday, love you," she said.

"Love you," he echoed.

"James," his mother said when he arrived at their house. "We didn't expect you until much later. How was the drive from Newcastle?"

"Wet and dreary," he said. "How are you?"

"We're both well, your father's out in the shed doing something, did you have lunch yet?" she asked. James wondered if all mothers assumed that their children, no matter how old, needed feeding.

"I haven't had lunch yet," he said.

"Just go out to the shed and see your father, he took a day off today to see you when you came. I'll make some lunch for us while you're out there," she said. James went out to the hideaway that was his dad's shed.

"Dad, what are you up to out here?" he asked.

"Oh, James, I didn't expect you so soon. What time did you leave Newcastle?" his father asked.

"Five this morning," James replied. "It wasn't too bad a run-down. So, what are you up to out here?"

"I'm trying my hand at home brewing," his father explained. "This is my second batch, I've still got some of the first batch in the house, come, we'll go inside and try one." They went in, and beer was poured. James had to admit, it was quite good. His mother tutted about drinking beer in the middle of the day and served lunch for them all.

"How are you getting on in America?" she asked.

"We're doing well," James replied. "Katrina likes her job, and I like mine. We've met some nice people. I've travelled quite a lot, going to twelve states already."

"When can we visit?" his father asked.

"We've only got one bedroom in our flat, but we could arrange a hotel that's close," James said.

"I think we'll wait until you've got a bigger place," his mother said. "Your father and I are going to South Africa this Christmas to see Will and Bridget. We're flying out about a week before Christmas and will be back the second week of January."

"I took my holidays over Christmas," his father said. "So that we could get a longer stay there. Will said that he's going to take us to a different park this time. He said that the rains make Kruger not so good, so we're going to a part of the country that doesn't get much rain."

"Sounds like fun," James said.

"When's your flight back?" his mother asked.

"I leave tomorrow afternoon. I need to turn the hire car back and check in, so I should leave here right after lunch," James replied.

"Oh dear," his mother said. "I wish you could stay longer."

"He is on a business trip, Dear," James's father reminded his mother.

"I know, well, I'm glad you stopped to see us," she said. "So, tell us about the places you've been." James went through his trips and talked about each state, the differences and similarities. There was quite a lot to tell, and they were still talking about things when tea time came.

"How are your folks?" Katrina asked when James called that evening.

"They're fine, Dad's taken up home brewing," he replied.

"Did you try any?" she asked.

"I did, and it wasn't bad," he said. "They told me that they're going to see Will and Bridget this Christmas, I'm a bit jealous."

"I know what you mean," she said. "I wouldn't mind a trip home, but I suppose we'll get to go back someday."

"When does John come back from Australia?" he asked.

"Thursday," she said. "Bobby told me that they get in at the same time that you do, you'll probably even bump into them in Chicago."

"Any more naked swimming?" he asked.

"I did last night," she said. "It reminded me of that time we went out to Milomfwe Falls, that was a lovely day."

"It was," James agreed. It had been the first time they had made love in a pool of water, and he still remembered the day. They had driven out past Kalulushi and then taken a dirt road that led off into the bush, and had actually left the road and driven through the bush itself to the waterfall and the pool.

"Bobby asked me if we might house sit for them some time," she said.

"That would be nice," he said. "Any dates?"

"Not yet, I think just testing the waters," she said.

"Okay, well Mum's getting antsy, so I'd better go, I'll see you at the airport tomorrow, love you," he said.

"Love you," she replied. "See you tomorrow."

James did meet John and Dan in Chicago. They had just flown in from Los Angeles.

"James, hi," John said. "Where have you been off to?"

"I was in England looking at a mine site and a dragline opportunity," James replied.

"Oh," Dan said. "How big?"

"65 cubic yards on a 310-foot boom," James replied. "We should get the request for a quote next week."

"Good, good," Dan said. "Things are looking up in England. Who else is bidding?"

"Our man says that he's seen the Bucyrus and Ransomes people," James replied.

"That's to be expected," Dan said. "Ransomes is a Brit company and Bucyrus has got the Ruston sub."

"How was the Australia trip?" James asked.

"Coal is big and so is iron ore, so draglines, shovels and drills, plenty to look at," John replied. "I think we'll do well out of this trip."

"Any family visits while you were in England?" Dan asked.

"I stayed with my folks last night," James said. "They don't live too far from Heathrow, so it was convenient."

"Okay, guys," John said. "That's our flight."

Katrina and Roberta were both at the gate waiting when the plane landed in Milwaukee.

"Katrina, this is Dan Wells," James said, making the introduction.

"Katrina," Dan said. "Nice to meet you. Roberta, nice to see you again."

"Let's go and get our bags," John suggested. North Central must have been truly organised that day, because by the time they had walked down to the baggage claim, bags were already appearing.

"That's mine," Dan said. "I'll see you guys tomorrow."

"You've been keeping Bobby company?" John said to Katrina after Dan had left.

"It was very kind of her to ask me,' Katrina replied.

"I think it's a splendid idea," John said. "Saved both of you from getting lonely. Ah, that's my bag. Will we see you at the office tomorrow, James?"

"I'll be there," James said.

"Katrina, James, have a good evening," John said. He and Roberta left, and then James saw his bag, and they were able to leave. They drove home, collected their mail and carried his and her bags upstairs.

"I'm glad to be home," James told Katrina. "I missed you."

"I missed you, too," she said. "I missed you in bed, I missed feeling you up close to me, and I even missed this." She had reached down and slipped her hand inside his trousers. He responded and peeled clothes off her as fast as he could, and then helped her pull his clothes off. They made love where they were, in the living room, it was passionate and sadly over too soon.

"We need a bath and then do that again more slowly," he said.

"Let's go," she said, leading him by the hand to the bathroom.

"So, how was the stay with Bobby?" he asked, as they sat soaking in the bath.

"It was lovely," she said. "I really like her, she's funny, she's smart, she can cook really well, and she's someone you can talk to and know that whatever you say will stay with her, like having a favourite aunt. She's in great shape, too. I can see why John runs after her. She was telling me that she's met the wives of most of the managers at James & Brown, but that she didn't hit it off with any of them. I think she was getting a little lonely. I know what she means. I like Amanda and Kathy, but I'm not ready to pour my heart out to them. Maggie and Dorothy live in their own worlds, and they probably wouldn't have time for me."

"I know what you mean," he said. "Tom and Kathy have been really kind and helpful, but I wouldn't go so far as to say we're friends. I'm warming up to Bill, and I like Amanda; we'll see there."

"I suppose making friends in a new country is always difficult, like when you first came to Zambia," she said. "You were lucky to meet Tom and Rita on the boat. Shame what happened to Tom, and we've lost touch with Rita. If you move far away, you really do have to work to stay in touch with friends and family. If I think about it, I've lost touch with all my old friends in Zambia, shame, I've been lazy and not tried to contact them, but they haven't tried to contact us either. I suppose you live your life wherever you are, and people you come across may become friends, but will it be friends for life? Which brings up a good point, you said something about us earlier, are you ready?"

"Any time you are," he said.

"Let's go then," she said.

Thanksgiving

"Are you ready for your big presentation to the board?" Katrina asked James.

"As ready as I'll ever be," he said. "Bill and I went through it with Hank Miller twice last week and once this week. Miller wanted a few changes, but there was nothing that changed the tone of the presentation."

"What time are you on this morning?" she asked.

"We go on at ten," he said.

"Remember that these *ouks* are just a bunch of old *oomies*," she said. "They probably don't know a whole lot about the competitors, so unless you say something outrageous, you'll be fine."

"I probably shouldn't say, look you *ouks*?" he laughed.

"Definitely not," she said. "So, best bib and tucker today?"

"I've only got the one suit," he said. "But I did iron my shirt last night, and I've got my RSM tie."

"Shoes polished?" she asked.

"Shoes polished, socks match," he said.

"Go and knock them dead," she said. "Will you be free for lunch to tell me all about it?"

"I've no idea," he said. "Miller was vague about that."

"Who's on the board?" she asked.

"Hank Miller, John Williams and Tom Sanders from the company and the outside directors are Graham Brant, he's the banker I met on the plane, Charles Bristol, insurance, Evan Eastwood, electrical switchgear, Hal Wainwright, money manager, Walter Collier, property management and Peter Burgess, medical equipment," he enumerated.

"No women," she commented.

"No women," he confirmed. "I suppose that will come in time."

"Are you ready?" she asked.

"Let's go," he said.

"Ready for this?" Bill asked James as they sat outside the boardroom, waiting to be summoned in.

"Do you mind doing the talking?" Bill asked.

"No," James said. "If they ask questions, I might throw them your way."

"No problem," Bill said.

The door to the boardroom opened, and Hank waved them in.

"These are James Martin and Bill Evans," Hank said in an introduction. "James is one of our application engineers, and Bill is one of our manufacturing engineers. They are in the management development program and are going to talk to us today about our competitors. Your slides are loaded and you may begin any time."

James launched into a brief review of the markets that they served and who were the major players in each segment. He then took each of the major players and gave a brief history of them, and then an analysis of their estimated market share, their mode of distribution and their financial performance over the past five years.

"That's pretty thorough," Graham Brant said. "Bill, any comments?"

Bill talked about the various companies and their manufacturing capacity, something that he and James had anticipated might be raised.

"And you guys are an application engineer and a manufacturing engineer?" Wainwright asked. "How did you put all this together?"

"It took some work on our part," James admitted.

"So, if I'm Joe Contractor, why should I buy from us rather than, say, Cat?" Collier asked.

"We've thought about that a lot," James said. He then went into a long answer about decision drivers and how those were different for different customers.

"You guys sound like the Boston Consulting guys," Burgess said. "Hank, hang onto these guys." There were a few more questions, but only a few. Eastwood then announced that he was ready for lunch and asked Hank if James and Bill were invited. Hank confirmed that they were. Lunch was brought in, and James and Bill were split up and spent much of the lunch time answering questions, not only about what they had just presented, but also about their careers. It was well after two when Jame and Bill finally escaped from the interrogations of the directors. They felt that they had acquitted themselves well, but would not really know until later.

"So, how did it go?" Katrina asked when she picked up James after work.

"I think fine," he said. "We'll see tomorrow if we get anything back from Miller or the others."

"We've been invited to Bobby and John's for Thanksgiving," she said.

"When is that?" he asked.

"Apparently, it's always on the fourth Thursday in November, which this year is the 27th," she explained.

"So, do we need to take anything, do anything?" he asked.

"No, Bobby said I can help her with the cooking and to take a bag to stay, because she said that people usually eat and drink too much on Thanksgiving Day," she said.

"I'd like a glass of wine, what about you?" he asked.

"Pour one of whatever you're having," she said. "I was thinking, it's been three months now since you had the snip, so we should make an appointment and take a sample in for a test."

"I'll call them tomorrow," he said. "What do you think, will everything be okay?"

"I'm sure it will," she said. "Then I can go off the pill."

"Tony," John Williams started. "You did us a service when you decided to hire James. He did us proud with the board yesterday."

"Great," Tony said. "I know he and Bill have been putting in the extra hours. Anything of great import come out of the board meeting?"

"A couple of things, James, would you give us a few minutes?" John asked. James wandered off and found Bill out on the shop floor.

"Hey, James," he said. "I just got feedback from Sanders, we did good, he's happy, apparently the directors are too, so for the moment we're the golden boys."

"I wonder for how long?" James laughed. "I'd better get back." James went back to the office, and John had gone, and Tony looked happy.

"Life is good," Tony said.

"Oh, what happened?" James asked.

"You didn't hear this from me," Tony said. "But I just got a grant under the stock option program."

"What's that?" James asked.

"The company awards you the right to buy stock at today's price, no matter when you exercise, so if the stock price goes up, then I exercise and pocket the difference, less tax," Tony explained.

"And if the stock price goes down?" James asked.

"Then you're screwed and it's not worth exercising," Tony said. "Unless you can't count."

"How do you get on the program?" James asked.

"When you've been here long enough and reached a certain level in the management, then they'll probably put you on as well," Tony said. "Say, what are you and Katrina doing for Thanksgiving?"

"We've been invited to spend it with some friends," James replied.

"Oh, okay, that's good, we were thinking it would be nice for you to see a traditional Thanksgiving, but you're already taken care of, that's great," Tony said. James was not sure whether the, that's great, was a comment on the fact that they were going to see a traditional Thanksgiving or relief that he did not have to add James and Katrina to what was probably a family affair. The telephone rang and Tony answered. He looked at James and nodded, then hung up.

"You need to go downstairs and see Hank Miller," he said. James went and found Bill there as well, waiting outside Miller's office. They were called in and given a summary of the reviews of their presentation. The reviews were universally good, but that was probably as much due to the critique that Hank himself had made of the presentation before it was given as to their own efforts. Hank told them that the board had asked to see more of them and would they put together a presentation on projected demands for mining machines over the next twenty years. He added that two of the other members of the development program had been tasked to do the same thing for construction machines.

After work on Wednesday, James and Katrina drove to John and Roberta's house, suitcases in hand. The company had given most people the Friday after Thanksgiving off as well, so for James and Katrina, that meant a four-day weekend.

"I'm so glad you came," Roberta said. "This will be fun."

"What is typical of a Thanksgiving dinner?" Katrina asked.

"Well, the origins are with the Pilgrims who came over from England in the 1600s, who probably just carried over the Harvest Supper tradition from England. The Plymouth colonists, as they were known, didn't fare well, but they were helped by the native peoples that were here, in particular the Wampanoag. In 1621, things looked up so they had a feast, and what was served is hazy, but they did serve fowl, probably turkeys; they also had venison, corn, fish, shellfish and vegetables," Roberta explained. "Over the years, the menu has settled on turkey, with cranberry sauce, yams, some kind of green vegetables, potatoes usually mashed, followed by pumpkin pie."

"I thought potatoes were from South America?" Katrina asked.

"What we eat today is certainly derived from South American varieties," Roberta confirmed. "But there are some theories that a different variety was found in North America and was certainly eaten in the west, whether or not it was found in the east, I don't know."

"So, what are we having?" Katrina asked.

"Turkey with stuffing, cranberries, roasted Brussels, and roasted potatoes. I'm not a big fan of pumpkin pie, so we'll have a Dutch apple pie instead. We'll probably be eating leftovers for the next four days," Roberta replied.

"What would you like me to do?" Katrina asked.

"You can help me with preparing the vegetables tomorrow," Roberta suggested.

"And what do you want James to do?" Katrina asked.

"Keep John out of the kitchen," Roberta laughed. "Too many cooks, what?"

"Is Thanksgiving the only holiday that doesn't have gifts and cards?" Katrina asked.

"Not quite, but almost," Roberta said. "Christmas, gifts, Valentine's Day, gifts, Mother's Day, gifts, in fact, if your man forgets either of those, he's branded as insensitive, unfeeling, uncaring and an all-around cad. The card, flower and lingerie industries have done a marvellous job of conning the nation into thinking that this is normal and expected custom."

"Is she on her high horse again about the commercialisation of holidays?" John asked as he and James came in from the garage.

"Well, you have to admit it's got a little out of hand," Roberta said.

"It has, I agree," John said. "It always amazes me at the billions we'll spend on those things, and yet we'll forego basic necessities for some."

"Thanksgiving strikes me as a time to get together with families," Katrina said. "You have no close family?"

"None," John said. "My folks died five years ago, and Bobbie's three years ago. Neither of us had any brothers or sisters; there are a few cousins out there, but we've never had anything to do with them. We've had to rely on one another. We lived here, then in Australia, in England, and now back here. It's been difficult to make lasting friends, so it's just been us. You'll probably find it much the same, unless you and James are close to your siblings."

"We get on well enough," James said. "But my sister and brother live far away, so we only see them rarely."

"I have none," Katrina said. "There are some cousins that I've never met, but I imagine they're all in South Africa. So, it's James and me."

"So, what do we have for dinner tonight?" Roberta asked.

"I could cook if you like," Katrina volunteered.

"Would you? That would be nice, have you anything in mind?" Roberta asked.

"I was thinking of a bobotie," Katrina said. "It's a beef mince dish done with curry and a milk and egg custard."

"Sounds wonderful," Roberta said. "Just tell me what you need and I'll help you find it. John, go and find us a nice bottle of wine."

The bobotie was a success, with none left. They sat and talked until late, and it was almost midnight when James and Katrina finally got to bed.

"I got the results of the sperm test today," James told her. "The count was down to nil, so you can go off the pill now."

"That's good," she said. "I have to admit I was a little concerned when the gyney talked about the long-term risks."

"Are we imposing on John and Bobby?" James asked.

"I asked Bobby that again tonight while I was cooking, and we had a long chat about it. The answer is no, she loves having us here, and whatever she wants, John goes along with; he just worships her. I said before that I thought we'd been adopted, I get that impression more and more," Katrina said. "Bobby also made the comment that family is often not blood family, but who you associate with and who you are comfortable with. I like them both, and Bobby and I get on really well. It really is like having a favourite aunt, but an aunt that's not so far removed in age to not understand how we're feeling."

"John and I had a brief chat, and I suggested that I not tell anyone that we stay here or are close to them, and he agreed," James said. "I also told him not to do me any special favours at work. He told me not to worry about that, he said that I'll make my own mark, apparently have already done so."

"Good, so here just treat him like a friend," she suggested. "Ask advice like you would your dad or an uncle."

"I'll do that. Now to celebrate a negative result, how are you feeling now, tired, too tired?"

"Randy," she said.

Thanksgiving Day started early, mainly to put the turkey in the oven to give it time to cook. Everything else could follow later. With the turkey cooking, Katrina suggested to James that they take a swim. With a nod to conventions, they both donned costumes and went to the pool house. James jumped in and started down the pool, then Katrina dived in and passed him quickly, doing two lengths to every one of his. They were joined by Roberta, who clearly was an expert swimmer. James climbed out of the pool while Roberta and Katrina raced up and down. It was a close match, and it looked to James as if Roberta had the turns down better than Katrina, but Katrina managed to catch her down the length of the pool. When they finally stopped, James was not sure if there really was a winner.

"I should get you a new suit," Roberta told Katrina. "This one is a new blend that I came up with that will probably be on the market for competition swimmers next year." It looked to James like a sleek extra skin that she was wearing; it was form-fitting to say the least, and it seemed to him that water just ran off it.

"You do work for the swimsuit makers?" James asked.

"A couple of them are my clients," she confirmed. "It's interesting work, you want flexibility, chlorine resistance, UV resistance, easy to sew, elasticity in its true form, so that it will cling and not provide for folds or bunching that would slow a swimmer down. I get to test all the designs, so have a cupboard full. Let's see, Katrina, what size are you?"

James left them talking about measurements and went and changed, and then went looking for John. He found him in the living room sorting out records.

"Hey James, where are the girls?" John asked.

"Deep in discussions about swimsuits and sizes," James replied.

"That's been a really lucrative business for Bobby," John said. "She makes more than I do."

"Does that bother you at all? I'm sorry, I shouldn't have asked that." James said.

"No, it's fine," John assured him. "I'm delighted that Bobby gets so much for her advice, I'm not threatened at all by it, my manhood is intact."

"Forgive me for asking, but is Bobby part Indian?" James asked.

"The politically correct term is Native American," John said. "But to answer your question, yes, her maternal grandmother was Lakota, one of the plains peoples that lived in what is now Colorado. She even has the costume that her grandmother wore, and her own that she made."

"Katrina has native African in her family on both sides," James said. "We probably shouldn't ask her to wear the costume of her ancestors; it would be a thin piece of cord around the waist with a very small apron at the front and nothing else."

"That would shock the neighbours if we ever had a fancy dress party," John laughed.

"What are you two laughing at?" Roberta asked when she and Katrina joined them.

"We were just saying that the mode of dress of Katrina's Bushman ancestors would shock the neighbours," James explained.

"I'm sure it would," Roberta said. "But then almost anything would shock the neighbours. So, Katrina, are we ready to go and get the rest of this dinner organised? John, you and James are in charge of setting the table and picking wine."

"Dinner is served," Roberta announced. She brought through a platter with the turkey on it, and Katrina followed with a dinner wagon laden with all the other dishes. "John, hack up the turkey, will you, and while he's doing that, let's just remember a few things that we're thankful for. James, tell us something that you're thankful for."

"There's so much," he said. "I have Katrina as my wife and friend, we both have jobs, we both have good health, and we have new friends."

"I'll echo that," said Katrina. "When we left Zambia, we weren't sure what we were going to, this has been wonderful."

"Well, I'm thankful for John," Roberta said. "He's been my rock for twenty-four years now. I'm thankful that we have new friends; I'm thankful that we have such a lot, it's sometimes hard to believe our good fortune. John?"

"I'm thankful for Bobby; she lights up my life. I'm also thankful for new friends, it is wonderful to have someone for us to share our good fortune with," John said.

"So, here's to new friends," Bobby said, raising her glass.

"New friends," the others echoed.

"Okay, dig in," Roberta said. They did indeed dig in, and at least some of the food disappeared. Roberta had been right; they probably would be eating leftovers for the next few days.

"It's tradition among many households to watch football," John said. "Do either of you want to watch a game?"

"I'm fine," James said. "But please, if there is a game you want to watch, don't worry about us."

"I actually don't have much interest in football," John said. "I was a skier in college, and I could never understand all the standing around in a football game."

"I watched a game at Tony's house," James said. "I have to admit to being completely lost."

"How did you two meet?" Katrina asked.

"It was a blind date set up by one of my friends," John said. "He told me that he had this amazing date for me, well, I was more than a little hesitant to go, because the past three blind dates he'd set up for me had been disasters. But this one was great, and we just continued after that."

"I was asked by one of the girls I knew if I would like to meet someone," Roberta said. "She was dating John's friend. As John said, we met and I just fell for him."

"I know the feeling," Katrina said. "When I first met James, I decided that he was the one. He was a little slow, I had to drag him off into the bush to get him to loosen up, but once he did, we had fun."

"Hard to imagine James as slow," John laughed.

"I was nervous," James said. "I had a hard time believing someone as gorgeous as Katrina would take me seriously. I didn't want to mess things up."

"So, how many years now?" Roberta asked.

"Five," Katrina replied. "James came out to Zambia in 1969, and we got married the next year. I think my folks were relieved, I think they'd given up hope that I would ever find anyone."

"When I told my folks that I was getting married and to an Afrikaans girl, I think my mother nearly died of fright, I'm convinced she thought that I was marrying a black African, I had no idea that my mother had such racist views, then they got the news that my sister was marrying an Italian, I'm surprised she survived. Since then, she's been a lot better, I think it all opened her eyes a little," James said.

"You speak Afrikaans?" Roberta asked Katrina.

"I do," Katrina confirmed. "With my folks, we use whichever language best expresses what we want to say, but most of the time, it's Afrikaans."

"Do you speak any Afrikaans, James?" John asked.

"Some," James replied. "I'm not fluent, but I can get by. I've been trying to teach myself Italian so that I can talk to Vincenzo, my sister's husband. His English is fluent, but to be able to talk to him in Italian would be nice."

"So, can I get anyone anything else?" John asked. He served out more wine and waited for replies. Everyone was full, James and Katrina both thought that if they ate another mouthful, then they would burst.

Washing up was done, turns around the garden were taken, and naps were also taken. It was a thoroughly lazy day, full of eating, drinking, talking and laughing. Roberta tried to sell more food and had only mild interest, so she told them all that they should help themselves to what they wanted when her duties as hostess were done; they were family now. James and John went for a quick drive in the jeep, but it started to snow, so they hurried back to find Katrina and Roberta in the kitchen, heads together, giggling about something.

"And what are you two up to?" John asked.

"Just girl talk," Roberta said. "Nothing for you two to worry about."

"That makes me worry," John said to James. "Do you play pool, James?"

"I've never tried," James said. "I played snooker a few times when I was in college."

"Well, let's leave these two to it and we'll go and play pool," John said. He led the way to another part of the house, and there was a room with bookshelves all around, full of books on chemistry, engineering, politics, history, you name it, and in the middle of the room was a pool table. John explained the rules, and they started. It was clear that John knew what he was doing, whereas James struggled. He did get tips from John that helped him improve a lot, but he knew that playing John for money would be a losing proposition.

"What were you two giggling about earlier?" James asked Katrina when they were in the bath together.

"Sex," she replied. "We were talking about sex, what we like, what we're less keen about, what gets us turned on and randy."

"So, anything new?" he asked.

"Oh yes," she said. "We'll try a couple of things out when we go to bed."

"You like her, don't you?" he said.

"I do," she confirmed. "I like her a lot, even though she's much older; she's very young at heart, I think it's not having children. I can talk to her and she talks to me, while you two were away, we spent a lot of time talking about separation, loneliness, and how to keep the spark alive in a marriage. From what she said, we're doing pretty well. She can be very direct. I was floored when she said that she and John liked to fuck in the pool, that's what she actually said, fuck in the pool. I always imagined PhD types as snooty, airy-fairy, but she's down to earth."

"What secrets of ours did you give away?" he said.

"I told her that we liked to fuck anywhere the opportunity presented itself, then we got onto what's one of the different places you'd fucked in?" Katrina said. "That's what we were really giggling about when you came in. Her place was the laundry room with her perched on the dryer while it was running, mine was up against the Land Rover at Kamfinsa while it was pouring with rain."

"So, shall we dry ourselves off and go and experiment with what you heard about today?" he asked.

"Definitely," she said.

Friday, they were lazy. James and Katrina talked about going shopping until Roberta pointed out that it was probably the busiest shopping day of the year, and the mall would be crowded. That ended any desire they had to go shopping. So, they stayed in and ate leftovers, and talked about Zambia. Roberta was planning a safari and wanted to know where to go, where to stay, what they might see and how to get there. Katrina knew people who ran safaris, so promised to get in touch with a couple of them to get rates, dates and so on. Roberta had maps, and Katrina was able to show her where the parks were and talk about the facilities that were available in each park. They also talked about going to Durango for Christmas. John showed them where the resort near Durango was and where their house was. The company was shutting down on Christmas Eve and not reopening until the 5th of January. James was surprised; he would have thought that they would be open for some time the week of the new year, but Hank Miller had decided that everyone needed a break and that they could attack the backlog in manufacturing with vigour in the New Year. So, John suggested that they book flights to Durango on Christmas Eve and fly out together and get one car, and all drive out to the house together. Roberta intervened and told them not to worry about tickets; she would treat them to tickets. She had just received a large payment from one of her clients and was feeling generous. James wondered just how much money was in polymers. Katrina asked what kinds of clothes they should take, and Roberta got out a photograph album and showed them at the ski resort, at home, dining out, and James and Katrina saw that apart from the actual ski clothes, they had no need to take anything special. For the ski clothes, Roberta suggested a shop in Milwaukee and told them that boots and skis would be rented at the resort.

Saturday was almost a repeat of Friday. Leftovers were eaten, conversations were had about politics, economics, history and a few other things besides. John and Roberta went out for a while to collect a new car for Roberta and came back with a new car, a Mercedes 450 SEL, a luxury car if ever there was one. Katrina went for a drive in the jeep with John, and Roberta took that chance of them being gone to talk to James.

"James, you know that I really like Katrina, she's like the younger sister I never had, do you know what a lovely person she is?" she asked him.

"I do," he said. "I knew the first time we met that she was special. I was afraid that I would not live up to her."

"You two are well matched," Roberta said. "Make sure you keep your marriage alive, don't let things go stale."

"It's been great so far," he said. "I'm not that keen on being away a lot, but we talk every day I'm gone and try and make up for it when I come home."

"John was away in the Korean War for over a year," she said. "We'd just got married and he got called up. That was a tough time. I was afraid half the time that he wouldn't come back. He likes you, he'll help you in any way he can, don't let us down, will you?"

"I won't," James promised.

"Don't let your love life with Katrina go stale, try and stay spontaneous, cater to her whims and desires, remember that women need more warming up to things than men do," Roberta advised. "She told me that you like to be spontaneous, that's good, don't get into a rut."

"I don't see that happening," he said.

"Not now," she agreed. "But twenty years from now, things may be different. Experiment, let her suggest things, dress up, act the fool once in a while, treat her like a princess. Support her if she wants to try something new, no matter how odd it may seem. What does she like to do apart from work and screw you?"

"She's taken up sketching," he said. "I think she's really good."

"Maybe we could get her to do some while she's here?" Roberta asked.

"We could ask," he agreed.

"I hear them back, one last thing, you can come to me for advice any time, advice on anything, think of me as your counsellor," Roberta said.

"Thank you," he said.

On Sunday, they prevailed upon Katrina to do some sketching, and John and Roberta both posed while she did facial sketches. The results were received with acclaim, and James guessed that they would soon be framed and hung somewhere. Roberta then dressed in the clothes of her Lakota grandmother and asked Katrina to do a sketch of her. That took a little longer than just the faces, but the result was as good. Both John and Roberta were delighted with the sketch and had a long debate about where it should be hung. While they were discussing that and wandering around the house, sketch in hand, trying it out on walls, Katrina and James put lunch together.

"You should do a self-portrait," James suggested. "Then maybe one with you dressed like your ancestor, Motshaba."

"You just want a nude sketch," she said, poking him in the ribs.

"Not nude, just dressed in typical Bushman clothes," he said.

"So, to all intents and purposes, nude," she reiterated.

"Well, it would be nice, you've got one of me," he said.

"I suppose," she said. "I'll give it a go."

"You'll give what a go?" Roberta asked, coming into the kitchen.

"A self-portrait," Katrina said. "I've never tried one, so we were just talking about it. I put lunch together. Shall we eat here or in the dining room?"

"I think here would be fine," Roberta said. "So, James, what do your parents do for a living?"

"My dad's a civil engineer, works for the local authority mainly with roads and bridges," James replied. "My mother worked in a bakery until Dad made enough that she felt that she could give it up. Now, she tends to her flower beds."

"And your sister and brother?" Roberta asked.

"My brother's a civil engineer, he works for ICI in their paint factory in South Africa, his wife is a chemical engineer, she also works for ICI, but in their explosives factory, my sister is a solicitor, she still practices in Italy, and her husband is now with the Italian secret service."

"And Katrina, you told us that your family had a transportation business, until they sold up and went to South Africa, and now grow grapes. Did your mother work in the business as well?" Roberta asked.

"Until I joined," Katrina said. "She did the scheduling and kept the books, and I took that over. Now she points out things to Dad that need fixing or addressing in some way."

"When did you last see your family?" Roberta asked.

"When we left Zambia, we drove to South Africa and took the boat from Cape Town, so we stopped in Calitzdorp to see them. That would have been about a year ago, in fact, a little more, we left Cape Town on the 12th of November and got to Southampton on the 25th," Katrina replied.

"That had to be fun," Roberta thought.

"We decided to do that rather than fly, because the boats are on their way out, the Jumbo Jet took care of that, so soon the service will end, so we wanted to take the opportunity. James had done it before on his way to Zambia in 1969, but I never had," Katrina said.

"You have led interesting lives," Roberta commented. "And there is so much more to come."

There was much more to come as James found out went he went back to work on Monday. Tony wanted him to go to Canada, to Alberta and the tar sands operations. It struck James that it was going to be cold, really cold there, and he asked what it was that he would be doing.

"Nothing too much outdoors," Tony assured him. "We need to take a look at the tar sands operations and understand how they're doing it. They've got draglines and bucket wheel reclaimers planned, we'd like you to take a look and give us a long-term assessment of that, and if that's the right way to do it, or should we plan for something else in the long term."

"How do I get there?" James asked.

"Fly to Denver and take Western up to Edmonton, then Air Canada to Fort McMurray," Tony said. "You'll meet up with Pat Edwards in Edmonton and fly up together, stay at the Peter Pond Hotel, I think that's your only choice right now."

"When?" James asked.

"Go up on Wednesday and back Friday," Tony said. "I'm off to Alabama to look at a coal mine there."

"So you get the sunshine and I get the cold?" James joked.

"Rank has its privileges," Tony laughed. "So how was your Thanksgiving?"

"I've never eaten so much," James said. "We thought about going shopping on Friday, but we were warned off that."

"Just as well," Tony said. "I think everyone and their brother goes shopping the day after Thanksgiving, stores have sales, so it's a madhouse. Okay, so call Pat and set things up with him."

"I'm going to Canada," James told Katrina. "I'm leaving on Wednesday and I'll be back Friday."

"Will it be cold there?" she asked.

"Bloody cold, I should think," he replied. "Let's look at that atlas you bought."

"So, where are you going?" she asked when she had the atlas.

"A place called Fort McMurray," he said. "It's in Alberta."

308

"Oh, here it is," she said. "It's way up to the north, don't freeze to death."

"I won't," he said. "Fort McMurray is where the tar sands operations are, you dig out this bitumen-rich sand, cook it and get the oil off it, then chuck the sand back in the hole. Apparently, there's masses of the stuff."

"Did anyone ask you about your Thanksgiving?" she asked.

"Tony did, I told him that I'd eaten too much and that we'd talked about going shopping on Friday, but had been talked out of it," he said.

"I said about the same to Fred Brock," she said. "I think it would be best if we just kept mum about spending any time with Roberta and John."

"It's almost like having an illicit affair," James laughed. "I suppose in time it might leak out, but it won't come from me.

"What do you think about this trip to Durango at Christmas?" she asked.

"I think we go, we say thank you nicely, and just try and enjoy it," he said. "Roberta told me that she looks on you as the younger sister she never had, and I think she just enjoys being with you."

"She really is nice," Katrina said. "Apart from you, she's the smartest person I've met."

"I think you're biased," he said. "I think she's smarter than me."

"I don't think so," Katrina argued. "And Bobby told me that you're really smart, she sees you as running the company one day."

"She told me that I could go to her for advice on anything," he said.

"I got the same," Katrina said.

Pat Edwards met James at the Edmonton airport once James had cleared Canadian immigration. Then they took the Air Canada flight to Fort McMurray. James sat and looked out of the window at the endless forest of trees that they flew over, and his mind wandered to Katrina and the fun and new ways they had tried making love. He was brought back to reality when he landed in Fort McMurray. It was a small town with what looked like an endless row of temporary housing for the construction crews that were building the tar sands facilities. Canada was cold, temperatures well below freezing, plummeting overnight to the single digits, and Pat said that it would get colder still as they went into January. James wondered what the cold did to the machines. He knew that steel became brittle at really cold temperatures, unless it was a special alloy developed for cold weather. Then what did it do to the greases and oils that were used? At those temperatures, normal lubricants would probably solidify. The Peter Pond Hotel was busy and noisy, but it was warm. James called Katrina and told her about his travels and his daydreams, and she laughed and told him to concentrate on his job, not fantasies. Pat had arranged a tour of the operation and an explanation by one of the engineers. James listened and asked questions, then more questions. Finally, he was satisfied that they had told him all that they were going to tell him, and he and Pat left to go back to Edmonton. The next day, he flew back to Denver and was surprised to find that he cleared the US immigration and customs in Edmonton, not Denver. Apparently, it was common for flights between the US and Canada for the US immigration people to actually be in Canada.

"So, tell us about the tar sands," Tony said when James was next in the office.
"On the face of it, it's the right way to go," James replied. "Dig off the overburden, dig up the tar sands and windrow them, then rehandle with the bucket wheel reclaimers and convey the stuff to the plant. Long term, what's going to get them is the maintenance costs of the miles of conveyors they're going to have put in as the face moves further away from the plant. The dragline costs may be low, but the system costs are going to be the issue. If I were them, I'd be running some simulations to see what happens with rising conveying costs."
"What's the alternative?" Tony asked.
"Shovels and trucks and then slurry up the stuff and pump it to the plant, dewater and then cook to extract the oil," James suggested.
"How long before that happens?" Tony asked.
"I don't know, fifteen, twenty years," James thought.

"So, not much we can do right now," Tony said. "We didn't get the dragline orders, and I don't see any more forthcoming for a while; we should write that off in the short to medium term."

"That would be my assessment," James agreed.

"Well, there you go! You can't win them all," Tony said.

Christmas

"We've been invited to a company Christmas party," James told Katrina.
"When?" she asked.
"Friday the 19th," he said. "It's at the Milwaukee Public Museum."
"I suppose we'll have to dress up?" she asked.
"I'm sure we will," he said. "I'll ask Tony, he got an invitation as well."
"Maybe it's us who got the invitation as well," she laughed. "You're not exactly high on the totem pole."
"I'm not sure how many people are going, but it's not a sit-down dinner, according to this invitation, it's cocktails and hors d'oeuvres," James read.
"I'll call Bobby and ask her what I should wear," Katrina said. "I wonder if American company parties are staid and sober affairs or wild shindigs with people kissing under the mistletoe?"
"No idea," he said. "I'll ask Tony tomorrow if they've done this in the past and if they have, what to expect. I wonder if it's time to lash out and buy a new suit?"
"You could do with one," she said. "You've only got the one and you're wearing it constantly."
"Maybe I'll try Gimbels and see if they have one that will fit," he said.
"We should go this weekend and see," she said. "I might also look for dresses while we're there. Can I see the invitation? This says Black Tie, what does that mean?"
"I wonder if it means dinner jackets?" he said. "I should ask, if it does, I suppose I could rent one somewhere."
"If it means dinner jackets, does it mean long dresses, or can I get away with a short dress?" she wondered. "I need advice, I'll call Bobby in the morning. You realise that I may have to actually wear stockings? God, I haven't worn stockings or tights in an age. I can't decide which is worse, tights because they're a pain if you need to go to the loo, or stockings because of the suspenders. At least wearing trousers to work, I don't have to worry about them, I can just wear socks with my boots."

James talked to Tony and learned that Black Tie meant a dinner jacket, tuxedo, as the Americans would call it. Tony even had some advice on where to rent one. Tony also told him that the party was something new. It had not been done before, so no one knew quite what to expect. Katrina talked to Roberta and learned that she could wear a cocktail dress. So, that meant a shopping expedition to Gimbels. The Gimbels in Milwaukee was an impressive edifice by the river and boasted quite a few floors. For James, it was relatively easy; he really did need a new suit, so they picked out one in grey, with a pinstripe that looked very professional. He already had black shoes, so he was set. Then it was Katrina's turn, and that took a little longer. She had to pick out a dress and shoes to go with it. The whole process took what seemed to James an age, but in fact was only just about two hours. The final pick was a short black dress overlain with lace, and some silver shoes and matching bag. Katrina grumbled and muttered, but also bought some black stockings to wear. They decided that coats would be surrendered at the door, so there was no point in buying new coats. The tuxedo rental shop was close to Gimbels, so they went there next and tried on jackets and trousers until a good fit was found. They could take it then and there and bring it back after the event. Katrina thought that a good idea, as the tuxedo did have a lingering hint of dry cleaning fluid. A week or so of hanging in their flat would give that time to go. James did not need to buy a fancy shirt and bow tie; he had those left over from his college days when formal balls were, if not common, not rare either. Their last port of call on the shopping expedition was Herman's Sporting Goods, where they got what they needed for the ski trip, everything bar boots and skis. They also debated and debated about what to do for John and Roberta for Christmas; they could hardly go empty-handed. They did have some copper bowls that they had brought from Zambia and thought that they might make a nice gift. They would get Will to arrange to get replacements for them. He did make the occasional trip to Zambia to the paint factory there.

"How do I look?" Katrina asked James as she got ready for the party.

"Smashing," he said, and he meant it. "You're going to need your coat, it's snowing out there. I wonder where the taxi will drop us? Will you have to walk in the snow? Should you take another pair of shoes and change them when we arrive?"

"I'll take a pair with me, in case," she said. "You look pretty good in that; you should dress up more often."

"Are we ready?" he asked.

"Ready, you have the invitation?" she asked.

"I do," he said, patting his pocket. They took the lift down to the ground floor, and the taxi that they had ordered was waiting. They had decided to take a taxi so that there would be no issues with drinking and driving. The season for Christmas parties was in full swing, and the police had been active and had been arresting people left and right. The taxi dropped them right outside the door, and the walk-in was short, and the snow had been trodden down by people coming before.

"Good evening," a woman said. "The James & Brown party?"

"We are," James confirmed.

"May I take your coats?" she asked. They surrendered their coats, and Katrina quickly changed her shoes and handed over the bag with the other pair to be hung with her coat. The actual entrance to the museum was guarded by another woman who asked to see their invitation.

"Please go in," she said. There were already people there, and just inside, there was another young lady, but this one had a tray of glasses of wine. James and Katrina took one each and wandered around.

"James, good to see you," Hank Miller said. "Margaret, this is James Martin, and you must be Katrina Martin?"

"Nice to meet you, Mrs Miller," James said. "Yes, this is my wife, Katrina. Thank you for inviting us."

"The Martins moved here from Central Africa earlier this year," Hank said to Margaret.

"How interesting, oh, please excuse me, there's Betty Ridings, I haven't seen her in an age," Margaret said, before rushing off. Hank looked at James in mute apology and went after her. James looked at Katrina and shrugged his shoulders. They wandered more and nodded to people that James did not know, and stopped and said hello to those he did. There were servers mingling with trays of good-looking things to eat, which they sampled as they went. Apart from the people, there were also exhibits to look at, exhibits that were dioramas of life in Wisconsin over the ages. James was pointing out things in one of them that he remembered from his childhood when they were joined by John and Roberta.

"Katrina, you're looking lovely tonight," Roberta said.

"I haven't dressed up in ages," Katrina said. "So, we went shopping. I like your dress, it really is pretty."

"John," a voice said.

"Hi, Roy," John said. "Roy, this is my wife, Roberta, and these two young people are James and Katrina Martin."

"Nice to meet you," Roy said. "This is my wife, Sonya. So, James, where do you work for us?"

"I'm in sales as an application engineer, and Katrina works in the Parts Department," James replied.

"I love your accent. Where are you from?" Sonya asked.

"I'm from England by way of Zambia, and Katrina is from Zambia," James replied.

"What were you doing in Zambia, Katrina? Were your family missionaries?" Sonya asked.

"No, we had a transportation business, moving heavy equipment, mainly for the mines," Katrina replied.

"John and his wife moved back from England not long ago, too," Roy said to Sonya.

"Did you enjoy living there, Roberta?" Sonya asked.

"I did," Roberta replied.

"Oh, there's Margaret, excuse me, I must go and talk to her," Sonya said. Roy looked at John and grinned, then trailed after her.

"He's fairly new to the company," John commented. "He joined two years ago while we were in England; he's the new treasurer. I gather that Sonya and Margaret are old friends, and that's how Roy got the nod to be the treasurer."

"Now now, John, no cynicism," Roberta cautioned.

"I gather from Tony that this is the first time there's been a party like this," James said.

"It's part of Hank's plan to bring the management team together," John explained. "Christmas parties here in the past were usually put on by each department, and then they were often employees only, no spouses, and I gather that some got out of hand."

"Are you ready for Durango?" Roberta asked Katrina.

"We are," Katrina said.

"Why don't you get out of work early on Christmas Eve, by noon if you can, drive straight to our house, and we'll take a car down to O'Hare," Roberta suggested.

"And who are these two lovely-looking ladies?" a man asked.

"Oh, hi Tom, Emily," John said.

"Hi Roberta, nice to see you, and I don't know this lovely lady," Tom said.

"This is Katrina Martin, James's wife; she works for the company too, in the Parts Department," Roberta explained. "Hi Emily, how are you?"

"I'm good," Emily said. "You know we've lived here for years, and I've never been here."

"Excuse us, we should go and say hello to Tony," James said. They did indeed say hello to Tony and Maggie and a few others who were in a corner gossiping about someone, and conversation stopped abruptly when James and Katrina joined them. James got the feeling it was Katrina who was the subject of interest, and they could hardly continue when she joined them.

"I wonder how long we should stay?" Katrina asked when she and James went off to find another glass of wine.

"Long enough to be polite, we've said hello to Hank and his wife, so we've done our duty. When you start seeing people disappear, we'll go," James said. They lingered for another half an hour and then left. The lady with the coats asked them if they needed a taxi, and she called for one for them, and it was outside the door in less than five minutes.

"So, that was interesting," James commented to Katrina when they got home. "I got the feeling you were being stared at, and the tongues were wagging much better."

"I suppose we are a curiosity," she said.

"I think it's you more than me," he said. "They're not used to seeing someone who could be a film star."

"You're just saying that," she said.

"Well, that's how I see you," he said.

"That's sweet," she said. "So, are you going anywhere this week?"

"Not that I know of," he said. "Tony hasn't said anything about any requests, and I'm up to date with all my reports, so it will be a lazy short week, only three days."

"What about your Hank Miller project?" she asked.

"There is that," he agreed. "I should take the chance of a slow week to get some of that done."

"Are you ready for a bath and bed?" she asked.

The days went by quickly, and by Christmas Eve, it looked as if everyone was taking off early, so at noon, James and Katrina left. They drove out to John and Roberta's house to find a huge black car in the driveway.

"Park in the garage," John said. "Let's get your bags loaded and then as soon as Bobby's ready, we can go."

"I'm ready," she said, coming out of the house. "He often accuses me of being late," she explained to Katrina. "But I usually have to wait for him."

"Are we set, good, Continental Airlines, please, José," John instructed. The drive to the Chicago airport was quite quick. There was traffic, but José seemed to know how to avoid it. At the airport, John signalled a porter who came and took all the bags and scuttled off to the check-in desk. He was back in short order with claim tags and boarding passes. They had seats in rows 2 and 3, seats A and B in each.

"Not bad," Katrina said to James. "Not as convenient as the LearJet, but more room and easy access to the loos." The rest of the passengers boarded, and the crew got quite festive, with Santa Claus hats and all.

The flight was quite short, as flights to Denver go, only two and a half hours. Then there was a wait, and finally the Rocky Mountain Airways flight to Durango, where they arrived at five-thirty.

"Let me just go and get the car," John said. James looked around, and many of the people who had been on the flight with them now came out of baggage claim with long bags that James could only assume were skis.

"It's very pretty here," Katrina said. "I like the mountains; we don't have any in Wisconsin. We didn't really have any in Zambia either, unless you went down to the Luangwa Valley and looked back up at the Muchinga escarpment. Where my folks live in South Africa, they do have mountains, but nothing like these."

"I'm so glad you came," Roberta said, putting her arm around Katrina. "It's so nice to have someone to talk to."

"But surely you and John talk?" Katrina asked.

"We do, about anything and everything," Roberta said. "But, to have a girlfriend to talk to about stuff that John wouldn't understand is so nice."

"Are we ready?" John asked. He came and got some bags, and James got the rest and followed him the short way to the car, actually a Jeep Wagoneer. James looked back at Katrina and Roberta, and it struck him that both of them had facial markers that told of their mixed heritage. It made both of them a little exotic and out of the ordinary; they made a good pair, both dark, with dark hair, extraordinary good looks and both with figures that many women would kill for. His musings were interrupted when John told everyone to climb aboard, and they would be off. The drive to John's house took about thirty minutes. It was beyond the town of Durango, off a side road to the north, set against red cliffs and looking down over the river valley, across to the hills on the other side of the valley. The house was not some great palatial affair, but a simple three-bedroom A-Frame house with a steep roof that John explained was good for getting rid of snow, of which there was quite a lot already on the ground. The driveway had been cleared, courtesy of a neighbour, John told them, the same neighbour also did shopping for them, so that there was food and drink in the house. Inside, Roberta showed them to their room and suggested that they come down to the kitchen as soon as they were ready.

"Are you ready for Christmas?" John asked.

"Not really," James replied. "It's hard to believe that a few hours ago we were in Milwaukee, and now we're here out in the Wild West. I ought to be ready; there's been Christmas carols being played in the shops since Thanksgiving, so I've had plenty of warning."

"Fancy a drink?" John asked.

"Thank you," James said. "John, do you have any advice on careers?"

"Take things as they come," John replied. "Don't be afraid to take on a new challenge, don't get too consumed with The Plan. Some have a great plan for their lives and may be disappointed if they don't achieve the plan, and may also miss out on great opportunities and adventures if they forego something because it's not in the plan."

"And marriage advice?" James asked.

"You don't seem to need any," John laughed. "But, support her in anything she wants to do, don't take her for granted, try not to fight, you can disagree and argue, but don't let that descend to name-calling and generalities."

"What's this?" Roberta asked as she and Katrina joined them. "John getting philosophical?"

"I was getting marriage advice," James explained.

"From John?" Roberta laughed. "What did he tell you, get up on the morning and say I'm sorry, hoping that would cover the sins you might commit in the coming day?"

"No, but does that work?" James asked.

"Of course," she said. "Anyway, while you two have been solving the world's oldest problem, we have been slaving away barefoot and pregnant in the kitchen, well, maybe not pregnant, so we can eat."

"What was the marriage advice John gave you?" Katrina asked James as they lay in bed. He told her, and she laughed and told him that it was exactly the same advice that Roberta had given her.

"I'm still bothered a little that we don't have much for them for Christmas," he said.

"I honestly don't think they expect anything," she said. Katrina was right, Roberta was delighted with the copper bowls when James gave them to her on Christmas morning. She apologised for not getting them anything for Christmas, but James pointed out that the trip was much more of a gift than they had ever expected.

"I was thinking that we'd be lazy and do Christmas lunch at the ski resort," Roberta said. "We can also get you set for your lessons."

"We can take care of that," James said.

"Nonsense," Roberta said. "I've already arranged it."

"Shall we take a drive up there?" John suggested. They put on outdoor clothes and drove up to Purgatory, which seemed to both James and Katrina as an unlikely name for a resort. John explained that it got its name from the Spanish name for the Animas River, which was the river of the lost souls in purgatory. As they drove up, they drove further into the mountains, which now loomed bright and snow-covered. At the resort, they could see the lift and the runs cleared through the forests that clung to the mountainside. James admitted to Katrina some apprehension about coming down what looked like a steep slope on two bits of wood. John took them first to the ski school, and they met Bethany, who would be their private instructor for the next three days. Then, lunch called, and they went off to the restaurant where John and Roberta were greeted as old friends.

"I rather feel like a favoured son," James said to Katrina that night.

"Like John Wells was in Mtuga?" she asked.

"A little, but John was nice as a favoured son, I hope I don't become like George Bullock, who was anointed from on high and who was an idiot," James replied. "I just hope I can live up to the expectations."

"I'm sure you will," she assured him. "Bobby says that you're smart and she should know, she's one of the smartest people I've met."

"I wonder what Bethany will be like as a teacher?" he said.

"We'll find out tomorrow," Katrina said. "Four hours seems like a long time. I think we're going to be tired tomorrow."

"We're also high up here, so I'm sure we'll feel some effects from that," James thought.

"I'm looking forward to trying things tomorrow," she said.

"I was rather looking forward to trying things out tonight," he said.

"You were, were you?" she laughed. "Well, what did you have in mind?"

"This and that," he temporised.

"Well, show me," she suggested. He did, and they enjoyed themselves.

John and Roberta delivered James and Katrina into the hands of Bethany and left to do their own skiing, promising to meet up in the bar at the end of their lesson. Bethany quickly fitted them out with boots, skis and poles and then led them out to the 'bunny' slopes where beginners slid, fell and eventually skied. James was surprised at how quickly the four hours passed, but by the end of it, both he and Katrina had managed the beginner hill a few times, and Bethany was talking about an actual slope the next day.

"So, good day?" Roberta asked when Bethany delivered them to the bar.

"They did brilliantly," Bethany gushed. "Tomorrow we'll try the main run. I'll see you guys tomorrow, gotta run, another lesson."

"She fancies you, James," Katrina said, after Bethany had gone.

"I don't think so," he said. "She's just doing her job."

"She fancies you," Katrina repeated.

"She does," Roberta confirmed.

"Do we need to get another teacher?" James asked.

"No," Katrina said. "She might fancy you, but I have you."

"You do," he confirmed.

"Do you two need a room?" Roberta joked.

"Sorry," James said. "What about you two, did you enjoy your day?"

"It was fun," Roberta said. "I even managed to keep up with John, first time ever."

Over the next couple of days, James and Katrina both improved on their skills and technique until they actually came all the way down the main slope, without falling, hesitating or straying off the beaten track. James was convinced that Katrina had said something to Bethany because she was professional, but not all like the first day when she had seemed to James to be merely solicitous; but to Katrina, there had been more.

"So, how do you like skiing?" John asked over dinner after their big day of skiing the main slope.

"It's fun," James said. "I'm not sure which I like better, the speed and thrill of the downhill, or the peace and quiet of the cross-country."

"We can do both here, so it's take your pick," John said.

"Katrina and I have been saving to buy a house. Do you have any suggestions as to where?" James asked.

"Oak Creek is as good as anywhere," John said. "As you move out to where we are, the prices go up. I wouldn't buy in South Milwaukee or Cudahy, just not my kind of neighbourhoods, I like a little more space, and you can still get that in Oak Creek."

"We should take a ride tomorrow on the train," Roberta said, changing the subject back to the present.

"Good idea," John agreed. "My dad worked for all his life for the D&RG, based here in Durango; he worked trains to Silverton. The line was built in the 1880s to get gold and silver ores from the mines at Silverton. Now it's a tourist train mostly in the summer, but in the winter they do run trains part of the way to Cascade."

"Dress for the cold," Roberta cautioned. "The line climbs from here, so it gets colder as we go higher. The train leaves in the morning at ten and we'll be back by three."

The train ride was an adventure. James noted that it was a narrow gauge line, 3 feet, a little narrower than the system that covered southern Africa, which was 3 feet 6 inches. The carriages were all enclosed, except for one that was open to the sides, and was for hardy souls who did not mind the cold. The train ran parallel to the road for a while, then ran closer to the river, with some spectacular sections where it ran on a narrow shelf hacked out of the mountainside, with drops of up to 400 feet to the canyon floor. With crystal-clear blue skies, snow-covered hillsides and tall pine trees, the scenery lived up to its billing and was spectacular. Added to that, they saw elk and deer on the way, and John told them that in the summer, they occasionally would see bears as well.

At the turnaround station, the whole train was turned around by reversing into a Y, and then they sat for a while for people to enjoy lunch by the Animas River, lunch that they either took themselves or bought as a box lunch from the company. While they ate lunch, Katrina told them tales about her trips to Rhodesia on the school train, two days on the train, with beds made up in the compartments and meals taken in the dining car. The train was divided with boys at one end and girls at the other, and plenty of teachers on board to act as chaperones.

On New Year's Eve, they decided to forego parties and driving and stayed in and saw the new year in while snow fell and blanketed the roads, the garden, the valley below and the hills beyond the river. James and Katrina wondered what 1976 would bring; certainly 1975 had been a year filled with new experiences, new places and new friends, so would 1976 top that? New Year's Day, they all went skiing again and rode the lifts together to the top of the slopes, then split up while James and Katrina made their way carefully down, and John and Roberta went racing down. The new snow had made conditions a little different, so James and Katrina were cautious, whereas John delighted in the new powder snow and was as happy as he could be.

"Good day?" Roberta asked when they met up in the ski lodge.

"Super day," James said. "I think I'll sleep well tonight."

"I'm sure you will," Roberta said. "Exercise and fresh air, a good recipe for sleep. Tomorrow we need to leave at seven-thirty to get the plane to Denver, so be up early if you want breakfast."

"We can't thank you enough for bringing us out here and giving us such a wonderful time," Katrina said.

"It has been our pleasure," Roberta assured her. "We've enjoyed having you here and, if you would like, we'd like to have you come out next Christmas."

"Thank you," Katrina said. "That would be lovely."

"So, shall we eat here or go home?" John asked.

"Here, then there's no washing up," Roberta suggested.

The flight back from Durango was on time, but James assumed that that was because the plane actually stayed there overnight and made its first trip of the day from Durango. In Denver, there was a little time to wait, and they watched people arrive and depart before boarding their plane back to Chicago.

"So, now we've been skiing," Katrina commented to James as they drank tea and ate another breakfast, this one provided by Continental.

"We have," he said. "I still am having a hard time accepting that John and Roberta are doing all this for us. Part of me just wants to accept it all and say thank you, part of me wants to ask why?"

"I talked to Bobby," Katrina said. "She told me again that she really likes us and enjoys our company, makes her feel young, she said, and she said that they have the means, so why not? She told me that she'd rather spend time with us than with the peers of John and their wives, she says that she doesn't have anything in common with them."

"But surely some of the wives have more to them than just being the wife of?" James said.

"You'd think so," Katrina agreed. "But I think when the conversation turns to children, grandchildren and the rest, she feels left out and also feels that they pity her for not having children, I think assuming that she couldn't."

"I like John and Roberta, they're fun, they're interesting people," James said.

"I like them too," Katrina said. "I'm really getting to like Bobby; she and I have found that we can talk about anything, so it's nice to have another woman to talk to. Mom is far away and I miss the times when we would talk."

"Talk about what?" he asked.

"Life, period pains, the prospect of menopause, sex, feminine hygiene, all the sorts of things you would probably talk to me if you had to, but which you couldn't bring any actual experience," she explained.

"And you and Roberta can do that?" he asked.

"We do," she said. "She's got a lot to share and she's not coy about discussing it, so it's really helpful. We even talk about you."

"Me, God forbid," he said in mock horror. "What about me?"

"Are you any good in bed?" she teased. "Mainly, we talk about where you might go next in the company."

"Do I have a bright and rosy future?" he asked.

"Bobby thinks you do," Katrina said.

On the ground in Chicago, they collected their bags and walked out to the area where cars picked people up. José was there, and he came over to help with the bags. The drive north was a little slow because of the snow, not the soft powdery snow of Colorado, but wet, heavy, slushy snow that stuck and clung to everything. At John and Roberta's house, James and Katrina stopped long enough for tea, then said their thanks and left to go home.

"Well, that was super," James said to Katrina. "And we have another day before we have to go back to work. What shall we do tomorrow?"

"Laundry," she said. "We've got clothes that need washing, but we might find time to chase each other around the flat."

"That's one drawback of staying in someone else's home, you can't just decide to make love in the living room," he laughed.

"They'd probably just politely avoid us," she said. "But it might be embarrassing for all of us. Talking of that, I'm feeling deprived and randy, are you coming to bed?"

"With an invitation like that, lead on," he said.

"So, James, how was Christmas?" Tony asked when James returned to work.

"It was wonderful, thanks, we went out of town for a few days, saw some of America," James replied.

"So, ready to get back at it?" Tony asked.

"Of course," James said.

"Two things came in over the holidays, one in Turkey, you can go there, and one in Australia, I'll take that," Tony said.

"What's the Turkish operation?" James asked.

"Coal," Tony said. "You'll have to get a visa to go to Turkey, and then I guess you'll have to go to London and then get a plane from there to

Ankara. Malcolm Frasier from International will meet you in Ankara, set it all up with Marlys."

"One of the chaps in my class at college was from Turkey," James said. "I'll see if I can contact him and find out more."

"Good idea," Tony said.

"I think most of Turkey's coal is in fact lignite, so probably good for draglines," James said.

"There you go," Tony said. "One thing, if anyone brings up the issue of how much we have to pay to some government official to secure an order, you know nothing, you say nothing, let the local rep handle all that."

"Do you think that's likely?" James asked.

"No idea," Tony admitted.

"I came across that a little once in Zambia," James said. "In the end, all it took was half a dozen grease guns and everyone was happy."

"Well, there you go!" Tony laughed. "Let's get on with things and set up these trips and go out and get some orders."

"I'm going to Turkey," James told Katrina that night.

"For how long?" she asked.

"I imagine that with all the messing about that I'll be gone a week," he said.

"I might just talk to Bobby and see if I can spend some time with her while you're gone," Katrina said. "Make sure you come back safely."

"I will," he promised. "It looks like 1976 will be an interesting year."

"1975 was a whole lot of firsts," she said. "I wonder what 1976 will bring. I can't believe that in just a couple of months, we will have been here a year already; time just flies."

"It does," he agreed. "We're lucky, we have jobs, a place to live, new friends, what more could we want?"

"Not much," she said. "We've got each other, which makes living in a new place so much easier, and now I have Bobby to commiserate with, the loneliness is not so bad either."

"I wonder if I'll ever get another job that doesn't involve travel?" he mused. "It seems to me that the Americans are constantly on the move."

326

"Maybe you should ask for the job running the J&B place in South Africa," she suggested.

"Do you think they'd give it to me?" he asked.

"Why not?" she said. "You've lived in Africa before, you know mining, you can count, so the accounting side of the business won't be that hard, you've managed people before, I think you'd be the perfect fit. I'd give us another year or so here, then ask for that job."

"I might just do that," he said. "Yes, that sounds like fun, great idea, plus we won't be that far from your folks or from Will and Bridget, if they're still there."

"Good plan," she said. "I suppose if you did do that, then at some point they'd bring you back here?"

"I'd ask for that," he said. "There's only so much that can be done in South Africa."

"Good, so for now, we have to make up for the days that you'll be gone to Turkey, so I'm ready whenever you are," she said.

"I love you," he said. "I really do, I can't imagine being without you."

"Just come back from Turkey safely," she said. "Now, no more talk, bath and bed!"

Select Bibliography

- Anderson, George B., 1980, *One Hundred Booming Years: A History of Bucyrus-Erie Company 1880–1980*, Bucyrus-Erie.
- Bauer, Alan, 1971, *Open pit drilling and blasting*, Journal of the South African Institute of Mining and Metallurgy, January 1971.
- Bureau of Land Management, *Coal Development: Collected Papers*, July 1983.
- Caterpillar Inc, 1975, *Caterpillar Performance Handbook*.
- Haddock, Keith, 2005, *Bucyrus: Making the Earth Move for 125 Years*, Motorbooks.
- Haddock, Keith, 2008, *Bucyrus Heavy Equipment, Construction and Mining Machines, 1880 - 2008*, Iconografix.
- Dessureault, Bill, *415 - Rock Excavation*, University of Arizona, Mining and Geological Engineering.
- Harnischfeger, Henry, 1985, *Harnischfeger Corporation*, Newcomen Society of the United States.
- *Marion Mining and Dredging Machines: Photo Archive*, Iconografix, 2003.
- Kahraman, S., *Performance analysis of drilling machines using rock modulus ratio*, The Journal of the South African Institute of Mining and Metallurgy, October 2003.
- Kennedy, B. A., ed, 1990, *Surface Mining*, Society for Mining, Metallurgy & Exploration.
- Langefors, U., Kihlstrom, B., 1973, *The Modern Technique of Rock Blasting*, John Wiley & Sons, New York.
- Learmont, T. and Chare, H. B., *Area Stripping Productivity in Deep Overburden*, AMC Session Papers, May 1980.
- Lewis, Robert Stanley, 1951, *Eighty Years of Enterprise 1869 - 1949: Being the Intimate Story of the Waterside Works of Ransomes & Rapier of Ipswich, England*, W. S Cowell.
- Martin, James, W., 1982, *Surface Mining Equipment*, Martin Consultants.
- Nichols, Herbert L., 1975, *Moving the Earth: The Workbook of Excavation*, McGraw Hill.
- Orlemann, Eric, C., 2003, *Power Shovels: The World's Mightiest Mining and Construction Excavators*, MBI.

- P&H Mining Equipment Inc, *A History of P&H Mining Equipment Inc.*
- Pfleider, Eugene P., 1968, *Surface Mining*, A.I.M.E.
- Rasper, Dr. Ing. E. h. Ludwig, 1975, *The Bucket Wheel Excavator: Development, Design and Application*, Trans Tech Publications.
- Williams, David, W, July 1974, *British Passports and the Right to Travel*, International and Comparative Law Quarterly.
- Williamson, Harold F. & Myers, Kenneth H., 1955, *Designed for Digging: The First 75 Years of Bucyrus-Erie Company*, Northwestern University Press.
- Wootton, David, 2012, *Opencast Images: An informal look at British opencast sites*, Fox Chapel Publishing.